1

SPINDLE
OF LIFE

C.L. QVAM

SPINDLE OF LIFE

THE FATED HEIRS

C. L. QVAM

QVAMINGTON

First published by Qvamington Press in 2023
Qvamington Press is an imprint of Qvams Forlag

ISBN 978-82-94035-00-7 (eBook/ePub)
ISBN 978-82-94035-01-4 (Hardcover)
ISBN 978-82-94035-02-1 (Paperback)

Dust jacket cover art by Evelyne Paniez, www.secretdartiste.be
Case laminate design by Franziska Stern, www.coverdungeon.com
Interior design created with Canva & Vellum
'The Passage' illustration illustrated by the Author

Publisher website: www.qvamington.com
Author website: www.chaselouiseqvam.com

FOREWORD

Dear reader,

As you're sat reading, these words might just be another couple of words on another couple of pages, but to me they are a miracle.

This book you're holding is a dream made tangible between a pair of binders (metaphorically or literally depending on which format you're reading). It is the first book in a series that has been more than one and a half decade in the making prior to this book's release.

It is the fantasy world of a girl who dreamed up stories to make sense of her own.

It is the work that many believed would never happen, and which some even decidedly said never could.

It is the purpose that kept me going in times I believed there was nothing more to keep going for.

Finally, it is my gift. From me to you, with a hope that it may inspire you, like books inspired me, to embrace the magic inside you.

Yours,

C. L. Qvam

Content warning:

This book, while fictional, deals with dark themes such as the abuse and indoctrination of young people, but in a gentle and sensitive manner. If it triggers something unhealed, please be kind to yourself; surround yourself with what gives you comfort and take reassurance in that the content serves a purpose.

To all readers, please note that this book is written and edited according to British style and spelling.

To all who have had their magic suppressed, and to everyone pushing through, taking the world by storm.

CONTENT

PART III

PROLOGUE

KENDAL, CUMBRIA, 31ST OF DECEMBER 1997

HER PULSE HAMMERED in her parched throat as she raced through the forest behind Hallows Grove. The sky flared up in noisy white, red, gold, and blue, but the fireworks couldn't drown out the sound of growls chasing after her. Charlie did not know whether she was running towards town or away from it, only that she needed to keep going. Keep pushing through the thick woods despite the tree branches slashing at her, ripping her cotton dress, and cutting her cheeks and arms as she ran.

In daylight, she had always found these parts of the woods mystical and enchanting. Now they felt like a threat to her life.

Roots slithered in all angles on the ground, as if attempting to trip her up and catch her. Like the dogs chasing her. The farther she ran, the closer she felt to being caught, and her desperation rose.

Get me out of here, please. Somebody!

As if it had heard, a raven swooped in over her head to lead the way, and Charlie followed it without question, stumbling once, twice, into a clearing, her muscles heavy and weary.

The sounds behind subsided. While attempting a glance over her shoulder, she stubbed her toe and finally went flying. Her lungs let go of what little oxygen they had left, and the taste of wet dirt and blood filled her mouth. Her tongue ached where she had bitten it, forearms burned as if they had been scrubbed with wire wool, and the bird took flight with Charlie staring after it, her breath grating against her throat with every drag. But these were the least of her worries.

The air filled with low canine growls, and yellow eyes shone in the thick darkness. For a second, she dared to hope that she had run into some secret clan of dog-shapers, that they were fellow Defectives like her and there to lend a hand. To harbour a fugitive from the evil that chased their kind. She took a shallow breath.

And the world exploded into barks and fangs.

Her scream ripped through the forest as the first pair of canine teeth sank into her leg, shortly followed by another set cutting into her flesh. A third dog caught her foot with its claws at the same time a fourth attacked her hand attempting to swat them away. All surely driven wild by the smell of her tainted blood. Over and over again they bit and mauled her, until her screams were nothing but gurgles in her throat. Her eyes flitted around the clearing, between the muscled bodies of fur, searching for an escape when someone ahead shifted in the dark.

Perhaps she was imagining them.

Out of the treeline stepped a boy and a girl, striking against the backdrop of blurring darkness. She was petite and beautiful, with long black hair and irises white like silvery ghosts. They dimmed and turned an emerald-green before she nodded to the burly boy by her side, his own eyes serious over a flat nose. He seemed to dissolve, to transform of sorts. To what, she did not see, but a beast snarled amongst more yelps and snapping jaws. The pain subsided, leaving a cold numbness in its wake while movements receded away from her on quick legs.

Another firework painted the sky. Blood red. Matching the heavy stench of iron. Silence returned, and a girl's face appeared above hers, blocking her view to the stars.

A wolf howled, sounding worryingly close. Perhaps he had come for her carcass. She mouthed for the girl to run, but she did not listen. Instead, she came closer, the dots on her forehead glowing like a constellation.

'It'll be alright, Sophie,' said the girl. 'Close your eyes.'

I'm Charlie, she thought, but did as she was told.

PART I

1

THE RAVEN GIRL AND HER BRUTE

BATH, SOMERSET, 30TH OF OCTOBER 2000

THE BANG of the front door closing caught Charlie by surprise, causing her to elbow a pot standing on the kitchen island. It toppled over the edge. Shattering pottery echoed through the empty manor like a burglar alarm, instantly giving away her presence in the house.

She held her breath.

Her heartbeat pulsated like drumsticks against her eardrums. Footsteps moved about in the entrance. Her chest swelled tight with anxiety at the thought of Agnus Dei searching the house. Relax. *It's probably just Maddison coming in from one of her nightly frolics.* That was far more likely, especially considering they had lived there for a whole year without being discovered. Although... it was bound to happen at some point. *No, it* must *be Maddison.* But the thought only made her stomach twist further as she observed the thin trickle of blood running from the cut on her arm. Unhealed. What if Maddison came into the kitchen and saw? How quickly would she understand that Charlie had tried and failed again?

Her eyes fell on the pieces of pottery. She could say it was an accident.

Urgently, she folded up the hem of her skirt and gathered the shards, bringing them back to the worktop. Her knife lay askew on the cutting board where she had left it, scarlet fluid drying at the tip of its blade.

She was just about to bring it to the sink when another loud crash sounded from the second floor. *Definitely not alone in the house*, Charlie thought, and if it was Maddison moving about, it didn't sound as if she was alone either. Which was odd, because she would always tell Charlie if she'd invited someone over – then tell her to stay in her room. Which meant whoever was here with her now was uninvited.

Turning the knife's handle in her hand, Charlie moved out of the kitchen with the sharp blade raised, shivering, but ready to stab in self-defence if needed.

The ground floor was abandoned, like always, save for the furniture covered in white sheets. Here and there the moonlight hit just right to illuminate a collection of cobwebs – the whole thing so large at this point, it could have its own exhibition at the Victoria Art Gallery. Her and Maddison had left the first floor like that ever since they occupied the house – like a decoy – in case any travelling Agnus preacher came knocking and peering through the windows. Anyone would think the place was deserted.

Up until now at least.

Rings and swirls covered the floor as if someone had dragged the hem of their cloak – or a body – around in the dust. Shuffles and footsteps sounded above her head yet again, and she peered up, wishing she could see through the floor of the living room upstairs. Perhaps the Agnus had caught Maddison outside the house. Whatever they would bring her inside for she could not say, but her emotions were running far beyond the rationality of her mind. She gripped the handle of her knife more firmly, the skin of her knuckles tightening, as she paused at the deafening silence – before an inhuman guttural scream cut through the night.

'Nooo!'

Charlie ran up the stairs, two steps at a time, then burst into the living room where she came to an abrupt halt. Her knife fell to the carpeted floor with a thump.

The room looked like it always did. Plush sofas and armchairs were strewn around the room with pillows and books, all of it basking in the warm light of the electric fire built into the original fireplace. Most of the people present were familiar to her as well. The silhouette sat shrouded in darkness. The four observing their alpha from the sofa and the alpha himself. She would almost have thought it a regular night in with friends if it weren't for the wretched creature in the middle of the room lying crumpled on the floor, face grimaced into countless silent '*O*'s. Over him towered Brimley Weston like a muscled giant, gripping the creature's thin wrist.

'No, don't!' whimpered the boy, but Brimley's square face was emotionless as he snapped another finger into a sickening angle.

'Transform,' Brimley growled. The lines and roughness of his face hardened as he furrowed his brows. But the boy only curled farther in on himself. Goosebumps rushed down Charlie's arms as she recognised him as the boy who had gone missing from Brimley's pack months ago. *Doyle*.

'Ah, there you are, Charlie,' lured the soft voice speaking up from the shadows, smooth like the velvet she wore. Maddison Quinsey watched her carefully from a cushioned armchair – her self-acclaimed throne – with raven black hair falling down one side of her face like a curtain. Her long fingers played with a tear-shaped vial permanently tied around her neck with a silver chain.

Brimley turned at Charlie, growling. 'Where've you been?'

'In the kitchen,' she murmured, unable to take her eyes off the bundled creature on the floor. 'Making soup for tomorrow.' A little white lie. She'd *meant* to make it... before she became distracted.

'And? Did you succeed?' Maddison drawled, seeing through her. Charlie shook her head.

'Shame.' The chill in Maddison's voice pierced Charlie's chest like an icicle from a ten-foot drop. 'They're counting on you, you know.'

As she pointed at Doyle, unease and nausea welled inside Charlie, making her feel much like the creature rocking himself back and forth. He looked nothing like he once had. Filthy skin hung off his bones like melted wax, evidence of muscles that had been and gone. A *Withdrawer*.

He'd been burly, like Brimley. Thick-necked and broad-shouldered. She'd always thought of him as someone who could run through walls. Brimley's only real competition for the alpha role. But Charlie suspected even the slightest breeze would knock Doyle over now, turning him into dust. *Physical powers, physical symptoms.*

Faces from Hallows Grove swam before her, particularly one belonging to a girl struggling to look away while her fellow pupil was caned.

'Charlie,' Maddison purred. 'Do you need some fresh air?'

It was a test. Despite the caring tone in her voice, Maddison's question required but one answer. Their life – this world – of being a squatter, of being on the streets, was no place for the weak. The weak would become captives of the Agnus Dei. The Withdrawer being an agonising reminder of that. She could not be weak. At least not – her eyes shifted to Brimley's pack members still lounging on the sofa – in front of anyone but Maddison.

'No.' Charlie shook her head, giving her the answer required, swallowing the bile threatening to come up her throat. 'No, I'm fine.'

A curl of her lips and the pleased expression on Maddison's face came and went before she turned back to the scene before her. Brimley, seemingly occupied with counting the birthmarks on Maddison's forehead, shook his head as he realised that she was expecting him to speak.

'He won't transform,' he repeated.

'Yes, that's usually the case when a shapeshifter has withdrawn, Brimley.' Maddison wrinkled her nose at the creature whose muscles had sunk in on themselves like deflated balloons. 'Have you asked him *why*?'

With his neck and ears blazing red, Brimley grabbed the boy by the shoulders and lifted him into the air, shaking him like a rattle. 'What happened?' he barked, thick saliva splashing on the Withdrawer's hollow cheeks.

Doyle sobbed, whimpered, and drooled all at once. 'Pl-please, I had no choice. There were screams. So many screams.' He appeared to slip back into the shadows of his mind, but then Brimley gave him another shake.

'Keep going!'

Doyle gasped. 'Our parents lay murdered in the hallway, gashes on their chests. My brother – I had to go with my brother. He's my little brother! I had to make sure he was safe.'

'Where?'

In his rage, Charlie could see the predatory gleam of the wolf in Brimley's eyes. His shapeshifter form threatening to come out. The other wolf-shifters in the room growled in anticipation, sensing the ire of their alpha. But the Withdrawer did not speak. He only blubbered and whimpered.

Maddison made one swift hand motion and rose, her dark dressing gown cascading down her slender body. Instantly, Brimley released Doyle onto the dirty rug, his eyes catching onto every glimpse of her legs as Maddison swaggered over to the Withdrawer, kneeling by his side.

'They took him to one of the *orphanages*,' she said shortly after, fingertips barely touching Doyle's forehead, still staring ahead as if she were watching a film none of them could see, the white in her eyes bleeding into her emerald-green irises like ink on paper.

Charlie's insides trembled. The hair on her neck stood up. There was no air to breathe, no space to move. She grasped the arm of the nearest chair and forced herself still, pushing back the blitz of memories.

'I need to talk to you in private,' Maddison said to Brimley, her voice keeping Charlie anchored to the present. He ordered his pack members to leave the room as he and Maddison stepped away from the Withdrawer and Charlie, into a corner.

Charlie, always forgotten, was left staring at the broken mess of a creature that lay before her.

'Please,' he whimpered. 'Help me.'

Despite her instincts telling her to leave him be and run the other way, Charlie inched closer, the helplessness in his voice pulling her towards him. As if his pain and sorrow had coiled itself like a rope around her neck, forcing her closer. It was like a reflex, something automatic after growing up amongst Withdrawers at Hallows Grove. Maddison used to say she had a saviour complex. This was one of those times where she understood what she meant. No sooner had she reached him and knelt by his side than Doyle's arm shot out and grabbed her wrist, foam frothing at his mouth. She yelped in surprise.

'Heal me!' he barked. 'I know you can!' There were shuffling noises from the corner, but no one came to help her.

'Let me go!' Charlie cried, horror rushing through her. She tried to push him off while throwing a glance in Maddison's direction. They were both watching, Maddison holding Brimley back from running forward. Doyle's cracked black nails bore deeper into Charlie's skin.

She whimpered.

Not so much from pain, but from the familiar tingles that awakened down her arm. Warmth spread throughout her veins like hot liquid. Her palm – pushed against his arm in an attempt to pull him off her – grew hot, and she could tell by the Withdrawer's instant silence and wide eyes that he felt it too. They stared at his hand where the finger Brimley had broken began to twitch. With a sickening crunch, it moved back into place and the blue tint that had begun to take form on his skin evaporated. The cuts on her arm healed as well, leaving pink lines. Then nothing else happened.

The boy continued to stare at his hand, as if he was still hoping for more – for the outline of his skeleton to disappear beneath replenishing flesh, for his bruises and scars to turn golden and smooth. Distress lingered in his glance as their eyes met, but also something else – a mutual understanding.

Charlie shivered, beads of cold sweat running down her cheek. Or were they tears? Something shifted behind her.

A flash of a cane, the stinging pain as it smashed down upon her shoulders. Healing warmth surging through her body. Traitorous. A slap to her face. Charlie threw herself backwards, whimpering as her breath came in rapid waves. 'No, no, no!'

In an instant, Maddison was there, her black gown billowing at her ankles. She hunched down and grabbed Charlie's wrists firmly. 'It's alright.'

Charlie shook her head. 'No!'

'You didn't do anything wrong. Breathe—'

'Please,' Charlie gasped, lips pulled back in a grimace, tears pressing at her eyelids.

'Shh—get him out of here, Brimley! Just breathe, Charlie...'

Charlie locked eyes with Maddison as her brain registered Brimley chucking Doyle over his shoulder. 'There now. Breathe,' Maddison repeated as they left. 'Look around. *They're* not here. You see? You're safe. Tell yourself that.'

'I'm safe,' Charlie stuttered, glancing left and right as far out into the hallway as she could see. No one. No tight hair buns. No unforgiving faces. No black suits with embroidered broken wands. No creatures beyond the ones she knew. The ones who had saved her and kept her protected. She exhaled a shivering breath, noticing at last the slackening gallop of her heart.

She nodded, her voice still trembling. 'I'm safe.'

2

A HERITAGE OF MAGIC

MELLOW MARSHMALLOWS DIPPED up and down in the light-brown liquid, tempting Charlie to take another sip even before she had finished savouring the last. Satisfaction coiled in her belly while the warmth of the hot chocolate seeped into her heart. She had often given Maddison a hard time and a few moral lessons for manipulating money out of innocent people, but right now she could not help but agree that it had its advantages – if only to afford such small luxuries.

After taking another sip, Charlie sighed and leaned against her bedroom wall, tucking her feet underneath her in bed and pulling a tired old book into her lap. She stroked its egg-white leather binding and gold foil title, feeling the smooth gloss underneath her fingertips. *The Encyclopaedia of Mythological Creatures.*

Maddison had gifted it to her shortly after they first met, using it to explain their world in a way Charlie had never heard it described before. She practically knew every word by heart now, but she kept browsing through it still. If only for the pictures.

A drawing fell out as she opened the binders, and her eyes caught on the charcoal girl, one of many she had made in those weeks following—

It came without warning. As if it had been waiting since Doyle, biding its time until she was off-guard. *The cane, as swift as a guillotine,* and a wave of memories washed over her like an ocean surge, drowning her from within. Her fingers clamped around the mug, but this time even the mild burn could not keep her afloat from the current pulling her under.

A searing agony announced itself in her bones and spread through her fingers from where the cane had hit, several fingertips covered in black ink. The Sister stared at Charlie with large, enraged eyes, but there was something else in them too, something that flashed whenever she did a double take at Charlie's stressed drawing of a girl, as if making sure the girl was still confined to the paper.

'What do you have to say about your actions, child?' thundered the black-clothed woman, gripping the cane, barely preventing herself from swinging it once more for good measure.

Charlie cast a glance at the other children around her. Eyes that had been following the spectacle now turned away and pretended they did not notice. One of the boys grabbed his arm, hiding a couple of nervous twitches. Some of the girls bit their lips, blood drained from their faces, looking ready to faint. Only one girl was able to meet her gaze, but perhaps more so because she was forced to – her muscle control low, her head lolling to the side with saliva pooling in her bottom lip. She'd been able to shapeshift into a bear cub when she came in at only six years old. They'd been on her for days. Breaking her down. Bit by bit.

Charlie blinked slowly at her, signalling a way to escape. The girl took the hint, closing her heavy eyelids, but then opened them again – as if upholding her resistance. In solidarity.

'I'm sorry, Miss...' Charlie mumbled, returning her gaze to the

woman standing before her. It was astonishing how she could keep the same frown for so long, as if she was moulded to look like a sourpuss from the get-go. 'There were so many feel--I-I felt,' she corrected herself. 'Frustrated. It calmed me down. I—'

'What frustrated you, child?' the Sister hissed. There was a new tone to her voice. An urgency, an ecstasy almost, and Charlie knew she had failed at finding the right words. She had heard the tone many times before, and always before a punishment. The Sister had picked up on what Charlie had been trying to hide; that her ability to sense – or rather absorb – everyone else's emotions had been activated. Here was a chance to not just discipline her but to make an example out of her as well – an opportunity to educate dozens of pupils with one striking cane.

'Was it the words of God that troubled you?' The Sister straightened her back, eyes popping. Not waiting for a reply, she turned to the others. 'Who, children, is it that find the words of God disconcerting?'

In unison, the room replied. 'Sinners, Miss.' The other girl closed her eyes.

The cane fell over Charlie's shoulders, leaving a lingering crunch resonating in her ears, sending jolts of pain branching down her back, skin searing even as the cane came away.

'And who forgives sinners, my children?'

'God, Miss.'

Another rap, so forceful that it shoved Charlie's forehead into the desk. Stars exploded before her eyes.

'And how, my children, does one receive forgiveness from God?'

'By abstaining from sin, Miss.'

A second rap over her knuckles, this time so hard that the skin cracked open and red drops rose to the surface. Charlie's mouth remained closed. Tears burned in the corners of her eyes whilst the Sister stared at Charlie's knuckles, her ecstasy and breath caught in the moment, like the tension emitting off the orphans.

Then, Charlie's skin healed itself.

Charlie forced herself to return to the present, her own brown eyes staring back at her from the mirror over her dresser. Her brows were heavy, her jaw set tight, and her hair fell in chocolatey waves down to her chest.

Three years had come and gone since she'd escaped Hallows Grove, and she almost looked like the girl she pictured when she thought of herself, yet at the same time she didn't. Along with thicker brows and fuller lips, her face had sharpened in places, erasing her more childish features.

But the eyes were still the eyes of a child. Young, naïve, frightened. As if something had broken inside of her long before, and she would always be caught in a loop of vulnerable adolescence. Never knowing what it would fully mean to be an adult; forever trying to fix what had broken. Always looking to others for the answer. Of who she was. Who she was meant to be. But what they *said* did not help.

A Magling. A Defective. A Human.

Those were the answers they gave. Labels. And she was each one of them depending on who was talking.

Amongst the Magless, left in the dark about magic, she was a fellow human. But unlike them, she had powers of sorts, and was therefore also, to the Agnus Dei, a Defective. One of God's creatures, alas woefully branded and corrupted by the Devil. A poor unfortunate soul they had to purge magic from, even if they had to squeeze it out of her. Squeeze and restrain until the Defective withdrew and became... a Withdrawer.

Like Doyle.

Like all her fellow orphans at Hallows Grove.

Like her. Almost. Except, she still had a sliver of unruly magic left. Not that it was much to brag about.

Charlie blinked, turning her gaze away from the mirror and to the open book in her lap. Maglings, as the Defectives called themselves, were listed in it too, except under the title *Mages and Magi-cians*, and she didn't think it near elaborate enough for her kind. For example, it didn't say anything about how some Maglings could learn to shapeshift into their spirit-animals. Nor did it say anything about how Maglings came to be. What their magic was like. That, according to Maddison, it all stemmed back to the gods and the four original species that came from them. The demons, the faeries, the nymphs – which were considered protectors of their territories – and the elves. The last of which was divided into Svartalfars and Liosalfars.

She touched the edge of her tipped ear. *'What do you think I am?'* Charlie had asked Maddison once.

'Part elf, at least with those ears,' she had replied. *'A Svartalfar, I'll say, considering your dark features and olive skin.'*

It had unnerved her at first; she'd read what was written about the Svartalfars, and the descriptions of their terrible power and cool intellect made the image of them incredibly intimidating in her mind. Brutal, like night itself. None of which were words usually used to describe her or her magic. If the Agnus knew about those myths, she imagined she would have been punished twice for the suspicion of her heritage alone.

Goosebumps rose at the thought, even now, when she had been around Maddison and Brimley long enough to wish that she would rather have terrible powers than no powers at all. But to believe that she was of Elvish heritage – it was hard. Maddison had once told her the elves had escaped into parallel realms and pocket dimensions during the Great Flood. Surely such an ancestry would be too far back in time to leave any visible traces on her now?

She'd certainly never seen another elf before. Except... perhaps once. On a mission for Maddison to steal a painting from a mansion short of a mile away from where they currently lived.

She'd failed, nearly being discovered as the people of the house returned earlier than expected, and she had just about managed to sneak outside and hide on the veranda as they entered the kitchen. That's when she had seen him.

Fair and beautiful, skin nearly as pale as his hair. His hands fumbling with some black masquerade masks the others had tossed onto the kitchen island. The subtle tilt of his chin while they talked seemed to still time. Her heart raced in her chest as she noticed the slightly tipped edge of his ear.

Even now, she reached up and felt her own just thinking about it, tracing the pointiness of it. The possibilities of her heritage. Her existence. There were other things, she supposed, that sounded more improbable.

Charlie turned the pages until she found an illustration of three old hags – the Three Fates. The ones more powerful than even the gods.

Maddison was beyond fascinated with them. Obsessed even. Kept on referring to them as their ancestors. Charlie supposed, as someone who suffered visions, that Maddison had a personal need to connect with the Fate of Fortune. To make sense of it all. Someone to idolize. Perhaps she wanted the same for Charlie too, likening her to the Fate of Life, whose powers were more like hers.

She studied the many names listed underneath the illustration. The *Encyclopaedia* contained all kinds of species from mythologies stemming from both the north and south of the equator, but for those who paid attention, it was clear that the majority were just a bunch of different names for the same beings repeated in folklores with a cultural twist. Same went for the Fates, with their Greek names listed as Clotho, Lachesis, and Atropos, while Nona, Decima, and Morta were their Roman equivalents. Urd, Verdandi, and Skuld were named as their Norse alternatives, but Norn, Moirai, Parcae, or simply "The Fates" were their collective terms.

It was enough to make her head spin.

Charlie shuffled through pictures of other beings, including the Banshee – a specific kind of faerie, one which the Quinseys apparently descended from – vampires, and... the werewolf.

Whenever she saw its picture, she always felt like she had seen it before. It tickled her memory, even though she could not place it. Not a human, like Brimley and his pack before they shifted. Not a wolf, like they were after. But something in between.

The phantom stench of rotten flesh and blood enveloped her, and she forced her eyes shut, feeling the hairs on the back of her neck rise. Feeling the presence of a demon, a beast, edge towards her bed. *Yellow lupine eyes, massive jaws, and fangs full of spit.*

She clamped the book shut and drew a shivering breath, pressing her forehead to the palm of her hand, her mug now cool to the touch in the other.

'I take it you're not feeling any better?'

Charlie looked up to see Maddison leaning against the doorway, casting a shadow over Charlie's tiny room the way she cast a shadow over most things.

It wasn't a bad room, really. Nothing spacious, but compared to the large empty room she had shared with the other orphans at Hallows Grove, it was quite nice to have her own intimate space. There were a few cracked spots on the walls where the plaster had fallen off and gaping construction holes lingered – holes from which she now and then felt the stare of beady-eyed rats waiting for her to fall asleep. She hated them. Hated the thought of them crawling closer when she was dreaming. But the wolves stationed to keep watch over them were quick to investigate whenever they heard her scream. Quicker than in the beginning at least, when Maddison had held them back to see if rat bites would trigger Charlie's magic.

Still, Charlie thought, at least she had a decent bed in this place. In other places they had squatted, she'd had to sleep on the floor.

'It's just been a long day,' Charlie replied at last, heat flooding her cheeks as she fidgeted with the sheets. 'I'm sorry for... for...' Her words caught in her mouth as her fingers twisted the corner of the duvet.

Maddison waved a hand. 'Everything was sprung on you. On me too.' She raised an eyebrow, seemingly lost in thoughts. 'When he told me he'd discovered something on his journey, I thought it'd be *her*. I didn't expect him to dump that boy on our living room floor. It was a bit of a shock.'

Not that anyone could tell, Charlie thought, admiring Maddison's skill at appearing completely unaffected by anything.

'I thought you'd been to see your fling again.' Charlie spoke into her cup, remembering a second too late that the drink had gone cold.

'No,' Maddison said pointedly. 'I meant it when I said that's over.'

'Right.' Charlie recalled now. Maddison had come home in a huff the other month, swearing off boys for the rest of her life. Charlie had discarded it though, having heard the declaration before. Then she added more quietly, 'Wish it was her.'

'You know, Charlie,' Maddison started, filling the silence between them, 'chances are we'll have to make peace with the fact we'll never find her.'

Charlie looked up from her cocoa again, her voice but a mere croak as she answered. 'I just... it'd be nice to know... you know?'

'I *know*.' Maddison twisted her lips contemplatively, as if she, too, was thinking back to the day she found Charlie, believing she was someone else.

Maddison had been flying high and low in her raven form, searching for that someone. Someone named Sophie Lou. It had not been until Charlie explained that she had been at Hallows Grove her entire life that they realised Charlie had to be Sophie's sister. That Sophie was Charlie's *twin* sister who, up until then, Charlie did not even know existed.

Ever since, she had marvelled about this girl, trying to wrap her head around the fact that a copy of herself was wandering around the big world on her own. Part of her wanted to find her, so that they could be a family. The other part speculated whom Maddison would like the most. Perhaps Sophie would be a stronger Defective than she was, and Maddison would be *her* best friend rather than her own.

That part of Charlie – the part she didn't like to acknowledge –

wanted to find Sophie too, but only to ask her if she knew what happened to their parents... and why they abandoned *her* at an orphanage.

She picked at a wooden pin on her sleeve, feeling the curve of the carved spindle against her fingertips and a crawl of an old, familiar insecurity in her belly. There hadn't been many belongings to bring with her from Hallows Grove. All she'd really owned was the pin. Clothes and toys were handed down to the younger children once outgrown, and even her baby blanket, wrapped around her when she was found, had been given away.

Had she been abandoned? Had her parents decided to keep Sophie before they died and Mrs Quinsey had taken her in? She had grown up with Maddison as her adoptive sister, that much Charlie knew, until the Quinseys had been torn apart too.

'If we don't find her,' Maddison said, eying the pin, 'I hope you know you still have family in me. It's not blood, but we're still sisters. Sisters-in-arms.' She studied her nails then gave Charlie a mischievous look. 'Us against the world.'

Charlie's heart fluttered at the words, but a concern kept nagging at the back of her mind. 'What if my magic doesn't get better?'

It had taken three weeks for Charlie's body to heal after she fled from Hallows Grove and was attacked. Three weeks where her mind kept her in a coma while her magic did its wonders. Now and then she had been aware though, aware of the sounds made and words spoken around her. *'Look at her, isn't she glorious? Look how her skin simply stitches itself together.'*

It had been Maddison thinking it was Sophie's magic on display and not her twin's.

Ever since she came to, Charlie's magic had been a fluke. An occasionally occurring event at best. All her life she had struggled to keep it hidden at the orphanage, with the Agnus Dei Sisters circling around her like vultures, ready to pounce whenever she used it, or whenever it belted out by accident. Now, when the people around her *wanted* her to use it, she struggled to bring it forth.

'It will,' Maddison said, her eyes cold and hard, and Charlie felt it was not an assurance, but an order. An ultimatum. Her space by Maddison's side dependent on her magic, of it becoming what Maddison expected it to become. She glanced down her arm to the pink and white lines. Some unintentional, others intentional, to see if they would heal after. Once upon a time, they would have. She looked up to see Maddison watching them too.

'Keep practicing,' she said, tucking a lock of hair behind Charlie's ear, her voice turning silky smooth. 'Or else we might end up apart. You don't want that, do you?'

Charlie shook her head, and the raven girl gave her a ghost of a smile before she rose from the bed. 'I have to go. Brimley asked me to come down to the Doghouse to discuss Doyle and the Halloween party tomorrow. You should stay in and get rested.'

Instantly, Charlie's body tensed. 'Tomorrow? But...' She grappled for an excuse as anxiety tickled up her shoulders. 'But we don't have any costumes?'

Maddison squinted and rubbed her temple, looking as if she was about to have one of her episodes.

'We don't need any costumes,' she growled, rolling her eyes as she paused on her way out. 'By the Moirai, Charlie, you're a Magling. You might want to start acting like it.'

Charlie sagged back against her pillow. A Magling yes, but also a Defective. She cast a glance at her Encyclopaedia. *A monster, corrupted by the Devil.*

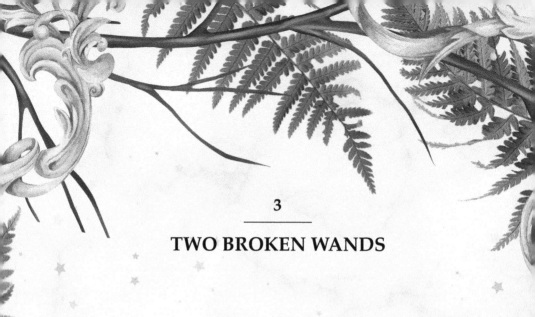

3

TWO BROKEN WANDS

'YOU'RE BREAKING MY HEART, Charlie, you really are, but please don't take too long filling their bellies, alright?' Maddison said, eyeing the Thermos in Charlie's hand. Damp steam from the hot vegetable soup rose from its mouth, cloaking her view of the homeless Withdrawer drinking greedily from the cup she'd handed him.

By his side on the bench lay dozens of newspapers that he'd used to keep warm, and a particular picture caught Charlie's attention. She felt as if a bucket of ice had been thrown over her head as she picked it up and stared into the familiar, cool glare of Mother Agnes – interviewed on the matter of an incident at an orphanage by a competing organisation.

'"We are struck with grief and disbelief at the tragedies of this world, and our hearts go out to our distant colleagues",' Charlie read aloud to Maddison, hearing the echo of Mother Agnes' imposing voice in her head.

'"We imagine that they, like us, try their very best, every day, to take care of these vulnerable children, but we are all merely servants of God with few resources. Sometimes the tools of the modern age overcome our Lord. And we can only pray that his lost children are now safe under his embrace. Although our own children's homes are at full capacity, we are opening our doors to our boarding school for young adults to those without a home. While we wish we could do more, we have found that every small bit of contribution helps in times like these".'

'A new attack?' Maddison asked with teeth gritted, reading further. Then she snorted. 'Can you believe that? They're blaming it on a gas explosion this time... and milking it for what it's worth.'

Charlie did not need to ask what she meant. Below the interview was an incentive and a bank account number for anyone wishing to donate in support of the Agnus Dei's charitable work. Without a doubt, the way they could squeeze a coin for all its worth, the Agnus would get enough money to fix both future gas leaks and uncontrolled Defectives alike. 'You think it's a cover up?' Charlie murmured.

Referenced in the article was a former home, Nettleheys, that was closed nearly eighteen years ago, in 1983. The reporter was linking the incident to patterns of children's homes and ragged schools from various organisations closing across the country – the common link being that no one was inclined to comment on the matter. A few more homes had shut down shortly after Nettleheys, but this new incident and closure was just the most recent in a wave of closures these past months alone.

'Might be a Defective.'

They looked up at the Withdrawer who'd stopped sipping from his cup.

'Who?' Charlie asked. But Maddison went to halt a couple passing by, then shortly after walked away towards the River Avon with one of their cell phones in hand, no doubt having compelled it from them.

'The reporter. Only someone like *us* would ask such questions.'

Charlie thought she understood now. She'd heard Maddison and Brimley discussing it before.

Throughout the years even before Nettleheys, there had been

hushed-up cases around the world where private homes – like Doyle's – had also been attacked, the parents murdered or vanished without a trace, leaving their children orphaned. The Agnus Dei, as a respectable charitable organisation, was usually the first on the scene after the police, taking the children into their care. Often, people wondered and worried that the culprits would come back for the children and attack their orphanages. But no one ever did, and people forgot about the events. Except from the Defective communities, where the general belief was that the Agnus stood behind the attacks because the families affected had been Maglings. Then the attacks on the orphanages began.

Suspecting them for this was a far more controversial theory. Some, like Charlie, struggled to believe the Agnus would go that far. There was evil, and then there was *evil*. Besides... word on the street whispered about monsters, not men, being the source of the attacks.

Then there were those who did not take much stock in these rumours and believed the Agnus Dei capable of doing anything to draw attention away from themselves.

'It was them then; it is them now,' croaked the Withdrawer below his rattling breath.

'Wouldn't it be reckless? And counterproductive? It's children! Someone is bound to be looking into it.' Charlie looked at the photo of Nettleheys, the memory of Maddison's words still sizzling in her chest, and studied the grand building, finding something familiar about the position of the trees next to its driveway and the intricate details of the door—

Abruptly, her mind jumped back to the children. Would any of them still be alive today and able to tell them the truth?

'*Orphaned* children,' Maddison said, appearing beside them. The couple stood by the pathway, their phone returned, and scratched their heads. 'We don't even have *parents* looking for us.'

Charlie drew a breath and scowled against the sharpness of her words, but she didn't say anything. It was true, after all.

With an impatient sigh, and without paying the Withdrawer a

second thought, Maddison hoisted her rucksack onto her back and headed towards the staircases that would lead them back to the streets above. It really shouldn't have surprised Charlie; as far as she knew, Maddison had only taken on one charity case in her life – *her* – and she hadn't shown any interest in taking on another since.

'Come on!'

Distressed, Charlie looked from Maddison's retreating figure to the Withdrawer with the cup still cradled in his hands.

'Thank you,' he wheezed, catching her expression. His lungs sounded frozen from the inside out, yet he returned the cup and waved Charlie along as she turned to follow Maddison, leaving him under the park bench where they had found him.

Yellow leaves swayed above, ruffled by the cool autumn air. She could feel the gaze of Prince Bladud's statue boring into the back of her neck as she walked past it, and she made haste, telling herself it was due to the cold wrapping itself around her limbs and buttocks, rather than shame.

An orange balloon on the loose rushed into the sky as they left Parade Garden behind them. Wafts of hog roasts, garlic butter, and red wine drifted out of one of the finer establishments lining the park, making her mouth water. They followed the roundabout, down a little side road, and past the gothic marvel that was Bath Abbey.

Charlie's head spun to take in the arched windows and detailed carvings, but her attention was quickly pulled back to a street performer playing music in the middle of the square, trying his hardest to serenade the few people present. Yet their faces remained as stoic as the old statues of Roman emperors and governors lining the terraces of the Roman Baths, eventually turning their backs on him as well.

Doorbells chimed as the pair continued down Abbey Street, followed by the sound of excited children yelling 'Trick or Treat', and surprised exclamations from adults.

'Trick,' Maddison hissed at a child they passed, snatching a sweet from his basket. He didn't even protest but instead shrank back frightened under her glare. The moment she walked on, the child made haste and disappeared back the way he came, the wind howling after him.

'Was that really necessary?' Charlie asked, the cold autumn breeze throwing her hair into turmoil as they turned the corner onto a quiet cobbled street square. Here as with anywhere else in the city, the golden Bath stone surrounded them. It had always been fascinating to her how Bath managed to keep the same façade, year after year, building after building, while other towns surrendered to the modern era bit by bit. It was as if the town simply refused to let its mask fall, covering up new buildings with the clothes of an era gone by. She empathised with that. Perhaps all Defectives did.

'Why are they out here if they can't handle a scare?' Maddison combed her hand through her long raven hair and tossed it back over her shoulder in one fluid motion. A green sheen rippled through it. Charlie opened her mouth to argue but decided not to. There was simply no point. Instead, she humoured herself thinking of how the Headmistress of Hallows Grove used to call *her* a headstrong girl. If only she had met Maddison; she'd probably have asked the High Priests for an early retirement.

Sensing Charlie's surrender, Maddison's hostile expression softened, and she hooked her arm with hers. 'Chin up, Hallows. Brimley has promised me an absolutely brilliant party.'

Of course he had, being as hopelessly in love as a puppy with its owner. Charlie would have rolled her eyes if she did not feel bad for him.

Somebody ought to. Maddison rarely noticed the emotional havoc she caused in others, clever and brilliant though she was. Charlie sighed, studying her friend as they walked around the grand old tree in the middle of the square, cautious to appear as carefree and casual as possible in case anyone was following at their heels.

She had to give Maddison a break, she supposed; no one else had to live with the burden she did. Charlie wouldn't be surprised if it was her way of coping with her visions. If it had been her witnessing grief and suffering at all hours of the day, Charlie would probably have withdrawn from her powers just to escape it. As such, she couldn't fault Maddison for using her coolness as a mask. And it wasn't like Maddison was completely void of emotion. Charlie had seen fleeting moments of warmth after all, although they were usually reserved just for her.

Charlie pulled her cloak tighter, taking in the funny little shops around her. Warm light filled the gleeful window displays full of pumpkin bulbs and skeletons hanging merrily wherever appropriate. The smell of warm buns, clotted cream, and strawberry jam made her mouth water, enhanced by the fresh air. She located the aroma coming from a little cafe with patrons walking in and out through its low-beamed threshold. There were people everywhere. A few, mostly students the same age, were dressed up while the rest scowled at those who were.

Charlie wondered how many of them were Defectives. How many currently ran the risk of detection by the Agnus because they thought they could blend in with the masses. *But the Agnus would notice,* she thought, certain that they could spot real horns or wings – "Devil's marks" as they called them – from afar; just like the old Puritan witch hunters who examined bodies for warts and the like during the seventeenth century. They were their forefathers after all. Spotting the unnatural was in their DNA just as much as magic was in hers.

Charlie dragged her beanie tighter over her ears.

'One day, I'd like to experience Halloween in America,' Maddison said enthusiastically as a witch passed them, clearly in a different mindset than Charlie. 'I hear practically everyone dresses up over there. The number of Maglings amongst them must be unreal! Then I'd like to participate in a proper Beltane celebration. A whole night dancing around bonfires and frolicking!' Her eyes shone with delight as she spoke, but Charlie only smiled nervously, silently thinking she wouldn't be any more relaxed in America when all she could do was look around for black suits and hostile eyes.

Usually, Maddison didn't care much for holidays, not even Christmas, and neither did Charlie, but for different reasons. The rest of the year was difficult enough without the added display of joyful parents and children ready to celebrate.

They passed an old sweet shop window when someone inside caught Charlie's attention. A pair of twins, whispering secrets and giggling to one another while their parents purchased sweets. Drawn to them, Charlie probably looked like a real Agnus creep with her nose pressed up against the red-framed glass. Yet, she could not help but stare. The twins gave each other a hug, and her stomach jerked, thinking of what might have been and wondering again what had happened to her own twin.

'Charlie!' Maddison called from farther down the street. Startled, Charlie jogged to catch up, her head racing with the thought of family, love, and companionship. By the time she reached her only friend, her heart was aching tremendously. It was practically a relief when she caught sight of the homeless hiding behind the bins and under rain-stained cardboard boxes, like a lighthouse on a stormy night. It wouldn't bring back her family, but at least she could help these folks.

She stopped before the men and women, unscrewed the Thermos top, then poured soup in its cup. None of them came forward. Instead, they remained in the shadows. Whether they truly were Withdrawers was hard to tell, but Charlie had learned to recognise them by the fearful look in their eyes. The one darting across the street as if expecting the Agnus Dei to appear out of the blue. The one that bore holes into her cup of soup while they waited to see if it was a trap. But hunger had a way of fighting fear.

One after the other, they staggered forward. Some she already knew from evenings spent wandering through town with Brimley and Maddison, picking up news regarding the Agnus, Defectives known to them, or other tales of woe from the streets. Their stories were many.

'My father himself sent me to one of those places,' an elderly lady told them once, nodding her head so that her toothless mouth ran over with soup. 'They declared me insane because I refused to marry the man he had chosen for me. Perhaps I was. Perhaps I wasn't. Would have been a much better life in the end than the one I got.'

The woman, like many others, had been healthy when drugged, but her free spirit had been smothered, along with the magic that roared within her, one inseparable from the other. And all of them recalled the burning fire of hope they had nurtured when Margaret Thatcher shut down the mental institutions. But no Defective could have foreseen the Agnus entering the scene, buying community houses and old orphanages still carrying the weight of the good name of noble organisations before them, despite the previous owners having nothing to do with them – saints, like the Old Sisters of Charity, doing their duty to care for the weaker ones no one else knew how to deal with. No one would believe them when the Defectives and Withdrawers complained about their new prisons. Surely, this time, their past ordeals had simply driven the poor souls mad for real.

Today, it was impossible to say how many of the drunks and homeless on the street were Withdrawers or simply just Magless having lost their way. In all honesty, Charlie did not think there was any difference. One way or another, society had driven them to alcohol or other substances, their spirits broken by the system, until their addictions had landed them on the street.

Tragically, there were always new faces as well. Faces from Bath or faces who had travelled from other cities hoping to escape the missionaries, without luck. The Agnus usually caught up in the end. It was why Charlie and Maddison never stayed in the same place too long. Many of their kind chose to withdraw instead, hoping to belong, to be accepted and live in peace with themselves and society. *Redemption.* The mere thought of the word made her heart sigh. How she wanted it, or her idea of it: the freedom to simply exist.

But it never came. Not as a Defective. Nor as a Withdrawer.

Most regretted the transformation, suffering physically, mentally, or both. Reconnecting with one's magic once it was lost was unheard of, or a myth at best. Instead, the Withdrawers she met told their stories like a warning, as if their symptoms didn't speak more than a thousand words.

The thought of sharing their fate scared her half to death, and she knew, if given the choice, she would never return to Hallows Grove, even though it meant she would live a life in sin with other Defectives – at least, if she did not withdraw. The irony was bitter in her mouth. Here she was, once an Agnus orphan with powers, broken and unfit to be part of society, now a Defective but not a strong enough one. Wherever she was, she didn't quite belong. But the Defectives were her best bet to eventually do so. If she failed, however, she might only belong to the streets.

Her heart bled with empathy for the homeless by the time they reached Lady Harietta's corner. Charlie only had a little soup left but took her sweet time pouring it into a cup, delaying their imminent arrival at the Doghouse. If only Lady Harietta wouldn't look at her so knowingly over the edge of her cup.

The fortune-teller had once travelled around Bath in her wagon, living on the outskirts of the historic town. Her clairvoyant powers were nothing to Maddison's, but she had managed to eke out a living for herself – until the Agnus appeared in Somerset.

At the same time, Lady Harietta had put the *closed* sign on her door and never saw a client again. Now she was on the streets, strolling through the alleys with her trolley and rubbish-filled bags, dirt and grime covering her clothes.

'Bless you, child. May Clotho be with you,' Lady Harietta cooed, blessing upon her the Fate of Life before she put the cup to her lips a second time. Eagerly, Charlie thought to ask her what she knew about the Fates but stopped mid-speech when Lady Harietta made a deep, satisfied 'Mmm' sound. Warm soup sloshed about in her mouth as she grinned back at Charlie, and she thought it better to let her enjoy it.

In payment, however, the old woman offered them fortunes between mouthfuls. Charlie listened respectfully, secretly hoping some would come true (the one regarding a prince, particularly). Maddison didn't even bother to pretend as though she was listening; she continued to stare in the direction of Brimley's lodging.

'You wish to be loved and praised,' Lady Harietta said, trailing Charlie's palm. Then she gasped. 'But you'll be betrayed.'

Maddison turned on her heels at the same moment Charlie shook her head.

'Pardon?' Charlie looked at her palm, trying to see whatever the old lady had seen, at least expecting red flashing flags of sorts.

'Come on, Charlie! We're running out of time and we're almost there,' Maddison groaned, tugging at her arm.

'But I—'

'Now!'

Annoyance and frustration lingered in her at being dragged away from Lady Harietta's corner. 'I really wanted to know what she meant, you know.'

'I wouldn't put too much stock in the ramblings of an old fraud,' Maddison sneered, keeping up her speed, eyes firmly fixed on the lodging coming into view at the end of the alley.

It was desperately in need of some tender love and care. Its misshapen, gothic façade made it quite clear why it was out of business; it appeared destined to attract only crooks and the homeless. No paying customer in their right mind would set foot across its threshold, if not for the lack of visual appeal, then at least for the repulsive odours of rotting garbage, waste, and wet animal fur. It was the perfect cover for a pack of wolf-shifters, spending their days clawing at furniture and barking into the long hours of the night – which they usually did.

That was why a sense of unease fell over Charlie at the tense silence surrounding the building. There wasn't a sound – not the clinks of bottles or even the rattling wheels of Harietta's trolley, which they should have heard pulling away.

'Wait!' Maddison held her arm out while her eyes darted left and right to the darkness gaping back at them from the alleys as thick fog rolled through. They were in the centre of a five-point crossroad where several back alleys met and melted into one another. The wind shoved litter across the ground and into the walls. 'Something's off.'

'Perhaps they're having a meeting?' Charlie asked, hearing the scepticism in her own voice. They were supposed to arrive to a party, not a funeral.

Maddison ignored Charlie's suggestion and cautiously approached the side entrance, which burst open as Brimley's pack members tumbled out.

Something was obviously wrong.

The pack clawed at their bodies and ears as though they had fleas. Brimley lost his balance, rolling around on the floor, fighting yet another involuntary convulsion of his body. Fur sprouted from his pores, covering his knuckles as his nails transformed to claws. The others were all undergoing similar transformations.

'Bri-Brimley, what's g-going on?' Charlie's fear rasped at her throat. Brimley stood before her, his thick eyebrows bent in confusion above his narrow eyes and thick, flat nose. A growl erupted from his vocal cords as he started clawing at his now-pointed ears, covered in bronze fur.

'That sound!'

'What sound?'

'*That* sound!' Brimley's voice faded into lupine yelps as he completed his transformation and crouched onto all fours. Seven wolves stood in the alley, barking at each other until they tensed – as one – ears alert, noses twitching, and paws tapping. For a brief moment, they froze, all seven muzzles pointed in the same direction. Then they rushed past the girls, knocking them over. An involuntary gasp escaped Charlie as her tailbone met with the cobblestones, sending a sharp pain ricocheting up her arms after she tried to prevent the rough landing with her hands. Tears welled up in her eyes, blurring her vision as the wolves disappeared down the alley.

Only one wolf remained, straining his neck and monstrous muscles as if fighting the urge to leave, looking back at them with large, familiar eyes.

'Brimley,' Maddison whispered.

Charlie blinked. For the first time in her life, she heard a soft whine from the alpha before he threw his head around and disappeared after the others.

Panic flared in Charlie's chest. 'What—where did they go?'

She scrambled to her feet, intending to run after them, when Maddison's voice – or something in it – made her pause, her blood turning to ice.

'Charlie.'

Chills skittered down her spine as she turned.

Maddison wore a faraway expression, staring with green irises turning white into the dark alleys beyond the fog and shadows. Charlie imagined the one thing she feared the most, but it was not imaginary when marching footsteps sounded, crunching litter underfoot. Dark shadows slipped out of the alleys through the fog. As they came closer, her eyes picked out crucial details: four cloaked figures with two broken wands embroidered on their pockets.

The Agnus Dei had found them.

4

A MEMORY OF HALLOWS GROVE

CHARLIE'S TIME after the escape had been plagued by nightmares. They woke her during the night, leaving her shivering and gasping for breath in pools of sweat. And they were always the same. Running wolves rising on two legs, turning into men, more men. Agnus Brothers closing in on her. Now the nightmare had come alive.

The dark figures marched towards them, tendrils of fog clinging to their cloaks, paving the way as the Agnus brandished their whips. Charlie spun around, clocking another four coming from the opposite direction.

'How many?' Maddison whispered through the corner of her mouth.

'Eight in total,' Charlie replied, and air went out of her as she said it. The Agnus always hunted in groups, knowing there was only so much magic a Defective could use at once. Maddison's body tensed next to her. Even for her it would be too many to compel at the same time without taking a break. Especially if one of those carrying a copper whip caught a hold of her before she caught a hold of him.

Knowing smirks curled themselves on the faces of the whip

carriers as their comrades revealed their crucifixes and sticks with nails at the end as if they were hunting vampires or pests – one equal to the other as far as the Agnus were concerned. A sudden click sounded, and Charlie imagined a pocketknife opening.

In her nightmares, she had always seen Mother Agnes standing before her, cane in hand, grinning in triumph, as though she'd caught a wild animal. Blinking, Charlie saw a real Agnus member; his cold eyes filled with disgust, studying her every move. Her heart raced, faster than ever before, nearly exploding in her chest. With numb, shaking limbs, she staggered backwards towards Maddison, until their shoulders were pressed together. They glanced at each other briefly through the corners of their eyes. Maddison's fists were up, her expression strained, her eyes white, but nothing happened. The Agnus came closer still. None of them attacked, but Maddison's ashen face said it all. Their chances were bleak; any defence would be futile.

'When I say the word, you run,' Maddison whispered.

Charlie gulped down shaky breaths. 'I don't want to leave you behind.'

'You won't... Now, run!'

Her legs reacted before her head could. She dived in between two of the men, dodging their outstretched hands, and bolted down a random alley littered with rubbish and rubble that crunched underneath her soles. Throwing a wild glance behind her, Charlie caught a glimpse of Maddison still in the same place, dodging the coppery whips as they came for her. Two other Agnus members were chasing down Charlie, closing in as she hesitated.

Run. She faced ahead, pumping her arms as fast as she could, her nails digging into her palms. Her throat burned as if it were on fire, yet she did not stop. She skidded around a corner, her shoulder crunching painfully against the rough brick wall. Her movements turned wobbly as she fought her way down the street, one hand pumping, one held to her shoulder, her legs drumming wildly. A gunshot sounded far behind, and Charlie stopped dead in her tracks.

Turning slowly, she stared past the men racing towards her, her mind conjuring an image of Maddison lying in a pool of blood back at the Doghouse. *She would have wanted to go down fighting, and they would have seen themselves forced to use... No, maybe she had manipulated the gun holder to shoot another... That's not really any better.* Her thoughts echoed through her head. Out of pure instinct, she raised her palms. Not to surrender, but to conjure something – anything – to fight back with. The men hesitated. Just for a second, but it was enough to make her feel slightly tougher; they had weapons, but she had one too. She just needed to control hers.

She shoved her palms towards the men and saw them flinch. She begged her powers to come, to simply show themselves. Throw the men against the wall. Fling fireballs at them. Shake the earth under their feet. Heal Maddison's gunshot from afar if there was one.

Maddison had always had faith there were hidden features to her powers. Now would be a good time for them to reveal themselves.

Charlie reached deep into the well at the core of her being... Yet...

Nothing.

She visualised nothing, and nothing happened.

As always.

The only thing she produced were bitter tears running down her cheeks as her failure washed over her. Rather than shaking with power, she began trembling with fear and grief at the thought of having lost Maddison. In exhaustion, she reached for the pin on her sleeve, but the coppery fall of a whip latched onto her feet and coiled around them, pulling her off balance. Her newly wounded shoulder exploded with pain as she hit the ground. Charlie grimaced, rolling side-to-side on her back, glimpsing a pair of frightened eyes staring at her from behind a pair of trash cans. A plea for help escaped her lips as four arms grabbed hers and hauled her upwards, but as a sack was pulled over her head, Lady Harietta scampered back into the shadows.

'Deep breaths,' Charlie murmured to herself, inhaled sharply, then exhaled.

Before her lay a stack of paper, a couple half-broken coal sticks, and a raven sat in the windowsill, cawing for attention. It was her only company in the room, which was a good thing because what she was about to do – if it worked – was for her eyes only. And the raven's.

She glanced down at the top sheet of paper, featuring a coal-drawing of a girl looking much like the way she pictured herself in her mind, but which never looked the same as her reflection in the mirror. This girl was prettier, the shape of her face sweeter, her eyes wider, and her nose barely a button compared to Charlie's real nose. Even her stance carried a sort of confidence and fierceness that Charlie had only dreamed of. She was so full of life! Almost as if she were *alive*.

Goosebumps travelled down Charlie's arm, and she hesitated ever so slightly. But it was better to do it now than risk it later. The Sister Assistant had notified Charlie that her presence was expected in the headmistress' office in promptly half an hour, and since she had been rather good of late, Charlie could only think of one reason for it.

Now and then, Hallows Grove held random assessments to test whether the children had withdrawn from their magic. The punishments upon discovering they hadn't were severe. Much worse than when being caught with magic on the daily. Most students withdrew by their second or third assessment if they had not already by their first. Charlie had lost count of how many she had endured, and it wasn't from a lack of trying to avoid them.

But her magic was a bit like a dandelion. No matter how hard she tried to quench it or cover it, it kept pushing to the surface. This time, though, she was optimistic – or desperate, same thing really – as it had been weeks since her powers last made themselves known. Possibly months even, although it was hard to tell. Time seemed to move so slowly here. She was just about to turn fifteen, and yet she felt eighty years old. Or at least how she imagined eighty-year-olds would feel.

The raven cawed again, calling out her stalling.

Sighing, Charlie picked up the drawing and prayed behind closed *eyelids before she blew on the drawing like she had done the very first time it happened. Then she dared herself a sneak peek.*

At first, relief flooded through her. Nothing had changed. But the reprieve soon turned to ice as the girl began to rise off her sheet, moving in swirling motions as if she was being uplifted by an invisible wind.

Startled, Charlie dropped the sheet of paper onto the others, staring at the pile in horror.

Her magic was as active as it had ever been.

A quick rap of knuckles sounded at the door, and Charlie jumped a second time.

'You are expected, Charlie.'

Kicking the drawings under her bed, Charlie rose as fast as she could despite her whole body feeling as if it had been steeped in lactic acid, just like the time she was punished with laps around the grounds from morning to evening.

The Sister Assistant barely deigned to look at her as she opened the door, waiting only long enough to give her a scolding glare before she turned on her heels and led the way down the staircase.

They walked straight into a thick wave of ammonia.

Buckling over on the lower steps, Charlie gagged on the smell and searched for its origin. She didn't need to look far.

Through the open dining room door, she spotted a fellow orphan standing on a three-legged wooden stool, a black mock-witch hat on his head. His legs were caked in two to three days' worth of dried excrement and urine, and a shiver went down her spine, her own legs turning heavy with the weight of phantom faeces. The boy caught her eye, grimacing mournfully as if to wish her good luck. Whether he meant with the assessment or her next turn on the pedestal she wasn't sure, but she clenched her teeth together and hurried after the Sister Assistant before she herself would make sure of the latter.

By some miracle, Charlie made it to the headmistress' office without puking. Mother Agnes, however, looked up from her papers as if she had come drenched in bile.

'Charlie. You've done magic again.'

It wasn't a question at this point, so Charlie didn't answer either.

On her bookshelf stood a plaquette used to prop up a row of Agnus' texts and pristine Bibles Charlie often wondered if ever had been read in full. The plaquette bore the words 'For Most Abnormally Normal Children' and had been granted to Mother Agnes just before Charlie arrived. She supposed it was some running joke amongst the Agnus Dei and their orphanages.

Their homes were known for taking care of children with special needs, like many other homes in Britain. What the public didn't know was that most children who came into the care of the Agnus developed their special needs after *their arrival. That was what the "abnormal" referred to, and it struck her worse than the cane every time.*

The headmistress sighed, stood from her desk, and walked towards Charlie, her cornrow curls braided in their usual halo around her head, framing her aging face.

'There is no use dissociating from the situation, Charlie. I can see it upon the flush of your cheek, the shifty guilt in your eyes.'

Charlie flinched as Mother Agnes reached out a hand, but she laid it gently against her cheek.

'If only you'd see we simply wish you well.' Her breath stung with bitter coffee as she trailed her thumb up to Charlie's forehead where Charlie's meeting with her desk some weeks ago had left a mark. It was still a little bruised, mainly because it had not been left alone since.

Mother Agnes pressed against it, and Charlie drew her breath sharply.

'Heaven is not a place for Defectives,' the headmistress said and let go. 'Nor is Earth. Your powers are an abomination. You know what you have to do.'

Suppress them, *Charlie thought. Mother Agnes nodded as if she had heard her. 'Only then will you be absolved from your sins. Or else your soul will go to Hell.'*

She retracted her hand – and struck. Hard. Charlie fell against the wall, her ears ringing like the bells of St Thomas' Church. The whole room seemed to be spinning. Spinning with one thought. Isn't *this* Hell?

When the headmistress spoke again, it sounded like she was miles away, and Charlie's head only stopped ringing when there was a knock at the door.

'The representative from Soli Gloria, Headmistress,' said the Sister Assistant, casting one look at Charlie.

Mother Agnes nodded. 'Send him in. I had hoped that I would be able to prevent this, but alas.'

Entering past the Sister Assistant came a tall man with sharp facial features and long buttery hair bundled into a ponytail with a greenish tint to it. He was the handsomest man Charlie had seen (granted she hadn't seen many yet), despite the dark robes he dressed himself in; the uniform of the Agnus Dei, his chest pocket embroidered with two broken wands.

'Is this her?' he asked the headmistress before she had the chance to shake his hand, ignoring her outstretched one.

'It is,' answered Mother Agnes, clenching her jaw tight. 'Marvella, will you see Charlie outside while the Soli Gloria representative and I speak?'

His lips curved into a saluting smile as their eyes met, earning Charlie a whack across the back of her head by the Sister Assistant once they were out of the office.

'Don't tantalise the poor man,' she hissed, trying so hard to be inaudible that it was perfectly obvious. 'Off you go!'

Charlie didn't need to be asked twice. In fact, they would have a harder job asking her to stay.

Soli Gloria. She knew that name. It was where those who had not withdrawn before the age of eighteen had been sent. The Agnus' missionary school for young adults.

But she was not eighteen yet. And yet, he was here. For her. That much had been clear. To take her away?

Soli Gloria had often been whispered about between those who shared Charlie's room. A place for the worst of the worst they said – with punishments that fit the bill.

Her insides trembled.

But how would they know? *She tried to soothe herself. It wasn't as if anyone had returned and told them... but was it because they wouldn't or because they couldn't? Were they even... alive?*

She glanced up at the Sister Assistant's unpleasant features and knew then that neither here nor there was an option. It was time. Time to make a run for it.

And she had. And she had gotten away too.

Until now... Charlie thought as she came back to her present self, feeling the moving vehicle under her coming to a stop. There was the sound of a door sliding open and the bustling noises of someone entering. Whimpering and pleading ensued. More feet shuffling. Finally, some rough fingers grabbed her arms and forced her to her feet, one hand on her head, keeping her back hunched low as they guided her outside. There was a rush of coarse fabric caressing her face, ruffling her hair, and the sack was removed from her head, replacing the blinding darkness with the blurred shapes of an unknown place.

The smells of decomposing leaves and wood struck her as she was freed, and it took her a moment to register the face lit up by the streetlamps above. Once she did, she recognised him at once.

'Ah, Miss Charlie, of Hallows Grove!'

He hadn't changed at all the past three years. Sharp facial features and long buttery hair with a greenish tint. 'You disappeared so quickly I didn't get to introduce myself last time,' the Soli Gloria representative said. 'I'm Brother Deimos.'

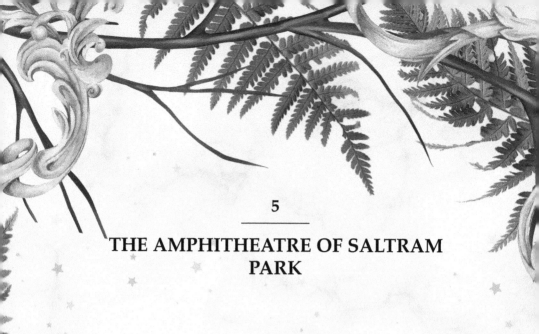

5

THE AMPHITHEATRE OF SALTRAM PARK

THEY HAD STOPPED at a car park surrounded by tall trees and darkness, empty of any other cars but the white vans parked with total disregard for the white lines marking up free space. Youths were herded out of them like school pupils on a field trip, but none of them appeared excited to be there. Each had a colourless face, trembling lips, and darting eyes. Some were rubbing their arms repetitively as if they were cold while others stood stiff and poised, as if ready to make a run for it.

She imagined she looked much the same. Brother Deimos had not said much, besides giving her a promise that they would become closer acquainted *very* soon, before he turned to a fellow Brother of his, murmured something that was received with a curt nod, and then disappeared down a broader path signed with "Saltram Park".

Tremors of panic went through her body, making it rapidly harder to breathe. She searched the car park for anything, anyone, to ask for help or hold on to – until Maddison appeared by her side and her panic intermingled with ripples of relief.

'You're alive!' Charlie breathed, her body poised for a hug.

'Of course I am,' Maddison said, making a sharp warning gesture with her hand. Charlie stayed put. 'Why wouldn't I be?'

'I-I heard a gunshot.'

'Ah.' Maddison rolled her eyes. 'That was a flare gun, Charlie, and it was a ploy to make you stop.' *Obviously, it worked*, her eyes said.

'Oh...' Charlie murmured. Cool shame ran through her body as she pretended to study their surroundings. Whether it was due to the icy wind or crude voice in her head was hard to tell, but tears soon stung at the corners of her eyes. *Of course it was.* And she'd stupidly fallen for it. One tear rolled down her cheek, and she dried it off before Maddison could notice, forcing her thoughts to take another direction. To think of *anything* more productive. Like how they could escape.

But it was a fool's idea. She had no clue where they were, unable to see past the vast green, closed buildings, and trees that bordered the car park. She wouldn't get a hundred metres down the road before caught hesitating at a crossroad.

She looked towards the Agnus Brothers. Some were watching them, whips at their sides. Others were busy diverting a guy that appeared to have come out from closing the site for the day. Her stomach tightened into a hard knot. Could she signal to him for help?

'Night-time field study you say?' she heard the man say. 'You'd need a special permit to enter the Saltram Gardens.'

'Oh, we're not going there; we're sticking to the public footpath.'

'Well, you do as you please then. It's public, innit,' the man said and walked off towards his car, clearly annoyed at being delayed from his return home.

Just as she stood eavesdropping, another vehicle pulled up and caught her attention. It was not a white van like the others but an expensive-looking black jeep. A short man with a snout of a nose jumped out from the driver's side, backpack in hand, and hurried on short legs, wild mane billowing around him. It made him look like a stressed-out lion. To her surprise, a boy around her age stepped out from the passenger side and received the backpack from his driver. Shimmering starlight painted his fair locks in white-silver and highlighted his cheekbones, sharp like a papercut. He hoisted his backpack over his shoulders and gazed around the site, meeting her eyes with his own steely blue. It was him, the boy she'd observed through a veranda door! The one with slightly pointed ears like hers.

Immediately, she felt her cheeks flare hot, and she became immensely interested in her feet, her knotted stomach easing a little with her budding curiosity. What was *he* doing here? She peeked up again, but the boy had turned his back to her, addressing his driver.

'Do I really have to be here?' His voice reached her ears. Annoyed. Not entitled or whiny but strained.

'It is your father's will.'

'But I rather want to help you with—'

'Not here, lad.' The driver shushed him, and both looked around, catching Charlie staring. Flabbergasted, Charlie turned and pulled at Maddison's sleeve. 'That boy doesn't seem to have been brought here by the Agnus, isn't that odd?'

'Not really,' Maddison said, looking bored, staring at her nails. No one would believe she was kidnapped against her will. 'Could be one of those odd families with a sudden appearance of magic.'

It was believed amongst the Defectives that all humans had magic at one point, but that generations of mixing with Magless and withdrawing had slowly watered down the genes until the majority were born without it. Yet, sometimes, a family member would prove to be Defective even though all of their closest relatives were not – which sparked many controversial debates ranging from magic being genetic to magic coming from something else and merely being dormant in a modern society.

Maddison continued. 'His family probably met one of those travelling Agnus preachers convincing them to send him here voluntarily. Religious families on the extreme end tend to take the bait, sending their

Defective children away in a desperate attempt to "drive the devil" out of them. Very hush-hush of course. Neither the families nor Agnus would want *that* to be widely known.' She grimaced and followed Charlie's gaze to the boy, her eyebrows lifting approvingly. 'But I sure hope the devil stays in that one.' Maddison nudged Charlie's shoulder with her own.

Charlie's eye sockets hurt by the force of her eyerolling, the taste in her mouth souring. 'I see you're over your partners in Bath already?'

'Don't hate the player, Charlie.' Maddison winked, remarking on the stink of Charlie's envy by a mere curl of her lip. Charlie couldn't help it. Maddison, like with everything else, flirted as if she was a born professional. Charlie could never even imagine pulling off a "Let's romp" without digging a grave and pushing herself into it. Worse was that Maddison didn't even need it. Boys looked at her whenever she walked by, simply because of the way she looked. No one turned when Charlie passed them...

A rustle like the sound of a stomping herd told her that people had started moving – or were being moved. Reminded of Maddison's suitors, Charlie looked amongst them for Brimley and his pack members, but none of the faces she saw were familiar. Perhaps she would find the pack at the institution. The boy, however, was moving to join them; the driver remained by the Jeep, staring directly at her.

'Pray, what is your name, lass?' the driver asked.

'Err, Charlie, sir,' she replied, taken by surprise. She pulled her jacket closer to herself and rubbed her fingers on the pin on her sleeve, as if checking that it was still with her. The man's eyes followed her movement and widened as they fell on the pin. But he said nothing. She debated asking why he'd asked, but the boy's voice cut through before she had the chance.

'There's no need to linger, Bes. I won't try to run.'

As if he'd announced that he'd actually try, or to demonstrate that there was no way he could, the Agnus Brothers closed in on the group, pushing the boy and Charlie to join the rest, and blocked their view to the driver.

The knot in her stomach returned, and her muscles trembled with every step. This was happening. The Agnus Dei had her, and she was returning to one of their institutions, far away from freedom. Her breathing quickened, and her nerves acted like a group of circus performers, tumbling about left and right as if they were trying to flee their bodily prison like she wanted to flee the site. Maddison, however, did not seem to share her emotions.

'It's a shame it's so dark,' Maddison murmured soberly, her eyes on the tree above them. They lined the path ahead on both sides, forming a tunnel, their leaves a deep shade of scarlet in the night. 'I think it would have looked spectacular walking through here with the sunlight flickering above. As if walking under a roof made of flames.' Reading her glare correctly, Maddison sighed exasperatingly. 'What more can they do to us, Charlie? They're already taking our freedom.'

'They could force you to suppress your powers, and they could...' Charlie paused. They could succeed in making *her* withdraw from hers once and for all, but what would that even be like? For once she would be hunted no more. Punished no more. If she withdrew, they would send her into society. Their duty of boarding only extended until she was nursed from her deficiency – but, she reminded herself, there would be no life awaiting her on the streets.

She thought of the Withdrawers of Bath, alone and forgotten. A life neglected and suppressed. Unloved, even by Maddison. She'd be free of one set of problems only to have another; one she didn't think she preferred.

The raven beauty clicked her tongue. 'No, they can only *try*. And they will. But it is up to us whether or not we let them.' An odd expression fell over her, which Charlie had difficulty interpreting. She had seen it before whenever Maddison hatched some sort of plan and was watching it come to fruition, but she couldn't imagine whatever the plan would be now.

'Then what about Sophie?' It had not been lost on Charlie that they would now be prevented from continuing the search. Surely, it wasn't lost on Maddison either.

'There was no guarantee we would ever find her,' Maddison said, her face hardening at the unspoken words. For all they knew, Sophie could be dead already. And facing Soli Gloria, Charlie wasn't certain whether or not she envied her if she was.

'Who knows what we're walking into. This is their turf,' Charlie muttered.

'Let's just focus on bringing Hell to their Heaven, shall we?' Maddison smiled slyly. Then they walked in silence, until a small hilltop rose by the side of the road they were following.

There was a folly on the top, partly hidden by the trees, looking like a little piece of Rome in the middle of Britain. It consisted of three mock Roman archways with a godly face carved above the arches, each tall enough to walk through, but they did not lead anywhere but to a rock wall on the other side. On the horizontal beam, there were some tiny words carved in a language Charlie did not understand. *Sanctuarium tuum, domus nostra.*

'Your sanctuary, our home...' drawled a boy, *the* boy, appearing by their side. Charlie and Maddison exchanged glances. Partly because of the boy, partly because of the words.

'That doesn't really make much sense though, does it?' Charlie whispered, taking in the antique appearance of the folly. A strong need to curtsy before it came over her, as if some ancient power still resided within the eyes of the faces. 'If an Agnus institution is... here, somewhere?'

'It didn't use to be,' Maddison replied. 'The school used to be a sanctuary for those with magic, protecting them from anyone wishing to hurt them, whether they be witch hunters or dark Maglings.' She paused, catching Charlie's questioning frown. 'A little birdie told me. Apparently, the grounds were enchanted to prevent magic from being used to attack someone, so that everyone would feel safe. It probably worked against Maglings with ill-intentions, but it made the Defectives unable to defend themselves when the Agnus found a way through and seized the territory.'

'This used to be the secret passage to the sanctuary,' the boy supplemented, then headed towards the folly. 'Another realm awaits on the other side, in case you didn't know.'

Both Charlie and Maddison stared as he and other students were ushered through, walking beneath the archways – and disappeared. None came out on the other side. Charlie gasped, feeling the hair rise on the nape of her neck as foreboding jumped up and down inside her.

'I'm frightened.'

Maddison squeezed her hand, her skin cold and dry against Charlie's sweaty palm – one of the rare acts that persuaded Charlie to think Maddison had a few empathic bones left still. 'Don't worry, I'm here.' Then they, too, stepped through the archways.

It felt like going through a purifying wall of water.

All of Charlie's heavy burdens lifted, like armour falling off a knight exhausted from battle. Something burst from her chest, like a roar, as if something else inside of her had awakened, causing panic to surge through her mind. At the same time, a new landscape cleared and appeared before her. They certainly weren't in urban Plymouth anymore.

She turned to Maddison, catching a glimpse of a surprised 'oh' as the raven girl's body convulsed and shrank with dark feathers sprouting out of her pores. Then Charlie's sight exploded with colour – yellow, bright orange, and red. Her blood was boiling, filling her with an inner fiery storm of agony that ripped through every organ, limb, and spots she didn't know she could feel before now. A terrifying wild scream erupted from her throat as the flames melted her skin, turning her body into an inferno. The stench of burned flesh threatened to suffocate her, forcing dry tears from her parched eyes. Then she tumbled out of the folly, a ball of fire.

PART II

6

SOLI GLORIA

DIFFERENT SETS of feet were running towards her before something heavy was thrown over her body like a blanket. Strong arms patted her down. Each blow like a club beating her bones to dust, but the heat subsided until there was nothing but tendrils of smoke snaking their way underneath the coarse fabric covering her.

Charlie stared at the grey twirls as they swirled into the night, barely daring to breathe. Her throat felt scratchy, and the smell of singed hair and burned flesh overwhelmed her at every inhale, the movement causing a kind of agony her mind struggled to acknowledge. And with it, the slightest kiss of the breeze stung like ten lashings of acid washing over her.

Maddison was calling her name, over and over. 'Charlie! Charlie!'

But Charlie remained quiet, staring up at the night sky. Unable to think. Unable to be. Unwilling to feel. The boy from earlier leaned over her, illuminated from the starlight above, still patting her down as if making sure all the flames were put out. He was beautiful. She was not. His eyes looked her over, the grimness of her damages reflected in them. Shame filled her like a cloud of darkness despite all the pain. A single tear rolled down her cheek, etching its way through craters of wounds.

'Get off her!' Maddison hissed, pushing him aside.

A rare sight. Wide, concerned greens stared down at Charlie below a diadem of stars. It was as if someone had taken the birthmarks on Maddison's forehead and lit them all with stardust. An ebony feather loosened from her head once again topped with long black hair. She was a raven no more, her rucksack returned to her back. Then she dug her nails into Charlie's shoulder – causing her to cry out with as much surprise as pain – and forced her to stand. A flood of tears blurred Charlie's sight.

'Hey!' the boy protested. 'You shouldn't—'

'We can manage on our own, thank you,' snapped Maddison, steadying Charlie. The grass beneath felt like heated nails under her sore soles, her shoes having burned apart as well as most of her clothes. Remaining pieces of fabric poked into her wounds as they began walking, each step sure to drive her mad. In the end, she collapsed, whimpering, in Maddison's arms.

Instantly, the boy was there, ready to catch her, but disguised his manoeuvre by grabbing his coat and pulling it tighter around her, shielding Charlie's burned near-nakedness from the others.

'Nice glow, Liosalfar,' Maddison spat at him before forcing Charlie to lean on her, ignoring her grimaces of agony. 'Why don't you use your magic and put her out of her misery?'

The boy gaped at her, eyes flickering wildly to see if anyone – any Agnus Brothers – had heard her.

Of course, Charlie thought. Liosalfars had light magic, healing properties being one of them. But to use it here... the Agnus would be upon him in a minute. She couldn't blame him when he pulled away.

'I can't,' the boy stuttered.

'Useless,' Maddison hissed.

Looking at him apologetically, Charlie took in the apparent glow surrounding him like an aura – not starlight, *him* – taking comfort in the fact she had been right in her suspicions. His light seemed to dim at Maddison's insult, but his was not the only trait on display.

All around, the Agnus Brothers were rounding up students who had become slightly altered, the light from their lanterns illuminating their new features. Some had dark green bark-like lines on their faces. Others had turquoise or lava-red veins that glowed underneath their skin. A few had skin that was an entirely different shade altogether.

Three petite youths with translucent wings stood bundled together, their long ears alert, eyes narrowed at their captors. Then there were a few animals. A Jack Russell terrier and a fox who transformed back into a boy and a girl, and a large cat, the size of a mountain lion, sneaking off into the woods. Apparently, some hadn't given up hope they could escape. Charlie doubted they would get far, but they might be able to hide. The grounds were a vast landscape where woodland, cliffsides, and sloping lawns met with the sea, a white strip of sand marking where firm ground ended and water took over. Her body shuddered as the waves rolled in, reminding her there would be little enjoyment for her at such a place in her current state.

'What happened to us?'

'It was the folly,' Maddison replied in a hushed tone, glancing back at the ancient construct, looking as out of place in this strange location as its twin had in Saltram Park. 'Back in the day, none were allowed to come in disguise, and so the folly forces Maglings to show the traits of their heritage.'

'Precisely,' said a crawling voice. Maddison's body went rigid beside her. Behind them stood Deimos, his eyes twinkling like emeralds in a cave. 'Which is why I propose you two come with me before you expose yourselves to even more prying eyes.' He gestured to the gothic, castellated mansion ahead, toward which other Agnus Brothers were already coaxing the other students.

Without waiting for an answer, Deimos headed towards the mansion and its orange windows, gleaming like a wickedly twisted lighthouse in the midst of the woods. Maddison and Charlie exchanged glances but trailed after, knowing it had not been as much an invitation as a demand. Her nerves, however, were threatening to send her heart into seizure. She would have turned and made a run for the folly if not for the fact she could barely move without Maddison in the first place.

As if noticing her unease, Maddison gave Charlie's fingers a little squeeze for comfort, which immediately made Charlie wish she hadn't. Sharp bolts shot through her already frazzled system, and she gagged on the nausea welling up, forcing back everything but a pitiful whimper. Looking at her swollen, scorched fingers, red glinting amongst the black, it was all she could do to keep on her feet. How did the rest of her look?

'How bad is it?'

Her flawless friend scrunched up her forehead, her birthmark dancing on the waves of concerned wrinkles. 'You're burned pretty bad.'

Yeah. She had figured that much. She swallowed and regretted it immediately, her raspy throat screaming. Her thoughts wailed in alarm. A boy at Hallows Grove suffered a third degree burn once, after he was unable to contain his affinity for fire. His skin had turned waxy white, almost leathery, and he never looked the same again. And with her powers near extinct, neither might she. The mere thought made her crumble until she was half-lifted, half-pulled, towards the castle by Maddison, her charred feet dragging and stumbling after – just like her consciousness.

'It hurts so much,' she whimpered.

'I know. Hold on a bit longer. We'll find a way to fix it,' Maddison urged through gritted teeth, but then Charlie stubbed her toe and tripped. The force of Maddison's hold tightened upon her wounds, and a new wave of hot flares shot through her body. Groaning, she couldn't help thinking Maddison was being too optimistic.

The only thing distracting her from utter misery for a slight second was the sight of Soli Gloria. Marvelling, Charlie thought back to her time at Hallows Grove and a field trip they had taken to an old ruin. It had risen like a fairy-tale castle amongst acres of gardens and wildflowers. The main building was a three-tier construction of arches and tall windows, towers and spires, but stripped of many walls and its roofs as history had required. Still, the remains of its disintegrated wings stretched both to the east and west like a dragon unfolding its own.

Soli Gloria was like a replica of the grand building, equalling its splendour, perhaps even exceeding it in its completeness; glass replaced the surfaces the original had been robbed off.

A rich smell of roses wafted towards them as they reached the main entrance and the gazebo that melted into the front wall of the castle. Vines and delicate flowers decorated the sandstone shell, poking Charlie curiously as she and Maddison followed the other students inside, through a wooden door, underneath a large coat of arms displaying the face of a lamb with two broken wands beneath it.

Inside, Charlie's eyes were immediately arrested by the stunning sight of silver stars twinkling back at her through the glass roof. Tears gathered in the corners of her eyes, although she couldn't tell whether it was from observing such beauty or from the agony still gushing through her body at every shift and turn.

'Come along.' Deimos pointed at the two of them and broke away from the rest of the crowd.

They cast only a quick glance to see where the others went before they followed his tall figure towards the second floor of the right wing and what looked to be his office.

Up until that point, Charlie had only been in one office, and much like Mother Agnes', this office shared the same simplicity as was to be expected of an Agnus Dei member. Only the essentials were present. A few bookshelves, a desk, a chair, and a waste basket belonging to the desk. A large crucifix hung over the window, and a thick Bible occupied the left-hand corner of the desk. Unlike most

Bibles she had ever seen though, this one was covered with dark ring stains, as if Deimos had used it as a coaster.

'Please,' the Agnus Brother said as he shut the door behind them, motioning to the visitors' chairs. 'Sit down before you both faint.'

Somewhat hesitantly, Maddison slipped Charlie into one of the chairs, and a new wave of pain caused her to wince pathetically. Maddison remained standing, poised and alert like a cat watching its prey. Something flashed in the Brother's eyes, and for a brief second, he seemed – no, he *was,* Charlie could feel it creeping through her bones – excited at the challenge the raven girl presented. Well aware that he was the real predator and she just another bird. Then his expression changed into that of boredom and polite hospitality, and he returned his attention to Charlie.

'It is lovely to see you again, Miss Charlie of Hallows Grove.'

It felt like a slap to the face. Being *of* Hallows Grove was a property label Charlie thought she had outrun. Now she felt it reattach, distorting the way she looked at herself, cutting away from the freedom she had become accustomed to. However small it had been.

'I suppose you don't remember me.'

Maddison slid into the chair next to her, catching her eye with a questioning glare. Charlie ignored it. 'I do. You were visiting Mother Agnes.'

'Precisely! I must say, she had quite a few more grey hairs then than the first time I met her.'

'Well, she was getting old, wasn't she...' Charlie's voice had been free of comedy, yet he laughed heartily, or humourlessly, depending on whether one was watching his mouth or eyes. Charlie squirmed in her chair, and it was as if every sound spun a spider's web to trap her in it and keep her there, and forced her eyes shut at the wave of nausea and electric stinging that followed.

'I knew we'd get along! I was very disappointed when I missed the opportunity to talk with you last. I was intrigued by Agnes' stories about you – see, you were the whole reason I was there really... but you disappeared so quickly!'

Charlie's heart skipped a beat as his eyes flashed at Maddison, as if he knew she had saved her. So, he *had* come to take her away. Did that mean she should be grateful for those three extra years of freedom or be bitter now that she'd had a taste and lost it?

'I wasn't all that interested in talking,' Charlie retorted.

'Ah, let's hope that'll change.' He looked at her for a long time, as if waiting for something to happen. Maddison's eyebrow rose higher for each second that passed by. Charlie wanted to disappear into the chair, realising the two of them waited for the same thing; the one thing she feared wouldn't happen. Unmistakably, Mother Agnes would have told him about her powers if she had told him stories about her.

'I can't do magic,' she said. This time, Brother Deimos looked like he was the one with all the questions.

He looked over at Maddison, as if hoping she would tell him something else. She merely crossed her arms and shrugged. 'She isn't lying.'

At last, with a disappointed sigh, Brother Deimos leaned back in his chair.

'Then perhaps you're not the person I thought you were after all. Or, perhaps, your journey has exhausted you. You should go enjoy your night. There's a Freshers' feast happening in the dining hall. After it, you'll be taken to your beds – or, perhaps, our nurse would want to see you before that.' He waved them off.

Charlie gritted her teeth as Maddison helped her rise, eager to leave his office, when Deimos' voice stopped them. 'I need to have some words with Miss Quinsey.'

Both of them paused, and with fear once again blooming within her like a bruise, Charlie opened her mouth to question why but fell silent under Maddison's look.

It'll be fine, it seemed to say. *Go.*

Trusting her, Charlie left the office hesitantly, knowing she was in no state to fight even if she would have had to. If Maddison was planning something, she was better off without Charlie standing in her way – and yet she braced herself against the wall, listened a little at the door, hearing nothing, before she decided to shuffle down the way they had come. It would not do if anyone caught her lurking. Eavesdropping was not particularly better received than magic. She learned that the hard way at Hallows Grove.

Luckily, it did not take long before the sound of murmuring led her to an entrance onto a grand balcony overlooking the grandness of a dining hall below. It stunned Charlie to the spot. Tables upon tables showcasing all the splendour of Halloween were pushed together in a horseshoe formation, all facing a head-table up at the dais, like a royal court banquet. Roof-tall curtains draped the windows lining the walls around them. They were shut, but starlight belted through the glass roof down on to the rich tables decorated with crystal glasses and bowls set between spooky pumpkins and filled to the brim with delicious sweets and cakes smelling of frosting and chocolate. Even one or two black witch hats were placed here and there on the white cloth, making her wonder whether or not she could be hallucinating. She was in extreme pain after all, and was it not an Agnus institution they had been sent to? It certainly did not look like one. The mere splendour almost made her wish she had come sooner (the whole being made into a human matchstick notwithstanding).

Each person sat by the tables looked as confounded as she, their hands firmly placed in their lap, hesitant to touch a thing for fear of punishment or it being a dream. Two elegant staircases curved from either side of the balcony to the ground floor. Staggering down one of them, fingers clutching the boy's coat in effort, Charlie snatched the first available chair she could reach, hoping that no one had paid her any attention.

It appeared she had succeeded; the majority stared wide-eyed about the room, and the rest muttered rapidly in hushed tones, commenting on the grandeur.

Only a few girls at her table seemed to have noticed her, throwing her glances and whispering amongst themselves. A tremble of discomfort went through Charlie's body, but this time it was not from the pain. Her ears grew hot under their stares, as if her burns had begun to simmer anew. Waves of cold broke out in sweat on her forehead and back. Mocking words about her looks, words she was certain they thought, ran throughout her head. *Grim. Vile. What a disgusting creature she is.*

Drowning internally, teeth clattering, she pulled the coat closer around her shoulder, wondering where the owner had gone, and distracted herself from the mortification and throbbing of her body by letting her eyes wander the room again. Some shoulders had begun to slump, as if their owners had decided there wasn't anything to be afraid of. Charlie didn't know whether to put it to the bizarre scene around her or their minds grasping for straws, but she couldn't shake the feeling that something wasn't quite right.

A glum-faced lady, with dark tarnished hair and a stubby nose, drew her attention to the teacher's table up ahead. She had that look about her, as if she could smell the stench of Charlie's singed hair from afar. Around her sat Sisters and Brothers, identically dressed in black attire and as miserable looking as those who had been at Hallows Grove. Only one Sister seemed different – the only one who wore a friendly expression under her bouncy white curls. Her hat, with an embroidered red crucifix, marked her as the school nurse. Something like concern filled her eyes as they rested on Charlie's burned face. An overwhelming wave of self-awareness washed over her once again, and she shrank in her seat.

It did not help that, in the silvery light, each and every one of the youths that had been brought in with her were striking. They were young adults of all sizes and colours, but the one thing everyone had in common was the brightness that shone from their vigilant eyes. Like Maddison, they radiated health with shimmery skin, toned muscles, and prominent bone structures. They were quite simply enchanting – like the magic they managed no doubt – and Charlie would almost have thought it an illusion of the fever she could feel coming on, if not for the transformations she had witnessed at the passage.

Envy stung deep within her chest, making her halfway swear she would train to be like them one day – before she remembered where she was. Immediately, her chest constricted with frustration.

Then she saw him. The boy. His wild, untamed blonde hair was short at the back and longer at the front. Its unruliness was reflected in the haughty look in his eyes as he leaned cross-armed against the back of his chair and studied his nails. Taking him in now, her pulse quickened. His slightly pointed face was youthful and chiselled like a statue, looking even more like an elf inside the castle than he had outside; like someone who would remain young forever because their beauty withering would have been a tragedy upon the world.

As if feeling her eyes upon him, the boy stiffened and looked straight at her. The delicate dent in his haughty appearance was masked by an arrogant dimpled smile and a raised eyebrow, challenging her to mischief. At once, he struck her as someone who would get detention before classes even began. She thought of his family. Was that why they had sent him away? Or perhaps he had agreed, only so he could cause havoc here? Like someone who answered to no one. Feared no one. Like a Pan amongst a bunch of Peters.

Her lips twitched in a nervous smile, but even this tiny movement caused pain to flash across her face. He turned away from her as she grimaced. *Of course.* She swallowed, reminding herself of what she came to realise outside. She was bound to be a disgusting sight to behold, and he certainly was not. And she wasn't the only one to have noticed.

'Hey, I saw you earlier, when you came out of the folly,' said one of the girls from earlier, her voice like smoke pulling Charlie's attention. She had hair the colour of blood and skin twice as dark as Charlie's. Glowing red veins shone brighter with the gleam in her eyes. 'Do you have an affinity for fire too?'

'No,' murmured Charlie, fingers knotting around her coat. 'Not that I know.' The girl's line of sight followed the slight movement.

'Interesting. And that boy, he gave you his coat. Do you know him?'

Charlie shook her head and winced.

'Don't bother either,' one of the other girls said and turned with a scowl towards Charlie. Somehow it seemed to reduce her glow a little. 'I've set my sight on him, and you'—she rested her hand underneath her chin, letting her eyes wander over Charlie's appearance— 'won't stand a chance.' As if to emphasise her point, she combed through her perfectly short hair with her fingers. It was pitch black and perfectly trimmed, which made Charlie's dark-brown locks look like a crow's nest in comparison.

Charlie blinked perplexedly. 'Who—'

'Am I? Venus Aurora Gillian,' the girl said and pointed rather rapidly to the girls sitting next to her. 'And this is Dia Vonsby, Ava MacLaren, and Gilly Jones. Remember our names. We're going to be everything and know everything at this school.'

The Fireling, Ava, smirked.

Charlie didn't know what to say, her tongue awkwardly tied to the roof of her mouth, unable to come up with a response. If Maddison had been there, she'd probably already have retorted with words sharp enough to cut through stone.

The girls started tittering, and Charlie heard Dia, a faerie, chirp, 'Maybe she is a bit dim.' The others chuckled louder. It was practically a relief when a woman's voice from the head-table cut them off before the strawberry blonde, Gilly, could chime in, and made them look away.

'Welcome, newcomers.' It was the glum-looking woman speaking. 'For those of you who may not know, I'm Mother Cressida Ratchford. I'm your Headmistress of Discipline, and may I say how pleased I am to see you all.' Even as she said it, her expression did not alter to show even the faintest trace of a twinkle or smile. 'You've been sent here because you are all special cases. Unruly, untameable, and unique—'

Someone roared a 'Yeah!' and Charlie half expected a fist to go into the air.

It seemed like the whole room held their collective breaths, and some people huddled closer to one another under the sound of shushing. But the headmistress' expression remained as unreadable as ever as she tilted her head and raised her hands.

'No, no. You are right. Come, show us what we have here. What powers you hold.'

Eerie silence.

Charlie barely dared glance at the person beside her, one eye on Mother Ratchford, the other on the hall, waiting to see if someone dared.

'I-I can grow flowers,' said a girl sitting close to the wall, and Charlie found her both ridiculously stupid and ridiculously brave as patches of green grass grew upon the rock where she touched it, pale buds popping open.

Mother Ratchford nodded and gave a polite applause, which the other tutors mimicked. The girl's pink-tinted skin deepened across her cheeks.

'I can bring forth the northern wind!' cawed a boy, bolting upright. He was extremely pale, more so than the Liosalfar boy. Like a ghost. And like a ghost, the wind came howling into the dining hall once he called upon it, causing more students to leap to their feet and teachers to clutch their chests. The nurse chewed her bottom lip, grip tight around her fork.

More students began chucking their magic about now. Filling jugs with water, transforming once and back again, making the candle flames rise tall until the wind grabbed hold of them and spun them for a dance about the room.

Mother Ratchford stood stoic and unmoving through it all.

Charlie's eyes narrowed in contemplation. So far, the Agnus had welcomed them with open arms and offered a feast. Maybe Soli

Gloria was not as bad as they had thought? As the worst of the worst, perhaps they had given up on changing them. Perhaps they just wanted to keep them safe and take care of them? Maybe, just maybe, Maddison, Brimley, and so many others had been wrong? Yet, there was a feeling in her gut... Charlie's train of thought was abruptly derailed as Mother Ratchford spoke again.

'Yes... you're all children of the beast, are you not? Marked by the Devil. Your magic...' Everybody stilled mid-action as she brought her palms closer together. 'An abomination.'

Before the word could settle in Charlie's mind, there was an explosion of things happening at once.

With two claps of Mother Ratchford's hands, the atmosphere in the room sank from jolly to one of panic. Men, Agnus Brothers, stormed into the dining hall and out from behind the curtains. They yanked the heavily laden cloths off the tables, sending students scattering and screaming as cordials and sauces spilled and stained the pristine linen red, yellow, and orange. Petrified, Charlie stood rooted to the spot, praying she wouldn't be trampled by people running in wild hysterics, their eyes darting with fright as they realised Agnus members were blocking their way, catching them one by one.

Ava McLaren balled her hands like a boxer ready to fight and pulled towards her the flames of the candles, turning them into a whirl of fire moving in an uncharacteristically controlled manner. Then she slashed her palm horizontally through the air and sent the spiralling flame thrower towards an Agnus member. But the fire coughed and died as though an invisible power had suffocated it. A sneering fox appeared out of nowhere and leapt, sharp glistening teeth bared, towards the Agnus member's throat. He waited, perfectly still, as she hit an invisible barrier and was hurtled backwards. Alarmed, Charlie remembered what Maddison had said about the enchanted grounds that prohibited Defectives from attacking one another – remembering it meant they could not attack to defend themselves either.

Immediately, other Agnus Brothers were upon the fox, forcing her to the ground until she transformed back. The same thing was happening to Ava. Disbelief still lingered in each girls' eyes.

'Please! Let go!' shrieked a voice so full of terror that it made everyone stop and look up. Three Agnus members carried a tiny boy with long sharp ears and glossy wings that flapped manically.

'Albin!' cried Dia Vonsby as she and another boy ran towards him, similar wings protruding from their backs, but they stumbled to a halt when Albin was forced onto the teachers' table.

'You have seen the generosity we are willing to bestow upon you.' Mother Ratchford spread her arms, gesturing to the ruined feast. 'And we ask so very little in return. We ask only that you leave your unfortunate bad habits, beliefs, and traits behind so that you may no longer pose a threat to society. Healthy, regulated, and obedient behaviour, beliefs, and personalities shall be taught, disciplined, and upheld here at Soli Gloria.' Her expression darkened like a brewing storm. Murmurs followed. Heads tilted towards one another in whispers, lips touching their neighbours' earlobes during the delivery. Dread had returned to everyone's faces, amidst angry defiance.

Mother Ratchford fished something up from the floor as the Brothers held Albin down on his stomach like a sacrificial lamb. Charlie's heart thundered in her ears, burns and pains momentarily forgotten.

'If you adhere to our request, you shall be rewarded with redemption.' Mother Ratchford's voice vibrated with some kind of elation as she raised her hands higher. 'But failure to do so will have you watch as it's all taken away. *"Behold, the Lamb of God, who takes away the sin of the world"!'*

There was a glint from a steel blade, and everyone stared in horror at the item held high: a pair of gardening shears. Only the nurse looked away, and Charlie wanted to do the same but somehow just couldn't. Time stilled with the passage of John 1:29. Albin thrashed against his captors, his fellow faeries once again trying to plough their way to his rescue. All of it to no avail before—

A terrible *snip* was amplified in the petrified silence.

A piercing agony shot through below Charlie's shoulder.

Soundlessly, Albin collapsed on the table, fainting on spot. Someone started to scream, and Charlie realised it was her when a strong hand covered her mouth and muffled the sound.

'Protest and they'll make an example out of you too,' a low voice whispered in her ear, pointing at someone else who had vomited and was then whipped with such force they fell into their own splatter.

'They know it's cruel just as much as they know it's effective,' said the keeper of her voice, who leaned over her shoulder ever so slightly, allowing her to see the blade of his cheekbones in her peripheral vision. It was the boy.

He nodded towards Dia, whose shiny wings had stopped flapping and now hung low on her back as if they were trying to grow inwards. The other faerie retreated against a pillar, shoulders thrown back to hide his own delicate wings. Charlie felt certain their ghostly white faces would haunt her for a long time to come. Then Mother Ratchford's voice demanded their attention once more, startling her so much that she jumped, feeling the boy's arms tightening around her.

'Magic is a curse, an abomination of nature. A curse, for which we'—she motioned to the Agnus members lined up like soldiers of war—'are the cure.'

Once again, she raised her arms like a priest calling everyone up from their seats during a sermon. 'Repeat after me:

> Agnus Dei, qui tollis peccata mundi, miserere nobis.
> Agnus Dei, qui tollis peccata mundi, miserere nobis.'

Apprehensively, Charlie's lips moved by habit, her ears catching the echo of defeated voices repeating the passage.

'Lamb of God, who takes away the sins of the world, have mercy on us.
Lamb of God, who takes away the sins of the world, have mercy on us.'

'Agnus Dei, qui tollis peccata mundi, dona nobis pacem.'

An odd tone laced the headmistress' voice, and a gruesome light filled her eyes as the Defectives repeated after her:

'Lamb of God, who takes away the sins of the world, grant us peace.'

With a shiver, Charlie realised it was a tone of delight.

7

DEVIL'S MARKS

ONCE THE DUST HAD SETTLED, and the students were separated by gender into quiet lines of submission, the headmistress gave the order for them to be taken to their respective sleeping areas. One of the Brothers was to lead the boys to a cavern while Sister Lucy was assigned to take the girls to the showers and "the Cliff" – whatever that meant. Perhaps this was it. They would simply push them over the edge and be done with them.

A spark of dark optimism lit up in her chest but drowned in its own pessimism. No, it wouldn't be that easy. The zeal she'd witnessed in Mother Ratchford told Charlie she would make their time at Soli Gloria as long and miserable as she could, and she'd enjoy every minute of it.

They were a rather subdued bunch, yet Charlie could feel the scuffling and pushing to leave the dining hall as fast as possible. One of the people behind shoved into her back, sending new waves of raging pain searing through her body, leaving her gasping in shock and despair. *Where is Maddison?*

She felt awfully exposed and abandoned after the Liosalfar boy had been ushered away with the other boys, her consciousness slipping in and out in blinding whiteness. As they ascended the stairs, she threw a glance back at the teachers' table. A couple of Sisters were carrying an unconscious Albin between them, following the nurse through another entry behind the table itself. A Brother listened tentatively to Mother Ratchford and picked up Albin's wings with a disgusted grimace.

Once out of the hallway, a sort of capitulation came over her. As if her quota of fear and anguish had been spent for the day. The pain was there, but her brain refused to acknowledge it, numbed by the warm haze that clouded her head. She couldn't wait to sleep – even if it was on the floor – and willingly walked as fast as she could, gritting her teeth together, until they neared the showers.

Her mind reared. What if the showers were a trap? What if something else awaited them, something painful or even... deadly?

So many – not only Defectives – through the span of history and wars had been persecuted and taken, never to be seen again. Had no one come to their aid?

Pulse pumping, she prayed someone would now, her own heart echoing those of the many who had been held captive before her, realising like they must have realised, that help would never come. They were entirely at the Agnus' mercy.

Her feet came to an abrupt stop, as if they were bound in concrete, while her instincts told her to run. People were bumping into her from behind. Ahead, Sister Lucy turned, as if sensing that someone was making trouble.

Her insides shivered, but she was frozen to the spot. Sister Lucy brandished her cane and started moving towards her. Girls turned and looked with anticipation. The girl who had spoken earlier, Venus, looked like a snake poised to bite until she saw that Sister Lucy was heading for someone else. Then her lips twitched with glee.

'What is the meaning of this hold up?' the Sister asked.

Fingers pointed towards Charlie.

'She won't move, Miss,' said a girl Charlie didn't know.

'And why won't you move?'

Charlie's lips trembled as she spoke. 'I'm frightened... of the showers.'

Someone snickered. Venus waved a hand under her nose, implying that Charlie smelled. Sister Lucy took in Charlie's wounds and the oversized coat covering her body and, to Charlie's surprise, her expression softened.

'It might hurt, girl. But hurt... builds character. Besides, your wounds need to be cleaned. I would send you to the nurse, but I believe she has her hands full with that boy. Come along now, better to get it over with.' And with that, Sister Lucy grabbed an excruciating hold of Charlie's hand and pulled her to the head of the line.

The showers were in a large room with toilet cubicles lining one wall and white porcelain basins, sunken into the rock, lining the other. The third and longest wall was missing. Instead, the space gaped towards a cliffside, a mountain shelf resting against the building. Water cascaded down from a hole in the stone ceiling above. The room was moist, carrying a scent of earth and mould from walls that never dried.

Charlie turned to look at Sister Lucy who only gave her a nod. 'Off with your clothes, then,' she said as the other girls peeked over her shoulders, staring at Charlie.

Wishing herself anywhere else, Charlie turned her back to them, hesitating for as long as she dared before gritting her teeth and letting the boy's coat fall. There were several gasps and a few giggles as the others caught sight of her charred back. Swallowing, Charlie stepped onto the mountain shelf and clenched her eyes shut as the icy-cold puddles of water numbed the sore soles of her feet.

'Don't linger around, girl, get on with it – and you! Stop gawking. Into the showers!' Sister Lucy thundered. The sound of girls hurrying to take their clothes off followed.

Charlie refocused on the water, contemplating her fate if the water was poisoned, a smidge of fear returning. *God or goddesses, protect me,* she thought and stepped in, letting the water pour over her at last.

The world turned silent but for the roaring noise in her ears.

Her wounds burned beneath the iciness, and the water merci-lessly ripped tufts of fabric out of her torn skin. Every part of her wanted to scream in agony, and yet she welcomed all of it; as long as she felt something, she lived. Then they were ordered to step out.

To her surprise and horror, the bathroom door swung open, and three Agnus Brothers marched in to the sound of the girls squealing and leaping over one another for their clothes and towels.

'Get in line!' barked one of the men, staring them down as they hesitantly dropped the pieces of fabric and huddled together. Then the men pulled them into a line and began searching their bodies. For Devil's marks.

Staring solemnly at the floor, Sister Lucy picked dandruff off the pile of woollen dresses she held in her arm.

'What happened to this one?' hissed the commanding Brother as he turned to face Charlie. 'She looks like she descended straight out of Hell.'

Into it, Charlie thought, staring at her bare toes grating against the rough stone floor. Blisters bloomed along the ridge of her bone.

'Perhaps it is the Devil raging within her. We should take her with us.'

'Or perhaps the Devil has left her?' Sister Lucy suggested, pointing at the open craters decorating Charlie's skin. 'Keeping her with *them* could tempt the Devil back in again. I'd like her brought to Sister Rowena – she might be ready for the path of light.'

'Very well,' the Brother said, walking towards Gilly to crouch by her feet, pressing his hand upward against the inside of her naked thigh. Nausea welled inside of Charlie, her own skin pounding in protest. He was being far more thorough than the men behind him, who barely dared touch the girls' arms to see into their armpits. Gilly's lip trembled, on the verge of crying, and Charlie turned her gaze ahead, seething with revulsion.

Nodding, Sister Lucy threw a towel over Charlie and ordered her to dry herself. While she did, a few of the girls were picked out of the line-up, their Devil's Marks too evident, and forced into their woollen dresses, the fabric sticking to their wet bodies. 'We'll be taking these with us,' the man said as Charlie, now dry, clothed herself. 'We'll drop her off on the way.'

The infirmary wasn't too far away from the showers, and she felt both estranged and relieved when the group continued without her, leaving her by the door. Parts of her wanted to stop the Brothers and ask them to let the girls warm themselves so that, at the very least, their teeth would stop chattering. The other part of her feared the retribution that would follow and was thus grateful she was not going wherever they went. Instead, she kept quiet and watched the men lead the girls away, their hair still dripping down their backs, her insides squirming in cowardice.

Inside, the infirmary was cast in the silvery light of the night. A statue made her jump, thinking at first it was a real naked person. But its smooth lines soon enthralled her, its delicate features making her think of the nymphs from her Encyclopaedia.

Several beds were lined up along the walls carrying roof-tall windows and a fresco painting, its shapes and figures a blur of peri-winkle blue, forest green, cloudy white, and golden yellow in the corner of her eye. Only one of the beds was occupied. Albin lay asleep upon the thick duvet. He must have been given a pretty strong concoction considering the peaceful look about him, the stubs of bone where his wings should have been bundled up in white bandages on his back. Maybe she would be able to have some too.

Sister Rowena looked up from checking his temperature, her nurse's hat slightly askew, and the concerned look in her eyes gave way for golden warmth as she left him to welcome Charlie.

'A most terrible thing what happened to him,' Sister Rowena said under her breath, observing Charlie staring, motioning for Charlie to pick a bed while she bustled to find her supplies.

'You think so?' The words escaped Charlie before she could hold them back, and she immediately shrank back on her bed. But when the nurse did not reply, a second set of words fell out, rushed by her curiosity. 'Why him?'

'Didn't have anything to do with *him*, only his wings.' *The traits that mark him as more of a beast than human.* Charlie didn't need her to finish the sentence to understand.

'Everyone has some sort of traits though,' Charlie muttered, recalling what Maddison had said when she taught Charlie about the necessity to hide her ears. *'They're hypocrites really,'* she had said about the Agnus. *'Every human alive – even they – have traits from the animal kingdom. From our nails sharing the same substance as animal horns to the hair that grows on our bodies.'* She had rolled her eyes and studied her own nails. *'But those are considered "normal" because the Agnus can't go capturing everyone.'*

'That is true,' Sister Rowena replied, overhearing Charlie's hushed mumbling, and returned with her supplies. Pausing for a moment, she studied Charlie's appearance then brushed a lock of hair behind her ear. Charlie stiffened as the nurse studied its slightly tipped edge. 'But some are more apparent than others.'

There was no judgement in the old lady's face but rather a wistful knowing in her large amber eyes. Her white curls framed her face, which was otherwise covered in thin facial hairs, like a soft layer of golden down. It gave her a sort of harmless appearance, but the harsh lines underneath told Charlie one would be a fool to underestimate her.

The old lady retracted her hand and put it around the pendant of a necklace around her neck. It was a pretty, round image, with a tree in its middle. Then she picked up the antiseptic and poured it onto a cotton pad. 'Now, bite your teeth together, dear, this is going to hurt.'

Charlie responded with a sharp inhale of breath and a quick whimper.

The cleanse felt like it lasted for hours, although Sister Rowena was surprisingly gentle for an Agnus nurse. Charlie knew – all too well – that she could have simply sent her to bed with painkillers, letting an infection deal with her instead. But Sister Rowena patiently cleaned all her wounds, picking out the remaining fluff with tweezers before carefully soaking Charlie's body in a soothing mixture of aloe vera. Once or twice, she caught the Sister looking at her in a peculiar way, but she quickly returned to her work whenever their eyes met.

At last, Sister Rowena applied bandages and handed her a plain, white dress. 'I'd like you to stop by regularly for the next couple of weeks so that I may check and change your bandages.' The gentleness with which she said it confounded Charlie to such a degree that she once again spoke without a second thought. 'You're not like the others.'

Sister Rowena raised an eyebrow. 'And how are the others?'

Charlie looked at her hands now, certain she had overstepped. What would the Sister do to her? She peeked at Albin, wondering if he had been nursed or aided into an overdose of medication.

'I understand it might be easy to perceive everyone as the enemy,' Sister Rowena murmured. 'Many things in your life have probably made you think so.'

'Are you going to tell me I'm wrong?'

'I'll only tell you to be mindful of who you say it to... and to remember some might see you as the enemy too.' Charlie didn't understand this. Did Sister Rowena imply she was dangerous? Or that her magic was? She was about to protest when the thought of Brimley shaking Doyle resurfaced. A *monstrosity*, she'd once heard Mother Agnes calling shapeshifters. Was that what she'd had in mind? Then her thoughts drifted to Maddison and the many times they had discussed her powers of manipulation, before they dissolved into an intangible mess, unable to explain to her mind the flux of conflating emotions that arose.

'Come now,' Sister Rowena said softly. 'It's time you had some sleep.'

8

MAGIC IN THE NIGHT

THE NURSE LED her out of the castle through an exit on the second floor, stepping out onto a soft carpet of grass. Crickets chirped between the steady crashes of the ocean waves, and once or twice Charlie saw a quick movement between leaves, painted silver by the light of the stars.

They were standing on top of a mound, elevated from the rest of the grounds. Ahead rose a wooden bridge allowing them to cross over to the cliffside. There was a familiar rumble, as if from a waterfall, nearby.

The showers! That must be where the water comes from, Charlie thought. Thank heavens. It was a large leap from all that she had imagined.

Whatever Sister Rowena had treated her with seemed to be working. Her fever and chills had broken, and she was able to move without too much pain. Yet, her body dragged with weariness. After a few more feet and turns, they reached the top of the cliff where several stone huts appeared, looking like scattered milk teeth waiting for the Tooth Fairy.

Sister Rowena knocked on one of them and poked her head in,

returning swiftly while informing her it was full. Charlie considered whether or not she should mention she'd like to stay in the same hut as Maddison... but the same thing happened with the next hut, and the next after that, and Charlie's courage dwindled with the apparent exasperation of Sister Rowena.

They were nearing the ones at the edge of the cliff when a figure hurried towards them out of the darkness.

'Oh, it's you!' Sister Lucy's vexed features softened as she recognised Sister Rowena with Charlie. 'I thought you were some of the girls. I've already caught a couple out of bed tonight!'

'Really? How odd,' Sister Rowena responded, her voice completely void of surprise. 'We're trying to find an available bed for this young lady.'

'Right,' Sister Lucy said, looking Charlie up and down, taking in her many bandages. 'There's one space left in number 13. I'll take you there—'

An odd sort of blankness fell over the Sister's face, and she gazed behind them. Both Charlie and Sister Rowena followed her line of sight without seeing anything but the dark silhouette of the castle. 'Actually, I'm needed somewhere else,' the Sister said and began to push past them. Charlie blinked.

'Me too!' cried Sister Rowena, her expression suddenly the same as Sister Lucy's. Charlie blinked twice.

'You'll find the hut on your own, won't you, Charlie?'

Staring in bewilderment after the two of them, Charlie wondered whether it was a test but decided, once it looked like they wouldn't return, that it was better not to linger. She would not want to be caught "out of bed".

Luckily, it didn't take her long to find number 13. Two bunk beds stood on either side of the hut, of which only the bottom left was empty.

Quietly, so as not to wake the others, Charlie crept closer to peek at the faces of her new roommates, but Maddison wasn't among them. With a rising panic pounding in her chest, Charlie hurried into her own bed, studying the room in deadly silence.

Its smooth, rounded surface and white cave-like appearance emphasised the strangest sensation of being inside a dented tooth. One tiny black stove protruded from the wall, momentarily making her mind wander to fuzzy autumn nights in front of crackling fire, its warm blanket shielding her from the crispy cold air outside. No logs of wood lay at its feet, however. The cosy thoughts morphed into dread, vividly visualizing cold nights settling into her bones.

She suppressed a shudder that had nothing to do with her wounds.

A frozen cage.

That's where she was. And it felt all too familiar.

Her thoughts wandered to the many sleepless nights lying in her dormitory bed at Hallows Grove, battling the worst winter nights with her thin old blanket.

She couldn't believe she was back again. Or as good as. *Worse* than.

She held up her bandaged hands for inspection. The dark shadows of the room crept closer, like the bleak thoughts in her mind, turning her heart into a bottomless well of misery. Only one wish remained: tomorrow, she would find Maddison – perhaps even Brimley – and together they would find a way to escape and go look for Sophie. The wish was snuffed out instantly by phantom growls and the memory of claws ripping through her flesh.

No, she would not dare attempt it again. Realisation hit her like a stone.

They would never be free.

The mere knowledge turned the air in her lungs into cement. A frustrated tear ran down her cheek. She quickly wiped it away when someone shifted in their bed.

'What's that sound?' one of the girls said.

'Hm?' murmured another, but no one responded, because now everyone heard it.

A deep tone, similar to the one she had heard from choirs during Sunday sermons, rose from the darkness outside. A blend of masculinity and vitality, as alluring to the ears as the depiction of an archangel was to the eye. The other girls were up now, moving towards the hut's only window, pressing against one another to see. One squinted into the night, her freckles dancing on the bridge of her cheeks. The second bit her lip nervously, eyes wide with trepidation, while the third frowned.

'I can't see anything...'

'Shall we go outside?'

The light tones of flutes and harmonicas mixed with the singing, sounding close enough as if someone was hiding behind the other side of their wall, squeezed between huts and bushes.

'I'd like to go,' one of the girls said, her hand already at the handle.

'Wait!' cried one of the others. 'What if it's a trap? What if they punish us?'

The girl at the door tightened her grip on the handle as she seemed to debate the question. 'Then let them!' she declared at last, her curiosity getting the better of her fear. And out they all went.

For a bewildered moment, Charlie couldn't understand why, until she found herself staring into the night after them, her nails dug into the doorframe, the song pulling at her to come outside. And before she knew it, she was standing amidst a large group of girls, all having abandoned their huts, all searching the darkness for the source of the singing.

A flapping sound beat through the air, and the first scream sent them bolting left and right. Panic coursed through Charlie's body as large shadows went over her head and landed amidst the stampede of barefooted girls. It was like the feast all over again.

She rushed to her cottage, motioning for them to follow her to safety, but no one listened. Reaching out, she grabbed at a girl's arm, tugging her towards her door. But the face that turned to her was not scared – it was thrilled – and her free hand was pointing.

'Look,' whispered the girl, her whole arm trembling in Charlie's grip.

She spun around to see cloaked figures drawing themselves to their full height, girls coming to an abrupt halt staring at the tall silhouettes bathed in starlight. A roused curiosity taking over the fearful glints in the girls' eyes, a thrill overtaking all as the figures moved in swiftly between them.

One headed towards Charlie and the girl, peeling a mask off his face with golden fingers. Creamy brown curls framed mischievous bright eyes, and the girl seemed to lose a bit of footing in Charlie's arms at the mere sight of him.

He reached for the girl when Charlie pulled her behind her, warning him off.

'What do you want?' The words trembled out of her like the rush of alarm through her body.

The boy's eyes smouldered, and his lips coiled into a pout. 'Only to free you.' This time he side-stepped Charlie and cupped the girl's chin with his hand, her eyes and body locked with his as if they were two. 'And,' he crooned in a whisper, 'your heart's desires.'

There was no refusal or hesitation between them as they walked away, just a mutual understanding of unspoken words, the atmosphere growing heavy with lustful expectations. Three steps away, they turned and made an inviting gesture.

Mouth open, Charlie shook her head. They shrugged, turned to each other, and had at once forgotten all about her. She glared after them, at the many couples that had already come together, engaged in exultant dancing of flushed skin and suggestive glances, feeling about as bewildered as Mother Agnes would have been had she been dropped in a den of sin.

What if the Agnus Dei came upon them? She needed to get away. Before they appeared. Before bodies came closer, hands ran wilder, and kisses deepened. But the song that moved them all into a euphoric cohort seemed to be moving within her too, belting through her bloodstream and overpowering the trembles of angst. A burn started under her own two left feet, itching to join in on the fun. To let loose. To forget and live for the moment.

Mortified even by the idea, Charlie threw herself around in retreat and bumped into someone running from the opposite direction. Strong arms prevented her from falling.

'I'm sorry, I—'

'No, it was my fault,' she stuttered. 'I really should watch where I'm going...' Sparkling dark eyes. Handsome lines. Strong chin.

The curve of his lips disappeared behind a mask covering the top half of his face. It was a beautiful matte black with sleek patterns marking the bones of a bat's wingspan, shrouding his identity in mystery. She felt a sudden urge to rip it off his face.

'Woah, what happened to you?' His hold around her released. Fortunately, her legs were steady enough to stop her from tumbling backwards. But the abrupt words made her cower, remembering her bandaged and patched-up appearance, and her eyes found her feet as she replied. 'I-I don't know...' She heard him shifting, as if he was about to take his leave. 'It was the passage.' She swallowed.

'The passage? How curious.'

She looked up. Eyes mystified, he seemed to contemplate whether or not he should move on or if he found her interesting enough to stay. Obviously, he would walk away. She was certain of it.

'Well, I suppose I ought to ask you for a dance now?'

Whatever she had expected, that was not it. 'Oh, please, no!' she blurted. His eyes widened. There was the deepest of blue in them when the light of the stars hit just right. 'I mean, I would love to, but I'm quite tired... and clumsy!'

He relaxed. 'Oh, well then, my lady, I won't force you.' His lips quirked up at the corner. 'I shall leave it for our wedding day.'

A nervous splutter escaped between her lips, waking a mini-Charlie inside her own mind who sat up, watching the scene unfold without being able to do anything about it.

'Where did you guys come from?'

'Apart from Heaven?' he asked, the mocking glint in his eyes so obvious that it ripped out what little confidence her heart contained. The nervous sounds erupted from her once again, and the girl in her head facepalmed herself.

'We climbed up the cliffside, except the show-offs flying in because they can. Airlings, ey? Damn posers the lot of them.' He scoffed at some boys behind him, floating inches over the ground and serenading girls, but he remained nonchalant and focused on her.

'Well, climbing sounds a lot more impressive to me,' Charlie murmured, fidgeting with her hair.

He bowed his head, and his short dark locks swayed and curled like the waves of the sea. 'I'm glad to hear that.'

In one way, she wanted him to leave, her consciousness reminding her of her own appearance and the peril of being discovered. Then again, she was extremely curious. 'Why are you guys doing this?'

'Consider it a demonstration against our supreme leaders,' he said, then took notice of her confused expression. 'We knew what they had in store for you tonight, and how they would attempt to put you on a fast-track towards withdrawal. We're here to show you what you'll miss out on… if you let fear control you.'

'That's *all* you're here to do?' Charlie nodded towards a girl dragging a boy into her cottage. The boy's smile widened with false innocence, and she crossed her arms to compose herself, hoping it would prevent her heart from jumping out of her chest at the same time.

'Coincidentally, I'll have you know, some innocent frolicking and exciting romance has always proved to be an efficient fuel for magic.' His devilish grin made her feel like she was once again on fire, melting from the inside out.

'Sounds like an excuse to chase girls to me,' Charlie said.

'Hey, the girls aren't any better.' He laid a hand on her arm and beckoned her to follow. Stopping just short of the tip of the cliff, the two of them glanced down at the sea below, and Charlie was able to place the soft alluring tones that didn't seem to stem from the boys' voices.

From the mouth of a large cavern, a flock of boys stood pointing and ogling towards the sea. Amongst the waves bobbed female heads, their lips slightly parted, singing like a choir of sirens as they swam towards the boys whose bodies turned more rigid the closer the water goddesses came. Even Charlie had to cross herself as the females rose from the mighty blue, soaked cotton dresses sticking to their bodies. Faces paled as they clasped the boys' hands in theirs, pulling them into the cavern until nothing remained from the scene but the sweet tones of their song.

Charlie straightened, realising that tall, dark, and handsome was studying her with a tilt to his head and eyes twinkling. Her stomach erupted into gnawing butterflies, making her uncertain whether or not she felt uncomfortable – or *too* comfortable.

'Erm.' She cleared her throat. 'I assume you're here to find someone, then?'

'I was, but she doesn't seem to be here.'

'Oh,' Charlie said, realising she had hoped he would say something cheesier.

'And now I'd rather stay here with you, perhaps get to know you better?'

'Oh!' Her mouth dropped open. 'I think that might have to wait for our wedding day too.' Genuinely surprised over her own cheek, Charlie struggled to keep her expression composed, her mini-self lifting a Quinsey-worthy eyebrow, nodding with approval. But the boy took a step closer and adjusted a lock of hair that had fallen before her eyes.

Oh, whatever could he see in her but horror? Blotchy skin and puss? Her bandages surely didn't cover every wound... and even so—goddesses, would he never stop looking at her like that? She looked away again, the fire in her cheeks threatening to swallow her entirely. She should walk away. Had she not been burned enough for one night?

Instinctively, Charlie stepped back. Perhaps the darkness had hid the worst of her damages from him. How awful he would find her if he came too close, noticing the craters of scars and blisters on her face? No, she didn't want that to happen.

With a quick apology and a goodbye, Charlie tore herself away from him and rushed back to her cottage, past the swirling couples intoxicated with one another, feeling the boy's eyes on the back of her neck the whole way. A storm of emotions flew frantically around her stomach like tumbling hot coals until she closed the cottage door behind her. At first, they were horrified, but then her lips cracked into a smile of joy in the mirror. A boy had spoken to her. *Two* boys had spoken to her, if counting the one she had met upon arrival. *Her!* They'd spoken to her, despite the way she looked... although... actually, her reflection didn't look *that* bad. She studied her facial features left and right. Flushed and red maybe, but honestly, she had expected it bad enough to cause a fright.

Her insides bubbling, Charlie dove into bed, biting her lips, half-heartedly scolding herself for smiling considering the state of things. On one side, the threat of the Agnus loomed over her, threatening to suffocate her. It didn't matter that she couldn't do magic. Romance... between Defectives! It would be her fall from grace, even if Heaven had decided to forgive her past sins. Yet... her smile remained. The masked boy's charming grin returned before her inner eye and remained there, his words making the butterflies in her stomach restless as they repeated themselves in her memory. If all else was lost, could she not let herself fall – even just a little bit more?

Thinking of the boy, she felt like the tiniest light had been lit within her. He had seemed to like her enough. Could he like her even when he saw her in daylight? Maybe he didn't care. Maybe he was a beauty-is-on-the-inside kind of guy. Although, as far as Charlie knew, those were a myth. *But,* Charlie pondered, tracing her pin while another thought occurred, *he seemed to know a thing or two about magic. Could he help me tap into mine?* It was a beautiful daydream if nothing else.

... until our wedding day.

A giggle bubbled within her. She had been flirted with. She, Charlie. And she had flirted back!

She held on to that. The moment they had shared. The thought of him, the potential of him liking her, and the daydreams that quickly spun from their meeting. Then she was dreaming for real.

The next day, as Sister Rowena unwrapped her bandages, the nurse stepped back in alarm, taking in Charlie's olive skin, freshly smooth like before.

9

MYTHOS

COMPLETE. Not a scab or wound to see. Every inch of Charlie fresh and bare, every lock of hair grown and repaired, every evidence of the incident with the folly gone. She should have been brimming with relief and happiness, should have been running to find Maddison. Instead, she glared at the nurse, who glared back, pulse pounding through her body.

Magic.

There could be no other explanation, no possible way Charlie could excuse it, and by the ghostly pale face of Sister Rowena, she knew it too.

Charlie braced herself for the punishment. The call upon the Brothers to take her to the dungeon.

But it didn't come.

Finally, the nurse regained her composure and, to Charlie's surprise, began laying new bandages upon her as if she had not seen her healed complexion.

'Remember to come by tomorrow for another change. Do you have any questions?'

Charlie did, but the nurse looked at her in such a way that made her think she shouldn't ask. Instead, she did as told and returned the day after, and the days after that, each time the same.

'It's odd, isn't it?' Charlie asked Maddison at breakfast a few days later. She had found her again the morning after their arrival looking well and rested but completely unwilling to spill where she had been the other night – in other words, her regular self. 'I mean, she knows I've *healed*, yet she doesn't say anything.'

'Do you *want* her to say anything?' Maddison muttered under her breath in turn, making the spoon dangling between her fingers do a slight, but deliberate, shift. Charlie looked up, seeing the sight everyone else in the hall appeared determined to pretend they couldn't. Five stools. Five pupils. Ten sets of red-rimmed and sleepless eyes begging for mercy, and the sickening stench of faeces that refused to leave her nostrils.

The antics that had happened the other night had been all anyone could talk about, and so it had reached the ear of an Agnus who'd reported it higher. Soon, students accused of being instigators – either by the Agnus or other students trying to avoid punishments – were placed on display for everyone to witness their penalty. Amongst them had been the couple that had asked Charlie to dance, all trace of flippant rebellion wiped from their faces and replaced with helpless distress. The girl fainted after the first day. The boy a few hours after that. Both were quickly replaced by new students.

'See him today?'

Charlie returned her attention to Maddison, feeling heat creep into her cheeks. She had told her about the boy. Of their talk. Their flirting. How that was the last thing she had done before going to bed, waking up fresh as a daisy. Maddison had been particularly curious about that.

'Not that I would recognise him if I did. He was wearing a mask.' Charlie scowled, ignoring the voice in her head reminding her that it hadn't stopped her from *trying* to recognise him. From searching the school grounds, the hallways, even lingering behind in classes when the girls were on their way out and the boys entered for their lecture.

Still, she had not spotted him, and she and Maddison were beginning to wonder if he had been a figment of her imagination; it was the only place he did show these days, in her daydreams. Which, for the record, were escalating to such a degree that she wasn't entirely sure she would be able to look him in the eye if they did meet.

Maddison groaned and planted her spoon in her sticky porridge, wrinkling her nose with eyes upon the teachers' table. 'See how they stuff their faces with bacon and eggs while we're left with this soggy paper?'

Charlie leaned past her to see Mother Ratchford and the other teachers enjoying their breakfast, looking as if they did not even see the students and their misery in the room. Maddison's expression was a feeble light of entertainment amongst it all. They hadn't exactly been able to eat luxury dishes while living in hiding, but with Maddison's powers, they never wanted for bread and butter or other tasty items they desired. The Agnus' porridge, however, contained neither nutrition nor taste, just as she remembered it. It was merely a quick fix, chewy sawdust meant to keep the Defectives weak and settle the hunger so they wouldn't complain.

'A couple more days with this and I'll start robbing the kitchens.' Maddison picked at her food again.

Charlie pressed her lips together, patting her compassionately on the back. Brimley would probably have offered to go on a hunt for her.

A stab of guilt surged through her thinking of Brimley and whatever had become of him. She had thought, even hoped at some level, that he would have been taken by the Agnus as well. At least that would have given them some kind of alliance. But it did not seem like he had. Then another wary thought fell into her head.

Had he heard the Agnus coming and made a run for it? Without them? Or... there *had* been something odd with how the Agnus cornered them... as if it was staged somehow. Could it have been? Could Brimley have betrayed them and then put up an act before their capture?

A bitter flavour filled her mouth. *No... he wouldn't do that to Maddison*, Charlie thought, gnawing her lip. *Unless...* Her heart dropped into her stomach. *Unless he knew about Maddison's fling.*

'You look like you've just seen your own death.' Maddison frowned, her eyebrow lifting suspiciously while Charlie kept racking her brain trying to remember if she had told him. 'And before you ask, no *I* haven't seen it. What's wrong?'

'I—' But before Charlie could share her troubled thoughts, someone's lush laughter drifted through the hall from the hallway. It sounded like rumbling water, trailing its owner as he appeared on the balcony with three other people. The four of them descended the stairs, giving off the same impression as if Hermes, Aphrodite, Apollo, and Ares themselves had walked in. One fair and familiar, the girl otherworldly, the tallest dark and handsome, and the fourth handsomer still, his laughter still on his lips, with ruffled black hair and blue eyes which she recognised instantly.

Her heart jumped back into her throat, overcome with a fluster and an immediate need to look away before he saw her too. But there was no way he would look her way. Why would he? And even if he did, why would he recognise or even *notice* her? Still, he passed their table, his head turning towards them as if he knew she was there, and gave her an ever-so-lingering smoulder.

Her heart stopped. The matte butterfly mask appeared bright and clear in her mind, placing itself over his face. A perfect match.

'It's him,' Charlie whispered, each word breathed with awe.

'Who?' asked Maddison, following her eyesight.

'The one in the middle.'

The four had picked a table and were sitting down, one of the other boys pulling the girl close to him. A sharp sensation of relief went through her. So, she was *his* girlfriend, not the other one's.

'Tyler McFade?' Maddison turned to face her, frowning. 'What about him?'

'He's the one I talked to before—' Charlie motioned to her bandages, her healed body underneath, feeling flustered and self-aware at the same time. Even before she burned, her looks hadn't typically drawn attention from boys – especially not with Maddison around – but if he had been interested in her while wrapped in white cotton and festering wounds and puss visible here and there, was it too far-fetched to think that he could, potentially, be interested in her now too?

'Tyler...' Charlie tested the name on her tongue. Tyler McFade, Maddison had called him. *Wait!* 'How do you know his name?'

Maddison cleared her throat and rearranged her spoon. 'I make it my business to know all the powerful families of the places we go. His family happens to be one of them.'

There was some benefit to having lived with Maddison for three years. One being that Charlie could clearly tell when she was lying. Looking back at Tyler, something clicked. She'd seen his features before Soli Gloria. One glimpse, with the other boys, when she had been sent to steal the painting, another when half of his face had been covered by Maddison snogging him earlier that summer. Something shot through her heart.

'That's your ex.'

'Oh, please,' Maddison drawled. 'He was a *fling*. A handsome little plaything.'

Yet serious enough that he came looking for you, Charlie thought, recalling the fact that Tyler had been on the clifftop to find someone else. Someone he knew from before... *But*, Charlie prompted herself, *you don't know why he was there*. Perhaps he had simply been there to convey a message? Share some information? *Or to get back with Maddison?*

'He was "the bird" you were talking about, the one who'd told you so much about this place?'

Maddison shifted uneasily. 'Yeah, but it doesn't matter, Charlie. It's over, and I'm glad of it. If you want, I'll even introduce you to him. He could be *your* little plaything.' She winked.

Charlie grimaced.

'No? What about his brothers? That's Jaden, the eldest, but he's already taken – and infatuated.' She nodded to the brown-skinned boy with wild locks of hair and the girl perched on his lap. 'I suppose that makes *him*'—Maddison contemplated, shifting her line of sight to the fair one, the boy they had met at the passage and who had kept her safe at the Feast—'Caden McFade, the youngest. He always went scheming with the butler, so I never met him, but Tyler said he'll turn eighteen soon too. Like us.' She licked the corner of her mouth and bit down on her lip. 'I might fight you for him.'

Just then, Brother Deimos sauntered down to the boys with a Bible under his arm and whacked Jaden on the head with it. Immediately, the girl leapt off his lap and settled on a chair beside him. Tyler said something, and Brother Deimos grabbed his shoulder, murmuring aggressively in his ear. Tyler sat rigid, as if reprimanded, but Charlie could have sworn his gaze – and Caden's, who looked to be eavesdropping – turned towards her. Warmth filled her all over, and her back felt particularly damp.

A gleam appeared in Tyler's eyes, while Caden's went cold and distant. He glanced away, as if looking at her was disagreeable to him. A knot curled in her stomach, and she let Tyler's warm, intrigued gaze pull her attention towards him instead.

Letting go, Brother Deimos straightened his uniform and tucked his Bible safely under his arm again before he turned to the teachers' table with a nod. Mother Ratchford dipped her chin ever so slightly in return before she turned back to her food as if she had not witnessed the scene at all.

Charlie's eyes followed the Brother as he left the hall. She didn't like him very much. 'What did he want with you the other day? And how come I've hardly seen you since we came?'

'He was merely giving me a dreary sermon informing me on the importance of the work the Agnus do here,' Maddison said, following Charlie's gaze. 'I think he watches me, so I've been busy trying to behave. Gives me a headache, though. Can't go to bed early enough,' Maddison whispered and stood up from her seat, gathering her school supplies. Yet another lie. Once she had figured out which one it was, Charlie had gone to Maddison's hut every night trying to get a word with her, but she was never there. She was up to something, and Charlie was determined to figure out what. She opened her mouth to argue, but Maddison cut her off.

'We better get going.' Maddison smiled. 'Won't do to make ripples by missing the morning sermon.'

———

That night, Charlie once again went to see Maddison and found her bed empty. Stuttering her apologies for disturbing them, Charlie closed the door on Maddison's scowling roommates and turned away from the hut. Speculating into the empty air, she went for a walk towards the very tip of their cliff and the panoramic view of the school grounds.

Just below her, she could see a treacherous path leading down from the girls' cliff that ended by some jutting rocks next to the entrance of the boys' cavern. Wafts of salty sea air drifted by as she took in the white beach, stretching on until it collided with the rolling fields. The grass, dull and minty green from the cold autumn weather, stood in stark contrast to the sand. On the other end, parallel to the girls', was another cliff. From where she was standing, there looked to be some old ruins of sorts located at its very tip.

She studied them when a flicker of colour made her still, but then nothing else happened on the darkening night sky. Had she imagined it?

Shaking her head, Charlie made to turn back when—*there, another light!*

It glinted teasingly above the ruins like a shooting star falling through the sky. She did not know why or how, but one word surged through her mind: *Maddison.*

Before she even had the time to think about it, her legs were carrying her down the rocky path, her hands fumbling and grasping for roots and rocks to hold on to. She nearly tumbled down the last bit but steadied herself quickly and snuck around the foot of the cliff, looking for anyone who might be walking around the grounds. It seemed they were all inside.

Trotting along with her heart in her throat, Charlie reached the other cliff and threw herself in between the bushes, breathing rapidly. Still, no one had stopped her. No one had shouted for her to get inside or called her over for an inquiry. The night was serene with silence, softly broken by the lulling sounds of the calm sea.

Standing amidst the greenery, with pointy branches poking her face and leaves scratching her bare legs, Charlie saw a steep and narrow hidden path reveal itself. Climbing it was a challenge. Her breathing grew raspy with every minute she spent hugged to the side of the hill. Yet it was worth it when she reached the top.

In wonder, she stepped out into a jungle of purple echiums and irises, silver trees, and aloes, all complementing each other and illuminated by the first quarter moon and stars above. Reaching the edge, what stunned her the most, however, was staring down upon a crescent row of grass-clothed terraces framing a podium elevated upon the rocks jutting into the sea.

A bolt of electricity flared up in the sky, coming from groups of sparring couples down at the make-shift arena, now bathed in white light. The McFades were among them, and Tyler moved about, instructing people on what to do. Robes and coats swung violently as some stepped back defensively and others moved forwards in attack. It was like watching a dramatic dance with wondrous magic as the background music. Flares of shimmering green bushes, glowing red flames, and translucent blue shot wildly left and right. A boy's feet were locked in snares, and a female Defective was completely drenched in a wave lifted from the sea and dropped on her head.

There were so many sounds, and so much light, and an instant alarming feeling told Charlie she shouldn't be there. *They'll get caught!* But as she took a step back, a twig snapped behind her, and a familiar voice spoke musically into the night. 'I see you've found the Grounds of Mythos.'

Turning about, Charlie saw two figures pulling off their hoods. Maddison, her eyes white like the stars above, and Brother Deimos. An intense need to run blazed up within Charlie at the sight of him, only held back by the sight of her friend.

The fighting subsided down at the arena, and Maddison cracked a smile. 'Welcome to the rebels' lair.'

10

THE CHILD OF LIFE

'I T ' S Q U I T E S P E C T A C U L A R, isn't it?' Maddison asked, walking Charlie down one of the staircases that split the terraces into different sections of seating. Down at the podium, students were milling about, discussing their latest combats. 'The original settlers of this realm left this space free from whatever is limiting magic at Soli Gloria, as a place to practice. A lot of the Maglings escaped here to defend themselves and jump off the cliffs when the Agnus Dei over-took the grounds. Deimos says the Agnus tend to stay away, thinking the place cursed.' With a suspicious glance towards Deimos talking with Tyler, Charlie turned back to her friend. 'So, it's perfect! Not only can we practice magic, but we can do it undetected as well—'

'How can you trust him, and why didn't you tell me?' Charlie erupted.

Maddison paused and weighed her words, as if she was about to speak to a small child. 'Because he told me he'd sent Brimley away to safety, and that he would send him to find Sophie.'

Charlie inhaled sharply. 'That's why you haven't been concerned about him?'

Maddison nodded.

'But... I saw Deimos reprimand the boys in the hall and – and you still should've told me!'

Rolling her eyes, Maddison sighed. 'He has to keep up appearances, doesn't he? And as far as telling you, he said you seemed too far gone. The rebels don't allow Withdrawers into their circle. Even previous rebels who withdrew have had their memories of their activities wiped by Deimos.'

'Memories wiped – Deimos has magic?'

'Uh-huh.' Maddison's eyes sparkled. 'He comes from a long line of Welsh banshees, like me.'

Apparently, that's what he'd wanted to talk to her about on that first day after recognising her birthmarks. Charlie studied the dotted freckles on her forehead, alight like the stars above.

'He's already taught me so much about my powers. Even on the first day I could expand my mind beyond this arena, to anyone on the grounds. That's our task amongst the rebels. Either we make nosy people turn away, or we'll make them think they've already been here and found nothing. But it didn't affect you, did it?'

A look of frustration and awe came over her. Charlie had seen it before, and many a conversation repeated itself through her mind. '*I hate that I can't meddle with your thoughts,*' Maddison would say.

'*I promise you, they are nothing worth meddling with,*' Charlie would respond. On the inside, she had been grateful for whatever quirk it was that protected her from the prying of Maddison Quinsey.

'I guess not,' Charlie answered, before something else occurred to her. 'Is that why... the night of the mayhem...?' Maddison's crooked grin was all the confirmation she needed.

She'd manipulated the Agnus to stay away from the girls' cliff and the boys' cavern as the rebels swooped in amongst the new arrivals, and she had known all along. While Charlie wondered and worried, Maddison had been safe and practicing magic. With others.

Maddison's smile faded as she studied Charlie's expression. 'I guess I should have told you. I was swept up by all of it. But you surprised us by showing up here, didn't you? I'm so proud of you.' She laughed and beckoned them towards a couple of free seats. Charlie gritted her teeth, feeling her fists tighten at her sides. She understood her reasoning, but it hurt not having had the chance to have a say about it. It hurt... that she had given up on her.

Feeling a soreness coil itself in her throat, Charlie diverted her attention towards the podium, seeing the McFades head towards it with Brother Deimos.

Eagerly, Maddison continued to point out how various sources – such as the torches for fire, the sea for water – helped the different Maglings connect to their elements. But Charlie was only half-listening and biting her lip, watching as Tyler called everyone's attention to himself.

'Rebels!' he began, the collar of his black coat shielding his neck and chin from the chilling wind that toyed with his hair. 'Tuesday night, you went out and caused a little bit of havoc.' A bit of hollering and giggling sounded. 'And today we have new faces amongst us. Curious faces. Faces tired of hiding. *Defective* faces.'

An increasingly aggressive murmur spread along the terraces.

'That is what they call us. Since the very first witch-hunts – even earlier – they've been trying to rid us from Earth as though we were a plague upon this world.'

Charlie bit her bottom lip, having heard this rant from Maddison before. Not in the same words, but with the same meaning – a message she would not want to be caught listening to by the Agnus.

'These cruel witch hunters attack at night, killing or abducting our parents. Never to be heard from again. How many of you are orphans?'

An overwhelming majority shot their hands into the air. It would be easier and quicker to count who hadn't. 'And how many remember the moment you were forced into their orphanages, greeted with false sympathy after one of their attacks?' The hands remained in the air.

'But we don't know it's them,' piped up a boy from a row farther above where Charlie sat. It was the Jack Russell terrier boy that came to Soli Gloria on the same day as her. Of course. Loyal, dependable, loud. It didn't come as a surprise that he was the one to speak on the Agnus' behalf. His voice, however, faltered at the many heads turning towards him. 'We don't know that it is them who attack us. The reports say nothing about men, but rather monsters tearing houses apart.'

Charlie thought of Doyle. He had mentioned monsters too.

The boy squared his shoulders and continued. 'The orphanages aren't safe either. Uncle was snatched from one almost two decades ago. He was never seen again. None of the children were.'

Charlie immediately recalled the news article she had read earlier that day, sensing where the conversation would go.

'Was the home one of the Agnus' institutions though?' Tyler smiled, as if he'd expected the counterargument.

'Well, no,' the boy stuttered, his neck and cheeks bursting red.

'And weren't the Agnus first on the site, trying to buy the place after it closed?'

'I–I don't know but... but there were monsters—'

'Ah, yes, the monsters.' Triumph painted Tyler's face now. 'That particular rumour has served the Agnus well, hasn't it, Deimos?'

The Brother dipped his butter-blonde head in acknowledgement. 'It has. Only the Defective children have been abducted, and the word always got out to the right places. Magling families who believed the Agnus' innocence would come out of hiding, begging them to take their children and have them withdraw so they would no longer be a target.'

'*Convenient*,' hissed Maddison in her best 'I told you so' manner, her eyes practically sparkling.

'Better withdrawn than dead, right?' Tyler asked his audience, now hanging onto his every word. 'Except, once you withdraw, the Agnus does not care what happens to you next. Damned be all the withdrawal symptoms that follow.'

Charlie could see how much everyone believed him, and she

believed it too, because he was describing her time at the orphanage down to an O. But she also understood the boy who had spoken, the one who sat chewing his cheek. How much she wished it would be different. That there really was a place – just *one* – where they could go and feel safe. A home. *Perhaps that's what these rebels are trying to make Soli Gloria?*

As if reading her thoughts, Tyler spoke again, more solemnly this time. 'We must stop them. We must find a way to fight back and make Soli Gloria ours again, like it once belonged to Maglings before us.' A wild stampede of people stomping their feet followed.

'Luckily,' Tyler said, commanding and obtaining immediate silence. 'Deimos has a solution.' He nodded for the Agnus Brother to take the stage, and Charlie's whole body tensed.

'Thank you, Mr McFade,' Deimos said, then gestured to the sky. 'As my heritage allows me, I've been consulting the stars, and they have spoken to me. The key to our salvation is a child about to enter into adulthood.' People whispered amidst themselves, wondering perhaps, who it could be. One of them? Themselves? 'With every supermoon lunar eclipse, there comes a tide that will change the world, and a martyr is born. Our child is a special one. She is the child of Clotho, the Fate of Life herself, and only with the child's powers will we be free.'

An eager murmur erupted. Apparently, it wasn't just Maddison who was familiar with the Fates, and the next questions made it clear most did not even question their existence.

'There are billions of children in the world – how will we know which one is the right one?' called a voice.

'I already know who she is,' Deimos answered. 'All that remains is to find her.'

'How would we search for her stuck here?' cried a second voice.

'Actually,' Maddison interrupted, 'we won't need to. We already have the *other* child of Life, here. Her twin.'

All eyes turned towards them, and it took Charlie just a moment too long before she realised Maddison was pointing at her.

11

TEMPTATIONS OF MAGIC

A HIGH-PITCHED SCREECH tore through the audience. 'That mummy?' Venus cawed, setting her slitted snake-eyes upon Charlie. 'You're telling me our freedom is dependent on someone who couldn't even travel through the passage without setting herself on fire?'

Charlie blushed, embarrassed at the reminder, but still not having processed the new information enough to take particular offence. It was not like she thought herself some destined child that could help anyone either. She could barely help herself.

Maddison, however, seemed to take the comment personally. 'No one can control what happens to them through the passage.' She sat up in indignation. 'That is the point of it. The mere fact she went up in flames should give you an inkling as to how powerful her magic is.'

Venus rolled her eyes in response and addressed Tyler down at the podium. 'She's clearly trying to elevate her friend's social status. Look at her! She's a hairsbreadth away from withdrawing. She shouldn't even be here.'

'How would we know she's born under this lunar moon thing?' Dia chimed in.

Tyler did not mirror their disbelief, but he did not seem convinced either.

Maddison's stare was so intense that Charlie was surprised neither Venus nor her friends burst into flames themselves.

'I know it because her sister and I were born on the same date, the 30th of December, year 1982.'

Deimos nodded. 'The last supermoon lunar eclipse.'

'Are you making the claim that *you're* one of these miracle children as well?' Venus' eyes popped. 'Aren't we lucky! One minute ago, we needed a needle in a haystack, now we have three.'

People laughed. Tyler's lips twitched at the corner. Charlie regretted finding Mythos in the first place.

'Don't be daft,' Maddison said, her sharp tone laced with the insinuation that she expected it would be a challenge for Venus.

Pulling herself up to her full height, it was as if all the light of the moon and stars above were absorbed into Maddison's eyes, which turned a silvery white. 'My mother was Lachesis, Fate of Fortune.'

The impact of her words was immediate. The Defective faces went pale and turned away, staring at their hands or feet. If this had been a non-believing Magless audience, people would have laughed and perhaps thought her a little insane for the claim. But these were Defectives. The worst of the worst; people who had held on to their magic with every stubborn fibre in their body, and perhaps, like her, soaked up every little scrap of information on myths and deities they came across. It looked like most were well enough acquainted with the fate-deciding Moira as to not test her alleged offspring. Even Venus' smirk faltered, yet she stubbornly crossed her arms as her friends shuffled a couple inches away from her.

Only Tyler did not seem surprised, which made Charlie wonder how much Maddison had told him... and not her.

Things were making more sense now. Maddison's infatuation with the Fates. Her clairvoyant powers and psychic abilities. Charlie wanted to catch her eye to see whether there was truth or lies hidden behind her frozen irises, but Maddison refused to meet hers.

'Well, it won't hurt to test the theory,' Tyler said, looking at Charlie.

A booming silence remained, and shortly after he began to bid everyone farewell for the night, seeming to acknowledge that he had lost his audience.

As soon as the closest people were out of earshot, Charlie twirled on Maddison. 'What are you playing at? I know I've been laughing at your jokes about the Moirai before, but this isn't funny, Maddison.'

'I'm not trying to be, Charlie,' Maddison said, one eyebrow raised.

'Is it some sort of plot then?' Charlie squeaked, her hissing transforming into solid volume. 'Something you've cooked up with Deimos to inspire the rebels? Am I meant to play along?'

'You're meant to be you.' With a pat on Charlie's head, Maddison leapt down the terraces towards Tyler before Charlie could say another word.

Baffled, Charlie watched them huddle together in hushed whispers, but their close proximity soon made her squirm. *Perhaps she just wants to make sure he's in on the plot,* she told herself. *Perhaps they're rekindling their fling.*

Prying her eyes from the sight of the two of them, Charlie observed how the rest of the group passed Deimos and the dazed expressions that fell upon their faces once they had. It unnerved her seeing how easily and readily the Defectives let themselves be compelled by the man, despite the uniform he wore, trusting him simply upon his word that he was on their side.

'So, you're the child of Life, then?'

Turning around at the sound of his voice, Charlie found herself staring right into Caden's steely blue eyes. He stood, hands in his pockets, watching her with a contemplating expression. As if he was weighing whether she was worth his time. *You're definitely not though,* said a low voice deep within, and she struggled at meeting his gaze. Then it occurred to her that he may have overheard her talk with Maddison, and that *maybe* he was trying to catch her in a lie. That was Maddison's sport though, not hers.

'I really don't know,' she said, and shrugged.

'Promising. How did you feel about the rest of the speech?'

Charlie hesitated before responding again, unsure whether he could be trusted with her answer. 'Like I've heard it before,' she replied in the end.

'Same,' said Caden, relaxing his stance a little. 'It would be intriguing to know, with Ty telling us what we want to hear, and the Agnus telling us what we don't want to hear, if Ty is right or if we simply want him to be?'

She felt like something had hit her. She had thought such things herself, but after spending all her time with Maddison, even voicing them would have been a betrayal to what they believed in. What they had fought for every day on the run, living outside of the Agnus' reach: freedom to be who they were. But what if their freedom really was the wrong thing? What if they *were* the evil, and the Agnus the good?

A hand clasped Caden's shoulder, and it was as if a veil of ice drew all the cordiality from his countenance, draining his face of colour.

'Is my brother bothering you?' asked Tyler, his half-smile cheeky, much like it had been the other night. Even the butterflies in her stomach blushed.

'No, not at all,' she stuttered, tucking a lock of hair behind her ear. It bounded right back again.

'I'm Tyler, by the way, and this is my brother Caden.'

'We've met before.'

Tyler's eyes widened, and he glanced at his brother. 'You didn't tell me that.'

'Yeah, well,' Caden muttered, not looking at either of them. 'Almost didn't recognise her without the blisters and scorched skin.' Then he walked away, the heat around her ears making her feel like she was catching fire again.

Looking bothered, Tyler turned back to her with an apologetic shrug, and his once-so-confident smile turned awkward. 'Sorry about my brother; he's not that great around girls. Especially not pretty ones.' He winked. And despite all the times she'd agreed with Maddison that cheesy lines were the worst, Charlie still felt her insides melt like butter. His words were like birdsong to someone only accustomed to deafening silence. She sighed internally. They were a little too much, these McFades.

'I have to go,' he said, taking her hand and kissing the back of it, 'but I hope to see you amongst our ranks.'

After watching him leave, the back of her hand tingling, Charlie caught Venus glaring back at her with a murderous expression. There was no need.

Charlie did not feel certain at all about joining any kind of ranks, and the days that followed did not change that.

'So, have you come to a decision yet?' Maddison's voice was innocent. Nonchalant. Her emerald eyes skimmed the glass roof as they walked down the hallway, studying the stone walls as if they were of particular interest to her, but Charlie saw through it.

'No, Maddison. I haven't.'

'Okay, no rush.' But it seemed there was.

Half a week had gone by since Charlie stumbled upon the Grounds of Mythos, and Maddison's probing and questioning had increased with each day. It had gotten to the point where Charlie spent most of her day avoiding her in places Maddison wouldn't want to be, doing things she wouldn't want to do. Like cleaning the stables or lighting candles in the chapel.

'Just... the rebels would like to have your answer soon, you know. I'd hate for you to get barred. We wouldn't be able to spend much time together if you were. I don't want that.'

Charlie gave her a strained smile. 'Me neither.' It wasn't that she did not want to join the rebels. To say she was not tempted would be a lie. For the past days, even in the chapel where she was sure it had to be some sort of sin to think that way, she caught herself daydreaming about practicing magic with the rebels. Imagining that some extraordinary force lingered within her just waiting to be used. Some days, she envisioned herself in some pretty, sleek robes, billowing in the wind, walking onstage of Mythos in a glory of controlled flames. Mistress of her own fear. Cause of mouths dropping everywhere. Tyler's handsome features lit up with amazement.

God, sometimes she even envisioned a musical taking form and the most delicate notes belting out between her lips, stunning everyone in sight. That was the point when she knew fantasy had long since replaced the reality of her situation. For one, she wouldn't know a good note if it bit her in the vocal cords. Second, she'd probably end up looking like a charred fish on a stick if she ever attempted reaching into that fire coiling in the pit of her stomach. And that was the crux of the problem. Either she would most likely fail and discover there was nothing special about her at all, or the Agnus' wrath, if they discovered the rebels, was a risk she wasn't sure she was willing to take.

'So—' Maddison began, but Charlie grabbed onto the handle of the infirmary door and pushed down.

'I'll think about it.' She grimaced, then disappeared inside, closing the door hard after her, exhaling.

Sister Rowena looked up over the rim of her glasses but said nothing, her focus remaining on her patients.

There were more of them now, keeping her so busy that she had stopped changing Charlie's bandages and rather set her to work whenever she came by to be "checked upon".

The girls that had been taken away by the Agnus Brothers had been brought up from the dungeons, congested with pneumonia. With their lips blue and eyes delirious with fever, Charlie could not help seeing Sophie in each of them. Had she been captured and kept in a dungeon too? No, she didn't want to think about that.

Grabbing an extra wash basin and cloths, Charlie headed over to the first bed. The girl's gaze was dazed and absent while Charlie dabbed her forehead, until they pressed shut when a seizure of coughs grabbed hold of her. Exhausted, the girl leaned back on her pillow once it was over, swallowing hard as if her neck was restrained, making angry red wounds at the base of her throat and under her chin bob up and down.

The others were sporting the same marks too.

'The Heretic's Fork,' Sister Rowena had murmured when Charlie first asked her about it. 'It's used until a confession is made, then they will take it off once the student has promised to begin their withdrawal process.' Whether aware of it or not, Sister Rowena had reached for the necklace resting around her own neck, clasping the pendant once before she continued adding salve on a boy's criss-cross wounds on his back.

Since then, Charlie had looked up the Heretic's Fork in the library, and the image of the device was the first thing that popped into her mind whenever she considered joining the rebels.

The lectures hardly helped. In history studies, the Sisters would tell them about gruesome incidents where Defectives had caused societies great harm. One Rasputin, known for his erotic lust and healing hands, brought such a fate onto the Romanovs that Charlie could not get poor Anastasia and her family out of her head for the remainder of the week. Unlike at Hallows Grove, they also had behavioural studies where the Defectives were encouraged to do magic, only to see it used against someone else. The class watched as Gilly was asked to fill mugs with water then forced to empty them over Dia's hands, who simultaneously was forced to keep flames in her palms. The sizzling pain of her fire being put out, hot water scolding upon her skin, revealed itself in her grimace. Next, a third student was brought in to force the water down Dia's throat. Only when Gilly pointedly resisted using her magic, despite the threat of the cane, did the Sister stop it all, pat her on the back, and congratulate her on making the right choice.

Each of these studies filled Charlie with such an apprehension for magic, conflicting with her inner desire to use it, that she even sought out the chapel for some guidance or piece of mind.

The chapel was a circular room, built with the same stone as the main castle and wooden tiles for the roof. Pews facing the altar lined the floor, surrounded by candlelight and chandeliers. Charlie supposed she should be glad that they weren't forced to kneel on the chilly stone floor, but the pews weren't tall enough to prevent the creeping cold from grabbing hold of her skin and settling in her limbs. Some days, she could barely pay attention, her teeth clattering, eyeing the boys' chinos and long-sleeved shirts with envy. She would have much preferred them to her own cotton dress, but that was not considered proper for a girl.

Despite this, she found herself lingering after the afternoon service when everyone had left, helping Sister Lucy put out the lights. The Sister eyed her contemplatively, before she sat down on one of the pews and patted an empty spot next to her.

'Come, child, tell me what bothers you.'

Charlie felt rooted to the spot, eyeing the seat as if some invisible monster waited for her.

'You may say whatever is on your mind,' Sister Lucy continued. 'We're in God's house, and you shall not fear any pain to be inflicted upon you here.'

Finally, fearing the Sister would take offence if she didn't, Charlie shuffled over and sat down. Yet, she did not speak. Not only were the thoughts in her mind a chaotic mess that she did not fully understand – not enough to put her emotions into words at least – but she did not really trust that she could voice them either.

As a result, Sister Lucy was the first to speak again.

'I see you've healed very well since your first day here.' She pulled at Charlie's bandages.

'Yes,' Charlie stuttered. 'Sister Rowena patched me up.'

'Her *powers* are a useful resource.'

Charlie frowned at the Sister, wondering if she meant what she thought she meant. Sister Lucy refolded her hands and sighed. 'She is allowed to use them in extreme cases – no more than necessary – as long as she repents afterwards.'

'She is allowed to use magic?' A spark of hope lit within Charlie's chest.

'Healing affinities are a delicate matter. They can do much good, as Christ himself did. What powers do you have?'

'I'm not sure,' Charlie said below her breath. 'I can heal... people. Myself. Sometimes. Can we keep magic if we—'

Sister Lucy shook her head. 'There's an exception to every rule. Sister Rowena is one of them. Magic is too volatile. It eats at your soul and darkens your mind. You must keep it pure, lest it affect your heart and lead you to a life of sin. Very few can do that. Especially you young ones.'

Charlie looked at her hands. They had folded themselves, perhaps out of habit from being in the chapel.

'How do you feel about that?'

'I feel like I don't want to be a bad person, but magic... it doesn't feel evil to me.'

Sister Lucy nodded. '"For I do not understand what I'm doing. For I don't practice what I desire to do; but what I hate, that I do. But if what I don't desire, that I do, I consent to the law that it is good. So now it is no more I that do it, but sin which dwells in me. For I know that in me, that is, in my flesh, dwells no good thing. For desire is present with me, but I don't find it doing that which is good." Romans 7:15-18.

'It helped me much before I withdrew, and so it will help you. Because I recognise those feelings. Thank the Lord, you need only shed everything you think you know from before and listen. We will show you the light and give you the ability to change. Will you let us?'

Charlie nodded, although she was not certain why. She was not sure whether the verse applied to how she felt at all. She could relate to some of the words, so maybe it did. The fact that Sister Lucy used to be a Defective confused her further. She could see no visible sign of withdrawal on her, but perhaps her symptoms were more of the psychological kind. Or perhaps her powers had been rather faint to begin with.

'Good girl,' Sister Lucy said, patting her arm and dismissing her from the chapel.

During dinner, Charlie imagined staying at the castle, working alongside Sister Rowena. If she gave in and denounced her magic, working towards withdrawal, she could become one of the Agnus. Would that be a life for her? If magic really was a sin, she could devote her life to helping others see the light too. She liked helping. How often had she wished that Maddison would feel compassion towards those who were weaker than herself? Perhaps being a Defective prevented her from doing that? But then again, Charlie was compassionate... at least she thought so.

Looking up from her watery vegetable soup and stale bread, Charlie caught Tyler's eye from across the tables and the teachings of the day melted away. With a flash of his smile and a maelstrom of ecstasy surging through her, she soon found herself daydreaming about joining the rebels, and all the while, something coiled and constricted in her chest, like a snake of sin.

12

ONE OF US

'I CAN'T,' Charlie blurted out, stumbling into Maddison on her way to leave the dining hall.

'You can't what?' Maddison muttered, keeping up her pace, taking a left from the staircases, and marched down the hallway towards the kitchens with Charlie in tow.

'Join the rebels. I—where are you going?'

'*I* can't take another porridge,' Maddison snapped and, to Charlie's alarm, snuck into the kitchen with a false apology about getting lost leaving her tongue. But the room was empty, except for Albin sitting on a stool in the corner, rinsing potatoes, hunched over a bucket.

'You're not supposed to be here,' he said, his pointy ears flat against his head.

'What are *you* doing here?' asked Charlie, dumbfounded. He acted as if he had not heard her, and Maddison, to Charlie's puzzlement, acted the same with him. She simply strutted over to the fridge and began rummaging for food. Charlie scooted closer to Albin.

'I'm so sorry about what happened to you,' she whispered, eying the stubs on his back protruding from underneath his sweater. 'I was there... when they did it.'

He gave her a slight side-glance but said nothing as Maddison reappeared with a slab of cheese and salami, stuffing both pieces into her mouth.

'I heard you withdrew. Is that why you're here, working?'

Albin nodded.

Charlie bit her lip. Sister Lucy, Albin ... that made two people who'd withdrawn and were now working for the Agnus. Would there be more? Charlie thought of the Agnus Brothers and Sisters, of the maids and other servants she had walked by, their faces looking down, their eyes refusing to meet hers. Could they be Withdrawers too, rather than Magless? And were they all as glad of it as Sister Lucy?

'Do you miss it? Your magic?'

'I'll get it back,' he said.

Charlie blinked, but the fridge was slammed shut before she could ask another question.

'Mmm, salty,' Maddison purred, gobbling up the last piece of salami and licking her fingers after. 'Just what I needed.'

Like a whirlwind, she turned on her heel to leave the room, and Charlie scrambled to her feet to follow. Reaching the doorway, Charlie paused briefly and looked back at Albin. 'After what they did? You still want it?'

Albin looked up, determination and fire in his brown feline eyes. 'Even if it's just for a day.'

A storm was brewing in Charlie's mind as she rushed after Maddison, throwing the words of Sister Lucy and Albin about until it was nothing but chaos. Even after all he'd endured, Albin still wished his magic back. The risk was a price he was willing to pay – but why? If it was sin, why endure all that to have it?

'Maddison, how do you feel after you've compelled someone?' Charlie asked, earning herself a questioning look.

'What do you mean how do I feel?'

'Do you ever feel... guilty?'

Maddison shrugged. 'No.'

'You don't think it's using your magic in the wrong way?'

'I think humans manipulate each other all the time. Whether it is with words or magic doesn't really matter.'

'Oh.' Charlie chewed the inside of her cheek, pondering as they manoeuvred themselves through the castle to get to the library.

'Where is this coming from?'

'I was just contemplating our powers... is it ethical?'

At that, Maddison came to an abrupt stop. 'Don't let them get in your head, Charlie. Is this why you say you won't join the rebels? This is what they do, and you're in no state to decide whether you want to withdraw. Not until you know what you'll lose.

'I've heard people talk about you. You really surprised them when you came out of the folly like that. They've never seen anything like it. *I've* never seen anything like it. You owe it to yourself to figure out what it was.'

Charlie clenched her lips together, chewing both of her cheeks.

Maddison raised an eyebrow.

'I just... I just...' Charlie said, but her voice drifted away, and Maddison harrumphed, signalling that the time to answer had run out, before she pushed open the door to the library.

Designed to impress, Soli Gloria's library consisted of two floors filled with white marble bookcases, vintage study tables, and floor-to-ceiling windows. However, like everything else in the castle, it had taken on a morbid air with books bound in baleful black leather, hiding their dry, rigid content of religious sermons and whatnot. It was also packed with students shuffling through papers and Agnus library staff clicking their heels across the polished floor. The sound of a page tearing and the whacking of a cane echoed through the room, but it all faded as hushed voices and an ocean smell pulled her attention towards a table by the windows. Tyler was sat with his brothers and Jaden's girlfriend, Vanilla Forth. Sunrays caught Vanilla's honey-coloured highlights, complementing golden eyes that illuminated radiant happiness and affection as she looked at Jaden. She was, in short, cute as a button.

As she thought it, the alabaster beauty threw her long white hair over her shoulder and looked directly at Charlie just as her jealousy reached its peak – and was washed away.

How? Charlie shuddered in surprise. Vanilla smirked in kind.

'*She's a Liosalfar too. Full-blooded,*' Maddison had revealed earlier that week as Charlie questioned her about the group. The hint of envy in Maddison's voice had made her raise an eyebrow. Was Maddison *also* jealous of other girls? Could such a reality exist?

'*Game respects game,*' Maddison had responded.

A full-blooded Liosalfar would be able to connect to and control every feeling in a room with their empathic gifts if they wanted to, and considering Vanilla's little trick just now, Charlie felt like she'd been entrusted with an immense secret – a confirmation of Vanilla's heritage; of the elves' continuous existence, one of them sitting in the very same library as her.

She'd understood that Caden shared in that heritage too of course, but seeing them side-by-side, there was a difference to them still. Where Caden was more human, Vanilla was unearthly. Then there was the fact Caden's brothers did not seem to share any elvish heritage at all. Jaden seemed to embody the spirit of the woods, his brown skin and minty green eyes reminding her of a sunlit clearing, his hair ruffled like the crown of a tree, trailing into one long, thin braid at the back. Tyler was like a fresh breeze from the sea. From the wet look of his locks to his piercing blue eyes and scent. Perhaps they descended from nymphs of some sort.

'Well, well,' Maddison chirped, pulling Charlie out of her thoughts. 'What are we talking about today?'

'The hypocrisy of the Agnus,' said Jaden, a laugh still lingering on his lips.

Tyler raised a challenging eyebrow. 'Did you know the robes and crucifixes of the priests were inspired by Maglings' cloaks and amulets? They wanted them and then claimed them.'

Charlie could feel her own brows shoot upwards, looking over her shoulder, half expecting Mother Ratchford or one of the Sisters to come upon them. This was dangerous talk.

'They might as well call themselves *Caecus Ovis*,' Maddison said coyly.

All of them laughed while Charlie grimaced in confusion.

'It means blind sheep,' Maddison whispered and tilted her head, then slapped on her best grin and dumped her bag on an available chair. 'Is there room for two more at this table?'

Leaning backwards on his own, Caden turned a page in his book – a page he had been reading since they arrived. 'Not if she's going to turn it into a bonfire,' he muttered below his breath. If only the ground would open and swallow her up.

'Caden, that's rude,' Jaden said and rose from his chair, pulling it out for Charlie to sit. 'That being said, I *would* love to have seen that.'

Tyler let out a loud sound of agreement and winked at her. Forget the ground, she would go to the sea and jump in instead.

'Boys,' Vanilla said, rolling her eyes without seeming condescending like Maddison, 'you're embarrassing her.' As if she was attacking him, Tyler held up his arms in surrender.

'Alright, alright. But in all honesty, that chair is reserved for...' He glanced around to see if anyone was listening, but no one was looking their way. Still, he lowered his voice to a whisper as he said, 'The child of Life. So... are you her?'

Charlie looked from one expectant face to another. Vanilla's and Jaden's smiles were the only ones that seemed genuine and optimistic. Caden didn't smile at all, and Maddison kept glancing between Tyler and Charlie, making her feel even worse than either of the others. From what she had seen, they were all pretty skilled at magic, and yet they were looking at her as if she held some secret power they did not. How would they react when they realised they were wrong about her? That Venus had been right? As if reading her mind, Maddison interrupted Charlie's train of thought.

'We can help you connect to your powers. They're in there.'

Charlie couldn't deny she wanted that. She did not want to poke at the Agnus' wrath, but she *did* want to become stronger. Like them. *More* than them.

If she was honest with herself, she wanted the others to look at her as though she was something special. Like they did now, but that they would have a reason for it. She wanted to hone her powers, learn how to control them, and use them in broad daylight. Freely. More than that, she wanted to be part of the group.

Tyler's group.

His immediate interest at the mention of her powers hadn't escaped her. Nor that it could be her ticket to get to know him better. And if they were in the same rebel group practising into the late hours of the night, what else?

If Maddison was right and she was stronger than she thought, could she impress him? She wouldn't know if she refused. But then it was the matter of whether Maddison *was* right. What if she was wrong, and the real child of Life was Sophie?

'Say I'm her and learn to use my powers, what then?'

'Then, as the prophecy will have it, our magic will be free from what binds it and we'll claim the school for ourselves,' Tyler answered, a sly smile pulling at the corner of his mouth.

Charlie looked at Maddison, pondering the coincidence that Maddison had found what she had always been dreaming of – an uprising – at Soli Gloria.

'Except they don't have a plan for that,' Caden said, looking out of the window towards the beach in the distance. Tyler shot him daggers.

'Whether the child's magic unbinds us or helps us figure out how to disable whatever prevents us from using magic against the Agnus, our numbers and strength will do the rest after. We'll attack and conquer. *That's* the plan.'

Charlie had to agree with Caden; it didn't sound like much of a plan at all.

Catching her frown, Tyler cast Maddison a glance, raising an eyebrow. 'Wasn't there a sister?'

'I'm her.' The words were out before Charlie could stop them. 'The child of Life. I'm her. I'll help, if I can.'

Everyone except Caden beamed at her. Especially Maddison. Her heart quickened in her chest as the others began to chat in excited whispers about the training to come. Tyler gazed at her as if she was an archangel descended from Heaven. Maybe she was? Maybe she was *the* child. That would be something. And even if she wasn't, would it not take a couple of weeks before they knew it for certain anyway? By then, they might even have found her sister. It would give her plenty of time with Tyler so that perhaps, by the end of it, he would not even care who she was... would he?

13

FIGHT OR FLIGHT

WEEKS OF PRACTICING and emotional turmoil ensued.

During the day, the rebels would sit amongst the other students, dutifully listening as the Agnus taught history, highlighting the crimes committed by Defectives and how the Agnus' forefathers exposed them, sentencing them to hang or burn depending on where the incident took place. For a few hours at night, however, long after the rest of the school was asleep, Charlie and other rebels would listen to completely different versions of the stories. In these, innocent men and women were tortured into a confession with different devices similar to the Heretic's Fork. While the Agnus taught them about biblical stories such as Noah and his Ark, Jaden added the history of magic, and how, in the instance of the Ark, the animals had been shapeshifters – their hides as varied as their personalities – saved by the One True Divinity from the Magless who hunted them. Jaden spoke this god's name with as much reverence as an Agnus' would God's. In his stories, it sounded like those without magic were the defective ones, while magic itself was something pure to be protected.

Despite knowing a little from before, Charlie savoured every word of his stories about the time when the celestial sphere and all its worlds had just been born, and multiple gods roamed the many dimensions and realms with their minor deities, the nymphs, by their side. Her insides tingled as he spoke about the elves and the faeries and elaborated on genetics, which provoked many conversations between Charlie's new group of friends.

'My mother is an Oceanid,' Tyler said one morning in the earliest weeks, staring affectionately towards the sea providing a mirror to the rising sun. His dark eyelashes cast shadows onto his cheek. 'That's why I have an affinity for water. Jaden's mother is a Hamadryad of a Willow, which makes him—'

'An Earthling,' Charlie finished, looking at Jaden, who was making a bouquet of daffodils grow from the grass on Mythos' terraces. 'Dryads are nymphs of the earthly element, right?'

Jaden dipped his chin affirmatively, plucked the flowers, and gave them to his girlfriend, whose tiny nose disappeared amongst the petals.

'You may say our father is a bit of a *nymph*omaniac.' He grinned. 'We're ten half-brothers at present. Mothers ranging from Alseids, an Oread, Naiads, even a Lampad. Only a few of us don't have a nymph for a mother.' He glanced over at Caden sitting close by but disengaged from their conversation. He inspected his nails, as if pretending not to have heard, the delicate curves of his ears flat against his pale hair.

'Ten!' Charlie spluttered, looking about. Were there another seven McFades running about the grounds she did not know about?

'Yeah.' Jaden cleared his throat. 'The rest are back home, in our, err—'

'Home country,' Tyler said, exchanging a hard, tense look with his brothers.

'It's more difficult now though,' Vanilla said. 'To tell what people are.'

Jaden nodded. 'The purer your heritage, the more specific magic you'll have. But races are mixed today, and most have different affinities as a result. Kind of like the gods, actually, only they are much stronger and immortal.'

'It makes them capable of doing more fancy stuff, but their magic is more unruly.'

'The gods?' Charlie asked.

'No,' Tyler corrected himself. 'The mixed races. Many struggle to know what they are, what they can do, and thus *who* they are.' He looked at her then, as if knowing something that had not yet occurred to her. Her fingers nervously tugged at her pin.

Even if she *was* the child of Life, she didn't know what that meant – whose genetics she shared or what magic she would have. And if she couldn't figure that out, would she ever know *who* she was?

'Then what do they do? If they don't know?'

'Focus on their magic.' Jaden smiled.

'Then they'll figure it out? Who they are?'

'More importantly,' Vanilla contemplated, studying Charlie, 'they'll *be* who they are.'

Focusing on her magic, however, when Charlie did not know what it was, was easier said than done. While she knew that she had healing affinities, it wasn't the sort of power you could chuck at someone in combat (unless she found a way to manifest a massive band-aid), and after watching power surge through the others like lustrous auras, she really wanted to uphold her own. To be able to fight back. So, when the others tried to teach her how to connect with her magic, she listened intently, all the while hoping it would help her reveal some new powers she had yet to discover.

'There are three outlets,' Vanilla said later that day while reaching for a pair of forgotten glasses by her side, putting them on and counting down with her fingers. 'Your psyche, catecholamine hormones such as adrenaline, and emotions.'

'You don't use glasses,' Charlie noted.

'Yes, but don't they look fantastic?' The Liosalfar grinned. 'They make me feel so... smart and capable—' She snapped her fingers, and a Defective who'd just had their ass handed to them in combat leapt to their feet, ready for a second try, their smile the exact match to Vanilla's. 'And that's me channelling my emotions.' She rested her chin innocently on her palm.

Charlie whistled, feeling a wave of Vanilla's confidence transmitting to her. 'How?'

'You have to think of magic as energy.' Vanilla pushed the glasses up the slim bridge of her nose. 'It's around all of us, and within.'

'Within the Magless too?'

Vanilla nodded. 'The biggest difference between us and them is that we utilize our magic. The Magless are always so restless!' She shuddered. 'Always running the rat-wheel and denying themselves, not knowing what to do with their energy, not knowing how to get more.'

'But we do?'

'We do. And we'll teach you. But first you need to learn how to connect with your energy within so you can harness the energy outwards.' And meditation became her first stop to learn that.

Following Maddison's instructions as she held the sessions with the rebels, Charlie closed her eyes, and a bomb of thoughts went off in her head. Things she had learned, questions she had yet to get answers for, and concerns regarding whether or not she was sitting correctly – should one of her legs rest upon the other? – or *doing* things right at all. Thoughts were flying left and right with such force that her eyes popped open out of sheer restlessness. Scowling impatiently back at her was Maddison, and Charlie quickly forced her eyes shut once again, focusing on one body part at a time, from head to toe. She tried to notice how her thoughts came and went... except they never left. They only increased. Growing louder until it felt like they were pressing on her eyelids to escape her head. Once again, her eyelids bounced open.

After session by session like that, Maddison gave up and handed her over to Jaden and Tyler to test for combat.

It did not go well.

'She's too afraid,' Vanilla said to Jaden, guiding a shivering Charlie down on the ground next to him, a sympathetic smile on her pretty face, before she turned back to a couple of rebels waiting to return to their training.

'I think I qualify as a blueberry.' Charlie sighed, gesturing at her bruised legs. For days now, the others had been using their elemental magic to throw branches in her way, make pebbles rain over her head, and stuff waves of wind down her throat, all with the sole purpose of triggering her defensive instincts. Charlie was beginning to think she had none.

Jaden wore the same empathic expression as his girlfriend. Every time one of his vines had lashed out at her, Charlie recoiled, visualising Sister Hilda or one of the Brothers punishing her for even trying to use magic.

With frustration, Charlie thought back to what Tyler had explained in one of his sessions.

Practicing or exercising magic helps activate the energy in your body and build your muscle memory. When the brain and body are connected, your magic will come almost instinctively, your bodily reactions responding to your neurological ones.'

As the others had nodded and eagerly paired up for training, he'd turned to her, adding more quietly, 'Normally, we'd start with understanding your heritage, but since we don't know it...'

She had looked down at her feet, feeling quite small. To her surprise, Tyler put a finger under her chin and raised her eyes to his.

'... we'll have to try and fail a little. And that's okay. Might take longer, and you may become sick and tired of spending too much time with me, but I'm certain we'll get there.' He'd smirked.

Even thinking of that smirk now made her feel warm and fuzzy inside, and she wondered if her bruises didn't seem to fade ever so slightly. Then her train of thought continued and derailed, and the feeling quickly evaporated. They had gone through so many hours of training already; what if Tyler was getting impatient? She could tell the others' patience was wearing thin. After all, many of the other newcomers had already learned to channel their adrenaline as an outlet for energy.

'I don't understand,' Charlie groaned at Jaden. 'If adrenaline is an outlet, wouldn't fear work too? I should be great at this stuff.' She hid her face in her palms.

Jaden shifted beside her, his voice gentle as he spoke. 'Not really. Adrenaline and fear are two sides of the same coin. Two opposite sides to your "fight-or-flight" system. Right here'—he tapped the back of her head—'is where our brains most closely resemble that of the animals we once were. When something happens, and it goes past your ability to think rationally'—he tapped her forehead—'your amygdala starts analysing your feelings. If you have too much fear, it can be overpowered. Think of it as a window of tolerance. As long as you're within your window, you have a certain control over your reactions. If you're overstimulated, you'll lash out. If you go under, you'll shut down. Training helps you widen your window, preventing the kettle from spilling and your powers fleeing.'

'Your metaphors amaze me,' Charlie drawled. Jaden's grin widened.

'Oh, I'm just getting warmed up. Nip this in the bud. Let your mind and body work together rather than fighting for control, and you'll see your adrenaline kick-start your defence mechanisms to stay and fight.'

'It sounds like a beautiful dream when you say it.'

He chuckled. 'It's only magic.' His eyes twinkled, as if he still believed she would find it. That little pool of powers and untapped potential within herself. He was kind to think so, and that was what she thought of him; Jaden was kind. Not nonchalant or haughty like Caden at times, not intense and overwhelming like Tyler. But kind. Pleasant. She felt safe around him – safe and alone. He and Vanilla together made her yearn tremendously for a special someone, and her eyes automatically scanned the rebels for Tyler. A cool dread ran through her once she spotted him observing Venus' transformation into a serpent. He was clearly impressed by the speed with which she could strike her opponent. Sensing a sharp sting of jealousy, Charlie felt time running out before one of Venus' poisonous fangs would puncture her heart.

As November ran into December, and the white blanket of snow grew thicker on the ground, Charlie was starting to panic. Any day now, Brimley could show up at Soli Gloria with Sophie. According to Deimos, he had picked up a fresh trail of her last time they spoke. And if Tyler – his family seemingly influential enough to send their children to Soli Gloria at their leisure – was to go home for Christmas, Charlie might not have another chance at making her daydreams come true by the time the holiday was over. Perhaps, by then, she might even have withdrawn, like one of the girls from her hut. One night they were four; the next Sister Lucy told them the fourth had withdrawn and secured a late admission spot at a school in Plymouth. Every night spotting her roommate's empty bed, Charlie wondered if the girl was happy being part of the society again or if she longed for her magic back – like Albin.

'Charlie, dear. You need to focus,' Vanilla said softly beside her.

Charlie sighed, opening her eyes. It was the second weekend of December, and except for the elf, everyone else sat still, the bright morning light thick around them as if the sun itself had ordered its rays to embrace them. Birds had come awake and chirped as they flew by, and yet the others remained still like statues, melted into the landscape as if they had been there since the dawn of time. Not far from her sat the McFades, and Venus appeared to have shifted close enough so that her knee was brushing Tyler's. It made Charlie feel hot and bothered, despite the frost lingering in the air. An empathic smile quivered on Vanilla's soft features.

'I don't know what I'm doing,' Charlie said, as if that was her only issue.

'Well first off, you need to stop fretting about the things you have yet to accomplish and be proud of the progress you have made. Second, think of the force, the matter, that exists within everything. What's inside of us is also within the trees, the wind, the waves of the sea... this is why elemental magic is so easily accessible to us. Energy. It'll feel differently, depending on where it comes from – like a language. Try and see if you can snatch up the vibe of one you understand. Does that make more sense?'

It did actually, more so than Maddison's vexing and moaning at her for not getting it at all. But Vanilla was more patient... and perceptive.

'It's not so much the understanding, more the doing, I think,' Charlie muttered, still eyeing Tyler and the snake beside him.

Vanilla followed her gaze.

'Perhaps you need a little motivation.'

Charlie frowned at her, but she didn't elaborate before the session finished. As everyone began scrambling to return to their dorms before the rest of the school awoke, Vanilla called for Tyler, ignoring Charlie's pleading for her not to once she realised what she was about to do.

Eyes alight and skin radiant in the morning glow, Tyler rushed up the terraces with Venus in tow.

'What's up?'

'Pray tell, Tyler, are you free at some point?' She gave Charlie a conniving look that sent heat rushing up her neck. 'Charlie seems to be struggling a bit.'

At this, Venus chuckled next to Tyler.

Ignoring her, Vanilla raised her voice firmly. 'And I thought you two could have a private session?'

'Of course.'

Charlie, at first focused on the death of Venus' smirk, almost dropped her mouth open in surprise as Tyler accepted.

'There's a full moon tomorrow that might help,' he added, eyes dancing. 'Give you a little more energy. I can meet you then if you'd like?'

Without hesitating, Venus turned on her heels and headed over to a group of girls that included Ava and Dia. She'd barely sat down before they started whispering furiously, staring at Charlie.

'Come on, let's head back to the dorms,' Vanilla said once she'd accepted Tyler's offer on Charlie's behalf, beckoning for them to follow Tyler as he left the site. Legs feeling like jelly, and with a circus of somersaults happening in her stomach, Charlie floated behind them on elated clouds until they passed the group of girls, and their whispers reached her.

'She's sleeping with him,' Venus told the others, and their eyes widened. Waves of hot and cold rolled down Charlie's back as she registered the words.

Ava made a sound as if this was nothing new to her. 'I heard she's slept with both brothers, Tyler *and* Caden.'

'I heard all *three*! And Vanilla doesn't even know!' said another of the girls, whom she didn't know, her voice full of indignation.

'What a skank,' agreed a third.

Shell-shocked, Charlie stumbled along the challenging path down to the beach, unable to focus on anything but what she had overheard. She wasn't surprised to hear foul lies being spread by Venus and her friends. But the others... there had been faces in that group she had never spoken to before, and yet they had been saying the same nasty things. That she... her chest contracted with humiliation and panic at the very idea.

'Don't tantalise the poor man...' The scolding voice of Mother Agnes' assistant resurfaced, as did the many sermons she had heard on intercourse, and suddenly her white uniform felt like a lie. Her whole body froze, and her mind turned impenetrable to Vanilla's questioning energy knocking at its walls.

Broken pieces of judgemental thoughts swiped at her from within, razor sharp like a barber's blade, taking on the voices of her fellow rebels. What if people believed them? What if *Tyler* believed them? How would she ever be able to prove the rumours to be lies? She could already see them, her new friends, turning their backs on her. A shadow over Tyler's face. Vanilla's golden eyes narrowed in hurt and betrayal. They would cast her out, leaving her alone in stifling despair.

A feeble voice tried to say something rational about truths and lies, that at least one of her new friends would recognise one lie and see the true colours of the others, but her panic swatted it away like a mosquito. Doubt of her character would be sowed no matter what they believed. *How* could she make the rumours go away?

She didn't know. But she did know how to not make them worse. Her heart dropped like a rock into her stomach.

She could not meet with him, not alone. Tomorrow night, she would have to stay inside and skip her training with Tyler.

14

COMING TO BLOOM

MONDAY EVENING, Venus blocked Charlie from leaving the bathroom. Her eyes scanned Charlie's body, as if she could see under her gown, a malicious and sarcastic grin playing on her lips. 'Whatever they see in you I'll never understand, but mark my words when I say this, Hallows.' Venus stepped closer, her slithering tongue clicking against her teeth as she whispered in Charlie's ear. 'I'll find a way to show them your pathetic true colours, you—'

'Unless you want to be forced to run through the corridors naked, I suggest you choose your next words carefully.' Stepping out of the shower cave, Maddison sauntered onto the tiled floor. She wrapped a towel around her naked body, staring down Venus with a feral purr. 'I don't take threats to my friends particularly well.'

Charlie's muscles relaxed at Maddison's presence, but her insides still quivered with unease. It was odd, considering she knew perfectly well that no one in the room was more powerful than Maddison – no matter how much venom their tongues lashed out.

Venus stepped back, eyeing Maddison with a calculating look, the ghost of her former grin still lingering in the corner of her lips.

'Whatever, Quinsey. I'm bored with you.' She tossed a malicious glare at Charlie over her shoulder. 'And the boys will be soon enough.' With her nose in the air, Venus joined her friends as they dried off and changed into clothes by the sinks. Clearly drawing strength from numbers, their laughter rang loud. Only Gilly didn't seem to laugh as merrily as the others. Charlie's discomfort rose.

'Don't mind them,' Maddison ordered as she finished changing. Yet Charlie kept her gaze fixed to the ground as they left the bathroom, the girls' laughter following them down the corridor. 'They're clearly idiots. Shouldn't you be off to see Tyler?' She dragged out his name teasingly.

Gritting her teeth, Charlie shook her head, bringing Maddison to a full stop.

'Why?'

Painfully embarrassed, Charlie recounted what she had overheard the girls saying. Unbothered, Maddison waved it off. 'They're only jealous. What does it even matter what they say? You know the truth.'

A heavy notion turned Charlie's chest into a knot. 'But everyone else doesn't, and I care what people think.'

'Too much.' Maddison scoffed. 'Have you cancelled on him yet?'

'No.' She had not been able to. Perhaps some part of her had held out for the possibility that she would be able to go. Perhaps some part of her had hoped Maddison would talk her into it. The knot slightly eased up.

'Go to him. Take control over your magic, then show them something else to talk about.'

Charlie frowned. It would probably be easier to live with the rumours than access her magic at this point.

'Okay, what about this?' Maddison said. 'I'll tell the school *I* slept with them. They're fine boys; I'd consider it an achievement.' Maddison pretended to dust off her nails, smirking. Then, without another word from Charlie, she sighed. 'Fine, if anyone starts talking, I'll tell everyone you hung out with me all night, not him.'

That might actually work. Charlie perked up a little. She would rather Maddison have compelled everyone to forget about the rumours, but she supposed that was not entirely decent. And she did *want* to see Tyler. Every fibre in her body tingled at the very idea.

Not ten minutes later, she found herself crawling out from underneath the bushes at Mythos, sweet fragrances of night-scented plants and dusk filling her nose, peering down at the terraces and the arena to see if the coast was clear. It seemed abandoned, with Tyler nowhere to be seen and only the sea beating against rocks for sound. For whatever reason, there was, however, a small hut not far from the podium with warm light filtering out from its window. She reached the door and hesitated with her fist raised to knock, the other girls' words echoing through her head, but she didn't get a chance to change her mind.

As if he'd heard her coming, Tyler opened the door, his face brightening like the full moon above the sea.

'Welcome.' He gestured her into the room, and she stepped inside, shyness filling her cheeks. Then her face drained of colour and her lips began to quiver.

'I heard she's slept with both... Caden and Tyler.'

In the middle of the room stood a large oval bed taking up all the space, an illusion no further helped by the tiny bookshelf pushed up against the wall, its driftwood shelves looking as if they were about to collapse.

'W-what is this place?'

'We think Mythos was once used as a theatre, and that the actors came here to change into their costumes or take a break.' Unaware of her slowly rising panic, Tyler beckoned for her to sit wherever she liked, and then went on to throw himself onto the bed. Without effort, he stretched out his arm and snagged a colourful book from the weathered crooked shelves. 'So, Vanilla thinks I can help, huh?'

Her voice trembled as she answered. 'I don't think anyone can help me at this point.'

Tyler looked like he was trying hard not to laugh. At her? With her? Out of pity?

'Do you know what struck me the first time I met you?'

If she could wager a guess, she would bet her blisters. Still, she only shook her head.

'The way your powers work. Some Liosalfars – mind you, you don't quite look like one – have healing properties, but none of them could have transformed the way you did before me that night. The longer we talked, the more you seemed to patch yourself together.'

Certain it had happened overnight, the thought of healing so openly in front of a stranger both excited and unnerved her.

'Then there was the fire I've heard so much about.' He paused as if contemplating her. 'The folly forces what's hiding inside of us to show itself. Earthlings tends to get more apparent markings with the characteristics of the greenery they stem from. For Waterlings, like myself, our blue veins stand out like the pattern of a Ming vase. Shapeshifters—'

'Turn into their animal shape,' Charlie finished for him, thinking of Maddison soaring like a raven, the Jack Russell terrier boy barking at the Agnus brothers, and the big cat slinking into the woods. She still didn't know who that had been.

Tyler gave her an approving nod. 'My point is, if Firelings reacted that way when they go through, you might have been one, but they don't.'

'Why do you think I did?'

'I don't know.' He smiled and shrugged. 'It's a mystery.' His gaze turned into one of his smoulders. 'I like mysteries.'

Avoiding the intensity of his stare, certain he could see the little fires sparkling at the top of her cheeks, Charlie's eyes drifted towards the empty spot on the bed next to him. Big mistake. The fires spread from her cheeks to her ears, evaporating every fluid in her throat, making her voice sound parched and throaty as she spoke.

'So... why the bed?'

He cocked his head, his fingers tracing the cover of his book. 'Training requires buckets of energy and time. Some days we train too hard. Other nights we've slept too little. And sometimes, a rebel might just need to hide from the Agnus overnight.' He patted the bed for her to sit next to him.

Sore from near all-nighters and (fruitless) battles, her body ached to stretch out on the mattress. And she could not deny that her heart, her mind – all of her – secretly wished for him to embrace her and pull her close if she did. There was no reason on earth why he would do it... except the look in his eye.

'I think I can relate to some of that,' she croaked and sat down, her eyes pretending to study a painting on the opposite wall to distract herself from Tyler's proximity. The closeness of his body. The cool chill radiating from his skin like a sea breeze on a hot summer's day.

'We'll only do a little tonight, then.' Tyler closed the book, having barely looked at it in the first place, as if he had picked it up just to keep his hands busy. Could he be nervous too? 'There's no point trying to wring a sleep deprived mind and body to do magic.' He paused, allowing her the chance to protest.

She had to shake herself to focus on what he was saying. It seemed surreal to have him there, sitting on a bedspread together, close enough for her to reach out and touch him. His dark locks curled around his ears as if they'd just dried after a swim, and she could have sworn she saw a shimmer of blue whenever the strands swayed with the movements of his head. She would have liked nothing more than to run her fingers through them. She blinked, reminding herself that he was watching her. If only he would stop smiling that way.

'So, why do you think you're struggling?'

Because I'm a coward. A talentless, waste-of-time chicken. She shrugged, picking at the duvet. 'I guess I'm scared of punishment – or of being rubbish.'

'Mastering magic...' Tyler began, one arm around his bent knee, rocking himself back and forth while he pondered his response, '... means connecting your body, mind and soul together. The methods we've taught you, in practice, help with the mind and body part, but sometimes the soul won't connect if your heart's not in it. Perhaps we need to work on that a little.' He leaned forward until their faces were mere inches apart.

Her heart was beating so fast she worried it would take flight and burst through her chest.

'Here.' His hand found hers and dropped something into her palm. She could barely take her attention away from his skin, cold against hers, long enough to notice the seed. She stared at it, puzzled.

'Jaden picked it out of one of his creations,' Tyler said, as if it explained everything. 'He said that it might be easier for you to start small than to try and connect with too much at once.'

He's been talking about me with his brother! The thought inflamed a glowing bulb of excitement within her.

He closed her fingers over the seed with his own, her eyes following the movement hungrily. Then he asked her to close her eyes. The moment she did, his skin became warmer against hers, and she became infinitely more aware of how each of his finger joints caressed her own. Her breath caught.

'Focus.'

Easy for him to say, Charlie thought, feeling him lift her hands until his breath brushed over her knuckles. 'Try and imagine the sprout within the seed. Imagine its little teardrop shape and how it strives to stretch and grow. Now imagine that same force within yourself. Tell me, Charlie, wouldn't you like to break out of your shell?'

His fingers were tracing her cheek now, running into her hair, down to the curve of her neck.

She shivered. All her senses felt alert, starving for more. The silky feel of the bedsheet. The drop of Tyler's hand. And the electricity that jolted up her leg as his fingers grazed her knee. A gulf of fire awakened inside her, and she gasped.

'Breathe. Inhale through your nose and exhale through your mouth. Notice the rise and fall in your body. Listen to it. Notice how your energy surges through you. Notice how it feels but let the observations pass. Accept it all. Accept your surroundings. Your feelings. Your fears. And let them pass.' His voice was a melodic hush, mixing with the soothing sounds of the sea.

Her insides shivered, nervous about making a fool out of herself. *Okay... concentrate... I'm focusing... I'm focusing... Row, row, row your boat... God, Charlie! Concentrate!* She listened to the beauty and kindness in his voice as he spoke to her. About her. Instantly, she thought of him watching her. Eying her with the same expression that laced his voice. She thought of him leaning forwards, his lips meeting hers, and the simple thought melted her insides into a bubbling waterfall of pink joy. Heat spread through her body, starting in the depths of her heart, and surged through her veins, across her chest, down her arm, until it reached her palm.

She gasped and opened her eyes. Tyler remained still, observing her with a knowing look. Holding her breath, Charlie opened her fist. The seed had cracked, and a tiny green seedling fled its shell.

'It's not much,' she mumbled, pride and shyness warring within her.

'It broke free, it's a beginning. And to be honest, the fact you could do anything with this element is another mystery.' His tone was full of triumph. Then he leaned closer, so close that she could count each one of his long eyelashes, his breath warm against her lips.

'Tyler,' she whispered. 'Why did you agree to help me tonight?'

He paused, a puzzled crease appearing between his eyebrows.

Charlie cursed her tongue. 'I just mean, you didn't *have* to meet me in private, at night.'

'Would you hold it against me if I said I saw my chance to be alone with you?'

'Why would you want to?' The mini-her was back, stomping her feet in frustration. Why did she have to ruin the moment?

He trailed a finger along her palm, sending an explosion of nerves up her arm. 'Because I have a lot of eyes upon me.' Humour laced his words, until it didn't. 'I hold most of the responsibility for the rebels. They see me as their leader, and I have to seem tough and serious.'

He looked up, his eyes tender and affectionate. 'I'm afraid I can't keep that façade up with you.'

She sighed, feeling in that moment as if she was finally seeing the boy behind the mask. She thought of kissing him, feeling the tingle in her palms grow stronger.

'Tyler.' Her voice was barely audible now. 'How do you connect your soul to magic?'

'Well'—he cleared his throat—'emotions and hormones are great amplifiers. The purer the better.' He edged closer, his own voice a husk against her lips. 'Art and love are pretty decent activities. Comes with a caution of intimacy though.' There was a ghost of a grin on his lips as his nose brushed against hers, his eyes searching one last time for permission before—Someone knocked at the door.

15

THE FINAL SPARK

CHARLIE FELT the blood drain from her face, scanning Tyler's expression for any signs of panic. If he felt it, he did not show it, but his expression appeared watchful. If they were caught by an Agnus member, the punishment would be severe.

'Erm, who is it?' he called out.

'It's Gilly,' piped up a soft voice. 'Gilly Jones.'

Even worse.

Perhaps she had seen them through the little window. If so, the rumours would practically be confirmed and Charlie's reputation finished. Rooted to the spot, she could not form the words to protest as Tyler stepped off the bed and opened the door ever so slightly. If Gilly was surprised to see the two of them, it was not evident on her face.

'Um, Charlie? Something's up with Maddison. I thought you...' Her words trailed off while she wrung her hands, as if she were nervous – or feeling guilty. At once, Charlie came to think of how Maddison had embarrassed Venus earlier on and the thirst for revenge on Venus' face. Had they done something to her? Was that why they had sent one of their own to get her?

She was on her feet at once. 'What did you do?'

'No–nothing,' stuttered Gilly, backing away as Charlie stormed past her and thundered back up to the girls' cliff and Maddison's cottage. Her anger came as a surprise, even to herself. But right now, it felt like a lifeline, keeping fear from overwhelming her with every step she took. *If they've hurt her...* she'd have no clue what she would do. Her anger started contemplating vicious actions she would take in retaliation, but her heart would not let her mind finish them.

The three girls sharing Maddison's cottage were huddled outside the little white tooth, looking as if a murder scene was to be found inside. 'She's gone mad!' cried one of them. Charlie rushed past.

After stepping through the doorway, however, it was pretty clear that no one had touched Maddison. She lay rolling in her bed, eyes white, and sweat beading on her forehead. Her beautiful red lips were twisted in grimaces and screams of agony. Instinctively, Charlie slammed the door behind her, barely registering that Tyler had been following at her heels and that he would probably be picking splinters out of his nose for the next hour. Then there was the talk and gossip that would be sure to ensue from his presence. But she couldn't worry about that now. Maddison was having one of her visions.

Calmly and methodically, Charlie rummaged through Maddison's stuff and then began the familiar process of soaking a cloth in a cool, prepared mixture of water, chamomile, and lemon balm. Once done, Charlie brought the mixture-soaked cloth over to the bed.

Feverish words escaped Maddison's lips in a faded whisper. At her chest, the vial pendant of her necklace glowed bright between her fingers.

'What are you saying?' Charlie murmured, leaning closer to put the cloth on her forehead.

A hand shot out and grabbed her wrist, causing her to jump. The cloth dropped to the floor with a splat.

'Monsters...' Maddison gasped. 'They're coming.'

Maddison remained restless after, caught between a dream-world and an awakened state where she seemed as distant as if she were still asleep. Charlie barely slept either. Shortly after her episode, perhaps by Tyler's suggestion, although she would not know for sure, the girls from Maddison's cottage had decided that Maddison was to be moved to Charlie's cottage and the empty bed. Before returning to Mythos, Tyler helped carry Maddison while Charlie brought her things.

Eyes followed them as they walked, and this time she shut the door in *their* faces. Satisfying at the time, but in the dark hours of the night, Charlie could no longer help but think about all the things that would be whispered and said about her throughout the morning. Even worse if Tyler were to hear any of it. Would he choose to stay away from her so not to be gossiped about? Their near kiss came to mind, and her stomach knotted with disappointment and concern. Concern it would never happen again.

Now and then, when Maddison thrashed in her bed, Charlie would throw her a glance while busying herself with sorting through her stuff. Her rucksack was oddly heavy considering the fact they'd been on their way to a party when she packed it.

She roamed through the clothes within until her fingers bumped into something hard. Frowning, she felt her way around the cool leathery surface and pulled it out. It was her *Encyclopaedia of Mythological Creatures.*

Why would Maddison bring this to a party?

Perplexed, Charlie started flipping through the pages. Most of them seemed unharmed, the familiar lively prints of nymphs and faeries as eerie as ever. Only one page had folded in on itself. The image of the *Moirai,* the Fates, as three old crones with crooked noses and evil eyes became visible as she flattened it out. She sure hoped the real Clotho, Fate of Life and presumably her mother, did not look anything like her haunting portrayal.

It was not until a ray of sunshine dashed through the window that she looked up from the book, realising that morning was dawning and Maddison was sleeping peacefully. Considering that, perhaps she ought to give Tyler her thanks for helping her, both with Maddison and the seed. Then she closed the book and headed down to the stage where she found him overlooking the meditating rebels.

'Do you ever sleep?' she asked him, stopping by his side, hands in her cardigan pockets.

'About as much as you do, it looks like.' He smiled at her, his forehead creasing. 'How's Maddison?'

She exhaled. 'Maddison has visions. She sees things. Things that will happen.'

He turned towards the sea while his mind seemed to dive into his own thoughts, his eyes turning soft upon the horizon. 'Non-elemental magic is so impressive. Caden can talk to ghosts. Did you know? It's extremely rare.'

And dark, Charlie thought, her eyebrows lifting in surprise, realising she had never seen Caden do magic. She had seen Jaden make thick roots erupt from the ground, giant green serpents Vanilla would leap and run upon – light on foot with the speed and finesse of the elves – as they coiled themselves towards the sky.

She had held her breath as Airlings manipulated the air to knock her off balance, and she'd felt the small hairs rising on her arm as Ava balled up her fists and then flattened them, lifting embers of fire from the torches of Mythos to devour Jaden's greenery. And she had seen Caden, always hanging about but never doing any magic of his own.

As if gravitating towards the source of the mystery, she looked over to Venus and her friends with Caden sat between them. His eyes twinkled like pale aquamarine crystals, and a cheeky half grin pulled at his lips as his joke made them roar with laughter. Would he be talking about her? Except for the times he saved her, he had never seemed particularly fond of her. The motions of his hands certainly looked like her flailing about in duelling.

'I guess,' Tyler murmured, 'if Maddison really is who she claims to be, then visions would only be expected. They say the most recent Fate of Fortune was handpicked from a line of banshees. Their clairvoyant gifts, particularly that of predicting death, make the species natural candidates for the role. I wouldn't want to have that responsibility though.'

Charlie had to agree. Every bout of visions tended to be followed by a few days where Maddison would sit in darkness, wrapped in a blanket, staring at the sky from her window. Although she never spoke of what she had seen, it was clear that the images had been grim or full of suffering.

Tyler glanced at her, his voice milder as if he thought he had scared her. 'All myths and religions come from something. At their core, they all share a piece of truth that has been moulded and retold until it's barely recognisable anymore.' There was a hunger in his eyes then, and she realised he wasn't talking about Maddison anymore, but her. As if there were a truth hidden within her that he simply had to uncover. Some key to their rebellion against the Agnus, if only her powers would reveal themselves to be more advanced than healing boo boos. There were so many expectations behind those eyelashes that it was almost too much. Perhaps she ought to go back and check on Maddison. She nibbled her lip, looking towards the girls' cliff and the scattered white lumps, homing in on one of them as the wind blew a lock of hair past her face. Then she felt a squeeze and looked down to her hand, seeing hers in his.

'You should try to meditate before the morning sermon. Your powers should still be rather potent after the full moon,' he said, the warmth of his gaze filling her body, making her feel fuzzy on the inside. He gave the others a quick glance, as if to check if anybody was watching, and leaned in to kiss her on the cheek, his lips grazing the corner of her lips. Her heart fluttered, and moments later she found herself cross-legged on the terrace, her eyes on him as he instructed the rebels, her mind filled with the moment they had shared.

At first, she thought it a good thing that her face was turned towards the risen sun, before she started to notice the warmth of it. Soon after, she also became aware of the way the chilly stone under her thighs thawed under the light.

Somewhere, someone started making an 'Aaomh' sound.

Like the keys of the same piano, the rest of the rebels mimicked it. The soundwaves travelled through them all, stringing them along as if they were threaded pearls on a line. It made her feel wholesome, lighter than air, and for the first time she felt like she truly belonged to something great.

The feeling remained as she walked with Tyler, his brothers, and Vanilla towards the castle. She even joined in on a couple jokes, bubbles of laughter filling her chest.

But the mood drastically dwindled amongst them once they reached the chapel for morning sermons. Particularly Charlie's when she realised Maddison wasn't amongst the crowd. Guiltily, Charlie regretted spending such a long time at Mythos, but there was no time to go check on her now. Agnus Brothers and Sisters were ushering the students inside with hawk eyes, prepared to catch anyone trying to sneak away.

'Come on,' Tyler said, taking her hand behind their backs and pulled her close, leading her inside to sit next to him.

The chapel had been overcrowded on their first Sunday after Halloween, near claustrophobic. Now it seemed more spacious; there were fewer students than there had been. Evidence of more withdrawals. More students that had been permitted to leave the school.

Once they sat down on a pew, Charlie felt her neck prickle as though her spirit was digging its way out. As Mother Ratchford took up her place before the altar, Charlie's skin began to crawl, and a restlessness strung her up from within. Her throat tightened like her muscles, as if there was no air to breathe in the chapel.

Tyler put his hand over hers. It felt large, like a glove over her tiny ones. 'You're shaking like a leaf.'

'It's these sermons I guess. I don't like them,' Charlie whispered, eyes on the Headmistress of Discipline. A phantom pain pinched her arm where Mother Agnes had used to grab her, forcing her to her feet with an iron grip despite her exhaustion after nights on the Stool of Infamy.

Tyler's jaw clenched. 'I'm the same.'

Then the headmistress spoke. 'I have some grave news to share with you all today. Last night, another attack occurred, the first to befall one of our own esteemed houses.'

Charlie's head shot up. She could feel Tyler's eyes upon her, but all she could look at was Mother Ratchford's lips as they formed her next words. 'All the Defectives yet to withdraw were abducted by the monsters. In fact, so many children have disappeared that the home fears it may not recover its footing.'

Monsters, Charlie recollected the word, picturing Maddison's haunted expression in her mind. *'They're coming'*. It was true, then. The Agnus weren't behind the attacks. Creatures – *magical* creatures? – were.

The room swam before her. She tried focusing on the details of the chapel, hoping it would calm the sudden wave of emotions erupting within, grappling against the thickness blocking her airways, the terror dozens of orphans must have felt at once. What if it had been Hallows Grove?

'This is what we try to protect you from. This is *why* you are here. So that evil like this will be purged from this world. Work hard to abstain from sin, and you shall be safe. Withdraw, and we shall extinguish the flames that draw the bloodthirsty gnats towards us.'

Mother Ratchford did not even need to ask the students to stand up for their prayers. Even the rebels were on their feet by a simple gesture of her palms, looking nervously between one another. Like one of them might easily have compelled an element to their will, she had moved them all in their fear.

Charlie fixed her eyes on the candlelight beneath the crucifix, her thoughts still on the children and her own fright. *What if the monsters come here?* The flames shivered in their place – like her insides, desiring once again to escape from their bodily cage. This life. The Agnus. Was Soli Gloria really any safer, or were *they* in danger?

She thought of the children of the attacked home, alone and scared. Had they been hiding under their beds? Waiting, hoping that the monsters wouldn't find them? Praying to something, someone, who would not save them?

'Now then,' Mother Ratchford said, 'repeat after me:

'I believe in God the Father Almighty—'

Charlie closed her eyes. Had the children been in a morning sermon like this, hearing the words of a religion they did not even believe in and which – even worse – did not believe in them? She didn't know about God or goddesses anymore, but she knew the suffering that happened. She believed in the rebels as they tried to fight back, and that she would fight with them.

She opened her eyes wide. Mother Ratchford's voice trailed off, and everyone remained quiet, following her line of sight towards the same candles Charlie had been watching.

Having almost gone out, they had now come ablaze with an extraordinary intensity. Growing tall, the flames convulsed as though something – or someone – was trying to break free from within.

Then it happened.

The candles spat out tongues of flames that landed on the chapel's stone floor. To the screams and frantic noises of the audience, the flames appeared to come alive, running down the aisle like gingerbread men on fire. Charlie could have sworn they grinned at her as they passed by and disappeared outside. Complete bewilderment hit her at who could possibly have been bold enough to perform that kind of magic – in the chapel of all places!

She looked around for the culprit but realised that everyone was staring straight at her. Turning to each other, they whispered, 'Look at her eyes. They're white!'

Tyler had gone pale. Understanding hit her at the same time as

Mother Ratchford yelled, 'Grab her!', and two Brothers had pinned her arms before she could react.

Mother Ratchford stared at her, her nostrils flaring like an angry dragon's. 'Bring her outside!'

They forced her out, half dragging her down the stone aisle, their grip so tight around her thin wrists that her feet automatically leapt and ran along, until she slipped on the icy ground. She heard the murmurs of the other students spilling out of the chapel behind them and caught a glance of her fellow rebels' distressed expressions. Tyler stood with his lips pressed into a thin line, his fists clenched at his sides. She would have savoured his concern had it not been for the lump of panic paralysing her insides.

They stopped by a tree for the Brothers to tie a rope around her wrists and throw it over a thick branch. Her arms forced over her head, she was kept in place, face turned towards the trunk. Another face seemed to be carved into its bark, its expression solemn as if it knew what was to happen, having seen it one too many times before.

Hot tears streamed down her cheeks as all her traumas from Hallows Grove rushed back: the shame. The whispers and pointing. The hours of trembling on a stool, faeces running down her legs.

'Thirty lashes,' she heard Mother Ratchford order behind her, her voice calling for blood. The words were followed by a whistle as the first lashing met her back, drawing the first blood-curdling scream. All her canings and whippings returned with the same force as the one happening in the present. The frosted grass and clouded skies blended in her vision until there was nothing but blinding white. The whip kept on coming, eating away at her flesh. Ripples of pain bolted through her bones, making her legs quiver and buckle underneath her, the ropes digging into her wrists until she scrambled back on her toes.

Give in, whispered the voice in her head. *Let go*. Her dress hung loosely at her chest, shredded by the force of the knotted cords. Involuntarily, she started whimpering. Praying she would not have to endure it anymore. Praying it would all stop, even if her life stopped with it.

Her body grew cold. Her legs gave way once again. This time she did not rise. A tickle of scarlet fluid ran down her arm. *Let go...* What happened if she did? Her eyes fell shut. Would Death come? *Give in...*

A male voice broke the horrified silence behind her, but in that moment the rope of her consciousness snapped, and she gave in to darkness.

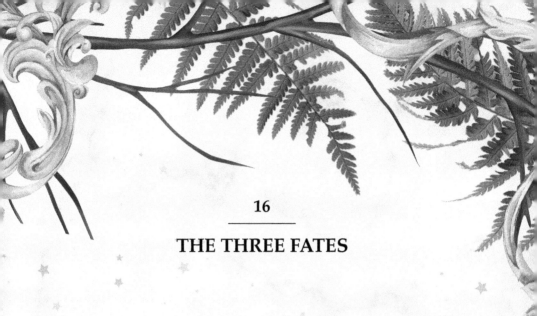

16

THE THREE FATES

COLD. *Cold seeped into her body like water into skin from a drenched piece of clothing. The smell of decaying earth and damp stone filled her nose. She wanted to pat the ground under her, to feel her way. But her arms remained elevated above her, weightless. Bloodless. There was a squeak and the pattering of tiny little claws. A mouse? A rat?*

She squinted to see, but through her fluttering eyelashes there was nothing but a black wall ahead. The wall of a dungeon? She shifted, but her limbs didn't work right, and her legs slipped out in an effort to sit straight, scraping over a stone floor sharp like ragged teeth. No. Take me away from this. *She shuddered, and the darkness pulled her back into its safe embrace.*

Mouth dry. Throat parched. A cough forced its way up and roused her; the explosion of pain that followed fully woke her. Something pierced into her chin, seizing her jaw with agony, forcing her head to jerk back. That same something dug into the soft spot where her collarbones met, sending excruciating jolts throughout her chest. Any attempt at lowering her chin brought on the same torment, and her sight blurred with tears, distorting the torch on the opposite wall. The flame grew out of its container. Swivelled closer. Took the shape of a woman made of fire, her flaming red hair like a halo around her.

'Help me,' Charlie whispered, resting her head against the cool wall behind her, the edges of her vision crumbling. The woman fading. 'Please. Help me.' But only darkness came.

Someone nudged her awake, sending a bolt of hot and cold shivers through her body. Cheeks aflame, she opened her eyes and saw the silhouette of a man.

'What are you?' he asked.

A bead of sweat rolled down Charlie's temple, her sight strained against the warm haze, trying to make out his features, struggling to free her tongue from the roof of her mouth. She cleared her throat to answer, whimpering as the device at her neck dug deeper into her chin and chest.

'Please.' She pressed her eyes shut, seeing Tyler's face in her mind, his gaze tender upon her.

'Charlie,' the man asked again, and his voice morphed into Tyler's. 'What are you?'

The words escaped with her breath. 'I am sin.'

Whirring *clinks* and *clunks* drifted in and out with her consciousness. Rays of light – was it the sun? – played on her eyelashes, trying to force their way through. Her eyelids fluttered, and a sound of shifting feet sounded close to her ear. The Agnus? She held her breath and braced herself. No, there was no falling whip. She let it out. Her hands twitched into the sweet space of air. No ropes on her wrists. No device strapped to her neck. She opened her eyes, seeing

Sister Rowena looking down at her with concern. 'How are you feeling?'

'Fi...' Charlie hesitated, searching her body for the pain she would have expected. 'Fine, actually.' She sat up in her bed, flexing her arms and back. A bit sore, but nothing compared to what she had expected. A sweet, familiar scent of chamomile hung in the air.

'I mixed a little sleeping draught for you. I expected that you'd need the rest.'

Charlie's eyebrows rose incredulously. 'That's all?'

'Your body did most of the work,' Sister Rowena replied with a straight face, but her voice was laced with meaning. Magic.

Exhilaration. Anxiety. Fear. Charlie felt both as she looked around the room.

Almost all the beds were occupied by sleeping, patched-up students, and she instantly felt silly for taking up another. 'I should probably leave.'

'No, it's only been a couple days since they brought you up from the dungeons. It will raise too many questions if you're seen up and about already.' Sister Rowena attended to the other students, some with their hands and backs bandaged, flecks of blood breaking through the white cotton.

'What's happened to them?'

'What happened in the chapel... your imprisonment... it's sparked a bit of inspiration around here. Those not afraid of their own magic have been pulling small stunts and acts of defiance all week, championing for their right to be able to defend themselves should the monsters come. Not without punishment, as you can see.' She shook her head. 'Desperation makes people do stupid things.'

There was a strain to her voice, an edge, as if ... as if she blamed her. Charlie's cheeks heated, and a strange feeling of defensiveness came over her. She could hardly be blamed for people wanting to fight for their freedom. Could she?

'I'm not surprised people are desperate. Either they'll be like you, servants of this place, or they'll be kidnapped by monst—Ah!' Gasping, Charlie clutched her chin and collarbones, feeling the burn from two wounds barely beginning to heal. The marks of the Heretic's Fork.

Sister Rowena frowned warily. 'I don't know enough about the monsters to express myself, but as for being servants, the alternative is often worse.'

She was, of course, referring to the streets, and Charlie hung her head, thinking of Lady Harietta and the other homeless people of Bath. How many had frozen or starved to death since she was taken away? Her cup of soup wasn't the most sanitary way to keep them fed and warm, but to many it was everything. Particularly when they had nothing. Some on the street had gangs. Others did drugs. But most simply lived in cardboard boxes, too sick to gain access to the job market. In light of that, staying at the protected castle of Soli Gloria would be the better option. But she did not want to admit that out loud.

'You might not like the Brothers and Sisters here,' the nurse said, as if catching the suspicion in Charlie's glare, 'but many of them were like you. The subjective reality of those whose withdrawal symptoms were light is different from those whose symptoms were worse. Their truth is that they were saved, and they thoroughly believe that they are saving you.'

'Does that excuse them?'

Sister Rowena gave her a look of meaning. 'Treat a person like your enemy, and they will become one. It only serves to reinforce their idea of you. A reason is not the same as an excuse, but an opportunity to understand. Until people learn that, we'll continue to treat symptoms rather than the disease that keeps us divided.'

With a final pause, perhaps noticing that Charlie's brain was going into overload, the old nurse excused herself and retired to her quarters, leaving Charlie deep in thought.

A wave of resentment washed over her at first. It was almost as if the nurse had implied that she, or the Defectives, were at fault, that they were making the Agnus treat them the way they did. If that was what she meant, how dare she turn all their ordeals against them? Did they not have the right to be angry? Hurt? Charlie's fury burned for a moment until it simmered out, and her thoughts took a new and uncomfortable direction.

Once again, she thought of Brimley and Maddison and the things she had seen them do. She thought of the rebels duelling up at Mythos and the thirst she had seen in their eyes. A thirst for revenge. An age-old anger itching to be let loose. She imagined herself as an Agnus witnessing the same display of power that she had seen over the past few months and could not deny that, to them, the Defectives would look every bit like the monsters they thought them to be. And if they did, could she blame them for the violence they used in return? If they thought that they were protecting themselves and other students?

She squirmed in her bed, the vicious circle becoming apparent before her. In doing what they thought best, the Agnus would also treat the Defectives as *their* adversaries, reinforcing the Defectives' impression of the Agnus as their enemy. Even turning the concept on its head resulted in the same outcome. More hate. Amplified prejudice. Further violence. It was like the chicken and the egg. The more she thought about it, the more impossible it became to pick it apart. Where did the fighting begin, and where did it end? Was magic at fault? Or religion? Were either of them?

Pondering into the evening, Charlie did not realise she had drifted off to sleep until she woke in the middle of the night, when the stars shone brightly with the moon outside, bathing the infirmary in a silvery light cascading in from the tall windows. A shimmer in the corner of her eye caught her attention, and she got out of bed to inspect it. It was the fresco of the western wall, a thin line of silver etched into multiple drawings from left to right. Numbers and letters were delicately carved above them, like a timeline. A timeline of time itself, Before Christ and After Christ.

There were some humanised, powerful-looking beings depicted, which she assumed were gods, looking down at groups of elves, faeries and nymphs of various natural elements. Three women – two of the elves and one of the Banshees, more extraordinary looking than the rest – stood out to her.

The Moirai.

They had the kind of dazzling beauty that made wonders happen in the hearts of mankind. Divine in every curve of their features. It made it hard to believe she was the child of one of them.

Charlie took a deep breath and let it out then jumped backwards. The moment her warm breath had touched the wall, a shiver rippled through the stone. Slowly, gracefully, the folds of the women's dresses lifted as though a wind had caught hold of them. A tingling sensation rippled likewise through Charlie's body, along with delight and incredulity. Next, the women themselves leapt from their spot and began dancing in circles around her, their thick, long hair swirling around their bodies. Their slender bodies rotated gracefully, and their delicate skirts floated like flower petals in the breeze. Watching apprehensively, Charlie stumbled backwards until she felt the cool surface of the wall against her fingertips. It softened underneath her touch, and she felt like she was free falling backwards into the light. The wall dissolved, and its final fragments disappeared around her.

Colours blasted in a blur of gold, warm pink, and orange. She saw images from biblical stories, mystical deities and humans going about their lives, nature, and dinosaurs – more and more darted all around, as if she had fallen inside a dimension made of time's own memories. '*At its birth, a divine energy descended upon Earth and created life in all its forms,*' said a female voice, her tone like the softest notes of a classical song; like a sunrise or a loving mother's whispers of a fairy-tale finding her daughter's ears. A sound her heart had longed to hear, although she could not remember having heard it before.

A low whimper escaped Charlie, and a lump clogged up her throat as she continued to listen.

'*The One True Divinity moulded the rocks, grew the landscape, filled the rivers and oceans with water, and lingered in the air for the living to breathe. Beasts lived and evolved for millions of years until the great collision; until the One True Divinity shaped life in divine forms, the origins of all myths. First came the gods, then the nymphs, elves, and faeries. Immortal in age, mortal in combat.*

'*They lived in peace and bred with one another, creating new kinds of magic and species. Some discovered that they could look like animals, and some even preferred to stay that way.*'

Shapeshifters appeared amongst the elves and faerie. Charlie watched as a child transformed into a cat and leapt between the legs of another laughing child. All around her, people loved, played, relaxed, and harvested crops. Some practised magic, but not all. Some shunned it, and then their own kind when they no longer remembered they used to be the same, their expressions sour with jealousy and bitter hatred.

A group of laughing women transformed into foxes and ran into the woods to play. The Magless people picked up their weapons: pitchforks, slingshots with stones, axes, and knives. Skin crawling, Charlie watched them hunt, murder, and hang the fox-women's crimson pelts to dry.

With nausea still churning in Charlie's stomach, she watched the three goddess-like women appear before her once again, more magnificent than before.

'*The three of us were handpicked from various species to become divinities, tasked with creating order, bestowing fate, and teaching all lives to value each other. To be the Moirai. The Three Fates of Life, Death, and Fortune. Our new names allotted to us with our titles.*'

One of the women, her skin pale as fog and hair as white as moonshine, remained cool and stoic as she received a pair of scissors. In contrast, the woman twirling a string of thread had long, flowy green hair and a forehead jewelled with a thousand stars. Her face was immediately familiar to Charlie, but the third, and most ethereal of the three, captivated her attention. The voice could belong to no one else but her. She radiated warmth, her dark-chestnut hair caressing her golden-brown cheeks, unveiling large doe eyes in a heart-shaped face.

'We became sisters-in-arms.

'Through millennia, we allotted the mortals their lives, their predicted fates, and their sleep in the underworld. We saw a war unfold between Maglings and the Magless.'

Translucent nymphs disappeared into their trees, waters, stones, or other places of hiding, or joined the other species into parallel realms and pocket dimensions.

'Then came the great flood.'

Charlie recognised all the things Jaden had taught them. The Ark, the shapeshifters boarding it, and other biblical moments with the inclusion of magic.

'The Great Flood changed the Earth's structure and foundation, making it seem younger than it was, but it has lived through and seen so much. And us with it.

'I spun life to be born, but I myself was also reborn into many a messiah or martyr, wearing their faces.'

Charlie saw it all as they had been taught by the Agnus, but it did not *look* like how it had been told, even by Jaden. Jesus was magnificent, with long hair and a face that radiated love and compassion; in Jesus' eyes, she saw the Fate, and her heart and soul in his every movement and action. Jesus' followers hailed their messiah, stared in admiration at her, quivered under her touch as she passed them by. Behind her walked the Fate with the thread, measuring a length for every person there, measuring a little more if Jesus blessed them.

'Lachesis, the Fate of Fortune, would always tell me why I was sent to Earth, my purpose, my identity, and remind me of where I would return in the end.'

The third goddess, however, remained behind in the Celestial Sphere, waiting in the realm of the afterlife with the sleeping souls. Charlie deduced she was Atropos, the Fate of Death, her expression grim as she cast long glances after the other two, their images resting on the watery surface inside a well, her fair facial features growing dark and wicked. She took her scissors and cut a hole in the air. Then she leaned in, cupped her hands to her lips, and whispered fervently through to the other side. Shortly after, Jesus was captured. Imprisoned. And – Charlie gasped even though she had seen it coming – crucified.

The Fate of Life returned to her dark sister and listened to her lamentations.

'Atropos was so lonely, forever cursed to roam those dark parts of the Underworld without us. I could not bear it. I broke the rules and let her go in my place at my supposed rebirth. But there were things I did not know. Things I did not understand. Such as darkness.'

Charlie's attention was brought back to the crowd of people gathering before a cave. From it descended Jesus on his day of resurrection, but this time, Atropos was looking through his eyes. During the day, she walked amongst the people, Clotho joyful on her behalf in the Underworld, and did what Lachesis told her to do. But in her own form, like an incubus at night, she did far more.

While the other two were unable to intervene, Atropos continued to whisper into a few ears, and when she finally returned to the Underworld, she continued to whisper through her hole. A shadow fell over certain people. Their expressions changed from hopeful to fearful, and the frightened began hunting the magical once again.

The gentle voice returned, brimming with melancholy. *'It was my punishment, for letting her take my place. My mistake hurt the very lives I guided into the world.'*

The damage Atropos had done was unravelling at a rapid pace looking back over the centuries. Systems were set in place to control those who could be perceived as a threat. Individuals were turned against individuals. Kidnappings. Murders. Witch-hunts. Polarization. Societies against societies. Genocides. Civil wars. Revolutions. Countries against countries. World wars.

Atropos led the mean and the wicked, the angry and frightened, dragging Lachesis along with her, arms bound by her own thread.

Monsters, wolves walking like humans, attacked and killed people in the woods. Inhumanly strong and pale people strode into houses with soulless eyes and scarlet lips, draining the blood of those asleep. Werewolves and vampires.

'Creatures of Night and Destruction were her creations, her soldiers, and all I could do was weep as I watched her undo mine,' the voice said throatily.

Charlie wept too while the next events unfolded.

A glowing thread floated towards Clotho, who stared at it, awestruck, and then reached out to softly cup it in her hands. She held it up and let its glow kiss her cheek. Then she held it to her heart and absorbed it. She vanished.

A crash sounded, and shock rippled through Charlie, followed by an intense jerk at her bellybutton, hauling her backwards like a fish on a hook.

Emerging out of the wall, Charlie stared around wildly, expecting an attack – perhaps from Atropos herself, her ice-cold eyes still vivid in her memory.

But the infirmary was empty, except for sleeping patients and Sister Rowena, standing in the doorframe of her chambers. A porcelain bed pan lay shattered by her feet, and she stared at Charlie, hand on her chest, with eyes wide in incredulity – and anguish.

17

BLASPHEMY AND TRUTHS

'I... I must be sleepwalking, I should—'

'Wait!' Charlie blurted out, mentally cursing herself in case she woke some of the others. But no one stirred. Sister Rowena glared at her with watchful eyes, like a deer caught in headlights. 'You've done this once before. You saw my wounds back then and my skin the day after. Still, you said nothing. You speak for them, but you don't speak *like* them. You know something, about this'—she beckoned to the wall—'about me. Please, tell me.'

The nurse seemed to consider for a moment before she disappeared into her quarters. Charlie's shoulders slumped.

Gutted, she started shuffling towards her bed when the door opened and Sister Rowena returned carrying what looked like a big album in her arms.

'I can't tell you much,' said the nurse and laid the album on Charlie's bed, the years 1982–1983 inscribed in gold upon the black leather. 'I've only seen powers like yours once, and their owner was the very same girl who painted me that fresco.'

Charlie turned the pages and stopped at a class picture where the eyes of a younger Rowena twinkled back at her, standing proudly next to two rows of stoic students. Next to her sat a girl whose facial features Charlie had just seen come out of the wall painting.

'Clotho,' Charlie whispered, touching the girl's hand which rested on her swollen belly. 'That can't have been popular.'

'It wasn't, but it was already done before they came here.' Sister Rowena tapped the face of a young man standing behind Clotho, her finger lingering a little too long. 'That's Thomas Kingsley. Her husband.'

A handsome man, reminding her of Tyler in many ways, his short auburn hair curling at his forehead.

'They ran away shortly after this picture was taken, knowing that their babies would be taken away from them and placed in a children's home as soon as they were born.'

'Babies...' mumbled Charlie, thinking of Sophie. Twins. It was too evident, seeing the characteristics of her own face staring back at her from the photo. 'They're my parents.'

Sister Rowena stared into the void, as if she herself had gone back to the past.

'Your likeness alone gave you away, long before your powers did.'

Her skin began to dry and crack in protest as Charlie snuck into the cold mid-December air under the cover of darkness and falling snow, trudging her way through the white matter towards Mythos and a new rebel meeting. To her pleasant surprise, it seemed that some of the Airlings and Firelings had come together to free the space from the worst of the snow, yet the sharp air kept those present huddled together in their robes, looking expectantly down at the podium. They were a smaller group than usual, but that was to be expected considering the number of rebels in the infirmary and the unknown number of people who were bound to have taken Mother Ratchford's warning seriously enough to withdraw.

'You sure you're well enough?' Jaden asked Charlie as she sat down next to him, his arms around Vanilla's shoulder. Crystals of frost had settled in Vanilla's fair slanted eyebrows, making her look like a winter angel.

'Yes.' Charlie waved them away, pale smoke swirling into the cool air from her lips. 'Rowena only kept me in there to be sure. I feel absolutely fine.' She didn't entirely. There were still wounds that her magic could not heal that played on her mind and woke her crying and sweating into the long nights, but somehow, she couldn't make herself speak about those. Then there was the matter of her parents, the fresco mural, all things she wanted to keep to herself for just a little bit longer.

'Did I miss something while I was away? Where's, um, Tyler?'

Jaden and Vanilla exchanged looks.

'He's recovering...' Jaden said. 'He, er, tried to stop them. The Agnus. When they whipped you. Ended up taking the last of your beatings and then some. Been licking his wounds in his cave.'

Had she imagined it or was there a smile lurking in the corner of his mouth? *Surely not...* but Charlie was not convinced seeing the mischievous sparkle in Vanilla's eyes.

She was just about to ask them what they found so amusing when two slim figures appeared by the bottom of the terraces. Deimos exchanged one last word with Maddison, who turned away, met Charlie's eyes, and came to sit with her.

'What was that all about?'

'He just wanted to go through tonight's lesson with me. He's taking over for Tyler, but he'll need to channel my energy to see it through.' Maddison gave her a quick scan before her attention returned to Deimos walking to the middle of the stage. 'Nice to see you in one piece. I heard what happened. Couldn't wait to step into the spotlight once I was absent, could you?' She said it with a grin, but somehow the humourless tone cast shadows over her hard eyes. Or perhaps Charlie was imagining things, letting her worries get the better of her. It hadn't escaped her attention that Maddison had not come to see her in the infirmary, and she had spent many a long hour pondering the fact.

'The spotlight isn't for me,' Charlie said, but Maddison didn't respond. Down at the podium, Deimos closed his eyes and pointed three fingertips to his freckled forehead.

'As you shall have learned from your seniors by now, the key to controlling your magic is to balance your mind, body, and soul.' He made a swift hand gesture, as if throwing something from his forehead to the sky, and everyone gasped. Up against the midnight blue was a silver image of a triangle looking like a constellation brought near. At its top was the word 'Mind', as if scribbled in neat handwriting directly on the night sky itself. On the bottom corners stood the words 'Body' and 'Soul'.

'This is the golden triangle of individuals. A perfect trinity. The world is full of trinities, and even the levels they come in can be split in three: micro, meso, and macro. Each trinity is a cyclical pattern of balance where there is no one direction, no *one* receiver or *one* giver, but mutual contribution. There are even lesser trinities, such as Freud's Id, Ego, and Super-ego. This is a trinity of the mind, perhaps more familiar to you if you attended school for the Magless.'

Charlie couldn't say she had heard of it, but then again, this did sound like something the Agnus would exclude from their curriculum even if it was taught to ordinary humans.

'Although a Magless himself, Freud was very curious about what I'll be teaching you tonight,' Deimos continued, then turned to the sky again. Two triangles appeared next to the first, one with the words 'Individual', 'Society', and 'World' and another with the words 'People', 'Nature', and 'Universe'.

'How does he do that?' Charlie whispered to Maddison, whose eyes had gone completely white, always resting on Deimos. Charlie feared her eyeballs would dry up due to the lack of blinking.

'It's an illusion. The pictures aren't actually in the sky, but in our heads,' Maddison murmured, her lips set in a thin line. 'It's genius.'

Charlie shook her head, yet she had to admit she was rather impressed.

'These are very simple trinities, and ones which don't mean much without context, a situation. Applied right – or wrong – however, they can steer the course of human nature and society as we know it. A trinity out of balance causes polarization, division, and disproportion, and the world is weakened by it. A complete trinity creates peace, prosperity, and purpose.'

Gilly Jones' hand shot up into the air. 'Are those trinities as well?'

Deimos dipped his head with a smirk. 'Very observant, Miss Jones. Those searching for it, will find traces of speculations surrounding the power of trinities since the age when men first walked on Earth. For pagans, three has always been a magic number. Alchemists used triangles as the alchemic symbols of the elements, and the early Christians made a whole religion around one specific trinity. Would any of you like to wager a guess?'

Looking at the shimmering triangles, Charlie was reminded of one in particular that felt practically imprinted on her brain, but... could it be? In all her life, Christianity and magic had clashed horns like two furious bulls. She could not imagine that one's theory was applicable to the other. And yet, did she not already know that at the core of every religion and myth there were the same principles of truth?

As Deimos put a new triangle up in the skies, she cursed herself both in surprise at being right and regret that she had not spoken. The Holy Trinity caused murmurs to erupt, everyone reading the familiar words of 'The Father', 'The Son', and 'The Holy Spirit'.

'Christianity, like so many religions and mythologies'—several triangles from different religions and mythologies appeared, and amongst them a large one saying the words 'Religion', 'Myths', and 'Ideology'—'is a euphemism for the trifecta effect. It's stories, metaphors, and allegories, its core principles a recipe to the secrets of life – of existence, of being – that is repeated throughout cultures. A theory of trinities that will guide us to our grand purpose as a collective.'

Just as she had learned from her *Encyclopaedia*. In the end, religions and myths were just the same lessons with different names from different places, carried across borders, over bonfires, and by bedsides. Continuing, Deimos listed and compared several Greek gods to Roman, Norse, or Egyptian ones; Christian heroes and events to Greek myths; and God's children, the angels, to Zeus' children, the gods.

'What use do we have of this?' asked Caden.

Deimos turned to the sky and set the Holy Trinity next to the individual trifecta. The 'Father' matched the 'mind', the 'Son' the 'body', and 'the Holy Spirit' matched the 'Soul'. It was blasphemy and universal truth as one and the same, twinkling back at her until her eyes burned from staring at such sin.

'There was another attack, and it scared you. I can tell by our fading numbers. You heard the words of Mother Ratchford and now you believe you've done sin. That you *are* sin in the eyes of a God.'

Although he was speaking to the crowd, Charlie could practically feel Deimos' eyes upon her.

'So, I ask you this. Are we made in the image of the gods, or are the gods made in ours? There'll come a time where the world will burn, and you can either burn with it – or help it rise from the ashes. Till kingdom come.' One final triangle appeared and melted with the others. 'Fate', 'Life', and 'Death', perfectly matching the others. 'The Hallowed Trinity, the one that speak of the Fated Hallows. People made saints through a holy purpose.'

A holy purpose... Like the child of Life? to set magic free?

'*With every supermoon lunar eclipse, there comes a tide that will change the world, and a martyr is born,*' Deimos had said, speaking about the child. About her or her sister.

Maddison's words from when they'd walked towards the folly resurfaced. '*Let's focus on bringing Hell to their Heaven.*'

If the child of Life set magic free, Maddison and so many others like her could quite literally set the world on fire for what it had done to them. Maybe it wasn't such a good thing to free magic after all... But then again, *if I'm the child*, Charlie pondered, watching the illusions on the sky, *maybe, just maybe, I could help the world rise again.*

Into a new heaven, where everyone was free and safe.

She would give anything to have that... or die trying.

They were a quiet and contemplative bunch leaving the theatre grounds down the steep pathway through the woods. Most looked like they didn't understand what had been said, and she, too, struggled making sense of it all – despite what she had been shown in the mural.

Magic seemed so infinitely delicate, like the light of the last quarter moon resting on the dark surface of the sea. Now and then, a ripple would move through it, as if it shivered at its own serenity.

That's when she saw him sitting on the beach, and Jaden's words echoed in her mind. *'He... tried to stop them... Ended up taking the last of your beatings and then some.'* She needed to thank him.

'I'll see you guys back at the cottages,' she said to Vanilla and Maddison, who were pausing to see if she was coming. They exchanged scheming glances with Jaden before the girls headed up to the castle and he towards the boys' cavern.

No doubt with pink roses in her cheeks, Charlie turned towards the beach.

Tyler sat with his arms around his legs, watching the sea as it rolled in waves towards him and back again. It would have been so easy to put a hand on his shoulder, to feel his muscles under her palm, but the very thought of it made her queasy with butterflies.

'You alright?' she asked instead and settled down next to him, taking some joy in his pleasantly surprised expression.

'Yeah, good, you?'

She gazed at the cool moonlight resting on the velvety smooth surface of the sea. 'Trying to be. Feels odd though, being out here while others are still in the infirmary. Unfair, almost, that I can heal myself and not them. I still haven't cracked that part. I tried though.'

He sighed. 'You're not like the others.'

She picked at the grains of sand, rolling them between her fingers, thinking he meant her magical abilities. 'I know, I'm pretty weak.'

'No. I was talking about *you*. You're not conceited or self-absorbed. You genuinely care. I saw your reaction when you heard about those children. What kind of magic it led to.' He clenched his jaw. 'And they punished you for it.'

'Yeah, about that,' Charlie mumbled, drowning in her shyness. 'Is it true you jumped in to save me?' He made a half-committed nod. 'Why?'

'I'd have thought that was rather obvious.' He took her hand, playing with her fingers. Jolts of electricity flared through her skin with every single touch.

All she wanted was for him to pull her close and kiss her. But what then? What if she never managed to live up to his expectations? What if who they needed was her sister? No matter how hard she tried, she could not become *her*. Although, for Tyler, she would try anything.

She cleared her throat. 'About the rebellion – is there anything else I can do?'

Tyler bit his bottom lip, turning his head towards the sea and the large rocks along the shoreline. For a moment she thought she had said something wrong.

'Let's go for a swim,' he said, suddenly lifting her hand to his lips, kissing it. A new and mischievous glint appeared in his eyes. He tugged her towards the sea, throwing off his shirt just as his feet hit the water. Out of the corner of her eye, she caught a glimpse of red lines, swollen against his skin.

She gasped. 'Your b-back!'

He stumbled in the shallow water as he followed her line of sight, comprehension appearing on his face. His eyes didn't meet hers.

'It's nothing.'

A cold dread snaked its way around her chest, squeezing her heart. 'It's from that day, isn't it?'

He stared ahead now, hard, looking at the blackness of the sea. 'I've never felt so angry. Every lash against you ...' His voice washed out with the waves. 'I needed it to stop, so I made him. With my fists.' He stood, like an avenging angel, staring back at her with a cloak of starlight wrapped around him. 'Had my powers been free, I would have made the Brother drown in his own bodily fluid.'

Without a moment's hesitation, Charlie stepped into the water, the icy cold submerging her feet and legs. A tiny part of her worried she might freeze to death, but the other part shrugged it off; at least she would feel his body against hers first if she did.

Determined, she marched towards him and threw caution to the wind and her arms around his neck, squeezing him tight with all the gratitude she felt.

'Thank you.' Her whisper was tender against his ear.

'You're welcome.' He grinned, shyly if she was any judge, before a glint appeared in his eyes. She interpreted it too late, shrieking as a splash of water showered her with icy-cold diamond droplets. He stood, palm raised above the water, never touching it, his eyes full of laughter. Then he pulled her back into his arms, bringing her farther into the depths of the sea.

'I don't have a lot of experience swimming,' she admitted, her fists clenched against his shoulders. She eyed the water nervously, the sea floor slipping beneath her feet the farther she went. Tyler smiled softly and swam backwards, holding one arm underneath hers, pulling her closer.

'It's okay,' he said. 'I have you.'

They stared into each other's eyes once they remained still, the chill forgotten, her legs wrapped around his hips while he treaded water. Tyler brushed a strand of wet hair from her face. Then the water level rose and spiralled around them, towering over their heads but never putting them under. Calmly, Tyler held her gaze as though it was nothing. As though being in the middle of a water storm was a perfectly ordinary situation for him. His confidence was contagious.

Closing her eyes, Charlie focused on the water, the feeling of Tyler's arms around her, and imagined the water coming alive, figures dancing out of the shimmering walls. Tyler's sharp intake of breath told her she had been successful. She opened her eyes to catch sight of life-sized animated water figures dancing amidst the wings of water.

'Incredible.' Tyler gaped, saltwater dripping from his locks. 'Imagine if the others saw this.'

Biting her lip, she glanced through a split in the water wall and towards the castle.

Warm lights shone from the windows. One of them would belong to Mother Ratchford's office, providing her with a full view over the grounds. Her territory. She would have control over every-thing from there... *Control...*

'What is it?' Tyler asked, perhaps noticing the surge of excite-ment in her eyes.

'How good are you at causing a distraction?'

He frowned. 'Depends. What did you have in mind?'

'Enough time to search Mother Ratchford's office for whatever is keeping our magic bound?'

Now his eyebrows disappeared into his fringe. 'That's pretty bold of you.' The way he looked at her, the way his eyes seemed to encourage every outrageous idea in her head, emblazed her courage until one urge turned into a thought, and she felt herself acting on it – fire coursing through her veins and sizzling against her chilled skin – before she could second-guess it.

'So is this,' she whispered. Leaning in, she kissed him, his surprised yet eager response sending the water wall shattering around them. In the midst of her utmost happiness and Tyler's crumpling magic, Charlie barely registered that her creations remained in their forms, like Oceanids brought to life, and dived far below towards the depths of the ocean.

18

THE DIVERSION

'TYLER WILL LEAD a diversion while I break into Mother Ratchford's office and search it for information on whatever's blocking us from using our magic to defend ourselves,' Charlie explained to the others. The waterfall rumbled next to them, hopefully preventing any unwanted listeners from eavesdropping.

Jaden and Vanilla exchanged uncertain looks with one another. Only Caden seemed mildly intrigued, but perhaps she was mistaking his sarcasm for interest.

'You've certainly done a number on her, Ty. She even speaks like a rebel now!'

'She's been a rebel for weeks, Caden. It's more than we can say about you,' Tyler shot back. Both boys' eyes darkened, and Jaden cleared his throat, changing the topic.

'If it works, it would be about time.'

Vanilla nodded. 'The rebels are desperate.'

'And stupid,' Caden chimed in.

Jaden rolled his eyes. 'But mostly desperate. Practising during the night can only do so much. They long for results, but at this rate they're only proving to others that using magic results in punishment.'

Vanilla's shoulders slumped. 'Four students have withdrawn in the past week, and that's not counting those still healing in the infirmary. Last night, Jack told me he couldn't shapeshift anymore.' She dragged a hand through her hair, the colour of her skin identical to her strands, like a piece of paper slicing through snow.

'Who's Jack?' Charlie asked.

'That dog-shifter that arrived when we did,' Caden said. So, the obedient Jack Russell had followed his master and withdrawn.

'We need to act now.' Tyler rolled up his sleeves. 'Today.'

'And what if she gets caught? That lashing will be nothing in comparison to the one she already had.' Caden lifted an eyebrow at Charlie crossing her arms in indignation.

'She'll manage,' Tyler said.

'Do you suggest I sit this one out?' Charlie asked at the same time.

Caden only deigned to reply to one of them. 'No, I'm saying I'm coming with you. I've always wanted to see the inside of that office anyway.' His grey-blue eyes twinkled against his pale skin as he stuffed his hands into his trouser pockets and tilted his head casually – ever the rebel he pretended not to be. 'Besides,' he said, his voice turning venomous, 'someone has to care for your safety when my brother doesn't.'

Tyler looked ready to attack him, but at that moment a rush of peace and tranquillity slammed into them like a giant pillow during a pillow fight.

'Peace and love, people! Aren't there enough conflicts around us?' Vanilla cautioned with a harmonious tone to her voice. Caden immediately looked down, like a kitten being scolded, and Tyler stepped back, hiding his face from the rest of them. Both of their bitter anger still simmered against Vanilla's emotional manipulation.

'Fine,' Tyler said. 'But let's get to it.'

It only took them a couple of hours to assemble enough willing rebels for the diversion and then create a plan as to how they would go ahead. Soon enough, Charlie found herself jotting down the last details on her chalk drawing with Caden standing guard at the end of the hallway.

'It looks as if it's about to come out of the wall this instant,' Vanilla gasped, stepping back with her own chalk in hand, admiring Charlie's drawn nymph now disrupting an otherwise spotless wall. Wistful smiles were exchanged between the girls. Charlie had wanted Maddison to help her – if only to hear what she thought of her plan – but Maddison had refused to get up this morning after another troubled night.

'Yeah, well hopefully any Agnus passing this way would be too busy trying to wash the graffiti away to continue down the corridor,' Charlie said, giving Vanilla's drawing of vines and flowers an approving look.

'Trust girls to make defiance look pretty,' Caden said, surprising her at first with his cordiality until he drawled, 'and take forever.'

Rolling her eyes, Charlie said her goodbyes to Vanilla and followed him down the hallway.

A loud commotion sounded from the first floor.

'So, it begins,' she said under her breath.

Caden turned around and pulled her along. 'And their sacrifice will be a waste if we're not successful. Let's hurry.'

Picking the lock with more efficiency than she would have expected, they soon stumbled into the gloomy light of Mother Ratchford's office. Waiting for her eyes to adjust, Charlie headed over to the windows and pulled back the curtains. As she suspected, the headmistress had a panoramic view of the grounds, but, to her relief, it would require quite a hawk's eye to see the path to Mythos or what happened around the beach.

Like Deimos', the office was sparsely decorated with only a few shelves, paper archives, and a large desk standing in the middle of the room.

'What's that stink?' muttered Caden just as it hit Charlie too, a scent of rot and iron. A large shiny item occupied one of the shelves amongst black leather books, looking like a pair of torn off wings from a giant butterfly. Dried coagulated blood and sinew were still attached to the bone. Albin's wings presented like a trophy. Nausea hit her with a blow. She did not even want to imagine Mother Ratchford observing them with pride late at night. The large golden crucifix on the wall seemed like a joke.

She held her breath and listened for any sound at the door, the mere thought of the headmistress making Charlie feel her presence in the room. But the hallway was silent.

'Let's search this place and get out of here,' Caden whispered. Hurrying towards the desk, he pulled open the drawers and rummaged through their contents. There was a slingshot, a pan flute, and other odd items she supposed had been confiscated at one point or another. Some letters filled another drawer. One of them carried a coat of arms: two broken wands above the letters *HG*.

Her heart stopped.

Caden continued to search the office, more frantically with every passing minute, but her attention settled on the letter alone. She picked it up and unfolded the crisp parchment, her eyes absorbing the words.

Dear Mother Ratchford,

Thank you for notifying me of your recent success in Bath, and of potentially holding one of our former escapees.

I believe you must be mistaken, as said escapee has just recently returned to us and is again in my care. I would send her your way were I not confident that we will succeed in making her withdraw ourselves. That being said, I was delighted to hear about the tip from a female caller on the whereabouts of the Defectives. It gives me great relief to hear there are still people who understand the danger of magic in a society more and more compelled by the idea of it.

Keep up the noble work you do,
Agnus Dei, qui tollis peccata mundi, dona nobis pacem

Yours sincerely,
Mother Agnes, Headmistress of Hallows Grove

'Did you find something?' Caden's voice interrupted her reading, bringing her back to the office. He peeked over her shoulder, quickly reading through Mother Agnes' words. She heard him pause, felt him contemplate what to say.

'I don't understand it,' he said at last.

Her fingers curled in on the paper and balled it up. 'Neither do I, but I will soon.'

Her body shivered with fury, threatening to explode. It felt dark and fantastic at the same time – as though she was finally coming alive. As though she could finally feel the full extent of every feeling she'd suppressed over the years. Her wrath over all the lies she had been told. *A female caller.*

There was only one other female that had known that they were going to Brimley's party in time to tip off the Agnus. Charlie recalled how she had suspected *him*, shame making her queasy. He had been a victim, guilty only of trusting the wrong person, like she had. But why now? Why, after all those years, had she betrayed them? Why even bother saving her from Hallows Grove?

Our escapee has just recently returned to us.

Maddison had once mistaken Charlie for someone else, and now it seemed Mother Agnes had mistaken someone else for Charlie.

Which could only mean they had her twin.

For once in her life, she held tangible proof that Sophie Lou was real, and an understanding dawned upon her that she hadn't truly believed it. It had been an alluring idea, whenever she felt lonely or insecure, but it had been just as easy to forget about it and think of herself as an only child. The *only* child of Life. The chosen one. Yet, here it was, the evidence. And not just that, an actual indication of Sophie's whereabouts. A rush of urgency threatened to overcome her at the thought of it. *I'm going to tear them down. All of them. Brick by brick. Starting with this one.*

High-pitched screaming and commotion sounded from the corridor, shaking her out of her rage. Her eyes met with Caden's, and she wondered whether he thought the same; had the Agnus figured out their trick? Were they fighting rebels outside the office? She followed him as he rushed out, crumpling the letter in her fist.

They saw no trace of Agnus members or rebels. Instead, they saw Charlie's and Vanilla's drawings come alive. Vines and flowers hugged the walls and ensnared statues. Tufts of grass jutted out between the stone blocks. A granite arm, like the arm of an Oread, a nymph of rock and mountains, protruded from the wall, holding four ankles in its stony grip. Held upside down in the air were Venus, Dia, Ava, and Gilly, their skirts around their shoulders, their under-garments on full display, their mouths still open in terror.

Dumbfounded, Charlie heard Caden double over in laughter next to her. Vanilla clasped her hand to her mouth, stifling her own. Rounding the corner were more rebels and Tyler, their faces flushed with excitement, who all came to a halt staring wide-eyed at the four girls. Shaking his head, Jaden looked right at Charlie. 'What *are* you?'

'That's easy, isn't it?' Tyler said, his eyes sparkling. 'She's special.'

Charlie, however, could only force a smile, her mind on the crumpled letter she held behind her back and her eyes on Venus, thinking how she'd rather see someone *else* dangle upside down, betrayed as she felt.

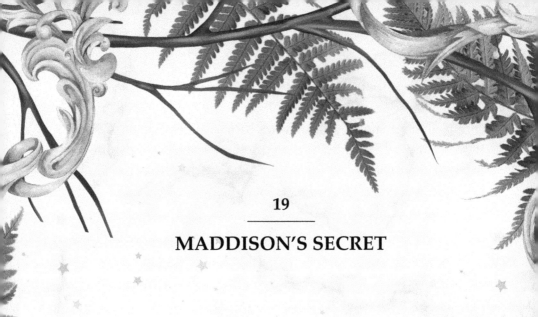

19

MADDISON'S SECRET

'DID you call the Agnus on us?' Charlie blurted out, storming into their cottage. The raven girl lay on her bed, hands over her face, and she shrank away from the light.

'Not now, Charlie—'

'Yes, now! You called them, didn't you? No one else knew we'd be there!' She had remembered the phone now, on her way over, the phone Maddison "borrowed" from the random people in the park.

Maddison glared back, lifting her chin defiantly like when she tried to make others feel inferior. But for the first time, Charlie didn't feel the pressure to bow.

'It's true, isn't it? How could you do that? To me? To Brimley? You're playing with people's lives, Maddison, and you have no right to. You're not God!'

Maddison scoffed and sneered at the same time, shifting out of the bed. 'No one is God. He doesn't exist.' She moved past Charlie and reached for the door handle.

'Where are you going? I have questions for you!'

'Not now,' Maddison breathed, sweat on her porcelain skin making her birthmarks shimmer. 'I need to clear my head.' At the same time, Charlie observed the flush in her cheeks and the tremble overtaking her hand. Recognising the signs, Charlie rushed to the door just as the raven girl lost her balance and collapsed into Charlie's arms.

'I have to go,' Maddison whimpered.

'Not like this.' Charlie gritted her teeth and supported the trembling girl back to her bed. This time, she did not make her a mixture nor tuck the duvet around her. Instead, she grabbed Maddison's chin, beads of sweat rolling down her temple, and forced her to look at her. 'Explain to me why you did it!'

Eyes as white as ghosts, Maddison clasped her fingers around Charlie's wrists, and then fragments of light exploded, turning her vision bright. It felt like staring into the sun. Colours moved like wet coffee stains on a paper towel. Then silhouettes began to form, and voices sounded as if speaking from afar.

'The Agnus call us corruption,' growled a voice. 'The stain on their pretentious society.'

Goosebumps rose on her skin. She knew that voice. Brimley.

He spoke to his pack, all seated on a tarnished sofa around a broken coffee table. They were at the motel, the Dog House. Maddison stood by Brimley's side, and Charlie was watching them all, standing by hers.

It's a memory, Charlie realised with a start, taking in the frost in Maddison's eyes and the way Brimley's appeared to be flicking from side to side, as if reading a script from one end to another. Was Maddison feeding Brimley the words? Considering Brimley was no wordsmith, and Maddison's powers, it was quite likely.

'They make it sound innocent enough,' Brimley continued, 'saying they're doing the right thing for the right cause, so that they can suppress us, hold us down and beat us. Until we become pathetic shadows of our former selves, unable to even put up a good fight. Unfit to do anything but lurk in the shadows.'

There was a brief moment of silence. Smoke from cigars forced itself through Charlie's nose and blocked her lungs. Looking over at Maddison, the girl seemed unaffected, her mask solid and unmovable.

The other pack members shifted uneasily, knowing Brimley was waiting for their response yet seeming hesitant to give it.

'What shall we do?' yelped one of the yearlings. His transformation had taken place that summer even though none of his family members had shown any signs of having powers. Magic had skipped a couple of generations in his family. And now their boy was with the Agnus – or Deimos – whatever that meant. Because of Maddison. Did they worry about him? Or feel relief at his absence?

Maddison once again watched Brimley intently, and Charlie was certain she was pushing for a declaration of war. But Brimley's fists trembled at his sides, as though they were resisting.

'We run before they can get their hands on us,' he said at last.

'What!' Maddison's mouth dropped open, breaking her cool composure. Brimley sent her a look of warning, a vein thumping hard at his temple. But hers was equally poisonous. If looks could kill, Brimley would have been skinned and flung upside down. Sometimes it had been hard to imagine that the two of them had grown up together like comrades in arms. This was one of those moments.

'You can come with us, Maddison – you and Charlie. I'll keep the promise my mum made to yours.'

'I don't care about the promise or my safety! What about the uprising? You're one of the largest remaining groups of shapeshifters left!'

'We're also outnumbered by the Agnus. Using our forms will only expose us and put us at risk.' He kicked at the banged-up sofa. 'I can't afford to lose anyone else. I'm sorry, Maddison,' he said, and she could tell it pained him to say it. 'But shapeshifters are more persecuted than regular Defectives. They're blaming the sheep killings on us, having farmers searching through the woods for wolves. I have to protect my pack.'

'You're a coward, Weston,' Maddison hissed. 'Your brutes might not realise it, but your mother did. She told you to fight!' Even Maddison had to know she was wavering into dangerous territory. The pack rose from their seats. Pack mentality. Protect and stand by the alpha.

'*My mother took her own life,*' Brimley snarled. '*You follow her if you feel like it, but the rest of us want to survive.*'

Charlie could practically see the wheels turning in Maddison's mind. It teared at her, she was sure, to see them preparing to leave the fight, to see the potential of an uprising slip between her fingers. Only then did Charlie realise why Maddison had stuck so close to Brimley all those years. To build up a pack – her own pack – of warriors. And now she was losing them. It was sure to set her on edge, accustomed as she was to getting her own way. Dependent on it, even.

'*But—*'

'*I'm the alpha, Maddison, and I've made up my mind. By the end of the week, we'll be gone.*'

Maddison simply blinked, staring open-mouthed, momentarily at a loss for words. Then she came to and put a hand on Brimley's arm, delicate yet controlling. '*I can make you stay, you know,*' she purred threateningly.

It was reckless, even for her.

It had been an unspoken rule between them all not to use their powers on one another without permission. Charlie suspected anger clouded her judgement like the thick smoke that filled the room. The entire pack stiffened at once.

'*And I'll be gone the moment your mind-craft loses its power over me,*' he snapped back, his face inches from hers. Maddison looked like she wanted to claw his eyes out but bit down the poison reserved for him and smirked. Extending one long leg, Maddison wrapped it against his hip. Her voice turned silky smooth in a way that brought men to their knees. '*Who said anything about mind-craft? I think it's time we found you a new trinket, don't you?*' She paused, breathing warm air against his earlobe. '*Considering your last one went and withdrew after all.*'

Brimley's eyes grew hungry. '*Careful, Maddison. Pack mentality, remember? We're linked.*' He nodded to the boys and girls looking at her with the same desire burning in their eyes. '*I'll do my best to control myself, but I can't destroy my pack to protect your virtue, can I? What little is left of it.'*

The tension in the lounge had finally peaked. This was how Charlie imagined it being inside of a pressure cooker. Maddison's body went rigid. Her fists tightened until her knuckles turned white. Resentment flooded both of their faces.

'How dare you—'

'You chose someone else to be your knight, Maddison, you always do. But the offer to come with us still stands if you choose me. Until then, however, I suggest you leave before we lose our cool.'

'You're all dogs,' she growled.

His lips twisted into a mocking smirk. 'That we are.'

His words echoed as Charlie was pulled from the memory, facing the Maddison of the present. Her eyes had returned to their regular emerald-green.

'They should bless the moon that I didn't force them all to snap each other's neck just for looking at me that way.' Maddison glared past Charlie, as if she was still stuck in the past. 'Our alliance was broken from that moment.'

'So, you betrayed him for disagreeing with you.' Charlie shuddered, the memory of that Halloween night returning to her. How she had seen Maddison try to fend off the Agnus, palms up. Now it made sense why nothing had happened. 'You put up an act. That whole night when they came for us, you were acting as if you knew nothing at all. The phone call... you arranged it all.'

'I needed us here. For the uprising.'

'Why?' Charlie whispered. Maddison's eyes shifted back to her, her hand fumbling with the vial at her neck.

'Because fate must run its course. That is the rule.'

'What kind of rule?' Charlie spluttered, throwing her hands up incredulously. 'What kind of rule can possibly force you to betray your best friends?'

'There are things far stronger than silly human friendships.' Maddison scoffed. 'Particularly with those who are becoming too similar to their fathers...' Pain flickered in her eyes, and she stared absentmindedly into the wall. Then they shot back at Charlie. 'How did you find out?'

'I found my book in your bag. I didn't understand why you would take it with you until I found this.' Charlie threw the letter she had found on Maddison's bed. 'Good to know how you feel about friendships.'

Frowning, Maddison picked up the piece of parchment, colour draining from her face as she read and reached the same conclusion as Charlie had. '*Sophie Lou...* Charlie, Charlie, wait!'

But Charlie was already heading for the door.

'There's another reason! Why I did it.' Maddison exhaled shakily as Charlie paused. 'I had a vision. I saw you at Hallows Grove. I thought... I thought they would manage to find you, and that this was the only way, but it wasn't you!' She shook the letter. 'It was Sophie!'

'So you sacrificed Brimley?' Charlie spun around, one hand on the door handle, pain hitched in her throat. 'What makes my life more valuable than his?'

Maddison didn't reply.

Realisation dawned upon Charlie.

'It's because you think I'm the child of Life, isn't it? The key to your rebellion?'

More silence.

'Answer me!'

'It's fate,' Maddison whispered.

Charlie glowered at her, her brows tightening with incomprehension.

'Lachesis had a vision about three children born to the Fates, destined to take their place. It was the only way to render Atropos powerless, and Atropos knew it. Taking her own and Clotho's child to safety, Lachesis raised them in hiding, as Desdemona Quinsey. My mother. The children were me and Sophie.

'But another vision told her Death would find us. She arranged for our safety, but we were separated both from her and each other, and I was left with one last mission to carry out, to make sure that fate would run its course.

'My search for Sophie began that day, and as you know I found you. *The* child of Life is more than just a key to take over Soli Gloria, you see.' Maddison picked up the letter again, her eyes scanning the words. 'One of you is foretold to free magic once and for all.'

She had suspected as much, during Deimos' lesson on the Hallowed Trinity. But having it made fact – it was a lot. 'Then we – I – need to find *her*,' Charlie said, feeling bitterness poison her from within at the thought of even trying to trust Maddison again. 'Helping the rebels is one thing but saving the world another. I'm not the one you want.'

Maddison looked at her with cold cynicism. 'Ironic then, isn't it, that to get out of here and save Sophie, you have to overthrow the Agnus – and if you do, you might very well be the one.'

20

A COLD HARD WINTER

THE NEXT DAY, Charlie found herself outside Deimos' office door, folding and reopening the letter in her hands. She never would have believed it if she had been told she would ask him for help one day but being stuck on the grounds left her with little choice.

Before yesterday, she would have asked Maddison if it were possible for her to somehow fly from Soli Gloria to Hallows Grove. Today, that meant chipping at the ice wall that had risen between them, one she was not certain she was ready to dent at all. The more she had thought about Maddison's betrayal, the more she had come to realise how Maddison had treated her as her inferior. And, comparing her to her new friends with their patience and kindness, that didn't seem like the right kind of friendship to her anymore.

She knocked and opened the door once she heard the 'Enter' from within. Brows rising above the frames of his reading glasses, Deimos seemed as surprised as she was to find her in his office.

'Miss Charlie, what can I do for you?'

'I, err...' She clenched the letter one last time before she handed it over. 'I think this should help you and Brimley find my sister.'

He accepted the letter, a gleam appearing in his eyes as he read its contents. 'This will help indeed. How did you get this?'

'I found it when Caden and I searched Mother Ratchford's office.' As Deimos frowned, Charlie added, 'You know, during the diversion.'

'Ah!' Deimos tapped his forehead. 'Of course.' He moved behind his desk, checking his planner, and pulled out a map from his drawer. 'Excellent. I will get on this immediately.'

Grateful relief flooded her, and she wondered if she had not judged him too harshly. Giving him her best smile, Charlie curtsied and thanked him and was on her way out when Deimos stopped her. 'Caden McFade. Do you trust him?'

Slightly confused, Charlie shrugged. 'I don't have any reason not to.'

'Aha.'

'Shouldn't I?'

'No, no. I just came to think of something,' Deimos deflected, already busy packing a small travel bag.

'What?'

He straightened, his eyes intense and penetrating as they imprisoned hers. 'Do you not think, as we have infiltrated them, that they may have infiltrated us too?' The words hung between them. 'No, I can see you had not thought of that. I will see you upon my return, Miss Charlie.' He waved her off, his eyes leaving her with an unspoken challenge, like he always seemed to challenge her, to trust – or distrust.

According to rebels who had been to see him after, Deimos had left the grounds of Soli Gloria almost immediately after Charlie's visit. There was nothing to do now other than to resign herself to the weekend, practice, and the oncoming week with more lectures. By Monday, there was still no news or sign of Deimos, and Charlie headed into Discipline and Manners where the other girls had lined up against the wall. Her head was so full, wondering if he would have found her sister by now, that she did not see the outstretched foot and went flying.

She landed, sprawled onto the floor, to a choir of girls laughing. Sister Hilda, on the other hand, did not.

'Honestly,' she snarled and whacked Charlie across the back with her cane. 'Get in line!'

Rushing to the nearest spot, Charlie found herself standing between Venus and Ava, both with angelic expressions plastered across their faces. Sister Hilda continued to prowl up and down the aisle, lecturing them about the importance of good posture. By habit, Charlie craned her neck to seek Maddison, but a shriek startled her back into position.

Next to her, Venus Gillian was clenching her arm, her pointed face contorted in agony. Red skin flared up underneath her fingers.

'Whatever is going on here?' barked Sister Hilda, nostrils flaring.

'Miss, Charlie burned me!' Venus cried, stretching out her arm for Sister Hilda to see. There was indeed a burn mark there.

'Wh-what?' Charlie stuttered, shaking her head violently. 'I didn't! I couldn't!'

Venus pulled a grimace. 'Oh, please, we all saw you coming out of the passage like an inferno!'

Sister Hilda turned white with rage. 'You dare use magic in my classes?' The cane met with her stomach, forcing her to keel over. Then a second smashed into her back, sending her muscle memory reeling from her past flogging and her body sprawling to the floor a second time. 'Posture!'

Breathing hard, Charlie caught sight of Venus and Ava, the snake and the fire-starter, smiling smugly back at her. They had staged it, she knew it, but how? In the same way that she couldn't have harmed Venus, there was no way Ava could have hurt Venus with fire... unless they had been at Mythos right before class. Angry tears filled her eyes, but looking over at Maddison's cool demeanour, she wasn't quite certain who she was the most furious with.

It had been their revenge for the upside-down incident, but it did not stop with that.

As soon as they realised she was no longer under Maddison's protection, Venus and her posse did their best to make Charlie's days miserable, their retaliation ranging from petty pranks at school to vicious attacks during practice, making her walk down from Mythos full of cuts and bruises.

Jaden and Vanilla did their best to protect her, but even they could not be everywhere at once. Tyler had his hands full keeping the rebels together as well under the absence of Deimos, so she supposed she couldn't blame him for simply sighing in exasperation while waving them away when they excused themselves with 'We're just helping her practice.'

Worse still, when she healed her visible wounds, the girls told on her to the Agnus, landing her both underneath the cane and, once, upon the Stool of Infamy. She couldn't look Tyler in the eyes for a good couple of days after that, and Caden didn't make her feel any better by spending more and more time with the girls – another fact they were sure to rub in her face, reducing their behaviour to sly smirks whenever he turned his back. It bothered her, seeing him with them, but not for the reasons they thought. Whenever she did, Deimos' words resurfaced, making her question his allegiance.

Christmas came and passed, and what one would think would be a joyous time was the most depressing of them all. Lessons were put on hold for the holiday, but the hours spent in the chapel were increased. They now spent seven hours a day kneeling on the chilly stone floor, listening to Mother Ratchford recite the Bible as if she was planning to read it from beginning to end before Christmas was over. Charlie could not imagine anyone wishing to spend another second in there, and yet she saw Gilly through the thick glass window as everyone left, still on the floor, her hands folded towards the altar. Perhaps she was praying for the uprising to happen?

To be fair, they needed all the help they could get.

Days passed by without any sort of clue as to how they could use magic freely on the grounds. The rebels speculated whether different objects could be enchanted to prohibit or allow it, but they soon realised they could remove and replace every loose article and item across the grounds and still be none the wiser.

On the plus side, Charlie was getting stronger. While she did not understand how, she now knew that she could animate things and natural objects. She could enchant Jaden's trees into making a battle face and claw at his opponents or make the practice dummy defend her. It even lashed out whenever Tyler threw her a sneaky little air-kiss.

Her balance and body strength had improved enormously under Vanilla's guidance, enabling her to dodge several moves and counter-moves. One time, Charlie used Jaden's tree to bend before her as a shield then hoist her up with its branches. Running up its trunk, she leapt into the air, hitting a manipulated platform of air with the tip of her toe like a ballerina. Her friends gasped as she leapt again, missing the next spot by an inch and crashed to the ground. They'd come running, muttering that they heard the sound of her ankle snapping, although all Charlie heard was Venus and her friends roaring from the terraces. Her pride hurt more than her ankle, which soon healed itself into a mere sprain. By the time Tyler had carried her up to the top terrace for a berry-dinner for two at sunset ('Courtesy of Jaden,' he'd said and winked), it was fully healed.

Despite the gloomy presence of the Agnus and the girls' bullying, this was also a time she valued. Although she did not say it out loud, she had begun to appreciate every day where the status quo was preserved. Every day that she had not heard from Deimos was another day alone with Tyler. Another day sneaking around the grounds, kissing under the rose pavilion of Soli Gloria when no one was watching, blowing rebellious raspberries at the Agnus' coat of arms, or stealing feverish moments on the trail to the girls' cliff – her back, pushed up against the wall of stone, his lips nibbling at her neck triggering quiet moans drowned out by the rumbling noise of the waterfall.

Every day was another day she did not have to face an uncertain future with either Sophie in the picture, the immensity of being the child of Life, or the pending revolution against the Agnus – and answering her own conscience on whether it was right or wrong. And so, she valued them.

Every day.

Until *one* day.

Jaden came running into Tyler's cave, his shouting rousing them awake. Charlie felt Tyler's arms around her and his body next to hers, realising they had fallen asleep like that. Last night, Tyler had invited Charlie to his cave for her eighteenth birthday. She had waited in her own cottage until the nightly rounds were done and the Agnus had seen her in bed. Then she left without so much as a 'goodnight' or 'happy birthday' to Maddison and made her way down the trail, entering the cavern and Tyler's cave to a surprise party made up of him, Jaden, and Vanilla. Somehow, they had managed to get their hands on a tiny extra-frosted birthday cake, and she was almost certain, based on Tyler's hints, that Albin had something to do with it.

They ate and laughed until late, when it was only her and Tyler left, snuggling on his bed, telling each other about their lives. His wish of making his father proud as the greatest war hero amongst his brothers. Her fear of being dull compared to, well, anyone.

'You're not!' he exclaimed and put on a dramatic flair. 'I mean, clearly I'm the big shot around here but...' His voice softened. 'You're pretty extraordinary.'

Charlie made one loud 'Pah!' while he ran his fingers over hers. 'I've lived with extraordinary for three years... believe me.' Her voice drifted into a mumble. 'I'm not it.'

His hand cupped her chin and turned her face towards him, his eyes tender upon her. 'I beg to differ.'

The warmth of his mouth filled hers as he leaned in for a kiss, and they stayed like that until Tyler fell asleep with her listening to his slow breathing, her heart throbbing throughout her body at the mere proximity of him. It was the last thing she remembered before the two of them sat up groggily, looking at Jaden's frantic appearance in puzzlement.

'What?' Tyler murmured, scratching his head.

'They've put guards on the path to Mythos,' Jaden said. 'And gathered up the rebels. They're about to punish them in front of everyone.'

21

GUARDIANS OF SOLI GLORIA

AGNUS BROTHERS BRANDISHING copper whips and tasers stood by the foot of the cliff blocking the entrance to Mythos. Shielding the sun from her eyes, Charlie looked up to see more of them standing up at the top. Tyler gave her hand one last squeeze before he let it go, and he, Charlie, and Jaden closed in on the herd of people standing by the forest edge. Screams filled their ears as whips curled in the air like serpents, slashing down upon the backs of rebels.

Vanilla, having watched amongst the crowds, turned and threw herself into Jaden's arms, a gleam of sweat on her forehead. 'I... can't...' she murmured into his shoulder, trembling. A new slash of wire meeting skin and bone sounded, and Vanilla's back recoiled as if she herself had been hit, her face etched with the rebels' pain.

'Let's walk away from here,' Jaden said, just as Mother Ratchford's voice rose amidst the crying.

'Reveal to us your leaders, and it will end.'

Dia's boyfriend, the other faerie from the day they had arrived, was on his hands and knees and raised a shaky finger towards them; towards Tyler stepping before her, raising his chin.

Voice caught in her throat, Charlie reached for and missed the sleeves of Tyler's shirt as he was dragged away, just like his brother was pulled out of Vanilla's embrace.

'No.' Vanilla gasped. 'No!'

An elbow hit her jaw, and she was knocked to the ground. Charlie rushed to her side, pulling the trembling girl into her arms as Tyler and Jaden were brought to the front, their hands tied over their heads to a branch. It was the same tree she had been whipped at before, its face staring solemnly back at her through hollow sockets.

'Sister Hilda,' Mother Ratchford asked, pausing before Jaden, 'what type of affinity has this young man shown in your classes?'

'Earth, Mother,' answered Sister Hilda. Mother Ratchford nodded to a man by her side, who turned to a barrel behind him and pulled out an iron stake; its heated triangle tip glowing red.

'It seems some harder measures must be taken,' Mother Ratchford declared, her voice carrying over the grounds. 'From now on, the use of magic will earn you a strike.' The Brother took the iron stake and set it against Jaden's back, the hissing sound drowned out by Jaden's agonised roar. Next to her, Vanilla went rigid, clawing at her hair and body, her scream echoing his. Charlie held her steady, vomit filling her own mouth. Forcing a swallow, she diverted her eyes. Ahead, Gilly and Ava held Caden back from rushing to his brothers' aid, his expression lethal.

Then the Headmistress of Discipline enquired about Tyler's powers, and Charlie felt herself numbly reaching for the ground, feeling so faint that she could not sit up straight on her own. As Tyler groaned through gritted teeth, her fists kneaded the earth in despair, barely noticing at first how odd it felt. Instead of frozen solid, the ground under her hand was warm and pulsating. Eyes on Tyler, his head lolling against his arm, his lips muttering comforting words to his brother, Charlie thought of all the times he'd whispered to her, telling her to listen to the force within. At once, all her fury and fear dipped from her body, as if flushed through her bloodstream, her lifeline extending underground, and she visualized herself as a bolt of energy going through the roots of the tree. She imagined it coming alive, protecting the boys from harm. And then—it did.

Like a projection of light, the carved face in the trunk stretched out from the bark then disappeared. She would have thought it a figment of her imagination had the Agnus not cried out in surprise. Even Mother Ratchford took a step back, eyes wide, as a near-transparent figure – tall, slim, and feminine – leaned out of the trunk with her upper body, looked at the people gathered around, then let out such a high-pitched cry that the ground convulsed and rippled like the waves of the sea, sending everyone into heaps and bundles.

No sooner had the woman appeared than she disappeared back into the tree.

Her eyes now wild with fury, tufts of hair sticking out of her bun, Mother Ratchford ordered everyone to their huts and caves, but not before Jaden was inflicted with two more burns on the assumption that his earthly affinities had been the cause of the appearance.

The boys and the wounded rebels were sent to the infirmary, along with Vanilla who had fainted. Avoiding Mother Ratchford's line of sight, Charlie snuck in under the pretence she was Sister Rowena's assistant and that the Sister would want her with her. To her relief, Sister Rowena confirmed it, her face wrought with such anger that the Agnus Brothers did not dare question her but rather rushed out of the infirmary after depositing the students.

Sister Rowena and Charlie bustled about throughout the day and into the night, trying to help where they could without magic. Even if they would have been able to use it, Charlie doubted either of them would have dared considering Mother Ratchford was on the path of war. The Brothers had been quick to remind them not to nurse the rebels more than necessary; there were more punishments to be given.

In a moment of quiet, when there was nothing more to do but observe the patients, Charlie lingered by Tyler's bed. Angry red downward-pointing triangles grimaced at her from his back, just like several downward-pointing triangles with lines through each of them decorated Jaden's. The alchemic symbols for water and earth.

Beside the boys' beds slept Vanilla, still but so tense that Charlie wondered whether she was only pretending. An idea occurred to her, and she pushed the beds closer. After a short moment, Vanilla's hand found Jaden's and squeezed it tight. Then her shoulders slumped, and her head sank into the pillow.

For the next hour, Charlie sat cross-legged before the infirmary's fresco. The phantom goddesses shimmered around her in rhythm with the comforting voice repeating their story, but Charlie was observing Clotho, deep in thought. She and Clotho had similar features, although Clotho's skin was darker, and her feline eyes much fiercer. Charlie turned her spindle-pin between her fingers, feeling the old wood underneath her fingertips. She recognised her powers now, watching as Clotho created and woke different life forms in hibernation. It made her think of the woman in the tree. What was she? And had it been Jaden who had brought her out, or Charlie? A knot of guilt tightened in her chest. If it was her, some of Jaden's marks should have marked *her* back.

'I see the magic of the fresco has captured you once again?'

Charlie jumped to her feet, twisting to see Sister Rowena standing behind her slipping a letter into her pockets.

'I–I...' Charlie stuttered, but her mind was blank of excuses. Which was okay, she realised, considering she did not need one with Sister Rowena.

The nurse's gaze turned blank, and her breath shivered as she spoke again. 'Eighteen years ago, I woke up to that imagery on my wall,' she said, looking small and frail. 'I'd never seen it change – until I saw you before it – but I always suspected, always knew it wouldn't be an ordinary mural either. After all, it was made by an extraordinary girl. One whose eyes turned white like yours whenever she used her powers.'

'My mother,' Charlie murmured.

Sister Rowena didn't answer. Instead, she studied her as if looking at a ghost from the past. Charlie's eyes escaped to the statues placed around the room and their smooth marble surfaces, like frozen milk. So lifelike that there could well have been nymphs buried underneath. *Nymphs!*

Something clicked in her mind, brought forth by the illusions of the fresco dancing next to the statue closest to her.

'Sister Rowena, you've been here for a while?' Charlie asked, too fervently to pay any attention to the look of indignation on the nurse's face.

'*Some* time,' she murmured.

'What do you know about the grounds? Do you know why we can't use magic?'

'You can.'

'But not against anyone?'

Sister Rowena shook her head. 'That's right. But I do not know why. I've only heard a myth. That the protective barrier is upheld by guardians of the grounds.'

Charlie felt herself light up like a lamp. 'Excellent. I'll be back soon!'

Not even five minutes later, Charlie was practically knocking down Maddison's door.

'I don't have time to explain, but you need to come with me,' she said as the raven girl opened the door, scowling once she saw who it was.

'Why would I do that?'

'You will if you want your uprising.'

At that, all defiance abandoned Maddison's face, and she followed suit as Charlie rushed down from the girls' cliff.

They snuck through the woods towards the tree by which she, Tyler, and Jaden had been flogged, making sure they weren't seen. Lines from her *Encyclopaedia* echoed in her mind. *Known as protec-*

tors of their territories... Nymphs sometimes retreat and dwell far within their element to ensure their safety.

They reached the tree and stared at it, the carved eyes gazing wistfully into nothingness.

'I'm surprised Mother Ratchford hasn't cut it down yet, after what you told me,' Maddison murmured, running her fingers over the immaculate ridges in the tree, like spoon-sliced ice cream. The tree bristled a little, shaking flakes of snow onto their heads. Whether it was the wind or something else, Charlie could not be certain. 'What did Sister Rowena say to you again?'

'She said there's a myth about guardians upholding the protective barrier. I think this nymph might be one.'

'And why do you need me if you brought her out already?'

'I've a suspicion I won't be able to communicate with her,' Charlie replied. She might not be able to tell the nymph about their problems, but Maddison would be able to *show* her. And judging by the nymph's reaction to the violence earlier, she was pretty confident that she would be on their side.

A moment went by before Maddison spoke again, her cool demeanour replaced by piqued curiosity. 'It's worth a shot.' She raised an eyebrow as if to say *go right ahead*.

A pang of panic hit Charlie at once. Exactly *how* would she wake her? She thought back to the morning and of the pulsating heat she had felt coming from the ground.

Hunkering down, she spread her fingers and pressed her palms to the dead grass. Frost-covered straws tickled her skin, melting against her body heat. She closed her eyes and calmed her breathing, recalling her meditative exercises. A minute went by where she connected with every nook and cranny of her body, then moved her attention underground. Weak at first, a slight pulse started drumming under her left ring finger. It spread out until she could feel it under both hands and followed it underground. Like she did when she brought an item to life, Charlie visualised some of her own energy following the connection and awaking the nymph within. A gasp by her side made her realise it was working.

Opening her eyes, Charlie saw the carving coming out of the tree, like a figurehead at the bow of a ship. It stretched and yawned, the sound reminding her of a tree creaking in a storm.

Then it began to move towards Charlie, a shimmering silhouette growing more solid for every foot it moved away from its tree until the Dryad stood towering over her.

She was stunning.

Her skin was a translucent, frosted green like the leaves of her tree, her hair braided in tiny enthralling plaits, and her face neither young nor old, but ageless. Charlie tried to speak to her, but she only frowned in confusion. This was what she needed Maddison for.

The Dryad shifted a little as Maddison came towards her, as if made uncomfortable by the sudden appearance of another human. But as Maddison's eyes turned white, the Dryad stood still, her own eyes sparkling like black beetles, turning angrier by the minute.

'My task has come to an end,' she said as Maddison's eyes returned to green, surprising them both with her speech. The sound of branches rubbing their leaves together trailed after her words. 'Earth will be free.'

The Dryad breathed in and lifted her chin to the sky, arms outstretched.

Once again, the ground convulsed, green, shimmering light emitting into the air like dust from a beaten carpet, leaving Maddison and Charlie grasping onto each other for balance.

'Thank you, Daughter of Life, for my awakening, and you, Daughter of Fortune, for the evidence. I might not have believed you otherwise.' The Dryad bowed to the both of them then turned back to her tree.

'You're not going to help us? What about the other elements?' Charlie called, but the Dryad only shook her head, already melting into her tree. 'By my judgement, our interference in the business of humankind has caused enough trouble. I wish you good luck.' And with that she was gone.

Our interference. There had to be more guardians. *One for each element*, she guessed as she and Maddison ran back to the infirmary, eager to tell the others.

Once they woke, the news alone seemed to invigorate the boys, infusing them with new energy, and the next night, the whole group – and a handful of rebels managing to lose their Agnus tail – met up in a clearing in the woods to test the Earthlings powers. Jaden sent a fallen branch towards Ava MacLaren, almost knocking her out in the process as she was still unable to defend herself, fire yet to be released by its guardian. Things happened a lot quicker after that.

Remembering from her own time in the dungeon – and reminded by one of the other girls that had been brought down there – Charlie and Maddison went through the dungeon's backdoor to study the mantles of the dungeon torches. Set in lava stone, they were shaped like curved women, the flames making their hair.

For a moment, Charlie wondered if the fire had ever gone out, and in the next she called upon the nymphs to awaken.

Two Lampades rose from the stone, and soon after, back in the forest, Ava had her revenge on Jaden by setting his trousers on fire. Face red as a tomato, Charlie brimmed with awkwardness as she healed the burn wounds on his inner thighs, the rest of the rebels snickering and chuckling in the background. But it was all in good spirit; even Ava fist-bumped Charlie's shoulder like a comrade.

All the rebels volunteered to help search for more nymphs.

There was the Aurai, a nymph of air, that had been one of the statues in the infirmary, and then an Oread in the old stables, tipped off by a withdrawn stable girl whose shapeshifting form had been that of a horse.

After those, there was only one nymph left to find: a Naiad or Oceanid to release the element of water. But no matter how often Tyler and his fellow Waterlings went diving into the sea, or how often the boys explored the deeper pockets of their cavern, there was no sign of any object that could mask a nymph.

One day, as they stood watching the Waterlings swim, Jaden leaned over and whispered out of the corner of his mouth, his breath white on the air before him. 'Maybe you and Ty should take another dip soon? It'd be nice if you found those two Oceanids again.'

The very idea made her stomach tingle, both with butterflies at the thought and embarrassment that she had told Vanilla who obviously had told Jaden in turn. But the fluttering was short-lived.

'I doubt it. He hasn't said much to me lately,' she murmured through chattering teeth. She had expected Tyler to be over the moon once she cracked the code to release their magic, but he'd rarely had any time for her since.

'Don't take it personally,' Jaden said. 'Tyler is... eh... Tyler has always been a soldier. He'll come around when the battle is done and the rebellion won.' His features grew darker. 'Right now, I think he's more consumed by the thought of revenge.'

Tyler had taken the worst of the punishments, both voluntarily and as the rebel leader. The dungeons. The Stool of Infamy. More public flogging, branding, and even near-drowning – the latter one of Mother Ratchford's more desperate measures to break his spirit.

He'd stoically taken it all, never saying a word, even though the Agnus had tried to make it out as if he had. Even though they told the general assembly that he had admitted to his sins and pledged to withdraw, before forcing him to kneel before Mother Ratchford.

Charlie would never forget the cold fury in his face that day. Perhaps none of them would; the insult burrowing into their very core. The burning promise of retaliation in his eyes consuming each one of them. Ever since, they'd all helped him dodge the Agnus' watchful eye in whichever way they could. Even Maddison, sticking close to him, as if she felt guilty about sleeping on the job the day the rebels were caught in the first place.

Frowning, Charlie nodded gingerly back at Jaden, an idea taking form. Perhaps Tyler couldn't go swimming with her anytime soon, but they had gone once before – and they hadn't been alone.

On a cold January morning, Charlie returned from a stroll on the beach with her eyes gleaming and fresh roses in her cheeks. 'I know where we can find the sleeping nymph of water,' she told Maddison and continued walking without another word or stopping to see if she followed.

She only stopped once they stood on the bridge linking the girls' cliff and the castle, staring into the centre of the waterfall cascading past. It had been obvious really, once the Oceanids she'd created had told Charlie where she could find her.

She focused on the curtain of shimmering water until a silhouette of sharp angles and curves took shape within. Maddison gasped as the freshwater nymph, a Naiad, appeared like a doll made of impossibly smooth glass. Diamonds sparkled on her body, which at closer proximity seemed to be solid water droplets embedded in her skin, reflecting rays of light.

'I thank you, dear child of Life,' the Naiad said after Maddison had shown her the same images as she had shown the other nymphs. But she did not retreat into her element like the others. Instead, she leaned in and whispered in Charlie's ear. 'The enemy is closer than you think.'

Confused and speechless, Charlie watched her melt back into the water.

'What did she say?' Maddison asked, but Charlie shrugged. 'That the enemy is closer than I think. But I don't understand; the Agnus is here. How much closer could they be?'

To be inside Tyler's cave was both intriguing and intimidating each time she visited. This was his comfort zone. This was where he lowered his guard and slept at night, resting his head on the pillows. It was also a place with a bed, which she couldn't seem to ignore no matter how hard she tried.

'You okay?' Tyler put a hand on the small of her back and moved her towards him. He seemed much more like himself again, now that the elements were released, and the rebels had set their plan to strike back at the Agnus.

She nodded. 'Yeah, just nervous about tomorrow, I sup—' The words stuck in her throat as Tyler took off his shirt. His shoulders were broad, the limited light within the cave casting shadows emphasising the lines of his muscles. He ran his hands through his tousled black hair and let himself fall onto the bed, just slowly enough that she caught another look at the many downward-pointing triangles on his back, more visible now above the white lines of his healed scars.

'Do they still hurt?'

'A little, but they're getting better.' Tyler grimaced. 'Joke's on them. I've come to rather like it. Makes me look macho, don't you think? Like tattoos.' He flexed, and she giggled. His lips formed a satisfied smile at her response, but it did not reach his eyes. Some wounds, she supposed, could not be brushed aside with a joke.

'Or like a birthmark,' Charlie blabbered. 'I've seen some on other Defectives.'

'Yeah, Venus has some snake stripes all over her body.'

Charlie blinked, immediately feeling as if Venus herself was on the bed with them. Nausea welled inside her at the idea of the serpent girl stretched out like a seductress, fixing her with slitted pupils. 'How do you know?'

'Um, Caden told me.' Tyler shrugged, and relief flooded through her. So, Tyler had not been with her. But it sounded like Caden had. At least enough to see her naked. Had she had her way with him after all and brought him to her bed? For some reason, the thought did not sit well, but Charlie supposed she had hoped none of the brothers would find Venus desirable.

'Caden doesn't seem very eager about the uprising, does he?'

Tyler laughed humourlessly. 'Caden would choose to be a Withdrawer if we let him.'

Alarmed, Charlie's mouth dropped open. She had known he was uncertain about magic, like her. But that he would choose to become a Withdrawer stunned her. '*Do you not think,*' said Deimos' voice in her head, *'like we have infiltrated them, they may have infiltrated us?'* At once, she realised they still did not know who had told on the rebels and had Mythos shut down. But that was a horrible accusation. She reprimanded herself, remembering Caden's rage and desperation as his brothers were branded with their elemental symbol. It did not seem likely to her that he would sell them out like that – unless he thought they would be pardoned.

Distracting her back to the present, Tyler wrapped his arms around her waist and pulled her down to the bed, his skin warm against hers.

'I'm sorry I haven't made much time for us lately. The moment we win tomorrow, I'll seek you out amongst the rebels and hold you in my arms.' His breath caught against her ear. She tried not to think of his front pressed up against her back as they lay spooned against one another. The heat in her cheeks inflamed the rest of her body when he nuzzled his nose against the crook of her neck. 'Jaden thinks you're good for me,' he murmured.

'I think you're good for me,' she whispered back.

He blew a sarcastic snort against the back of her head, and then after a while added more softly, 'You can sleep here again if you want.' His voice was low and husky. She turned and looked at him, his pupils wide with tender eyes. There was no goofy grin on his lips or any other hint of sarcasm. It sparked a tingle below her navel and took the wind out of her chest. Her heart was going wild, pumping blood faster than it would run through her veins.

Before she could answer, Tyler closed the distance between their faces. His mouth was warm and soft; his tongue skilfully manoeuvred its way around hers, making her melt in his arms. Something gnawed at her mind, like a warning bell in the distance, until his body shifted, and she ended up beneath him. Her pulse quickened with the eager movements of his hands. But when his lips let go of hers to brush against her collarbone, oxygen rushed into her lungs, and voices crept into her head. '*What a skank...*'. High, mocking laughter drummed against her skull. She pressed her eyes shut, trying to block them out, but they only grew louder as her chest tightened. His fingers traced the length of her leg, reaching a sensitive spot of skin underneath the hem of her skirt, and the alarm in her head sounded at full volume.

Tyler suddenly cried out.

She jerked upright, eyes wide, just in time to see him being pulled off the bed by large hands of rock jutting out from the roof of the cave. He hung between them, looking utterly tangled and shocked. It was the episode with the Oread drawing all over again, except this time no one was laughing. She felt infinitely mortified.

'I'm so sorry—I don't, I mean, I'm not... ready.' Words failed her. What if she had read too much into his kisses? Was she presuming he had wanted something more with her than he actually did? What if she had misinterpreted him? She barely dared to look at him.

Tyler opened his mouth just as Jaden poked his head into the cave. He stopped short, with his mouth forming an open 'O' as he took in the scene before him. 'Um, bad timing I suppose. You seem quite caught up, Ty,' he said, hardly able to contain his laughter.

The arms of rock let Tyler go, dumping him on the floor with an 'Umph', and retreated into the wall. Tyler stood up and dusted his trousers down without looking at her.

'I was just offering Charlie a bed for the night.' He turned to her, eyes still averted. 'I hope you have a good night's sleep. Don't worry, no one will disturb you ... I'll stay at Jaden's.'

'You will?' Jaden's expression was a mix of surprise and bemusement, but Tyler pushed him out of the small cave and, with a quick wave from Jaden, the brothers disappeared.

Trembling, Charlie hoisted herself back towards the pillows and hugged one tightly against her chest, her nerves still rattling throughout her body. Her panic came in convulsions. She buried her face in the soft fabric and breathed in the scent of sea spray and sand. Disbelief of what had just come to pass surged through her, and she closed her eyes, cursing herself as the image of an embarrassed Tyler dangling from the roof flashed against her dark eyelids. Goddess gracious, what had she done?

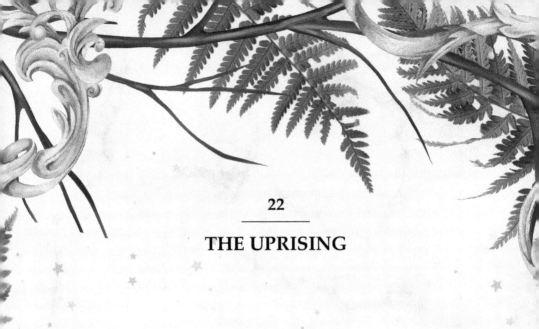

22

THE UPRISING

TENSION RADIATED from the rebels throughout the dining hall. They were spread out amongst the tables like any other morning, but now the anticipation in the air was so thick she could practically touch it. Next to her sat Vanilla and Jaden. Both eating breakfast. Both seeming relaxed and still. Yet it was the lack of intimacy between them that tipped her off. No secret hand squeezes. No tender glances between them. Others weren't quite so inconspicuous and sat picking at their food, their legs shaking restlessly underneath the table.

Venus and her gang sat with Dia's boyfriend and one of his mates, Callum, a boy with an Oread lineage. For once, the hatred in the girls' eyes was not focused on Charlie but at the head-table above. All but Gilly looked like Amazons, warrior women ready to burn down the world. Gilly, however, looked how Charlie felt. Uncertain and worried.

Tapping her nails impatiently on her plate, Venus' stare shifted to Tyler, observing him for the signal that would set them off.

Tyler remained calm like the sea before a storm. Only his loose tie and taut muscles straining his shirt were a sign of the vigilant warrior within. Whether on purpose or not, his gaze did not meet Charlie's.

After he left his cave last night, she remembered that she had originally come seeking his promise to help her find her sister. But now she worried he would not even talk to her again. *The moment we win tomorrow, I'll seek you out amongst the rebels and hold you in my arms.*

Looking away, Charlie caught Caden watching her, throwing her back to the night they had arrived. Of the trap that had been laid for them and the wings being cut from Albin's back. If this mutiny failed, she doubted there would be any mercy left within the Agnus, and they might very well leave them in the dungeons to rot.

For now, it did not look as if the Sisters knew something was wrong, or at least they did not show it.

There was the scraping of a chair at one end of the room, and an Agnus guard stepped down from his post at another.

Charlie held her breath, listening to his steps as he marched between the tables, heading for the staircases.

Tyler raised his gaze.

Mother Ratchford met it as if he'd called her name.

The guard left the room, and Charlie exhaled.

Then Tyler dipped his chin.

An explosion of movements ensued as people rose to their feet, plates and cutlery swivelling across the room.

A storm blew through the hall, guided by one of the Airlings – the same who had conjured the northern wind on their first day at Soli Gloria. Except this time, it did not dwindle into nothing but erupted at the head-table, sending the teachers' breakfast crashing into the walls. The Sisters shrieked and scrambled away, clutching the crucifixes around their necks. Non-rebels squealed as well and dived under the tables. Mother Ratchford's face stretched in white rage, but it did not stop the rebels.

The floor started groaning, and a loud crack like a mountain coming apart made Charlie jump. The ancient flagstones split open, ground trembling. She followed the crack to its source and saw Callum sitting underneath a table, his palms pressed to the floor. Jaden and the other Earthlings with greener thumbs leapt at the chance to work their magic. As one, they raised their palms, and a green glow filled the gaping holes in the fractured stone. Roots sprang forth from the earth underneath and crawled along the floor, ensnaring tables and human legs alike.

Frightened non-rebels crawled out from their hiding places and ran towards the exit, but they were met by armed Agnus Brothers running towards them. Unable to distinguish between them and the rebels, the Brothers' whips lashed out indiscriminately. Students' mouths gaped in agony as their bodies shook, but the Brothers just smirked. Taser whips – an upgrade.

Charlie racked her brain trying to figure out how her magic could help, while searching for Tyler, certain he would have the answers. Then out of the chaos appeared Caden, an aura of dark power around him. Eyes entirely silver, his hair ruffled by the Airlings' storm, Caden pressed his fingers together and slashed the air. Odd, infrequent buzzing and sizzling noises erupted from the Agnus' tools, as though their electrical currents within were interrupted.

One of the Brothers tossed his whip aside and, with a flick of his wrist, pulled out a stick which unfolded to twice its length. He ran, baton at the ready, straight towards Gilly Jones, who raised her hands helplessly. No magic occurred. She stumbled backwards until she stood pressed up against a statue of a tall muscular soldier – and the idea struck Charlie.

Pure instinct guided her as she swivelled her hands, hoping it would wield its sword in the same manner. Blood pumped in her ears while she imagined the marble man stretching his stiff limbs, her life force surging through his silvery veins. The stone creaked and rumpled, and the knight leapt off his pedestal and landed in front of Gilly, knocking the Brother unconscious with the flat side of his sword. An overwhelming fierceness surged within Charlie; a feeling of heightened power, pride, and triumph all at once.

Caden threw her an appreciative nod before a deep rumble caught their attention. Now was not the time to linger on moments already passed. More Agnus reinforcements were running down the stone staircases from the upper balcony. They clutched the marble banister as the massive structure shook and groaned, and their feet flew out from underneath them.

'Callum! No!' Tyler's voice called. Charlie sought him out and followed his gaze to the Oread boy who stood, feet splayed and fists clenched, glaring at the enormous staircase. 'Bring it down and we can't get out!' The fire in Callum's eyes made it obvious he didn't want to stop, but he, like the other rebels, followed Tyler without a doubt. The staircase shuddered before it stilled, and Callum threw himself into a nearby battle instead.

Behind Tyler, Jaden's roots had reached the head-table and wound themselves around the few remaining Agnus' ankles. A thick vine swirled down from the roof and caught Sister Lucy heading towards the dungeon door, trying to escape the chaos. Halted by her frantic screeching, Dia Vonsby turned towards her with a horrible grin of malice spread over her lips, her wings once again unfolded. With every beat of her wings, Dia made snipping sounds with a pair of breakfast knives in her hands. 'Let's see if you like being cut any more than we do.'

'No!' The word surprised Charlie as it came out of her mouth, but not nearly as much as the rash movement of her animated statue. In one motion, the stone knight grabbed the faerie with both hands and tossed her into the wall where she fell to the bottom, her body still and wings crumpled underneath.

Cold ran down Charlie's spine. What had she done? Inaudibly, she spun around, nausea welling within, mouthing for help but unable to form the words needed. Her breath caught in her throat as her eyes locked with Tyler's. Was it shock that she saw? Or fury?

'Tyler!' someone screamed, a voice that vexed Charlie on a regular basis but now drowned her insides in tar. Dodging a passing ball of fire, Charlie hunched down and looked for the source of the sound loaded with dependency. As was Tyler. Then she saw Venus caught in the arms of a Brother following his brethren as they carried away bound Defectives. Tyler seemed to have seen her too.

Grabbing a jug of water, he yelled for other rebels to follow. With a stinging feeling in her stomach, Charlie ran after them.

The entrance hall was in chaos as Agnus Brothers desperately tried to hold the rebels off. The air flickered with lashes of electrical whips and canes. Withdrawer servants sat hunched behind statues or corners, shivering with fright, while Albin stood protecting them, flinging potatoes at friends and foe coming their way.

Callum lifted his hands, and the ground shook beneath them all. The Agnus members cried out and hunched against their brethren, trying to regain their balance, dropping their captives. A smug smile crept over Tyler's face as he manipulated a surge of water to rise from his glass and shower the Brothers. Their howls as the liquid connected with the electricity made the hairs rise on Charlie's neck. She closed her eyes, feeling sickening waves of pain and dreadful fright rolling towards her. Then the rebels followed Tyler's lead and ran into a physical fight with the Brothers. Fists punched chins, and hands strangled necks. In between it all, she tried to watch Tyler as well as searching for something that could help.

Two tall figures appeared by her side.

'Let's finish this,' Maddison said, Deimos smiling next to her. Apprehension went through Charlie at the sight of him. He was back. And she would hear news of her sister. After the battle.

Staring intently at the few remaining Brothers, Maddison's irises turned white. One by one, they went limp and let their weapons drop.

No one resisted as the rebels ran forwards to bind their hands.

'Take them to the hall,' Tyler ordered, but he was interrupted by a slim figure with short dark hair who jumped into his arms and kissed his cheek.

'You saved my life!' Venus cried. 'I owe you, *anything*.' Her eyelashes fluttered, and Charlie felt a sharp pang of jealousy. *The moment we win tomorrow, I'll seek you out amongst the rebels and hold you in my arms.* That's what he had said, but Tyler didn't even look at her, even though the Agnus members were being rounded up and bound by cheering rebels, triumph written all over their faces.

'That's alright,' Tyler said, his eyes glorious as he flashed Venus a crooked smile. A smile he'd previously reserved for *her*, the one that made Charlie feel like the luckiest girl in the room. She *knew* then. Precisely what, she was not sure, but she knew that something had shifted. Something had gone horribly wrong, and it wasn't the uprising. The floor underneath her felt as if it were trembling, but Callum was happily celebrating with the others. The air around her felt thick and unbreathable, yet all the Airlings were hugging their friends. She needed a hug, but the one she had needed it from was following a happily skipping Venus into the dining hall.

She looked for Maddison, Vanilla, Jaden – Caden even – but they were all up at the front. All of the Agnus teachers, except Sister Rowena and Brother Deimos, were on their knees and bound by roots. A seething Mother Ratchford spat in Tyler's direction as he neared the dais, but he only paid her a gloating sneer in return and clasped Jaden's outstretched hand.

'Well done, brother!' Jaden smiled, pulling him in for a hug and a pat on the back. 'What do you want us to do with them?'

'We'll discuss it together,' Tyler replied, holding himself like a general before his squad, and squared up to the Headmistress of Discipline, her face swollen red with anger. Triumph danced in his. 'Lock them up in the dungeons for now. Let them suffer like we did at their hands.'

Jaden nodded and appointed nine rebels to execute the order. Unease filled Charlie, watching as Sister Lucy was manhandled along with the others.

'You won't get away with this,' cried Mother Ratchford as

Callum came and pulled her to her feet. 'You are filth, curses on the world!'

Tyler stepped up closer, stopping at eye level with the Headmistress of Discipline.

Loathing flew between their steely glares, and the hall vibrated with anticipation. 'You thought you could play gods, but that requires power,' he said. 'And you? You're *powerless.*' He waved her away, and everyone revelled in the sight of the protesting woman being dragged across the floor, wriggling and snarling.

Charlie tried to catch Tyler's eye and bask in his happiness, but soon after, someone shouted in warning, pointing behind him at an empty-handed Callum and Mother Ratchford's black hem disappearing through a side door.

'I-I lost my grip,' Callum stuttered, but Tyler had already shot after her with Jaden and Charlie following behind, up the winding staircase of the tower; the sound of the headmistress' clunky shoes against the stone steps reverberated over their heads.

There were no elements to aid them in this part of the castle, and it was all they could do but chase her. Charlie could not understand where she was hoping to escape to, until she realised she was heading towards her office. Her mop of hair in disarray, Mother Ratchford bashed through the door and threw herself over her desk, the boys reaching her ankles just as she pulled out the top drawer and grasped an item, fumbling to put it to her lips. But the boys dragged her down to the floor and knocked it out of her hands before she had the chance, both of them restraining her and glaring as she reached and clawed the floor for it.

'And you say we're the abnormalities,' Tyler hissed and grabbed the flute, tossing it into a corner, shaking his head at the madwoman before them.

'Demon filth!' Mother Ratchford spat. 'They will come, just wait and see. When they realise what has happened here, they will send help, and they'll come for you like they attacked Hallows Grove not two weeks ago!'

Her words knocked Charlie from what little stable ground she stood upon. Had something attacked Hallows Grove? *Sophie...* 'You lie!'

Mother Ratchford cackled. Jaden and Tyler stared between them, uncertain what to say or do.

'She doesn't,' said a voice, and Charlie turned around, facing Deimos' solemn expression. It seemed he had followed them and was watching Mother Ratchford with distaste. It was true, then.

'Where's my sister?' Charlie asked him.

'By the time I located Brimley, the attack had already happened. We tried to follow the trail of the attackers for a couple of weeks, but it went cold.' Deimos paused.

Mother Ratchford's eyes were popping, glaring at Deimos. 'What are you talking about?'

But Deimos did not respond. Instead, he guided Charlie out of the office while Tyler and Jaden locked it shut behind them. Mother Ratchford kept yelling and shouting declarations of doom from inside.

'We might simply have to consider her gone,' Deimos said, giving Charlie's shoulder a stiff squeeze. 'Although, the loss feels easier to bear knowing we have you amongst us.' Charlie did not think it made anything easier at all but said nothing.

Many eyes waited in anticipation as they came downstairs.

With an encouraging nod from Deimos, Tyler turned to the crowd and raised his arms, a radiant grin of triumph on his lips. 'The castle is ours!'

Cheers and shouts broke loose in the hall, but they all sounded far away. Rebels clapped and hugged each other, yet none paid Charlie any notice.

She tried to catch Tyler's eye, hoping he would give her the stability she desired, sweep her into his arms and tell her they would go and save her sister. Tell her he was certain Mother Ratchford had lied and that Deimos was mistaken. But instead, he waved for his brothers to follow him and left the hall, walking right past her. Her surroundings started to swirl, and she staggered back, leaning against a column. They had defeated the Agnus Dei of Soli Gloria, yet she felt like she had lost everything.

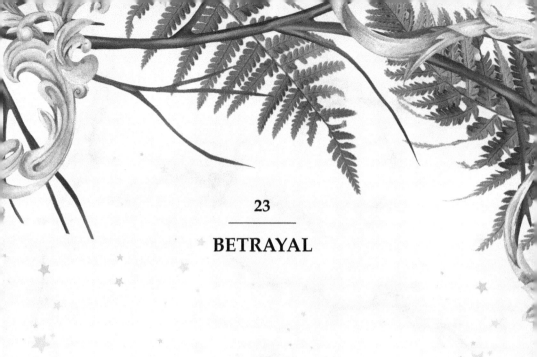

23

BETRAYAL

THE BEACH HAD NEVER BEEN MORE crowded, and yet people kept spilling out from the boys' cavern or coming down from Mythos, the celebrations branching out in both directions. Shortly after the castle had been secured, the different Defectives had grouped together to change the grounds. Some Firelings and Airlings heated the temperature in the air, while other Earthlings created firewood. Three major bonfires now blazed along the beach as a result, one made entirely out of stools.

The teachers' long table had been brought outside as well, which Tyler and Maddison marched back and forth upon, stamping their feet and riling up the crowd. Firelight flickering on their faces, eyes alight with power.

'Never again will we be starved!' Tyler pumped his fist into the air, and his audience cheered with him. 'Never again will we be tortured!'

'Yeah!'

'Never again will we be kept in frozen dungeons!'

'Never!'

'But they will be!' someone shouted, and others laughed and cheered, high fiving the speaker.

'We are free,' Maddison shouted, and the chorus of 'Yes!' boomed even louder. 'We will revel as if Dionysus himself is with us!'

'Yeah!'

'We will drink—' A couple of Earthlings squeezing juice out of grapes raised their beverages in salute. Cider and other treats had already been shared and consumed by many. 'We will dance—' People took each other by the arms and swung about. Maddison chuckled and added a purr to her voice. 'And we will frolic as if every day is Beltane!' Someone wolf whistled, and everyone laughed.

Jaden, sitting in the grass with Vanilla, chugged his beverage and covered her mouth with his. They rolled backwards into the grass to the awkward chuckles of people watching. Caden rolled his silver-blue eyes next to Ava and Venus, the setting sun casting a blanket of gold over his pale features. Tyler, on the other hand, shook his head, rubbing his neck with a sheepish grin until his eyes met with Charlie's. He gave her a curt nod then whispered something to Maddison who cast Charlie a glance over her shoulder. There was something odd in her expression which Charlie couldn't quite read. Then she turned back to the rebels and continued egging them on.

Jumping down from his makeshift stage, Tyler walked over to the chorus of 'The Agnus will lick our boots!' and gave Charlie a fleeting hug long enough for her to breathe him in – short enough to make her feel the chill of his absence as he let her go.

... I'll find you amongst the rebels and hold you in my arms.

Had that been it? Had he meant nothing more by it?

'How are you?' he asked.

'Bit overwhelmed,' Charlie admitted, rubbing her shoulders. His smile, radiant as the last of the sun kissing his cheek, should have made her feel at ease and yet... Yet, his eyes held the depths of the sea, and she feared he would slip between her fingers like water.

'Maybe you should go have a lie down? There'll be plenty of parties to attend later on if you feel like tonight's not the night.'

'Maybe.' Charlie bit her lip. 'I was hoping we could have a chat? Maybe in your cave?'

His smile dropped ever so slightly. 'Chat about what?'

'That I need to find my sister. And, well, *us*...'

'Right.' He glanced after Maddison, now heading towards the path of Mythos. 'I have a meeting with some of the rebels. We need to discuss things going forward.'

'Should I come?'

He shook his head. 'Nah, you don't need to bother with it. Go to bed. We'll talk later.' He gave her a friendly pat on the back and followed Maddison. Watching him like a predator on prowl, Venus tossed aside her cup and slithered after him.

'Where's Ty off to?' Caden asked, appearing by Charlie's side.

'To discuss rebel matters,' Charlie murmured.

He studied her while sipping his drink. 'Probably trying to figure out how they'll keep us here once we all become bored with their mayhem, or how to keep the Agnus out.' He sounded amused by the idea. Her old suspicions came creeping back.

'You don't think we can?'

'I think Tyler has no idea what we are up against.'

'But you do, don't you?'

'I beg your pardon?' A flash of lightning passed in his ice-blue eyes.

'You've never seemed keen on the uprising.'

'I don't see why my magic is more important than other people's safety,' Caden chided.

'So, you'd rather we were powerless?'

His expression fell, the cockiness barely lingering on his lips underneath his frosty glare. 'Funny, I didn't know I had the choice to be. Not all of us can be chosen ones, *Giver of Life*.' His tone pummelled into her chest, knocking the air out of her.

'You resent me,' Charlie said, lifting her chin stubbornly, hoping the warmth in her cheeks did not betray the insecurities she felt. 'Because I helped the rebels?'

'I resent the state of things.'

'And I resent a double agent,' she snapped.

At that, Caden threw his head back and laughed. 'And you think I'm one?'

'Deimos suggested there would be one – and you fit the bill.'

Caden lifted an eyebrow apprehensively, his jawline cutting the air as he pursed his lips together. 'Deimos did? That's interesting...'

Charlie narrowed her eyes at him. If he was a spy, he didn't seem surprised or concerned at having his cover blown. 'You don't seem bothered by it.'

'It's not real, so why should I be? Don't believe everything you hear.' He winked at her, the blonde locks of his fringe dancing before his eyes as he leaned in closer. 'Or else I'll have to believe that you viciously stole Dia's moment in the uprising.'

'Right.' Charlie rolled her eyes. Then exhaled. 'It's true that I hurt her though.' Guilt nibbled at her, recalling the image of the crumbled faerie as she slumped against the wall. She was in the infirmary now, but from what she had last seen, her worst agony was missing out on the celebrations. Still, it couldn't be good if people were talking about it. A snide voice crept into her mind. *Perhaps that's why Tyler's keeping his distance.*

Caden shrugged. 'I bet she had it coming. I'm not supposed to say – in our kingdom, everyone is equal – but faeries, in my experience, tend to be particularly malicious. Dia didn't seem any different. You won't believe the things I've heard coming out of her mouth.'

'Your kingdom?' Charlie frowned at him, watching what little tan he had received from days spent outside in the winter sun drain from his face. 'You're from a kingdom?' She recalled now, how Caden had called his brother "general".

'Actually, our father is the king.'

A sarcastic guffaw escaped her. 'I thought he was a nymph fanatic?' she tittered. But when Caden didn't laugh with her, she realised he was serious. 'Where is this kingdom?' What country had Defectives as monarchs, and were they even aware of it?

He tilted his head, eyes avoiding hers. 'Somewhere far away from here.'

'I think you're having me on,' she said, bitter resentment creeping into her voice. 'And to be honest, I'm not interested in being another joke between you and Venus' gang.'

He looked at her then, and after a moment his frown vanished as he sighed in realisation. 'You know, the best way to make sure they didn't harm you was to pretend to be their friend and distract them.'

'Now you're definitely mistaking me for a fool.' Charlie shook her head and stepped away, a coiling sensation of unease striking at her chest. A resistance to believing him, a gut feeling saying that maybe she should. 'And if you'll excuse me, I'm going to bed.' He let her go and said nothing until she was almost out of earshot.

'Believe what you want, Charlie,' he called after her in the end. 'But unlike my brother, I've never mistaken you for anything.' With a haughty smile, Caden turned back to the festivities around him.

After her conversation with Caden, Charlie was unable to sleep. She spent a few hours tossing and turning before she decided to seek out Tyler in his cave and went back outside to see him. But Tyler had not returned for the night. Perhaps he was somewhere on the beach still, partying with the others. She could go and look for him, but the idea of people seeing her leave the boys' cavern kept her firmly planted. All of the rebels knew there had been something between her and Tyler by now, but she did not want to feed the rumours.

'Thought I might find you here,' a voice drawled from the doorway, making Charlie jump.

Venus stood watching her, eyes agleam.

'What are you doing here?' Charlie asked, and Venus' eyebrows disappeared into her jet-black hairline.

'I'm here,' Venus sighed exasperatedly, 'to take you to Tyler, actually. He asked me to go find you and bring you to him.'

Charlie glared at her.

'Oh, come on. I don't have all night. He's in the costume hut, waiting.'

Rising, Charlie left the cave, refusing Venus' company as she passed her. 'Then I can find him myself, thank you.' She'd risk the rumour rather than accept Venus as her guide.

But to her surprise, the serpent girl proved harder to shake as they passed one long-stick torch after the other along the beach. Adding to the bonfires, the flames cast light against the dark sky, fuelling the stars above. It would be nice to watch it all with Tyler, and her stomach tingled once again with impatience for everything between them to return to normal.

Ava, her hair swirling around her body like fire engulfing a tree, stopped briefly in her dance-off with another Fireling sporting fiery red streaks down his skin, like veins filled with lava, but neither Venus nor Charlie stopped to explain what they were doing together. The latter kept marching with the former in tow, and they did not exchange a word until they reached Mythos. At that point, it seemed Venus was unable to keep silent.

'I told you they would grow tired of you.'

Charlie glared at her, but Venus' face and voice were free from the malice she usually reserved for her, making it impossible to read her intentions.

'No one's grown tired of me,' Charlie muttered and continued walking, but the snort behind her told her she hadn't been very convincing.

'Sure, tell yourself that. It only makes it worse that they don't let you know where you stand. At least you and I have always been open with each other about that. You know I can't stand you, and I know the feeling is mutual, no?'

Charlie nodded. Venus sighed, taking on a dramatic flair. 'There are so many things they haven't told you! Did you not wonder where Tyler slept last night?'

Charlie's breath stopped in her chest, the memories of the evening before returning vividly. Venus waved her expression away. 'Just as I thought. Ah.' She sighed dramatically and took Charlie's hand, patting it as if stabbing her a thousand times with a needle. 'I've been so unfair to you. I always thought you were the enemy. I even felt sorry for you thinking he could love you, while I knew the truth.'

They were within reach of the hut now, its yellow window giving away a warm light into the night. Someone's shadow moved inside. *Tyler.*

'He should have told you already that he stayed at mine.'

Charlie stopped dead in her tracks with one hand reaching for the door handle of the hut. Finally, Venus' fangs had punctured her heart, her words seeping in like poison.

'But,' the other girl continued, setting her slit pupils upon Charlie, 'it seems we've both been played for fools. There's always been someone else for him.'

Without a moment's hesitation, Venus pushed open the door, and something shattered inside of Charlie at the sight before them.

Tyler lay propped up on his side, his white cotton shirt open, exposing his chest, the zipper of his trousers undone. *He was a fling. A handsome little plaything.*

Stretched out, with her leg bent against his hip, lay Maddison, only wearing her underwear.

'Charlie.' They both spoke as one.

Paralysed, Charlie could only stare at them, the two she had held most dear to her, feeling as though something had forever broken inside of her. Feeling stupid that she had not paid closer attention, that she had ignored little red flags that all of a sudden seemed so blatantly obvious. The intimate image of the two burned before her eyes even though they were moving away from each other.

'I'll give you guys a minute,' Maddison said, throwing on her tights, crop top, and boots. She did not even care to say anything to

Charlie as she passed her by but paused to address Tyler instead. 'Come find me at the party.'

He remained silent.

Charlie took one step closer as the other girls left, but Tyler only turned away and dressed properly.

'What is this?' Her voice trembled in her throat, and she feared she would not be able to keep it under control. 'Are you back with Maddison now?'

More silence.

Frustration rose within her. She wanted to grab his shoulders and shake the answers out of him, but the idea of touching him now felt as forbidden as playing with fire. She was bound to get burned. Instead, her voice rose several painful octaves.

'What about me? You said... you said I was special!' She winced.

How childish those words sounded to her now.

She tried again, remembering what Caden had told her. 'Did you trick me? Didn't you think I deserved the truth?'

'It's not that simple,' Tyler finally said, but it wasn't nearly enough.

'Not that simple? Is she manipulating you? Because Maddison is *great* at that.'

'No, she's not.'

She put her hands to her head. 'So, then... so, then everything was a lie? What about *us*?'

'Come on, we weren't serious!' Tyler snapped. He might as well have slapped her. Speechless, she stared at him, frozen still by the ice in his voice.

'But this thing with Maddison, then, that's real is it?' She couldn't help the raspy hurt sneaking into her voice. 'You want to be with her?'

'Listen, Charlie. I'm not a relationship kind of guy; I just don't do them.'

Confusion and misery marred within her, and a quiet desperate plea rose to the surface. 'Maybe you just haven't given it a chance – with the right one?'

'I need to be free. Free of any sort of restraints. Please understand.' He pushed his palms to his knees and stood up. 'I'm going to join the party. Feel free to hang around here if you want, or perhaps you should go and enjoy yourself too, shouldn't you?'

Speechless, Charlie followed Tyler out of the hut and down the path, all the while wondering who this new person was walking in front of her. Could she have been this wrong about him?

Once back on the beach, Tyler joined Jaden and Vanilla and stopped with his back turned to her, blocking any space for her to join them. Both studied each of their faces before disappointed understanding seemed to dawn on their own. Still, none of them came to her side. Instead, Charlie was left entirely alone.

Maddison was standing farther away, drinking cheerily from her cup while sending seductive glances at the boys gathered around her. The moment she brushed her long hair over her shoulder, Charlie's vision turned red. She stormed up to her and grabbed her wrists, forcing her to spill her cup and face Charlie at the same time. 'How could you do that to me!'

The boys and other partying Defectives within earshot turned and looked at her as though she were crazy, but Charlie did not care.

'You need to relax.' Maddison waved a hand at her. 'It's just meaningless canoodling.'

'But he was more than that to me,' cried Charlie, her heart now bleeding out into her voice. The nearby listeners exchanged looks; a few regarded Maddison with disdain while others seemed to find the whole scene entertaining.

Maddison lifted her chin and spoke with a solid voice so everyone within range could hear her. 'Honestly, I thought Tyler deserved to be with someone true to the cause. Someone who doesn't attack their comrades and call them *Defectives*. Say, was it you who told on the rebels? So that you could keep him all to yourself?'

It was like a slap in the face, and Charlie remained stunned. She could feel the judging eyes and whispers turning towards her.

'I don't know what you're up to,' Charlie said at last, her voice shaking with suppressed anger and embarrassment, 'but you've gone too far this time, Maddison. After *everything* you've done, now you've taken him away from me and—'

She didn't get to say any more before a firm hand grabbed her arm, hard, and pulled her away. Tyler marched her from the beach towards the castle, his jaw clenched and lips pressed into a thin line.

'Go, Charlie. Stop harassing Maddison. You're making a scene,' he said and let go once they were far enough from the beach so that no one could hear them.

'Why are you protecting her? You think she cares for you?' To her horror, her voice was but a whine at this point.

'Enough, Charlie.'

'She doesn't care about you like I do.'

He stomped his feet and looked away, but not before she saw a flash of conflicted emotions in his eyes. Maybe he was just embarrassed and too proud to admit his mistake. Maybe he had been hurt by her rejection and sought comfort with the others. She took a deep breath and touched his arm lightly, speaking in calm tones. 'I *want* to be with you.'

The look he gave her was poisonous. 'But I don't want to be with you.'

He retracted his arm with such force that she felt burned with shock and dismissed with disgust in one sweep.

He seemed on the verge of saying something more when Caden appeared between them. 'I think you need to leave, Ty.'

Tyler scoffed. Looking from one to the other, his forehead creased, and a dark shadow possessed his face. 'This is too good. You're here giving me a hard time while you've been off with my brother. I didn't believe the rumours.' He chuckled, heartlessly. 'I thought you were better than that.'

His accusations left her dumbstruck, despair welling up in her chest. She shook her head feverishly.

'Leave,' Caden snarled.

Tyler only waved a hand mockingly in the air and walked away to re-join the party. With a sigh, Caden turned back to Charlie, but his sympathetic look was too much, and she ran from his side back to the castle, tears streaming.

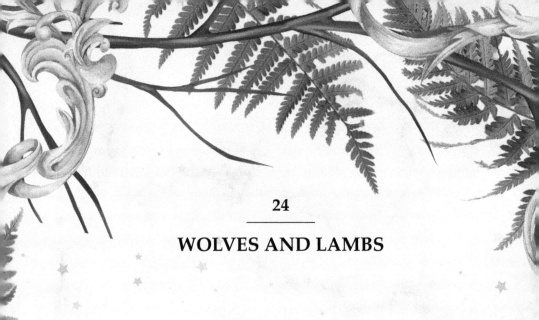

24

WOLVES AND LAMBS

'THEY'RE GETTING ROWDIER DOWN THERE,' Gilly said, turning away from the large infirmary window. Bonfire light shimmered on the glass like a hellish mirage. They'd been burning for days, kept alive with magic. So had the rebels.

Sister Rowena huffed and fussed over Sister Lucy, the burn-ish rashes caused by the vines having turned infected. After a couple days, the old nurse had straight up demanded Tyler allow her down to the dungeons to check upon her fellow Agnus Brothers and Sisters, and thereafter ordered the guarding rebels to help her carry the most wounded upstairs to the infirmary. Tyler hadn't objected or refused her, but he had not seemed happy about Sister Rowena commanding his rebels either.

Sister Lucy's wounds did not seem bad enough to warrant a stay in the infirmary, but Sister Rowena ordered her to change into one of the infirmary gowns nevertheless. As she pulled off her shredded black robes, Charlie gasped at the scars and gashes decorating her back.

'Did this happen to you recently?'

Sister Lucy stared at her hands while her colleague's lips set into a thin line.

'Contrary to popular belief,' Sister Rowena said, 'punishing students is not a favourite pastime for the majority of the Agnus, even if they believe it is for the greater good. Many here will avoid it if they can or turn a blind eye.'

'But, to him "who knows to do good, and doesn't do it, to him it is sin",' Sister Lucy said. 'James 4:17.'

Sister Rowena sighed and continued to dot anti-inflammatory ointment on the Sister's most recent wounds while Sister Lucy kept on talking.

'Like I told you, when an Agnus sins, they must repent with the mortification of the flesh.' Sister Lucy pointed her chin towards another Sister, whose black robes hung on her thin build. 'She's been fasting since that day Mother Ratchford used the branding iron on those two boys. She believes she was the one who gave Mother Ratchford the idea, since they talked about branding the horses not many days before.'

Sister Rowena looked at Charlie with meaning. 'Your boy might do well to know these things when they start chanting for blood.'

It sliced through her heart. Tyler was not *her* boy, would not be *her* boy, and apparently had never considered himself such either. The image of him and Maddison flashed before her again, and she squeezed her eyes shut against it, the lump in her throat growing and blocking her airways once more. It had been there since that night. Since then, she'd spent every hour walking around in complete disarray and confusion, going over the moments they had shared over and over again and asking herself how she could have misunderstood. If she had done anything wrong. Her mind always returned to the moment in Tyler's cave, the one with the cave wall coming alive and the shock on Tyler's face.

Shame coursed through her. *If only I hadn't...* But she didn't finish that thought. Wouldn't hear it. And perhaps, also, wouldn't believe it. Because even if she had embarrassed him and ruined their moment, she had thought that he cared more about her than that. That he wanted to be with her enough to wait. Now she felt like she didn't know him anymore. Didn't know the rebels going wild outside.

She glanced at the broken people in the infirmary. Some starved and sick, some having suffered wounds at the hand of a vengeful rebel taking advantage of his or her time guarding the prisoners. This was not what she had fought for. Or was it?

Something prickled at the back of her neck, and she turned to meet Gilly's gaze, her expression a mirror to her own thoughts. Perhaps they had not imagined the end result to be *this*, but they had both spent enough time with the rebels to know that they wanted revenge. Were they at fault for what they were doing now? Were they at fault if the Defectives became worse, turning into the precise monsters that the Agnus believed them to be? Had they enabled it?

Gilly turned her attention to the tray in her hands. A muscle twitched in her arm, causing the tools and cotton pads to shake on the silvery surface. The jerk continued along the right side of her body, culminating into a violent spasm of her jaw. Her whole face contorted into a grimace.

'Gilly, are you alright?'

'Yes, sorry,' the girl apologised, putting down the tray, shielding the lower part of her face with her hand. 'It's been like this for a... for a while.'

Withdrawal symptoms.

'That's why you weren't able to defend yourself?' Charlie asked, walking over to pick up a cotton roll that had fallen off the tray. Gilly nodded with another twitch.

'Yes. If you hadn't come...' Gilly's voice faded, leaving her eyes glossy with gratitude. They moved over to Rowena's work desk where Gilly settled the tray, and Charlie grabbed some tools. Slowly, they fell into a rhythm where Gilly cut the herbs and Charlie grinded them into powder, preparing medicine for the patients.

'You know,' Gilly said softly, 'Venus is telling people that you simply stepped aside and let everyone else do the dirty work.'

It didn't exactly come as a shock, but Charlie tensed nevertheless. 'Is she, now? Maybe it would have been best if she'd been right.' She looked out the window and down to the grounds where an Earthling was currently using vines to control an Agnus member like a puppet. Tyler was nowhere to be seen, and she hated how her mind immediately went to his cave, wondering if someone was there sharing his bed. Quickly, she looked away, blocking the thought, and the rebels, from her mind. Gilly's hand came over hers.

'Venus is actually quite threatened by you. It's the only reason she does it. She would have done anything to have your powers. To be the one that would turn the tides for the uprising. But she knows she never could. She's not *good* enough. She doesn't care to be either.'

'What use does it do to be good if this is the result?' Charlie gestured to the window.

'I think you underestimate what you can do, Charlie, when you lead with your heart,' Gilly said, her voice kind and non-judgemental.

It took Charlie by surprise to hear the faith and encouragement in Gilly's voice, and part of her felt shame at not having tried to get to know her sooner. That she had not tried to see past the groups they both had decided to stay with. If she had, perhaps she at least could have avoided exposing Gilly's underwear to the rebels.

Gilly merely laughed as she apologised.

'I think I was so amused with seeing Venus dangle that day that I didn't even think of myself. I stayed with them so I wouldn't get bullied. Being made fun of for a day was a small price to pay.'

Charlie looked at her in amazement. Suddenly, all of Gilly's laughs and mocking smiles seemed more and more forced the longer she thought about it. It was odd to learn how much of her assumption of Gilly had coloured her impression of her as a person.

You know, the best way to make sure they didn't harm you was to pretend to be their friend and distract them.

Caden's words hit her with a pang. It was the same explanation

Gilly had just confessed to, but unlike Gilly – who'd joined Venus' group for herself – Caden claimed to have done it *for* her. Perhaps that was true as well.

But she didn't know what to do with that.

Once again, she thought of Sister Rowena's advice. *'Treat a person like your enemy, and they will become one.'* Perhaps, if she didn't treat Gilly – or Caden – like enemies, she would have a friend in both. She needed friends right about now.

As if reading her mind, Gilly gave her a dimpled smile, followed by a new twitching grimace. Finding it rather endearing, Charlie gave her a smile in return, hoping she was right. And that Gilly was right. In that she, Charlie, really could make a difference.

'I come bearing your dinner,' Charlie murmured and entered Mother Ratchford's office, but she did not mention that she had asked to take the tray or voice her reasons for doing it. She hardly knew her reasons, only that she needed to change what had gone wrong. Starting with the uprising.

The former headmistress of Soli Gloria scowled at her from her chair by the window where she was chained in such a manner that forced her to witness the mayhem outside, without being able to do much else.

'Is it poisoned?'

'No, I'm not a killer,' Charlie responded, setting the tray on the desk.

'It'd be a grander mercy than what you do to my Sisters and Brothers out there.' Mother Ratchford nodded towards the glass and the beach beyond it.

Charlie gritted her teeth. 'If you had only treated us as humans, none of this would have happened.'

'Are you certain about that?' Mother Ratchford crooned. 'Are the Defectives you know nothing but good and virtuous? Have none of them surprised you, turned around and shown another side to themselves you did not think they were capable of?'

Charlie swallowed. Thinking of Brimley. Thinking of Maddison. Thinking of Tyler.

'No, I can see they are not. Who are you, then, to predict what they would or would not have done?'

Charlie struggled for words through her thickening confusion, feeling that there was a response but that it evaded her for Mother Ratchford's logic.

'But I'm not unreasonable. Help me put things right and I will take your advice.'

Charlie looked up, mouth open.

'Help me take back control over the school, and things will change.'

'How?'

'We will treat you like you are the same as us.'

'No punishments for doing magic?'

Mother Ratchford's strained smile quivered. 'No punishments.'

'Not for the rebels either, for what they did?'

'If you desire their pardon, I'll grant it.'

'Why should I trust you?'

'We've never pretended to be anything we are not, have we? Never have we beaten you without a reason why?'

There were so many flaws in Mother Ratchford's statement. Charlie could have pointed out that a reason wasn't always justification, or that pretending to be virtuous while committing sin was still a sin. But none of it mattered in this. It all came down to one thing, one preference. She would rather have the monsters she knew, the ones that would slash her front, than the ones that would stab her from behind.

'What do I need to do?'

The former headmistress' eyes flitted over to the corner where Tyler had tossed the pan flute. 'Use the flute, and help will come.'

Charlie went to pick it up and turned it over in her hands. She

raised it to her lips tentatively but caught sight of Albin on the beach
– dancing, laughing – and the hunch of his back. Her gaze jumped
back to Mother Ratchford, remembering what she had done,
remembering the wings she still kept in the glass cage on her shelf,
and she dropped her hand.

'No, I can't do it,' Charlie muttered. No sooner had she said the
words than Mother Ratchford sprang from her chair – the dinner
knife and her binds falling to the floor – and snatched the flute from
Charlie's hand. The mere force knocked Charlie out of balance and
into the wall while the former headmistress blew and blew into the
thin cylinders, her cheeks like red balloons. No sound came from it,
and Charlie stared incredulously at the woman whose skin popped
with strained wrinkles around her eyes.

'It doesn't work.'

'Oh, but it does,' Mother Ratchford cackled, eyes wild. 'They
will come for you now. Mark my words, they'll be here.'

Shaking her head, Charlie retreated out of the room, locked the
door, and left the former headmistress cackling to herself. She rushed
to her hut, trying to block out the growing unease within her one
moment, struggling to decide whether or not she should warn Tyler
the next. But nothing had happened, had it? Even if the flute did
something, it hadn't given a sound, and *she* hadn't blown it. If she
went to see him now, he would only want to know why she had gone
to see Mother Ratchford in the first place – and then he'd never look
her way again. She had almost jeopardised everything they had
worked for. No, she couldn't say anything.

And yet, as the hours went by, her head gave her no peace.

With her heart pumping and her mind frenziedly trying to
convince herself that Tyler would understand, would even realise
how badly he had treated her for her to take such measures, she left
her hut and let her legs lead her towards wherever she needed to go.
She came up short by the beach, spotting Maddison with her arms
around a couple guys, and Tyler not far from them standing with his
own group, watching her.

Charlie took a deep breath and made to march towards him, words already forming on her tongue, when someone grabbed her wrist and turned her around.

'That's not a good idea,' Caden said, his blonde fringe falling into his calm eyes.

'What is? You don't even know what I was going to do.' Charlie shrugged, attempting, and failing, at appearing nonchalant. Caden looked over her shoulder in the direction of Tyler and Maddison.

'You're planning to say something, anything, that will make Ty pay you attention again.'

Ouch. 'But...' Charlie stuttered, looking back at the beach before she let out a deep sigh, accepting, at the heart of it, that was what she was hoping to do. Nothing had happened up at the office. The grounds were still save from the party, people were laughing, and Mother Ratchford's threats were the threats of a madwoman.

To say something, anything, to Tyler was just an excuse to feel tied to him again. To have him pay attention enough to *listen* to the ache in her heart.

'I don't understand. It doesn't make sense. She must have... compelled him, or something.' Her teeth chattered as her whole body convulsed with jitters.

The discomfort on Caden's face was clear, even through her teary vision. 'She hasn't.'

Hollering and music thumped in her ears, screeching through her head so loudly that she almost didn't catch his next words.

'I... Jaden thought he would be different with you. He talked about you all the time. He was attentive towards you. I almost believed it myself. He honestly seemed to care more about you than he ever did about anyone else. But—'

Her shoulders slumped. 'Why didn't they warn me? Why didn't you?'

'He's our brother.' Caden hesitated. 'Jaden wanted to give him the benefit of the doubt. We all hoped he would come to his senses. Do the decent thing and be serious with you or at least tell you the truth before you were hurt. But...' He sighed. 'There are some people, like Tyler – and I suspect your friend Maddison – who thrive on manipulation and control. Not always on purpose – I like to believe he isn't aware of it – but it's a quick fix to gain energy, and more volatile and addictive than energy channelled freely.'

She glared at him, her heart threatening to bleed out onto the grounds. 'He's used me... for magic?'

He opened his mouth to reply when several things happened at once.

Someone screamed. Vanilla leapt from her pillow by the bonfire, and grasped Jaden's arm where he stood, eyes locked upon the sea. Everyone turned their heads in the direction she was pointing. Large creatures were moving through the sea towards the beach. Some had already crawled onto the sand and stood to their full height, their muscles alert. They weren't human. Their arms and legs were impossibly long and muscle-packed, attached to bodies covered in fur. Not an imaginary monster under the bed. Not a fairy-tale. Real, appearing before her as if they had stepped straight out of her *Encyclopaedia*.

Werewolves.

The pack leader threw his large wolfish head towards the moon, his howl reverberating through her body. Full-blown panic broke out on the lawn. Screams drowned out the stampede of feet scrambling and running. Some ran towards the castle, others into the woods. The shapeshifters transformed into their animal forms, hoping to be harder to catch or strong enough to fight, but the majority of the students ran in circles, blinded in horror, hoping for something to save them. Only the toughest of the Defectives stood their ground; roots of trees burst through the lawn, grabbing werewolves as they passed; giant waves belted over the creatures still swimming; and balls of fire sizzled past their ears until the air was filled with the nauseating smell of burned fur.

No matter how hard Charlie tried, she could not help. She held her arms up, but nothing happened. She could not even concentrate on what she *wanted* to happen. Her mind was blank with panic and fear. Caden fought by her side, knocking down werewolves as they came, purple orbs jutting out of his palms. But she barely even registered that he was using magic when she saw Maddison squaring off against a werewolf, her white eyes strained, and her jaw clenched as she stared him down. Yet, despite the werewolf's sluggish movements, its large eyes remained firm on its target, and his large arms, covered in dirty hazelnut fur, clawed hungrily in her direction.

A gasp escaped Charlie. She recognised that fur. Without thinking, she ran closer, Caden shouting her name, his voice drowning in hers.

'Brimley! Brimley!'

Maddison's arm shot out to her side as though to stop her. 'Stay back!'

'But it's Brimley!' Charlie cried, glaring at the werewolf's body, scars, and patches of fur missing where he had obviously been cut and stitched back together.

'What did they do to you?' she whispered, a sharp jab of guilt punching through her heart as the wolf threw his head back and howled to the sky once more.

'Charlie!' screamed a familiar voice from the direction of the castle, and she instinctively turned around just in time to catch a glimpse of Gilly running towards her, face scrunched up in fright, before something bony and furry slammed into Charlie's head and knocked her to the ground. A ringing sounded through her ears while she strained to see people running, fighting, with monsters at their heels. A big hairy back blocked her view to Gilly. Mind racing and skull throbbing, she searched for someone, like Caden, to call upon, but only found Vanilla balancing at the top of a tree while chucking spear-tipped branches upon the beasts fighting Jaden.

Then someone grabbed a hold of her, forcing her around. She screamed, and a furry fist cracked her face into oblivion.

PART III

25

RETURN OF AN OLD FATE

BARE TREES STRETCHED *black spider-leg branches towards the night sky. Some were topped with fresh snow.*

A doe-eyed woman leaned into Charlie's view, her wavy dark hair falling like a curtain around them. Clotho. *She cooed and whispered kind words then straightened to reveal a sleeping baby in her arms. A man's voice spoke a few words to the woman, and Charlie peeked up at him from his arms, the auburn in his hair glowing like embers. Her father.* Thomas.

The woman, her mother, knocked at a door and, almost as if he had been waiting behind it, a man opened it at once. He was short, with a broad, flat nose and a thick flowing mane of auburn hair – the same auburn as the younger male carrying her. A sense of recognition tingled before she was able to place him as the man who had dropped off Caden at Soli Gloria. Bes, *hadn't that been his name?*

'She told me you'd come,' he said to the couple, his eyes glancing at the bundled babies in their arms. The sleeping one and her.

'Hello, Father,' the young man said. 'How are the children?'

'In bed,' Bes responded, but he seemed troubled and grave, as if it pained him to say it.

'We figured Beset would guess where we had gone by the time our absence was noted, but we needed her surprise to be genuine,' the woman said.

Bes nodded. 'No need to explain, Hazel,' he said and looked at her, addressing her with what must have been her chosen name in this life. 'And no time. Come on in, I've ordered the staff out for the night.'

'Is she here?' Her mother's question was answered the moment they stepped into the living room.

It was dimly lit, but out of the shadows and into the firelight stepped another tall and lean figure. Her eyes were green like emeralds, and her long hair cascaded down to the small of her back. Desdemona Quinsey. Her resemblance to her daughter uncanny now that her long hair was coloured raven-black instead of the green Charlie had seen in the mural.

'Lachesis,' Clotho said, using the woman's allotted name. 'How is Maddison?'

'Safe,' answered the Fate of Fortune. They embraced, but Desdemona did not linger. Instead, she gave the other woman a nod before taking the child from her arms. Then she gestured for Bes to take the other. The old man reached out his arms, looking somewhat uncomfortable as Thomas handed him Charlie.

'Are you sure about this?' Bes looked to his son, who looked to his wife.

'Hazel?'

But Clotho – or Hazel – didn't look certain at all. She glanced pleadingly to her fellow Moira, eyes swimming with tears.

'We must set things straight, Clotho,' Desdemona said. 'And you must go now, or all will be lost. She has him and knows our plans. They'll be here soon.'

A boy with sharp pointy ears, mousy hair, and big glasses settled over the bridge of his nose came from the kitchen carrying a couple of canvases. He set them up against the wall. Two different images were painted on each, but Charlie couldn't quite make out what. Then Desdemona turned to one of them, with Charlie's twin on her arm and *the boy close behind. 'When all of us have gone through, burn the paint-ings and leave. Be brave, Clotho.'*

Thomas went to put his arms around his wife's shoulders as they watched the three disappear. Then, as her mother's tears finally spilled, Bes headed for the other painting with Charlie. With one foot through, he turned around for one last look about the room, his eyes travelling to the hallways, perhaps up to the dorms and his sleeping wards, and nodded as Thomas raised his palm.

Then the door burst open, and a monster stepped through. Tall and hairy, with saliva dripping from its chin. A werewolf, shortly followed by another.

Instantly, Hazel and Thomas took up the fight, swivelling out of reach of the furry arms and teeth but never wavering away from the painting. Dodging a swinging paw, Thomas twisted around to see that Bes and Charlie had gone through the painting and set it on fire.

Flames erupted around the corners of Charlie's memory as Thomas turned back around, a moment too late, and was clawed through from his ear and down his front.

Hazel's scream curdled Charlie's blood as he fell to the ground. He did not move again. Distracted by her grief, Hazel took a blow to the head and collapsed by his side, blood pooling out underneath them. Charlie cried out and shifted in Bes' arms, while the werewolves gath-ered around her parents' bodies, eyes upon Charlie as the final bit of the memory burned up into ashes.

Charlie gasped and sat up, her sight exploding with stars before a pounding ache filled her head, falling into rhythm with the throb-bing of her face.

She groaned and felt the back of her scalp. It was sore but whole. She checked her hand for blood, but her palm was bare and clean. Her sight, however, was somewhat blurry, as if she was dreaming still, or inside a cloud.

A thick white duvet covered her body. It hit her then that she was in a comfortable bed surrounded by baby blue walls. A fresh breeze blew in from open windows dressed in lace curtains. Everything was so pale, so pastel, that the woman sitting in a chair, watching her intently, stood out like a sore thumb.

Her bronze skin made the wooden arms of her chair look old and tarnished, and her heart-shaped face was framed by chestnut hair painted rich by the sun, like a halo of melted chocolate.

'Mother?' The word escaped Charlie's lips like a parched man's prayer for water.

The woman exhaled and nodded, looking at Charlie with big teary eyes. 'Hello, sweetheart.'

Charlie pinched herself, but nothing changed. Still, she couldn't believe her eyes, her mind fighting to make sense of what she saw and what she remembered. Had it been a dream rather than a memory? The werewolf attack an allegory of what had happened at Soli Gloria? She could believe that if she ignored the uncomfortable truth in her heart – the one saying it was a memory of her first and only visit to Nettleheys, her narrow escape and the death of her parents. Or at least one of them.

'I can see you have a lot of questions, dear,' Hazel said, her eyes shimmering with unshed tears.

Charlie nodded, all of them racing in her mind, fighting to be the first one asked. Where was she? Was she dreaming *now*? Why was Hazel alive, and if she was, why had she not come looking for her? Her throat and eyes burned.

'I'll answer all of them,' Hazel said, her eyes penetrating, as if she could read Charlie's thoughts. 'When you're strong enough. But for now, wouldn't you like a bath? I think it will do you good. You were so filthy when they brought you back from that wretched school.'

A bath. She heard them, but the words made no sense. *When they brought me back...* they. *The Werewolves! Caden, Vanilla. Gilly!*

'What happened to my friends? Those creatures – are you working with them?'

Once again, her mother shushed her. 'No need to be frightened. You're safe and so are your friends. They have had their own baths and are being fed as we speak.'

Still in shock, Charlie let Hazel lead her to a warm bathroom. It had red tile walls with pink towels hanging next to the white sink, making Charlie crave the taste of sugared strawberries – although that could very well be due to the scented bath before her.

What happened next nearly had Charlie convinced she *had* to be dreaming. It was something so unexpected it hurt her very sense of reality. She even pinched herself once more for good measure. In the end she had to accept what was happening to her. She was being *pampered*.

Gently, Hazel helped her strip off her filthy dress and cooed over the scars on her daughter's back, her scent rivalling that of the bath. *Water lilies.*

Savouring it, Charlie poked her toe into the steaming water, tentatively at first, but after an encouraging nod from her mother, she let her weight pull her under. She ducked her head, washing away her newly shed tears. Easing the aching of her face. When she surfaced, she kept her eyes closed, afraid of finding that her mother had disappeared. Then Hazel's fingers were in her hair.

Charlie luxuriated in the moment, wishing that everything else had been a bad dream and that she had finally woken to reality; a childhood home with her loving, tender mother alive and well.

She felt the sensation of invisible burdens lifting from her shoulders, as though all filth from nights on the Stool of Infamy was finally being truly washed away. The hot water sloshed against her body as she shifted, massaging sore muscles. Every ache seemed to seep out of her pores. For a second, Charlie's shoulders tensed as she heard the scrape of a chair on the floor. But, to her surprise and delight, when she opened her eyes, she saw Hazel's reflection in a steamed-up mirror reaching for the shampoo bottle. She hummed lightly, just how Charlie imagined a mother would hum to soothe her daughter. Charlie tilted her head and glanced at the woman behind her, still doubtful she was really there. Hazel merely smiled back at her. Again, tears welled up in her eyes. Happy tears.

Hazel dressed Charlie in a clean white nightgown after her bath before guiding her to a large dining room. There were no windows breaking up the panelled walls, the only light coming from lit candles and lamps about the room. The air hung thick as a result, adding to the sense of fog around her. Only a few pieces of furniture decorated the room, but the ones that were there were old and rich in appearance, such as the mahogany cabinets at either wall and the holstered sofa and end-table pushed against the longest. In the middle of the room was a table looking to be of the same wood as the cabinets, large enough to fit twelve people. The soft carpet tickled her freshly scrubbed feet, and the twinkling lights from the chandelier made everything on the table look twice as delicious. The flavoured smell of the roast beef dinner caused her mouth to run rich with saliva. She only had enough self-control to enquire about her friends one more time, noticing the table was only set for one.

'They have gone to bed, my dear,' Hazel replied and pulled out a chair, beckoning for Charlie to sit.

They were here somewhere, then. She would have to try and find them. After.

Charlie's stomach growled with the effort it took to sit down with dignity, her muscles aching with restraint. Yet, she looked up at Hazel questioningly until the woman nodded. 'It is all for you, and it is safe. Go ahead.'

Perhaps it was the small assurances, despite them coming from a woman she did not know, but hunger, as she knew from the homeless, also had a way of fighting fear. Without further consideration, Charlie grabbed her knife and fork and dug in, her insides crying out with relief at the first bite.

The meat practically melted on her tongue, its coat of gravy setting off her tastebuds like fireworks. Her stomach cried with exhilaration. Her knife sliced through the golden potatoes as though they were lumps of butter. Steam swirled off her plate, carrying the sweet odour of parsnip to her nose. She couldn't eat fast enough.

Walking seemed out of the question by the time she finished her plate. For a small belly, which had never tasted such a rich and full meal, it was almost too much. She sighed and rested her hands on her bloated stomach, slightly relieved when her mother announced it was time for bed. Hazel led Charlie upstairs to her room.

'There, dearest. Are you comfortable?' she asked after helping Charlie into bed and tucking her in.

'Very comfortable,' whispered Charlie, still afraid it would all be taken away. Her thoughts felt a little clearer now, but she was so tired she didn't have the energy to ask the questions that buzzed around her head. Where were they, her friends? And why was her mother in company with the werewolves?

Hazel smiled and turned to the night table. She picked up a glass of water and held out a small pill. 'This shall help you sleep a dreamless sleep and draw as much energy as possible from your rest.' Charlie raised a brow with uncertainty, but Hazel only thrusted the items forward. 'Please, darling, do as you're told.'

Carefully, Charlie placed the pill in her mouth and took a sip of water. Hazel eyed her knowingly. 'Open your mouth, please. Lift your tongue.'

Charlie winced, knowing that her mother would see the pill hidden underneath her tongue. She closed her eyes, expecting to be punished. To her surprise, she wasn't even scolded.

'Shall we try this again? I promise you, sweetheart, nothing bad shall happen to you under my care – as long as you do as you're told.'

It wasn't what she expected her mother to say, but then again she had little experience with mothers. Charlie swallowed the pill and emptied the glass of water. There was a thump from above, like a cat landing on the floor of a loft. 'Could I cuddle with the cat?' she asked, resting her head on the fat pillow.

'There are no cats here,' Hazel said, tucking her in. Charlie wanted to ask what the sound had been, but she forgot what she was going to say when her mother started singing. Sleep claimed her before she could even grasp the notes of the song, and she drifted off to the lullaby.

She woke up after what felt like only two minutes, but judging by the clock on the wall, she had slept for two hours. Not nearly enough, but a troubled dream about Sophie had startled her awake. Then her consciousness burned with shame. How had she not thought to ask her mother if she knew her sister's whereabouts?

Limbs heavy, head still groggy, she looked around the room, her vision blurred by a thick haze, and felt a sting in her arm. A needle was fastened with a piece of tape, feeding blood to her body through a tube – or taking it. The blood-bag hanging by her side seemed to be filling rather than emptying. Unnerved, she yanked it out, hissing at the sharp sting, and half-climbed, half-fell out of the bed still clutching her arm. Then she waddled over to the chair with her dirty old clothes, pulled off her spindle pin and refastened it to her nightdress. A different kind of pins and needles shot through her legs, but she shook them off. It was time to find the others. Surely, they would be in one of the other bedrooms.

The hallway was deserted as she poked her head out, looking left and right. 'Hello?' No response. Disappointment surged through her body. Where was her mother? Shouldn't she want to be as close as possible now that they were finally reunited?

A creaking from the floorboards above reminded her of the noise she'd heard before. Quietly, she made her way down the thin corridor, the smell of old furniture, velvet, and wood growing muskier the farther she went. She passed a few bedrooms that all seemed unoccupied at the moment, but one had a ladder descending from a hatch in the ceiling. Grabbing hold of a rung, splinters already digging into her soft skin, Charlie started climbing.

The loft was huge and, somehow, smelled fresher than the rest of the house. The scent of water lilies was strong despite the dust and cobwebs suspended from the rafters. Drapes of gauzy fabric also hung from the beams and brushed against her cheeks as she passed them. Low-burning candles were placed around the room, casting eerie light towards the iron-framed double bed in the middle of the room. The tall silhouette of a woman stood by one post, looking down at the prone figure of another.

Charlie froze, staring at the bedbound – an old body, completely void of colours, features wrinkled and unrecognisable. She could be just about anyone.

Glancing at the other woman, Charlie took a startled step backwards.

Just like in her memory, it was like seeing Maddison standing before her, only more mature, as if she had aged a decade. The teenager turned into a woman.

'Desdemona.'

Maddison's mother, the Fate of Fortune – *Lachesis* – stared at Charlie, her eyes set underneath thick, wavy black hair. There was a piercing gleam in her eyes. Like a cat watching a mouse.

Her presence was every bit as ethereal as Charlie had come to expect from the infirmary mural, but there was something sickly still to her bone-white skin.

'What are you doing here? What happened to her?' Charlie glanced at the body in the bed. 'And where's my mother?'

'This *is* your mother,' Desdemona said.

'No, I've just seen her. She—'

'You saw what my husband wanted you to see.' Desdemona set her gaze upon Charlie once again, hard and threatening like rolling thunder. 'But you have a chance to make it real. Wake her.'

Charlie frowned, walking closer to the bed, the body – towards Desdemona – as if she could not help herself. 'Wake her?' She stared at the old skin, unable to process that it was supposed to be part of the same woman she had spent the day with. It seemed implausible.

Unreal. Unless... unless everything had been a dream. Her insides jerked in longing.

'I don't know how.'

'I'll help you.' A sort of crazed expression fell over Desdemona's face, and before Charlie could move, she had grabbed her wrist and forced it up to her mouth. Two glistening fangs appeared as she gaped over it, and Charlie tried to pull back, a cry of fright escaping her. But Desdemona did not care for her resistance. The tips of the fangs pierced her skin, and a hot tornado of anguish tore through Charlie, like poison filling her veins.

'Will you wake her?' whispered Desdemona, a drop of blood lining the pearly white skin at the corner of her mouth. Her eyes a mesmerising light of swirling emerald. Urging her to say yes. Charlie felt her chin dip.

With determination, Desdemona pulled Charlie's arm towards the bed, slapping her wrist over the grey lips of the other woman. With a sigh, they parted and began to drink, suckling on Charlie's wrist, scarlet smearing.

The effect was rapid.

Charlie's body blazed as the changes began to take place, causing every instinct in her body to scream for her to pull away. The pruned skin smoothed out, and its dull grey colour was replaced by the radiance of life. But it did not turn a rich tan, like Hazel's. Instead, it remained ivory, like her hair now flowing with healthy strands. Neither did her facial features turn soft and dark, but pale and sharp.

With dread, Charlie realised her instincts were right. This woman was not Hazel.

Gravity suddenly felt too strong, pulling her towards the floor. Dread, then true terror, ricocheted through her body. With the kind of strength that only comes from desperation, Charlie ripped herself free, the skin on her forearm tearing.

Just as Atropos' eyes flew open, Charlie's closed, and she collapsed into a heap on the floor.

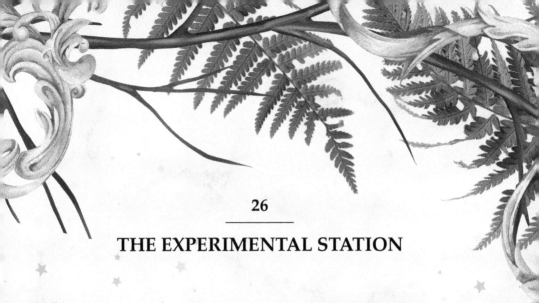

26

THE EXPERIMENTAL STATION

SOMEONE WAS CRYING. The echoes of her sobs bounced off the walls as if they were farther away, just beyond Charlie's reach. Still, her eyes would not open. An icy chill spread along her back while a musty scent of dirt and animals laced the air, increasing the distress growing inside her. Something told her she wasn't in the loft anymore, yet she had no idea where she was or, more importantly, how far away the Fates were from her.

The Fates... Lachesis. Atropos.

Had she really seen the Fate of Death rise from the dead, or had she imagined it? The latter, it had to be.

Her fingers dug into the ground as her muscles tensed, dirt gathering under her nails.

'She's awake!'

Cold fingers touched her skin, giving her a shake. 'Come on, Charlie. Open your eyes. Sit up. There you go. Good girl.'

Heart pounding, Charlie half pushed off the ground, half let herself be pulled up, and waited for the world to still, before her eyelids fluttered open.

Like a startled cat, she hissed and scrambled away. 'Get away from me, Desdemona!'

'Desdemona?' Youthful green eyes narrowed in confusion then opened wide. 'You've seen my mother?'

Maddison. It was Maddison sitting before her.

'You're here.' Charlie gasped, grasping the raven girl's hands, momentarily forgetting about their feud. 'Are you alr—'

Footsteps sounded behind her, and she twirled around to see Tyler, his face pale and fatigued, moving towards them, leaving Jaden sat hunched against a wall. It all came crashing down on her then. Finding them together. The words they'd said and the sneering and leering.

'Charlie! What happened? Are you okay—' Tyler reached for her, but she cowered away as if he would harm her. He froze with his hand still in the air.

'What are you guys doing here? Who's crying?'

'We were captured, like you,' Maddison replied, eyeing her as Charlie took another step away from them, rubbing her shoulder, checking her pin. Trying to piece together what had happened since she last saw them and now. 'We've been cooped up here ever since. You were brought in unconscious a few hours ago, she'—Maddison nodded to the crying girl—'half a day before that. We don't know who she is.'

'And we can't make her stop,' Tyler grumbled.

Charlie ignored him, looking around. It was a large rectangular space with the floor covered in sand, like some sort of arena. Rows upon rows of tables lined up throughout the room, their sturdy wooden surfaces used as mattresses for the distorted subjects and – was it coats of fur? – laid on top. She could not see the source of the crying.

'Where's *here*?'

'An equestrian arena, god knows where. But I don't think it's used for showmanship. No, Charlie, don't—'

But Charlie was already shuffling closer to the tables, the animal smell intensifying the closer she came, wafts of decay and faeces hitting her like a force field attempting to keep her back. Were those... hooves jutting over the table edge? Human skin and fur... fingers reaching towards the ground belonging to a limp arm dangling from its body.

She held her breath, pushing forward, the sound of her beating heart too loud in the large room. When she reached one of the first tables, it dawned upon her what she was seeing, what her mind had refused to believe. A horrified cry escaped between her lips, and she clamped a hand to her mouth, stifling the rest of it.

Black tufts of hair protruded everywhere from the near-human body. It was a boy, looking as if he was caught mid-transformation, shapeshifting into a bull. Not quite human, not quite animal. He looked like a half-breed from her *Encyclopaedia*. A Minotaur. The very sight made her legs go jelly, and the cuts and wounds along his skin – oozing with pus – were close to making the roast beef dinner rewind through her system.

'What is this?' She shuddered, turning towards the others. Tyler looked a little greener while Jaden kept staring ahead. Only Maddison seemed unaffected, her emotions cool and collected, but it was the faintest tremble in her voice that exposed her.

'Shapeshifters. Mutated.'

'Are they from Soli Gloria?'

'A few, some who left Soli Gloria months ago.' Tyler grew quiet, his silence saying more than words. They had all assumed that people who disappeared from school were Withdrawers being permitted to leave.

'Any of the rebels?'

'No,' Jaden said without blinking. '*None.*' And it occurred to Charlie that he must have looked at each face, searching for Vanilla. He clearly hadn't found her, but that did not mean she was safe. Even worse, maybe she was next in line.

The strange sobbing increased, and she moved farther down along the tables until she found a form huddled by the wall, her front and legs covered in dirty sand like Charlie's. For a moment she thought it was her mother, but this girl seemed shorter, stockier, and her hair hung like lumpy strands of a mop down her skull. When their eyes met, Charlie knew it wasn't Hazel. But who could she be?

A door swung open, and Deimos was brought in with a couple of werewolves, one of them Brimley. The girl scuttled closer to the wall at the sight of them, as if hoping it would swallow her whole.

Deimos! Charlie rushed forward, alarm jolting through her at seeing him captured too. But then she slowed, noticing something odd about the way the werewolves stood by Deimos' side. Like a couple of soldiers to their captain, not captors.

'Charlie!' Deimos beamed, spreading his arms wide as if he was to give her a hug but instead walked towards the table closest to him. A few things began to shift into place, although she struggled to believe it. 'I see you've been introduced to my experiments?' His hand fell on the ankle of what looked like a faun's leg. 'What do you think?'

'*You're* behind the attacks,' she stuttered, 'not the Agnus.' She turned her stare towards Brimley and the other werewolf. Mutated shapeshifters. The monsters that attacked orphanages. The monsters that had attacked her parents. The monsters—

Her memory of running through the woods behind Hallows Grove resurfaced, and the dogs morphed into one shape, half wolf, half human. *Deimos had been there that day.* She glanced at Maddison, who looked down at her feet. She knew then. It hadn't been dogs, and Maddison had *known*. Had not thought to tell her despite the many times Charlie kept seeing phantom werewolves. But there was something else in Maddison's guilt, something more, beyond that of being caught in keeping secrets, yet Charlie couldn't quite make the connection. The McFades' faces mirrored her own sense of betrayal.

'Not entirely right.' Deimos chuckled, brushing dust off the embroidery on his chest pocket. 'The attacks might be executed by us, but the Agnus know. At least their High Priests do – and approve for their own gain. We send the monsters; they reap the benefits. Loads and loads of families sending their children to their orphanages for protection. To be...' He tasted the words on his tongue. 'Converted? That's the contemporary word for the withdrawal programme, isn't it? Meanwhile, we harvest our payment when required.'

He gestured to the tables, to the dead shapeshifters upon them. 'We had many more. Unfortunately, the others have already... withered away – come now, don't give me that look. No ground-breaking discoveries have ever been made without a bit of experimentation.'

Charlie bared her teeth at him.

There was a roar that didn't stem from her, and Tyler shot past in an attempt to reach Deimos. Instead, he collided into a wall of muscle and fur. Brimley snarled and grabbed hold of him, lifting him above his head as if he weighed nothing but a feather, and tossed him six yards down the hall.

Catching himself, Tyler's body skidded and tumbled across the sand, but he quickly scrambled back to his feet, his breath ragged and winded. Wincing with pain, he raised his hands with palms crunching into fists. Yet nothing happened.

'There's no water in these pipes, boy,' Deimos sneered smugly. 'Only copper. You might as well save your energy.'

'You betrayed us!' Tyler spat in return, his knuckles tightening. 'We trusted you!'

'And? Betrayal shouldn't feel too unfamiliar to you, should it?' Deimos chuckled darkly.

This time, Tyler's face turned white as well, and his whole stance changed into a slump, his hands dropping to his side. Charlie's brows furrowed, looking from one to the other. She'd missed something, and she would figure out what, but first there were more pressing questions she needed answers to.

'Where is my mother?'

The boys glanced at one another. Maddison frowned in confusion.

Deimos' malicious grin widened, and Charlie's heart dropped into her stomach. 'What have you done to her?'

'I'm afraid she was never here, *sweetheart*.'

Charlie blinked. 'But I... I saw her... I—'

'I *made* you see her.'

She wanted to argue that he was lying, but there was a deep plunging realisation that told her he wasn't. Hadn't Desdemona suggested that her time with her mother hadn't really happened? Despite remembering the woman and her touches clearly, there was something else that prickled at the back of her mind. A knowing she had felt, even then, that something didn't add up. For one, her mother would never be working with the Agnus, and thus she would never have been free to walk about. Moreover, there was the haziness. The thickness that seemed to have clouded her mind. That it had been make-believe didn't only seem plausible; it felt more realistic than if it had been real.

But that didn't explain that she had *felt* her mother too. A compulsion could only affect what she *saw*. If her mother had not been there, then who... Her eyes landed on the sobbing girl again, huddled against the wall like a wrought-up, dirty old cloth.

Deimos' grin became unbearable. 'Yes, you see it now? She was promised her freedom if she put up the act. Although,' Deimos drawled, moving his hands as if weighing pros and cons, 'I did do all the heavy lifting...'

He moved swiftly, impossibly fast – faster than she had ever seen him move – and appeared beside the girl. Pulling her by the hair, he dragged her kicking and screaming back to where he had stood, her nails clawing at his grip. Lifting her to her knees, he put his slender fingers around her skull, the girl's teeth chattering while she pleaded for her life. Then he twisted her head, and the crunch of bones sounded before a deadly silence followed.

'I guess I don't have to keep my promise,' he said, letting the now-limp body fall with a thud into a cloud of dust.

Somewhere, the ghost of a horse whinnied, and Charlie's mind placed the girl upon its back, telling herself she got away. That she escaped.

Maddison stood paralysed to the spot, drinking in the sight of the girl with bloodshot eyes.

'Why?' Charlie asked, her voice trembling. 'Why would you do all of this?'

'To make you strong.' Deimos strolled next to a table, glancing at the dead body upon it. 'Strong enough for this.' He folded a hand behind his back and held up the other as if he was lecturing. 'You see, while our queen figured a way to freeze wolf-shifters transitioning, the pain it induced on other shapeshifters was enough to kill them – or make them go mad, at which point *she* killed them.' He made a bobbing gesture with his hand, indicating that those were one and the same. 'A few years ago, the project was put on hold. We realised we needed the gift of Clotho before we could continue, and we only started it again when my daughter brought you to Soli Gloria.'

Charlie spun to face Maddison, whose mask had crumpled entirely into a pained mixture of shame and despair.

Of course.

Deimos, who had addressed Maddison on their first day as if he knew her. Deimos, who was of a Banshee heritage. Deimos, whom Maddison had trusted almost instantly even though she hardly trusted anyone. Of course. It was all so evident now.

'I'm sorry,' she began. 'I didn't—'

'That's quite enough.' Deimos sighed, and Brimley sneered, causing Maddison to clamp her mouth shut, eyeing him warily. Deimos rearranged his cufflink. 'Pardon me, I see you've only just made the connection. I'm indeed Deimos *Quinsey*, and I believe you've already met my wife, Desdemona, the great Lachesis?' His top lip peeled back, showing the glint of fangs.

Charlie gasped, feeling the bite at her wrist burn, but as soon as she clamped her hand around it, something else simmered and cloaked her fear. A burst of anger, refusing to let him see how terrified she really was.

'None of this explains why you made that poor girl pretend to be my mother,' she hissed.

'I needed to fix Maddison's mess.' Fury flashed in Deimos' eyes, and Charlie could sense Maddison taking a few steps back. 'I worked so hard to have you reconnect with your magic, and then the two of you were about to let your teenage squabbles get in the way of things.

'Your Achilles' heel, much like your mother's, is love, my dear. It weakens you as much as it empowers you. I used this knowledge creating a happy moment for you today, like we created several at Soli Gloria.' He glanced up at Tyler and smirked, the latter looking down in the sand, his ears turning red.

The room seemed to grow smaller, her throat tightened, and whatever fight that had begun to boil in her was doused off with an icy chill. Jaden looked from one to the other, appearing to come to the same realisation as Charlie. It had all been a ruse. Tyler's affections for her. An act to indulge her into power.

She stared at the girl with the broken neck, tricked like she, too, had been tricked by everyone. They might not have physically harmed her, but her spirit felt broken still. Shattered. There was a terrible, bitter churning in her chest, grinding whatever was left of her heart into dust. Maddison had lied. Tyler had pretended to like her. Her mother had never been there. And Charlie had never been cared for, touched with affection, or loved. It occurred to her then how easily she had believed her mother to be alive because she so desperately needed her to be, but there was no room for naivety in this world. She thought she had already learned that by now.

Staggering backwards, her arm brushed against a cold limb and spiky fur. Her insides trembled with nausea, and she braced herself before glancing over her shoulder at the mutant lying there. This one had the upper body of a young boy and the bottom part of a horse. A centaur. If he'd been alive, Deimos would literally have made the myths of the past a reality of the present, part of the future.

A bullet of realisation tore through her, exploding her chest with dread and understanding. An understanding of why Deimos needed her strong.

'You want me to awaken them, don't you?' she whispered. 'Bring them back to life?'

'You can't do that!' Tyler erupted, looking as if he was about to have another run at Deimos. Even Jaden had risen now, shock scrawled over his features.

'I do.' Deimos nodded, pressing his fingertips together with an air of impatience. 'They'll be part of the new army.'

'An army? Against who? The Agnus? Didn't you just say you were working with them? And if you're playing them, you had the rebels more than willing!' Charlie gestured to the McFades scowling at Deimos with undisguised hatred.

'There's a much more ancient war raging than the one between petty, prejudiced, old men and what they fear.' Deimos scoffed. 'They are but a means to *her* end. One that has failed many times. This time will be different. *She* may have lost some of the battles, but she will win the war. With these.'

'Who is *she*?'

'Haven't you already guessed?' Deimos' mouth curled into a mocking sneer, the full length of his fangs showing, glee in his soulless eyes. An expression she had seen before.

The images of creatures roaming streets for victims to drain in another place, another time, returned to her, and she heard Clotho's voice in her head. *Creatures of Night and Destruction.* Her *soldiers*. Not Desdemona's. *She*.

Eyes cold as death opened in her inner mind amidst a face of ivory features. 'Atropos,' Charlie breathed, the final pieces falling together. 'You've done all this for her? Created half-breeds, groomed the rebels, trained me to—' Her words got stuck in her throat, a tear rolling down her cheek as she turned to Maddison. '*Everything* was lies, wasn't it? The prophecies? The three children born to the Fates, to stop Atropos?' She turned back to Deimos. 'Me, the child of Life, destined to set magic free?' There was no way these mutants – or any

Defective – would be free if she did this. 'You only told me that so I would connect with my magic? So that you could use me? Well, I'm sorry.' She spat at Deimos' feet and shook her head. 'I won't do it.'

In an instant, Deimos was by her side, his slender arms around her shoulders, first paternally like a father then tighter like a straitjacket.

'Oh, but you will. You see, the prophecies are real, which is why I've taken the necessary measures to protect my mistress.' He locked Charlie with his stare, and her vision began to swim, as if she were watching a faint glimpse of a film.

There was a room with axes and swords of iron, bronze, and steel hanging down from the roof where saddles and bridles should have hung. Partly hidden by racks of heavy vests and large shields was a large cell door with an observation window. Moving closer, she saw two familiar people on the other side: Caden and a girl looking like the one she used to draw, as if she had taken on a life of her own outside of the paper – her sister.

She was as filthy as her sheets, her thin white nightgown faded to yellow. This, Charlie realised with a bitter lump in her throat, only seemed to make her look more eerie and beautiful. Caden kneeled by her side, murmuring soft words while stroking her messy hair, shimmering like roasted chestnuts, with a gentleness that struck Charlie's heart. Was that... a tenderness she spotted in his eyes?

Something surprisingly akin to envy shifted inside her.

'Wake up, please,' whispered Caden, and a guilty pang hit Charlie as she realised she had not even considered that her sister could have been badly hurt. Dead, even.

No, not dead.

At the sound of Caden's voice, Sophie's nose wrinkled. Long-lashed eyelids fluttered open to reveal warm eyes like melted caramel. She gasped, her words coming out in a whisper. 'Please, help me.'

And then Charlie's sight returned to the arena, with Deimos' triumphant face before her.

'You have my sister?' she whispered. 'How?'

'Thanks to you of course. When you gave me that note, I made sure to send your friend here to collect her.' He motioned to Brimley, a statue by his side. No hint of emotion flashed across his wolfish features. No hint of his former self being present.

'So you see, my dear Charlie, you'll do this little favour for me, and if you can't or die trying, I'll add your friends to the mix, nurse your sister back to health, and have her do it.'

27

CLOTHO'S DUTY

SHE WAS GIVEN until sunset to finish the task. Not that Charlie knew what time it was and whether that meant an hour or a day; and not that she thought it would matter. She was only too glad Deimos had left the hall.

The moment they went, Charlie twirled on Maddison.

'You need to tell me everything. Now.'

'I had no idea that... that—'

'That your father is a monster? Your mother too?'

Maddison cringed at the word.

'You told me they were dead, remember? Ages ago! You said Brimley's parents had taken you with them to the UK from Norway after Atropos found yours hiding and killed them.'

'I thought she had! That's what Mrs Weston told me, but—'

'Well, they don't look dead to me!'

'But I saw *him* when I was looking through Doyle's memories.'

Charlie recalled the moment in their old living room, how Maddison had kneeled by the Withdrawer, eyes silver. 'You said he'd been at an orphanage.'

'I lied. I saw glimpses of my dad. Of a castle. Of Tyler. I knew

Tyler had spoken about a resistance building at Soli Gloria, that someone was teaching them, so I figured Doyle must have been sent to and withdrawn at Soli Gloria, and that my dad was there, teaching the rebels. It made perfect sense to me that he would be fighting against the Agnus Dei, not...' Tears ran down her chin.

'You know I have no reason to believe you anymore?'

Maddison nodded. 'It doesn't change the truth though.'

Charlie gritted her teeth, certain Maddison didn't know what truth was anymore.

'When I saw his werewolves attack Hallows Grove and you told me Sophie was there, I confronted him. But he used compulsion. I couldn't stop him after that.'

'That's your excuse, is it?' Charlie hissed. 'Has he used compulsion on your mother too? Because she forced me to awaken Atropos!'

There was a sharp intake of breath. 'You lie.'

'Come now, Maddison,' Tyler muttered. 'I think we've established the liar is you. Tell us what you know.'

Maddison scoffed bitterly. 'You don't know what you're talking about, none of you. My mother has always fought the Agnus! She's *always* fought Atropos. Atropos must have... *done* something to them when she captured them. Maybe they were experiments too!'

Tyler exhaled sharply, crossing his arms with a stubborn look on his face.

Charlie did not know whether she believed Maddison. She didn't even know if she cared. Parts of her felt like she wasn't present, merely watching it all from a distance. Tyler and Maddison as they kept yelling at one another. The mutants. Jaden staring into empty space. Fates. Creatures of Destruction. Creatures of Night. What mythology described as werewolves and vampires. There were a lot in her world that just *were* now, whether she believed in them or not.

After minutes with more quarrelling, Maddison threw her hands up. 'Whatever, just gang up on me.'

Charlie's body acted before her mind even registered what she was about to do. Her pointed knuckles swung up and landed a solid right hook under Maddison's chin. Shrieking, the raven girl lashed out as well, sinking her long nails into Charlie's shoulder, pulling her down to the floor.

She saw red.

An overflow of emotions erupted like a volcano, channelling into each blow all the guilt she'd felt when she'd failed Maddison's expectations. All the fear of being discovered by the Agnus and the pain induced when they had. All the heartache and grief and throbbing pain.

They were both yelling now, crying and screaming, tugging each other's hair, scratching, and punching.

'Get off! Get off! Get off!' Maddison roared and gave Charlie a rough shove to the chest, removing her momentarily – in dazed incredulity – before Charlie's anger returned and she leapt at her again, hissing like a wild cat.

'Alright, that's enough!'

Strong arms pulled them apart, Charlie snarling and Maddison panting behind a disarray of frazzled dark hair. While Jaden had grabbed a hold of Charlie, Tyler held Maddison, and the sight of her in his arms made Charlie's legs wobble and give way.

The raven girl tore herself free from Tyler's grip, checking the severity of her scratches. 'What are you having a go at me for?'

Charlie tasted salty tears running down her cheeks. 'Every time my life goes to shit, you're there! And it's your fault, and you don't even care. About anyone!' She pointed at Tyler, whose grave expression immediately changed to an awkward frown. 'You took him, and you... you broke my heart!' Large sobs ripped themselves from her chest, and she hid her face in the sleeves of her filthy nightgown. Jaden walked over to his brother, nudging him backwards to give them some space.

'Yes, I'm always there,' Maddison growled. 'When you finally made your escape from that god-awful place, I was there. When a werewolf attacked you, I was there. When you woke screaming in the night, afraid it was under your bed, I was there. When you needed someone to lie and tell you it had been mutts, I was there. For three years I've been there, and we were meant to take on the Agnus Dei together! Instead, you fell for my leftovers, some garbage not even worth a lick. It was only supposed to help your confidence. You weren't supposed to *fall* for him and forget about me!' Her nostrils flared as she paused, breathing hard. 'I did what I had to do so you'd see him for what he really is.'

'You *did* pretend to love him, so he'd leave me?'

Maddison barked out a humourless laugh. 'Tyler doesn't need *love* to go to someone's bed. He just needs someone stroking his ego, that's all.'

Tyler shifted behind them, shoulders hunching, and his brother looked at him soberly.

'Sounds like someone else I know,' Charlie hissed, her own conscience stinging at the venom in her voice.

Maddison's upper lip curled into a snarl. 'He's rubbed off on you already. You were always the better of us.'

Charlie stepped forward to lash out again when Jaden jumped between them.

'This isn't helping! You can beat each other up later, but I'd like to get out of here and make sure Vanilla is alright. So, can we please figure out how to do that?'

He was right. Presently, Charlie didn't know what she felt about Tyler or Maddison. But there were other innocent people she needed to focus on. Sophie. Caden. Jaden. Whatever she spent her time on until dawn would have to be to find a way of getting them to safety.

'Can we fight our way out?'

'If Caden had been here, perhaps. But I can't use my magic,' Tyler said between gritted teeth, as if it hurt him to admit how vulnerable he was.

Jaden sighed, scratching his head. 'I might have enough energy to kick up a sandstorm once the evil lord returns, but I think it would trip us up as much as them.'

They looked to Maddison, who stood with her arms crossed and chin raised, her pinched expression and matted appearance ruining the illusion of dignity. 'I can't manipulate the brutes. It must be something about their mutation. I don't know. There's no will there for me to bend.'

So, they had no powers. Which meant there was only one thing left to do.

Charlie turned and walked up and down amongst the tables, taking in the grotesque forms and the lives she would be condemning them to if she brought them back to life.

Long fingers encircled her wrist. 'Charlie, there's another thing I haven't told you,' Maddison murmured, so low it was as if she barely dared speak the words. 'Not long ago, I saw you waking Atropos. I saw... and I didn't want to believe it. I didn't want you to become stronger and make it real.'

Charlie said nothing, afraid what would come out if she opened her mouth. She thought she followed. If love made her stronger, and Maddison took it away, she would also become weaker.

'But now that we're here, Charlie, you have to do what they ask. If my parents are doing this, there must be a reason. Fate must run its course.' Maddison's eyes were round, deep, and desperate.

'As if she has to! We can't be dancing to their tune,' Tyler barked.

'Give her a break!' The harshness in Jaden's voice startled everyone. Maddison and Tyler blinked and shook their heads as though awakening from a stupor.

Charlie hurried away from them all, stopping next to a ginger-haired girl, about their age, whose whole body was almost completely covered in spiky red and white fur. Her heart sank, and she wanted nothing but to sink into the ground with it, bawling her eyes out. It was the yappy fox girl from Soli Gloria, the one who had thrown herself into the fight on their first night there. Would she ever have guessed that she would end up on a table, mutated, and having the rest of her fate decided by one of her classmates?

There was the sound of a limping step, and Jaden appeared next to her.

'You're the only one who can make this decision,' he said, pausing for a long time, as if trying to find the right words.

He looked at Tyler and Maddison standing silently apart, refusing to look at one another. 'Maybe I knew, although I wanted to believe better of him.' He sighed. 'I... I know I failed you. But if it'll help in any way, I'll stand by your decision today.'

Charlie let her eyes wander over a mutant. Ripped clothing hung loose where the person's muscles and limbs had taken on animalistic shapes. 'But you'll all be tortured and killed if I don't bring them to life. You'd really be okay with that?'

Jaden shrugged. 'If it's for the greater good. If it'll keep Vanilla safe in the future. There are worse ways to die than as a martyr.' He winked, but his smile didn't reach his eyes. She missed it, the warmth and laughter usually present in his twinkling circles of jade. The thought of that sparkle never returning tugged at her heart.

'Vanilla would be mad if she heard you talking like that, you know.'

'Yes, but she would understand. And so do we, so take your time and figure out what you think is right.' He patted her gently on her shoulder before returning to the others who'd now settled, shamefaced, onto the floor. They barely looked up as he reached them.

What *was* right?

Charlie turned back to the mutated shapeshifters spread out before her. On one hand, they had suffered enough. They *deserved* to rest in peace, and everyone else deserved to be protected from whatever hell would be unleashed if she awakened them. Deimos had said it himself. They needed the gift of Clotho to bring them to life. Maybe even heal them before they died if they tried to make more. She could refuse to use it, and his plan would end there.

On the other hand, so would her and her friends' lives too. And maybe they all were prepared to go to their graves with that knowledge, as martyrs, thinking they had died for something good. But that would only be the case if Deimos didn't use her sister.

Charlie sank to the floor, her back against one of the table legs, staring towards a circular window underneath the slanting roof of the arena.

She had no idea what moral compass her sister had. All she truly knew about her was that she had been raised by Desdemona along with Maddison, which was hardly a promising start. Either way, Sophie could be nursed back to health and forced.

Charlie wondered whether Caden had been placed in her cell to accomplish the first. His kindness alone... gods, she had only recently had her eyes opened to it, but her heart already ached with the regret that she had been blind to it. Blinded by Tyler treating her as if she was something special. She groaned internally and hid her face against her knees, wrapping them closer with her arms.

Special. "The child of Life". It all seemed so ridiculous now. More of a curse than a blessing; and remembering the pride she'd felt upon realising her heritage was equally painful to the humiliation she felt thinking of Tyler.

It had lit a hope in her. That her magic wasn't what she had been taught. That it wasn't dangerous, monstrous, or devilish, but pure. Godly. A saviour's magic. With her gifts, she could give people life. But this—Charlie looked towards the table ahead.

If she used her magic for this, no one would be safe. Deimos and the Agnus would never stop hunting Defectives and shapeshifters if this worked. And they, in turn, would be used to scare new people into the waiting arms of the Agnus, ready to hand them over to Atropos.

Atropos.

Charlie thought of the rebels and how quickly the Defectives at Soli Gloria had turned cruel in their revenge, fuelled by their power trip. It was nothing compared to the bitter bloodlust she had seen in Atropos' eyes in her mother's fresco. There was no doubt in her mind that if Atropos gained a big enough army, she would lay waste to the world as they knew it. She would not rest until everyone was under her control. Charlie's magic would not liberate Defectives as the prophecies had claimed, it would chain them to a fate worse than withdrawal. Like her friends.

But she did not want their blood on her hands either.

Many more could die if she brought the mutants back, yet... there was one undeniable fact: *could* was the key difference. Everything that could happen after she awakened the mutants were ifs and maybes. And any of it could happen without her if Deimos found another way. The only thing she knew for certain was that not doing anything would risk the lives of people she cared about, no matter how angry she was with some of them. Maybes would have to wait for later. Now she needed to rescue those she could by awakening the mutants. With magic.

A chill ran down her spine, followed by the sensation of cold, clammy hands tugging at her limbs as she realised it might not matter what decision she made. She might not be able to do it either way.

Reaching for her magic, she felt something, but that something quivered and hid like it had done since the uprising. Hiding underneath layers of shame and guilt.

She had believed helping the rebels with the uprising had been the right thing, yet everything had seemed to go wrong after it. Dia. Tyler. The attack. Atropos.

The latter by far the worst her magic had done. *But it* is *done.*

Perhaps the only way to make up for it was to use her magic for something good. Not only to save her friends but also to give the mutants a second chance. Who knew what side they would be on once they woke? Perhaps they would be grateful. And perhaps they wouldn't, but something occurred to her then. No one had ever described Clotho's magic as good. Good or bad, that wasn't her duty. Her duty was to create life. A duty that was now Charlie's, for better and for worse.

Her knowing turned swiftly into determination, spreading through her veins. *But* how *would she make her magic work?*

There was no mystery about why they had used her blood to

awaken Atropos rather than Sophie's. Hers would have been potent with magic, from a heart full of love – of hope – after seeing their mother. Orchestrated by Deimos, yes, but it was what had been needed. So how would she access her magic again without that love? When her heart felt like a cracked, empty shell? *Depleted, again.* She stared at one of the mutants, wishing it alive. Imagining her energy flowing through its body like she had imagined with the statue during the uprising.

Nothing happened.

She grabbed a handful of sand and chucked it away in frustration.

A second pair of footsteps sounded, and she wondered if Jaden had come to hear her decision. But it wasn't him.

'Hey, may I sit?' Tyler's voice was soft, barely audible, and she stared at him as if she hadn't heard. A visible flush crept over his neck and face as she didn't answer. 'Right...' His shoulders sagged, and he glanced towards the others, shifting as if to make his way back.

'You may,' she said into the void, hearing him stop. After a moment of hesitation, perhaps giving her the chance to change her mind, he sat down. But he didn't say anything. Not for a while.

'I never meant to hurt you, you know. Deimos told me a bit of romance would help you, but then you grew attached and... perhaps I let it go on longer than I should've. I guess the revelry and the bloodlust got to me as well.' He scouted the tables, a bleak tinge in his appearance. 'I've been a fool and a pawn in their game, haven't I? And I still don't understand how it happened.'

'They used your fear. All of ours. Even the Agnus'.' Charlie stared ahead, the steadiness of her words mirroring the certainty in her heart. The Agnus had always been about exerting power over the Defectives, yet Atropos had created their need for it. She remembered it now, from the fresco; the way Atropos would scheme and whisper in the ears of High Priests and dictators. 'That's why they've treated us this way. The Agnus. They've feared us. All this time they've tried to make others fear magic, but they truly do.' And the Agnus had started hunting them, just as she had seen in her mother's fresco.

They had made up lies so Defectives would believe themselves abominations. Shamed them and broken their spirits so they wouldn't fight back. But they had forgotten that violence also bred violence. She thought of Sister Rowena's teachings and of the rebels and their actions of revenge after the uprising. 'They've filled our hearts with hatred and our heads with suspicion so that we wouldn't know – wouldn't realise – that we're the same. Humans. Instead, we became precisely what they were afraid of.' She shook her head. 'And Atropos benefits from it all, playing us right into her trap. Silver lining is, we might not be abominations after all. Just pieces in a game of chess.'

'Not you though,' Tyler said, looking at her. 'You can decide the course from here on.'

She scoffed and dipped her chin. 'Are you saying it to sway my decision?'

Tyler chuckled, his smile genuinely amused. 'Jaden says he'll have Father remove my title if I try.'

'Right.' Charlie leaned her head back against the foot of the table. 'The royalty thing.'

Tyler regarded at her, perhaps deducing that Caden had told her. 'General, actually. He can do whatever he wants with my royal title.'

Always the soldier, Charlie thought, remembering what Jaden had said, and pressed her lips together. It was sad, really, if he did not see that he could be so much more.

Look who's talking, said her inner mini-self. And maybe that was the key. Maybe she did need to look at how she was talking to herself.

She believed herself entirely incapable, her magic depending on others' approval of her to use it. She believed it all too readily when Deimos had said that *love* was what she needed to do magic and that she couldn't do so without it. But was that the truth? Yes, her powers hadn't been strong, but they had been there at Hallows Grove even though she had spent every day emotionally neglected and worse. She thought of the state she had been in when she arrived at Soli Gloria as someone who, by all accounts, could be defined as withdrawn. She thought of Albin, determined to do magic again even though, for all they knew, he had withdrawn. How did they know that either of them had truly done so? How did they know that *anyone* had withdrawn?

They saw withdrawal like a sickness and the absence of magic as a symptom of it. But if a painter became ill, their talent of drawing wouldn't go away. If a writer lost their hands, it would not take away their ability to invent stories.

She had been incapable of doing magic at will, yet when she had needed it, it had come. Healing Doyle. Healing herself after the folly. Despite a lack of love, her magic had been strong enough to do *that*. How strong could it be if... if she believed it? If her body, mind, and soul worked together to make it happen?

She rose, taking Tyler by surprise, and strode back to the others with him stumbling to get up and follow.

'I need your help,' she said, hating the eagerness in Maddison's eyes.

'With what?'

'Did your mother ever tell you how Clotho would raise people from the dead?'

'She didn't. That was forbidden,' Maddison said instantly, then grimaced as though kicking herself. Great, so Charlie had to do something illegal as well. 'But she *created* life by placing energy into new lifeforms. It'd probably work the same way.'

'How?'

'She'd spin energy with her spindle, made of wood from the Tree of Life itself...' Maddison's voice trailed off.

Frowning, Charlie followed her line of sight towards her pin fastened to her dress, perfectly carved to resemble a spindle. 'This? It can't be... It's tiny!'

'Let your energy guide you; see if it can grow,' Jaden said, his eyes urging her on. 'If it is *the* spindle, surely it'll respond to you.'

Still uncertain, she unfastened the pin and held it in the palm of her hand. She didn't know where to begin but decided to let her instincts take the reins. Closing her eyes, a prayer took shape in her mind, like a whisper, and she felt her own blood carry it through her body. She began to itch, as though all the energy in her body was vibrating at a higher-than-normal frequency. She felt the wooden pin against her skin, the light weight of it, and imagined it growing. She pictured her energy pouring out of her pores and connecting with the energy within the pin.

Her hand became heavier.

Where before there had been what felt like an empty space, now a larger and sturdier object nestled in her grasp. She opened her eyes. A spindle, a rounded-rod, as sleek and smooth as though freshly made, lay in the pin's stead. Somehow it felt like her arm was complete, although she hadn't realised something had been missing.

'Clotho's spindle,' Maddison murmured in awe.

Charlie didn't need to ask what to do next. She had seen her mother at work. She took the spindle, already familiar in her grasp, and stood next to the first table, where the large black bull-boy lay on top. Warmth spread like a shawl over her shoulders and poured out of her like golden dust. *Time to wake... Batallion.*

The name came to her as a hunch, as if her mother was there, whispering in her ear. Telling her what to do. Holding the spindle high above the boy's mutated body, Charlie let go of it and stood back. It lingered in the air on its own. A thin glow connecting her to the spindle and the beast hung in the air like a spider's web, tying them together. She focused with all her might and visualised her magic working inside of the beast, kick-starting his heart and filling his lungs.

Again, nothing happened.

She found Tyler's eyes, a tingling sweeping across her face, shoulders, and arms. He gave her an affirming nod. *You got this.*

It sent a bolt through her chest, and she wanted to resist it, push it away, but instead she bit her teeth together and held it.

Her strongest source of magic was her emotions.

Emotions...

Emotions didn't have to be positive. They could be negative as well, and she had plenty of those, pent up in thoughts raging through her mind. Locked up in fear of what it would mean to let them loose. She unlocked that door now and thought of the heartache she had felt at Tyler and Maddison's betrayal. How everything around her had intensified, reminding her of all that she could not share with him again. The biting winter wind. The revellers' laughter underneath the night sky. The heat of bonfires upon her cheek. The smell of iron and wood. She felt her heart being torn in two, over and over again, begging for it all to be a bad dream. Begging that the way he looked at her now, in this moment, would never change. Had never changed. Begging that he was hers, not Maddison's.

She thought of her fight with the raven girl, every emotion still raw and trembling within her bleeding heart. She let all of it flow from her mind, acknowledging every hurt and how they ached as they went through her body, pooling into streams of energy.

A sharp wind whipped up a storm around them.

The hairs on her body rose, her hair twirling with the force around her. The golden thread between her, the spindle, and the beast glowed brighter – until it stopped and disappeared as if it had never been there, leaving her shivering and clinging to Tyler, who had swooped in to support her.

'Charlie,' Tyler whispered, but he wasn't looking at her. She followed his line of sight to the black face of the minotaur, its grey eyelids opening to reveal pitch-black eyes. Batallion's nostrils flared tentatively, testing the novelty of breathing again.

Tyler exhaled sharply, his face lit with wonder, as though he had not quite believed she could do it. Perhaps he hadn't. It did not change the fact that *she had*. She, Charlie, had brought a creature – a huge one at that – back to life. She allowed herself to exhale and step closer.

Batallion's hand flew out and caught her throat.

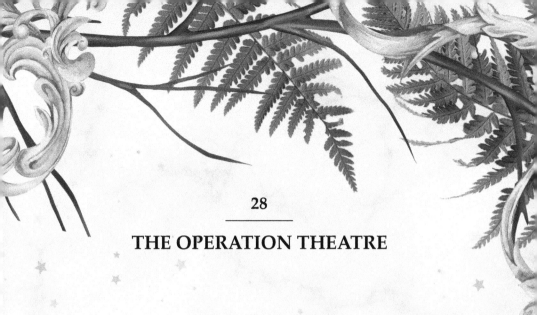

28

THE OPERATION THEATRE

CHARLIE'S EYES rolled into the back of her head, and everything dimmed. The others cried out, the sound of their voices drifting in and out along with her awareness. A sharp crack, like wood splintering, was the last thing she heard before the world came rushing into focus at a dizzying speed. Her lungs couldn't cope with the onslaught of air forcing its way back into her body, and she dropped to her knees, clutching her bruised throat. Her shaky limbs took their time to obey even the simple command to sit up.

Thick roots had erupted out of the table and tied around the beast's arms and legs like ropes, pinning him in place. His large nostrils flared with every heavy breath. Jaden relaxed, wiping his forehead.

Tyler kneeled in front of her. 'Are you alright?'

She nodded, still too weak and shaken to do anything but breathe. Her throat sore and scratchy.

'Good.' He helped her up. 'Because you've got plenty more to go.' Her stomach dropped.

. . .

Time became insignificant as they kept on. She didn't know if it was night or day outside, and with every resurrection she grew certain that she would not survive the next. Each one took its toll on her. At one point, Maddison went off to have a second go at reaching Brimley's mind through the walls and whatever space lay between them, but she returned with a defeated expression. Instead, she sat down and took Charlie's hand. 'Let's see if my energy can help yours. Channel it, what little is there.'

Having no time to waste on pettiness, Charlie thought back to her meditation exercises and reached for the glowing force within Maddison. She pictured it with her mind. It felt temperamental, and she imagined her own energy patiently coaxing it to connect with hers. Strength flooded to her as she succeeded.

Soon the boys joined in, each taking a shift and sleeping in between, making the task feel more bearable, although she didn't know how long it would last.

By the time Deimos walked in with Brimley and a group of men clothed in Agnus robes, Charlie was huddled in Maddison's lap, weeping and shivering while Maddison stroked her hair. Asleep by their side, the boys were roused awake. Twenty-three beasts lay breathing on the tabletops, bound by wooden ropes. Brimley and his crew were ordered to release them.

'Line up!' barked Deimos, his smirk growing fanatically as the mutants did as they were told. Next to Charlie was the fox-girl, standing motionless on command with blank, emotionless eyes.

What have I done?

'Perfection.' Deimos licked his lips and stooped over Charlie, picking up the spindle, forgotten on the floor. With feeble attempts, she tried to grab for it, but it was fruitless.

'Very clever, Charlie. Where there's a will, there's a way.' He looked at her then, like he'd done in his office, as if he was saying more than he let on. 'You know, I do think that with your blood, we can do this without you. The spindle will be a good precaution though, should we push the shifters' bodies too far again.'

Without answering her questioning frown, Deimos rose and addressed Brimley, gesturing to the mutants. 'Prepare them for battle. They shall march upon Soli Gloria first thing in the morning! Our mistress needs this army to grow *bigger!*'

'No!' Wobbling like a baby deer testing its legs for the first time, Charlie tried to stand up – only held up or back by Maddison grabbing onto her arm.

Deimos shot them a glare and snapped his fingers, ordering guards to their sides. Her fragile bones felt like they were being ground to dust underneath Brimley's grip.

'What are you doing? Let us go!' Charlie yelled.

'Let you go? I think not.'

Charlie stared at Deimos, baffled. 'What do you mean? You promised!'

'Did I?'

Desperately, Charlie combed through her mind, palpitations attacking her heart once it dawned on her that he never had; he had said what he would do if she had not wakened the mutants, but that was about it. Going limp in Brimley's arms, Charlie cast one last look at the mutant line-up as she was pulled out of the arena and into the stables. Her thoughts stilled into a numb mass, her body weak with exhaustion and capitulation. The others kicked and shouted profanities to their own guards, but the Agnus men simply ignored them, forcing them down the concrete alley, past animal boxes and cells reeking of urine and decay, up a rusty old staircase, and onto the second floor.

Heavy sheets of dirty plastic hung from the ceiling, casting an ominous air around the room. She could see shadows moving behind the thick material, setting off an alarm in her head.

An Agnus Brother brushed the sheet aside as they slipped through between two folds, and Maddison buckled over and vomited.

More tables lined the room; steely ones with odd machines and instruments ticking and whirring next to their respective tables. Most tables were empty, save for patches of dried blood and things Charlie would rather not identify. Others were occupied with a few lifeless bodies, sprawled on top like grotesque pieces of carved meat dishes. Youths and children who had not transformed. Failed experiments. Tubes attached to needles pumped green and yellow liquid into the veins of their buckled arms. Their heads wore crowns of metal, ornamented with screws fastened to their skulls. They still sparked.

One or two tables were crowded by people with clipboards in their hands and a mystified, calculative expression in their eyes, taking note of young ones gasping towards the roof – not quite dead but begging to be.

Charlie felt drowned by panic as their new fate became apparent. She hadn't won their freedom. Not one of them. The Agnus would experiment on them, torture them, and either transform or kill them. Ice filled Charlie's stomach, but she was too drained to fight back. She heard the others hissing and spitting as they were each laid and bound upon a table, but her eyes remained fastened on the curtains of plastic, imagining someone coming to their rescue, already giving up that anyone actually could.

She had tried. She had fought. And she would, most certainly, never know her sister. Most likely, she was too late. The fate she was about to meet was already hers; but at least in death they would be united.

A tear rolled down her cheek as a woman dressed in a lab coat fastened a metallic headband around her skull and stuck needles into her arms. Her teeth were chattering. She sensed the despair from the others and felt it wash over her like grave dirt. Somewhere close, Jaden started whispering his goodbyes to Vanilla, as if his mere love for her could be carried with the energy in the air and find her wherever she was. Charlie doubted anything that pure could move beyond these walls.

From the corner of her eye, she saw another man in a lab coat walk to a panel of buttons and switches.

'Charlie,' Maddison whimpered. Whether she was at the table

next to her or farther away she could not tell, her head firmly bound to the table. 'I'm so sor—'

A chorus of howls and screams erupted as the first bolts of power shot through their brains. It felt much like the force that had blasted her body when they walked through the passage between Saltram Park and Soli Gloria, only concentrated to their heads. Her sight went blindingly white, and something wriggled inside of her, like a beast on fire trying to break free. Licks of heat curled upwards and stretched into her limbs and joints, grabbing hold of her nerves and muscles. Then she went cold. Through blurry tears, she saw the man pausing at the switch panel, as if listening for something.

She listened too. To the faint and raspy breathing of the others. The murmurs of the ones with clipboards as they discussed the results. The roar of a lion. The—

Wait.

At first, she thought it was her imagination. *But there!* She heard it again.

Yelling filled the corridor on the other side of the double doors. Charlie's eyes flickered to the other tables, but the prisoners were still, listening as intently as she was. Loud bangs erupted, and the commotion increased in volume. Clunks of metal against metal mixed with a bashing and smashing.

The Agnus Brothers who had led the group to the operation theatre ran towards the staircase to investigate, but no sooner had they reached it than one of them toppled over backwards, his scream drowned out by a booming roar. A massive golden lion with a wild mane and gigantic paws pinned him to the floor, roaring once more, sending the other Agnus men fighting to descend the stairs first. They soon returned, a bunch of grey-cloaked men and women following at their heels, overpowering them with slight effort. Seeing its comrades, the lion stepped off the pinned man and let a red-bearded man take care of him instead. Then the lion set its golden eyes upon the youths on the tables and the laboratorians huddled together behind them.

With a shake of its fur, the beast transformed into a short, elderly man, his mane of dark auburn hair hanging heavy on his shoulders.

Bes!

Caden's butler. Her grandfather.

'Are you hurt?' he asked, leaving the utter surprise in her eyes unanswered.

She shook her head, too stunned for words, as he unbuckled her from her restraints and removed the tubes.

'Good. I believe this is yours?' He snapped his finger at one of his comrades who immediately stepped up by his side, handing him a wooden object. Her spindle. Questions milled in her mind about how he had retrieved it. Had he fought Deimos? Was Deimos hurt? Dead? But Bes did not give her the chance to ask.

'Order it to shrink and make sure it's well attached. There'll be chaos once we step outside these walls, and the spindle will need to come with us. Do you understand?'

She nodded and did as told, pinning it as securely as she could while grey-cloaks ordered the lab-coats to release the others.

'We need to move quickly,' Bes said. 'While we have the element of surprise.'

Everyone started moving without question, leaving only a few men to tie up the laboratorians and Agnus Brothers, when Charlie put on the brakes. 'We need to get a couple of our friends. My sister and Caden.'

Tyler and Jaden went extremely pale at their brother's name but clenched their jaws decidedly as Bes' eyes met theirs. They would not leave without him.

'Do you know where they are?' Bes asked.

'In an armoury, I believe.'

'I saw it on the way here,' the red-bearded man said, carrying Maddison in his arms. She seemed barely able to keep her eyes open, her dark, raven hair matted against her sweaty forehead.

'Then we'll get them on our way out,' Bes said.

They moved quickly down corridors, passing more cells. One

wooden door stood ajar, exposing a cadaver. For a brief second, Doyle came to mind, and her mouth filled with acid. Then she was pulled along by her grey-cloaked saviours.

Mutants and Agnus Brothers had caught up with them now, and the group of rescuers fought valiantly to hold them back – their eyes wide with disbelief at what they were seeing. Still, they did not let it distract them from making balls of fire leap from the torches, and the walls and floors to shiver and groan as wind howled through the hall. *They're all Defectives*, Charlie realised. *Adult Defectives.* Her own hands started to itch for something to protect herself with.

That's when she spotted the glint of a blade and snuck through a door slightly ajar. She beckoned for Jaden and Tyler to follow her, and soon found themselves surrounded by the same weapons she had seen in the vision Deimos showed her. Her eyes landed on the door, and she contemplated how Deimos could have shown her a fake image. What if it was a trap? And something far worse awaited them? A mutated Sophie? Caden? She did not know if either of them was a shapeshifter, but it did not mean they weren't.

'Whew, someone hasn't left the Age of Crusaders behind,' murmured Tyler, picking up an old-fashioned nail bat and waved it at Jaden. 'How primitive.'

'Ty?' said a voice, and Charlie picked up a small dagger as a reflex. Looking back at them between the bars of the window was Caden, and Charlie exhaled in relief.

Without even attempting to break the lock, Jaden put both his palms against the door and closed his eyes, connecting with the wood it was made of. It creaked and rumbled until it fell in planks and wooden pieces to the floor, revealing Caden with Sophie in his arms.

'Took you long enough,' he said, but his eyes were void of snark.

'Doesn't seem like you minded.' Tyler's eyes rested on Sophie.

Jaden rolled his eyes. 'You ready to get out of here?'

'Thought you'd never ask.'

'Great, but Tyler needs to carry her. We need your powers, Caden, for what's waiting outside.' Caden did as he was told, but tension emitted between the brothers as Sophie's body exchanged arms.

'Don't you drop her or leave her behind,' Caden hissed, and Tyler's features darkened in indignation.

'I wouldn't.'

Caden didn't seem convinced, but they all left the armoury still – and not a moment too late.

Batallion bellowed as the group shot before him and then kept on running, but he was quickly on their tail. Now and then, Caden sent a purple orb in his direction, but they only seemed to daze him.

'He's too strong!' Caden called and sped up.

'There's the exit!' cried Charlie, and they burst through the double barn doors, barely registering the golden beast waiting outside.

Back in his lion form, Bes leapt at Batallion, claws slashing, until he was aided by the rest of his group, giving the youths a moment to pause and catch their breath. Or so they thought.

Charlie had barely managed to gulp down a batch of fresh air when a soft snarl reached her ears. The man carrying Maddison shouted for Charlie to get behind him before his voice changed from a rough warning to a high-pitched cry of recognition.

'Roxy!'

He put Maddison down on wobbly legs and held out his arms to the fox-girl padding towards him, like a father about to embrace his long-lost daughter. Roxy cocked her russet head to one side, her ears prickling. It was monstrous to see how much of her human features were still evident in her mutated appearance. Slowly, she approached his outstretched hands, carefully sniffing the air.

The man's eyes shimmered with tears. Tears, perhaps, at what she had become, and Charlie felt the stab of guilt deep in her bones. Then she shrieked.

Rising like a human girl, Roxy leapt into her father's arms in a hurl of red and snapped her glistening jaws around his thick neck. Blood gushed from the puncture wounds, spraying Charlie's nightdress with scarlet blobs. Someone pulled her arm and forced her to run, but she could barely gather her legs. The man's screams were just a thick gurgle as Charlie doubled over, stumbling against a ball of hay. Maddison was by her side before she hit the ground.

'Come on, you need to hurry!' She pulled Charlie to her feet, nearly falling over herself. Then she grappled with the chain around her neck, lifting her necklace over her head and fastening it around Charlie's instead.

'What are you doing?'

'I need to figure out how to save my mother. This is hers, take it. Now, remember, "Fate *must* run its course", but *where there's a will, there's a way.*' She held Charlie still and paused for a moment before pulling her in for a hug. 'He is not worthy of you,' she whispered into her hair, 'but neither am I. I'm so sorry for everything. Now go!'

She pulled them apart and pushed Charlie onwards, shouting for her to run. When Charlie looked back over her shoulder, however, Maddison had not moved. Instead, she stood with eyes completely white and blood pouring out of her ears, the Agnus Dei slowing down behind her. At the sign of her overexerting her magic, Charlie realised she was attempting to keep everyone back so she and the others could escape.

Charlie opened her mouth to protest, but a man rammed into her and tossed her over his shoulder. She screamed and struggled, but the stranger was completely oblivious to her pounding fists. As he carried her towards the trees, she watched Maddison growing smaller in the distance, a glint of steel in her hand. Instantly, Charlie realised she was no longer carrying the dagger she picked up in the armoury. Would Maddison use it to defend or harm herself? Would Charlie even see her again?

The fragmented light of the forest glimmered through Charlie's tears as the trees closed in, and the sound of her own cry lingered in the hollow of Charlie's broken heart, like a wind wailing through shattered windows.

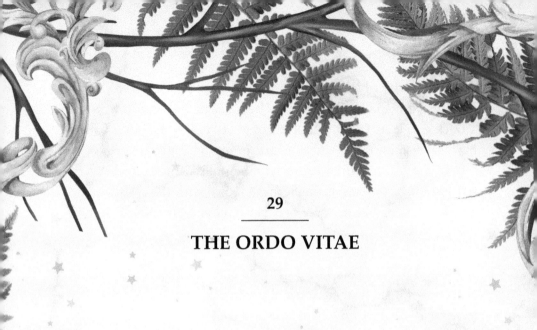

29

THE ORDO VITAE

CHARLIE LIFTED her head and rubbed her face, her skin tight over her tear-stained cheeks. The steady rhythm of her carrier's movements slowed down, the muscles of his shoulder relaxing slightly, her body bouncing less as he trudged along. Majestic trees creaked above her as squirrels leapt between their branches. Several flickers of sparkling orange appeared behind their trunks. A camp.

Some people sat next to the fire; others were busy around small tents pitched nearby like wayfarers. All wore grey cloaks, except for her classmates from Soli Gloria.

Her carrier stopped before Bes and Caden, who helped lower her down. Swaying on the spot, Charlie let herself be led over to the bonfire and had a cup of hot soup thrust into her hands. She looked up, right into a familiar, kind face framed by bobbing white curls.

'Sister Rowena! What are you doing here?'

'Oh, my dear, that is a long story,' the school nurse said, exchanging a soft, pensive glance with Bes.

'I saw the werewolves run off with you, so I slipped into my form – I'd be quite vulnerable in this old body, you know – and followed after.'

'Your form?' Charlie stuttered, her eyes heavy from all the crying.

Sister Rowena faced her but said nothing, and little by little, Charlie could see her face start to shift. Her nose turned flat, extending with her jaw, and the soft down hair on her face grew longer and golden. Both Charlie and Caden jumped as her claws scraped at the metallic cup in her hands before her nails returned to the regular human shape of white crescents.

'You were the big cat.' Charlie shuddered, staring at Sister Rowena once again looking like her regular self. 'The one that went into the woods the day we arrived. A lioness.'

Sister Rowena dipped her chin, and Bes put his arm around her. Two lion-shifters.

'You know each other well, don't you?' Charlie asked, taking in the closeness between them. The new sparkle in Sister Rowena's eyes.

'We are husband and wife,' said Bes, pausing.

Caden let out a low whistle, looking as equally taken by surprise as Charlie.

'When I saw that they were taking you to that old stud farm, I sent note for Bes and the rest of the Order,' Sister Rowena added, and Charlie was reminded of the letter she had pocketed earlier this winter. So, it was Bes she had corresponded with.

'The Order?' Charlie croaked.

Bes gave one firm nod. 'This is the Ordo Vitae, the Order of Life. Your mother's Order from the time of the Salem witch-hunts. Unfortunately, there's not many of us left, and we're spread out across the world.'

'All of you have been members from the beginning?'

'Only me and Beset.' He smiled solemnly, putting a hand on his wife's knee.

Charlie nodded, as if accepting the age of the people before her to be several hundred years was normal. But she supposed with mutated mythological creatures and Fates walking the Earth, it was just another thing that could be.

She took a sip from her cup, letting the hot fluid slip down her throat. 'And you're my grandfather.'

'Wait, what?' Caden asked, looking from one to the other, before shifting uncomfortably in his seat as it dawned on him that this talk was far more private than that between strangers meeting in the night.

Bes didn't deny it. Nor did he apologise for leaving her at the doorstep of Hallows Grove, which she presumed had been him. She did not return his smile but turned to her school nurse instead.

'Does that make you my grandmother?'

Sister Rowena – or Beset, apparently (*That'll take some getting used to,* Charlie thought) – gave a small nod while frowning slightly. 'I know, there's a lot I should have told you—'

'My father... what is he?'

'A demi-god, like us,' Rowena replied, faltering at her abruptness.

Charlie scoffed. 'Should've been harder to kill, then.'

A pained expression came over Bes, and he sighed, showing his first sign of regret. 'I shouldn't have looked back. How long have you remembered that moment?'

'I only just recently remembered it, so you're fine.'

His voice hardened then, perhaps aggrieved by her tone. 'Then you should know it was their way of protecting you, by sacrificing themselves.' Bes shook his head, and the light of the fire cast shadows over the odd wrinkles in his face. He looked more like a lion now than ever before. It should have unnerved her, but she was tired of being frightened.

'If you say so. I need to see my sister. Where is she?'

Caden, who'd remained awkwardly silent since the revelation of their family ties, offered to take her to her sister's tent. They left the old demi-gods sitting on their lumber seat, staring into the fire, and some part of her felt sorry for the cold front she had created between them. Then she reminded herself once again that one had left her at Hallows Grove and the other had kept secrets from her, and the little guilt became easier to bear as they walked towards her sister's tent.

'When we first came to Soli Gloria, I heard you tell Bes you wanted to help him. Was that with the Order?'

'Yeah,' Caden said, pine needles crunching under his feet. 'They've been trying to trace the children abducted ever since the first attack at Nettleheys to figure out who and what was behind it. Now I understand why. I had no idea Bes had a family of his own.'

Had *is the word*, Charlie thought as they stopped outside one of the tents. She stared at it as if it were a Fury.

Concern crept over Caden's features, perhaps wondering if she would treat Sophie the same way she had treated her grandparents. 'She's here, but she might be sleeping. It looks like she's been through hell. Go easy on her.'

'Don't worry,' Charlie said, reaching for the flap of the tent. 'She didn't leave me at an orphanage.'

Once inside, Charlie started thinking coming had been a big mistake. At first, it seemed as if her sister was sleeping, but then her eyes opened, and she simply watched her without a word. She had a delicate face punctuated with feline doe-eyes and a button nose like their mother. She was stunning. Already, Charlie could feel jealousy churning deep, deep within her. Jealousy for this person everyone had been looking for, even though Charlie had been around. This person they had all whispered about and who seemed to possess Caden's protection already.

She wanted to ask where she had been all these years, how she was separated from Maddison, and why she had ended up at Hallows Grove. But all of those questions seemed too big to push upon her now. They had time. Time to get to know each other and time to feel love for one another – if they ever could. Time to be a family again.

'How are you?' Charlie asked the first question that would come out.

'Alive,' Sophie murmured through chapped lips.

'Yeah... Do you know why? Do you know why he didn't torture you?'

Sophie shrugged, pulling her sleeping bag closer around her. 'He tried but said I was too weak and that I was worth more alive, either to force your hand or keep me as backup if you failed.'

Charlie's jaw tightened. 'I didn't fail.'

'I'm sorry about that.'

They stared at one another in understanding; an understanding that they both knew what they were capable of, who their mother was, and the responsibility that lay upon their shoulders. It was the kind of understanding in which a silent awkwardness grew, and Charlie excused herself, going outside, craving the easier conversation that seemed to flow between her and someone she knew, like Caden. But Caden had returned to the bonfire and was eagerly catching up on everything with Jaden. Opposite them sat Bes, with his arm around Rowena. *Beset*. Her grandmother.

Charlie marched towards them.

'Why didn't *you* tell me?'

Rowena stood up, hands folded over her chest. 'For your own protection, love – and mine.' She frowned. 'I haven't been a spy all these years by being careless.' Then, as if seeing Charlie better, she added more softly, 'Dear child, you need to rest.'

Shaking her head, Charlie stepped back, voice cracking with exhaustion. 'No, we need to go. Deimos will attack Soli Gloria with the mutants. We need to protect the others.' She wrapped her arms around herself, her teeth chattering. Fatigue wasn't helping at keeping her blood circulation going.

Bes' forehead wrinkled in concern. He murmured something to a man by his side and nodded. 'Very well. We'll just have a quick rest and recharge and see to any injuries.' He eyed her shivers. 'And then we shall hurry. Hopefully we'll be strong enough if it comes to a battle.' His features filled with sadness. 'We lost a few good people in the rescue mission. Nothing could have prepared them for seeing their long-lost children transformed into such beasts.'

Charlie thought of the bearded man and the fox-girl, Roxy, and swallowed the bile building within her. It was her fault. She had brought their children back to life as monsters. Rowena mistook the paling colour of her face to be a sign of her fatigue.

'You best pick that tent; it's closest to the fire. Sleep now. You'll need your energy when we leave.'

Charlie obeyed, though she doubted she would manage to rest at all. And yet, she fell asleep as soon as her head hit the pillow.

———

The fire was still crackling when she woke, guarded by Bes.

'I'm glad to see they fit,' he said, meaning the cotton shirt, deer-skin trousers, woolly cloak, and leather armour she had found on the floor of her tent. Now she saw she wasn't the only one who had been distributed new clothing. Everyone in the camp was wearing the same clothes. *A new Order, a new uniform*, Charlie thought, accepting her breakfast.

Shoving a spoonful of porridge into her mouth, she spent the better part of five minutes trying to chew and swallow while Bes watched her. Another ten minutes of tense silence followed – in which Rowena had joined them and added to the tension – before Charlie put down her bowl and stood from her seat. 'Think I'll go catch the sunrise somewhere,' she said and turned her nose towards the woods before anyone could say anything or try to stop her.

Just outside the clearing, when she could no longer hear the bustling of the camp or feel eyes at the back of her neck, Charlie paused in her tracks, let her shoulders sag, and looked up to the sky. Exhaling, she uttered a soft thanks to the gods above.

Fresh air filled her lungs and circulated through her body with every breath, leaving her with the wet dew of dawn hanging in the air. Then she kept wandering down a path dividing thin banks of grass covered in blankets of snow, passing evergreen trees and trees undressed by winter. Here and there, snowdrops had sprung forth, signalling spring's budding defiance against winter. She picked one up and put it behind her ear, feeling the clouds in her mind ease little by little as she trudged past heather and bushes.

At last, she spotted a rocky outcrop and marked it for her solitude. But someone else had beat her to it. Tyler turned his head as she came up behind him.

'No sleep for the haunted?' he asked.

She shook her head and sat down next to him, folding the thick cloak around herself. He was so familiar, with his black hair standing on edge and blue eyes twinkling harder than the streetlights below. But he also seemed like a ghost of who he'd been before the rebellion. She supposed she looked different too; it was hard to imagine anyone coming back from what they had experienced without a few alterations. Physical or psychological.

Stepping to the edge, she gazed down at the spread of grey brick houses, tall buildings, and a church spire in the midst of it all. She hadn't realised just how close to civilisation they were.

'Plymouth,' Tyler said. 'We'll be back at Soli Gloria in no time.'

Saltram Park lay east of the city centre, and from her perch she could just about make out its undulating expanse, slumbering in the tranquil hours of the dawn. She had forgotten how much she enjoyed these hours before sunrise; a new day, a blank page, with no colour to taint it yet. She preferred it that way. Simple. It felt like a gift. Occasionally, the sky would treat them to some of its raindrops too, leaving the air thick with the smell of petrichor and new promises.

'Maddison, did she ...' His words were barely audible, as if he didn't dare to say them.

Her heart skipped a beat in dismay and then guilt. 'I don't know.' She shrugged. 'She stayed behind to save her mother.'

His body slumped slightly forwards, as if he was going to hide his face in his hands but stopped himself from it. Was it because Charlie was sitting there? 'She always had a warrior heart.'

Even now, in the midst of her sadness, it stung to hear him speak so reverently of Maddison – and not her – which ignited a whole new tidal wave of guilt. How trivial and petty all their issues seemed now that she could be gone. Or dead, even. The vial of her necklace hung heavy against Charlie's chest.

'Yes,' she whispered. 'Yes, she did.'

'At least she managed to get you to safety. I didn't think she had it in her,' he said.

Charlie almost gave herself whiplash turning to look at him, eyes wide. 'How can you—'

He shifted with a grimace and shrugged. 'We are selfish beings, she and I.' He paused, rubbing the back of his neck and staring at the lights below. 'I'm not proud of how we—how I—treated you. It wasn't right. None of it. But,' he added, most likely seeing the spark of hope come alight in Charlie's eyes, 'I probably wouldn't have done anything differently given the chance. I'm not a good guy, Charlie.'

Her heart ached. He'd done so much to confirm what he said that it struck home. On the other hand, she also didn't want to believe that she had once fallen for a guy with no goodness in his heart. She thought of the faith he had inspired within her, of the care he showed whenever he trained the rebels – it was hard to believe that someone like that was a "bad" guy. There had to be something good, hiding deep inside of him, and the lost expression in his eyes only supported her theory.

'I don't believe that.'

'You should. You deserve better.'

She didn't know what to say to that, so they sat in silence, caught somewhere between something old and something new, while they watched the sun break through the grey dawn. As the rain started falling in earnest, Tyler patted her arm and stood up to go and get an hour's sleep. Her head full of thoughts, she continued to watch the shifting horizon and listen to the rain, reminding herself of her meditation exercises. *Inhale through the nose, exhale through the mouth – be in the moment.* She wasn't sure when they started, but she could hear the birds chirping clearly now. A gentle smile formed on her lips; apparently, even on rainy days, you could still hear the birds sing if you listened closely.

30

THE BATTLE OF SOLI GLORIA

Saltram Park.

Charlie struggled believing it had only been about three months since she and Maddison had looked upon it from the car park. Three months since she had eyed the passer-by with desperation, hoping that he would see more than just a girl on a field trip. The feeling of Maddison's reassuring touch as they walked towards the folly still lingered on her skin, mingling with the cold breeze.

But they weren't walking that way this time. Instead, they found themselves on the other side of the river – nearly dried up by the ebb of the tide – observing Saltram from the Laira Embankment.

'We need to find another way to the passage,' Bes said, conferring with one of his co-leaders of the Order. 'There might be guards stationed along the path, and they'll warn the opposition that we're coming.' The other man dipped his head in agreement and appeared to think of a solution. The rest of the Ordo Vitae waited with bated breath, staring ahead at Saltram Park on the other side of the shallow river. For most of them, what lay beyond had only been a rumour.

Jaden turned to Tyler. 'What about going by the sea, like the werewolves did?'

'We'd spend all our energy swimming from the sea passage to the beach. Besides, we'd need a boat just to get to the passage, and if we had one, we might as well take it over this river.'

'We do have one,' Caden said, eyes on a large object looking as if it had been washed ashore on the embankment years and years ago. Determined, he waded his way through the mud over to a de-masted hull – the remains of a fishing ketch which most definitely had seen better days. The smell of murky water and decaying wood tore at their noses as they all moved closer, but Caden merely grinned. 'A fine beauty, *Miss Antelope*, is she not? She's seen a thing or two in her days. Maybe we'll show her a third.'

Charlie saw it then, a reluctance, just before he squeezed his eyes shut and focused, hiding it. They all remained quiet watching him gather his powers until he gasped and collapsed knee-first into the mud.

'Caden!' Jaden ran to his brother, hunched down, and grasped his shoulder. But Caden only shrugged him off and stood up again. Breathing hard, he then proceeded to shut his eyes one more time and raised his palms towards the hull.

The Ordo Vitae exchanged confused glances, and Charlie caught herself biting her lip. Then the air turned thick and clammy.

The hair on her arms rose as a dense fog rolled in above the river surface, painting everything around them in a ghostly light. Gentle at first, then harsher.

A collective intake of breath followed the sound of breaking water.

A thin gleam appeared in the midst of the *Antelope*, the January night dimming as the light grew stronger, folding outwards until the fishing ketch was veiled in a silvery glow.

The smell of ancient dust and sea spray wafted towards them, and Charlie could have sworn she heard seagulls cry in the distance as the boat stood before them like it would have a hundred years ago, before it began to rot.

Jaden whistled, his eyes radiating with delight. 'I'll never get used to that!'

A man, his features shimmering in and out of focus in the same ghostly light as the boat, stood on the *Antelope's* deck. 'Who are you to disturb my sleep, young man?'

'I'm Caden McFade, and these are my comrades.'

'If you say so,' answered the ghost. 'But *why* are you disturbing my sleep?'

'We need to cross the river.'

The ghost shook his head. 'I'm afraid my sailing days are over – you shall have to take the highroad, like the others do.'

Charlie contemplated whether she would have to bribe him with the promise of a new life. *Could* she even bring a ghost back to life? She had no idea.

'It has to be this way. The other way is treacherous for us,' Caden said.

'And yet the tide moves for no one,' chuckled the old sailor, his beard flopping lifelessly against his see-through chest.

'It will for me,' Tyler said and held out his palm towards the river. In one quick motion, he closed his hand, and the group stepped back as the water rose and sloshed, threatening to wash over the tips of their shoes. Through the back of his head, Charlie could see the ghost's mouth drop open at the water now high enough for the boat to cross without scraping its bottom on the riverbank.

The sailor turned wide-eyed as the rising stopped. 'Now's not the time to be sleeping.' Awe slurred his voice.

He beckoned them all on board the *Antelope*. While her floors looked like vapours of smoke, Charlie set foot on solid ground. Thick waves lapped against the boat's side as they drifted across the river. By some miracle, the boat was large enough to contain them all.

As they sailed, the ghost scrutinised Tyler and Caden. 'You're some of those lost ones, aren't you? They spoke of you being sent to a school around here, back in my days when I was a handsome fella such as yourself.'

Caden shrugged. 'I certainly feel lost,' he muttered, low enough so that only Charlie heard.

She studied him, her hair flickering in her face, and realised how troubled he seemed. Was it because he had used magic? She made a mental note to tell him everything that had come to pass at the experimental station. Perhaps it could ease his mind about being a Defective too. *A Magling*, Charlie corrected herself. Maddison had been wrong, but she had been right too. If she wanted to be one, Charlie needed to change the belief ingrained in her: that having magic made her broken somehow.

'If I could control the waters,' said the sailor, 'I would be king of the sea.'

At that Caden snorted. 'Yeah, you and Tyler both.' Then his features paled, looking mortified.

'Brother,' Jaden urged, apparently having observed Caden too. 'What is it?'

'I sense another spirit. A familiar one.' His words were barely a whisper, his eyes sparkling with flickers of silver, locked onto the bank of Saltram Park. But there was no one there.

'Who?' Charlie asked, looking at Caden with concern. Was he hallucinating? Had he used too much of his powers? They had yet to stop and disembark; it would not do if Caden collapsed on them now. But his stare remained transfixed on a spot in front of the rock wall, just to the right of the folly.

'It's trying to connect.' He closed his eyes and focused intensely. A shimmer materialised, taking the form of a petite female.

Charlie's breath caught in her throat as she heard Rowena's gasp behind her. 'Goddess!'

The girl's features were excruciatingly familiar, despite her washed-out appearance. Her once strawberry blonde hair was drained of colour, now undistinguishable from her silvery-blue complexion.

'Gilly,' Charlie whispered, tears filling her eyes.

'What's wrong?' asked Bes, joining them at the front of the *Ante-*

lope, stopping next to Tyler and Sophie, who were quietly observing. His stern eyes opened wide, and he looked to Rowena as if she could confirm what he was seeing.

They were a quiet bunch moving onto shore and disembarking, nearing Gilly in a grave manner once Caden had returned the sailor-ghost to his realm. She became more solid after that, with Caden's energy solely focused on her.

'How?' Charlie asked, her voice barely a whisper.

'It happened during the werewolf attack,' Gilly answered, her own voice like a fading echo. She swallowed. 'I was running for help when one of the werewolves jumped me.'

Vividly, the image of Gilly running out of the castle, calling for her, emerged from Charlie's consciousness.

'I didn't suffer,' Gilly said, urgently. 'And I have something much more important to tell you. Mother Ratchford took over the school again after the attack, but something else changed this morning. It's as if a dark shadow has come over the place; the energy is all sorts of wrong.'

Charlie exchanged glances with Tyler. Had Deimos reached Soli Gloria before them? It was more than possible if he set out the moment they made their escape.

Gilly continued. 'I feel a certain grief emitting from the castle. As if something terrible has happened to someone I love – except I don't have anyone there. I think'—she cast Jaden a nervous glance—'they're using Jaden's absence to manipulate Vanilla for her powers.'

Of course, Charlie realised. Vanilla's ability to affect everyone's emotions would be perfect to subdue and weaken the others with her grief.

Jaden clenched his fists at his sides as if to stop himself from shaking.

Gilly gazed towards the folly, her chin trembling. 'They've been cooped up in the dining hall for days.'

'We *have* to get to them. Right now,' Tyler said.

'What if there's an ambush on the other side?' Charlie looked to

Sophie, hovering with uncertainty on the side-lines. This wasn't her world. Charlie needed to get her somewhere safe; she didn't want her in the midst of it all.

But Sophie only crossed her arms. 'I'll be fine.'

Jaden and Tyler didn't wait for more, already beginning to coax Order members through, two and two disappearing underneath the archway as if the space on the other side had swallowed them whole.

Charlie stared at Gilly. There were so many questions she wanted to ask her. How did she feel? *Did* she feel? Was she at peace?

Behind her, Caden laid his hand on Sophie's back and guided her through the folly, disappearing after her with one final nod at Charlie. The moment he was gone, Gilly disappeared too, as if sucked into a realm where Charlie could not see her. Tyler gave her a look of sympathy. It was time to go.

He went first, but as she started to follow, Charlie turned towards the spot where Gilly had stood and whispered, 'I'm sorry this happened to you,' hoping the ghost would hear. Then she stepped through the archway and felt a cool whirl of air encircle her, followed by the familiar sensation of something hooking into her navel and jerking her forward.

As she had expected and dreaded, her insides began to blaze with fire, but she closed her eyes and took deep breaths through her nose and mouth. Smoke and the smell of singed hair was quickly replaced with seaweed and fresh air as she imagined her own energy coating her body like a fire blanket. She opened her eyes on the other side, holding up her arm in amazement. For the slightest moment, she was covered in blazing flames that did not so much as tickle her skin, spreading like wings behind her. Noticing all the eyes upon her, she let it die down, the last embers dancing along her fingers before they extinguished.

'Nicely done.' Jaden grinned, with Tyler looking equally impressed next to him. Caden gave her a gentle smile as well, his arms protectively around Sophie, having wrapped his grey cloak around her. Sophie's own clothes underneath were a little singed, but nothing compared to Charlie's after her first go through the folly.

'Looks like you managed quite well too,' Charlie said, walking up to her sister.

'Honestly, I have no idea what just happened or if I did anything at all.' Sophie shook her head, looking from Caden to Charlie, a soft hiss escaping her lips as her dress shifted against her body.

'Let me help,' Charlie said, but Rowena laid a hand on her wrist.

'Save your energy. You'll need it. I'll take her to Mythos and heal her there.'

'I'll come with you,' Caden said. 'To keep guard.'

'We need you in the fight, Caden.' Tyler grabbed his brother by the arm, but Caden pulled it away.

'Don't ask me to be your weapon!' He bared his teeth.

Silently, Jaden reached for Tyler and asked him to come away.

They watched them go, Charlie with her arms clamped over her body while the waves broke against jutting rocks at the foot of Mythos' cliff. There were no other alarming movements, making it unnaturally quiet for a place in disarray.

The Order members stood, spread out, weighing their weapons. They seemed on edge, either from having dodged this place in their teens or knowing that their children were inside the walls of the castle.

'Okay, if they're in the dining hall, our best shot will be to split up into two groups,' Tyler barked. 'Charlie and I shall lead the first group through the main entrance. We'll distract the Agnus and give the rest of you a chance to free the students. Jaden, you'll lead a group of the strongest attackers through the dungeons.'

Both Jaden and Charlie nodded with resolution, but the Order members looked to Bes for confirmation. After a moment of contemplation, he made a curt dip of his head and began delegating his comrades to different groups.

Her stomach turned into a knot as Jaden, Bes, and other stealthy Order members disappeared into the woods, heading for the dungeons, while she and her team crept up towards the castle. Eyes on the windows, her heart thudded in her chest with the feeling of being watched, but no silhouettes moved behind the glass.

Neither did anyone move against them, although she had come to expect it, each moving shadow causing her to jerk to a halt and scour the landscape, listening intently. For the roar of beasts. For the screaming of men being captured in the woods. Yet she heard nothing but her own shaky breath.

She cast one last look at the sea behind them, wondering if she saw something move, before they entered the courtyard. It was as eerily empty as the grounds, made even more macabre with the summer's dead roses still clinging onto the gazebo.

As Fortune would have it – or maybe not, considering who she'd shown herself to be – they made it to the main doors without seeing a soul. Only when two Order members pulled the heavy doors open did they understand why.

A wave of despair hit them like a truck, knocking them backwards and forcing several down on their knees. Struggling, they attempted to crawl through the hallway and onto the balcony of the dining hall, the storm of emotions growing stronger the closer they got.

Tyler reached the banister first, grasping it with one hand while he grabbed Charlie's wrist and hauled her closer with the other.

Gasping, Charlie's fingers slipped, and she took cover, huddling on the floor as if that could keep the negativity at bay. Her skin felt like it was split open, all the energy, hope, and strength being drained out of her. It was Vanilla's work, she was sure of it, and she needed to find a way to counter it. Closing her eyes, she took a deep breath and opened up to Vanilla's hurt, thinking of her own heartache and how she had done magic despite of it – by accepting it.

Each razor-sharp stab penetrating her heart was a mini grenade of sadness, but she didn't block them out. Instead, she focused on distinguishing Vanilla's feelings from her own, intensifying the latter.

Vanilla, please... Charlie thought. *Can you sense me? I want to help.*

The storm of raging grief grew stronger, as if Vanilla's mourning was blocking out anyone who tried to soothe her. Still, it was something. *She senses me!* Charlie sighed, an elated thrill fluttering in her chest. This could work.

At the same time, Tyler's knees buckled next to her, his fingers dragging down his cheeks, his chin, down his pallid neck until they began to squeeze, blue veins popping down his arm, his mouth gasping for air. Feeling as if she herself was choking, Charlie gritted her teeth and tried her best to redirect her focus away from the spiking adrenaline in her body. Panic was the last thing Vanilla needed to sense in her now.

Think... Think, Charlie, think. Fighting her shortness of breath, Charlie sorted through her haze of disoriented thoughts, trying to remember what Gilly had said.

They were using Jaden's absence to hurt Vanilla. Vanilla believed Jaden to be hurt or dead, even. She needed to know he was okay. She needed faith.

Vanilla... Charlie focused all her mental energy on picturing Jaden just as she had last seen him, alive and breathing. *Can you sense this?* The wave trembled. *Can you see what I see? Feel what I feel?* Vanilla's emotions quivered, almost hesitantly. Grief and despair turned to distrust and denial. Still, Tyler's hands were slowly retracting from his throat. *He's alive, Vanilla. He's coming for you.* Tears ran down Tyler's cheeks, but his body language was still, as if listening. This was her chance.

For many years, Charlie had tried to imagine how one would go about interfering with the mind like Maddison did. Now she put it to the test. Charlie repainted the image of Jaden, this time adding Vanilla to the scene, reuniting them. She drew on her own belief that they would see each other again, gathering up all the joy and warmth she would feel at seeing them united, bundling it and pushing it back against Vanilla's denial.

Turning her face to the sky, Charlie watched the clouds through the glass ceiling, picturing the many starlit nights she'd looked up, wishing for her happiness with Tyler, willing to give it all up for Vanilla's. A tear rolled down her cheek, not because she was sad, but because it was possible, and it made her happy in an entirely raw and honest way that she had never felt before. She felt the rosiness wrap around her heart like a warm blanket – and with it the turmoil within finally abated and drifted away.

Panting, Charlie grabbed hold of the banister, hoisting herself to her feet. Her group lay devastated on the floor behind her, propping themselves up to standing positions through trembling, slow motions. They stilled and stared open-mouthed, causing Charlie to spin around.

The floor of the dining hall was littered with bodies spread about on top of one another as if it were the aftermath of a Beltane celebration gone terribly awry. Some rested their heads on the legs of others, while others rested on theirs. Charlie had the sickening sensation that she was looking at a mass grave. But they weren't dead yet. Dozens of eyes blinked up at her, some as if awakening from a nightmare, some still grieving, others vacant, but most wide with terror.

A large bird cage stood where the head-table once stood. A tiny girl sat slumped at the bottom, like a pearly skeleton against the black metal frame. *Vanilla.* Next to her lay another girl with raven black hair, her eyes white, a bird truly caught in a cage of her own making. Maddison.

Instinctively, Charlie wanted to call their names, but a man stepped out in front of the cage and took the air out of her lungs. Her insides went cold, as if frozen by his cruel glare. *Deimos.*

His Agnus robes were replaced with a black suit, his blonde hair cut short and coloured pitch black like his wife and daughter's. Looking like night incarnate, he grinned and clapped his hands together.

'Why, Miss Charlie, you left us so quickly, we didn't have the chance to say goodbye. Thought you'd come and have a little chat with the headmistress, did you?'

Mother Ratchford's body was tossed onto the stage like a rag doll, with Desdemona rising from the floor, revealing herself.

'Come to join my feast, daughter of Clotho?' She licked the scarlet of her pointy fangs. *Creature of Night.* A vampire. 'Or have you come to offer yourself with the others for our army?'

Tyler stiffened next to Charlie as Brimley and the werewolves appeared from the dungeon, moving into the hall between the frightened youths who gawked and rolled away in fright. Had they disposed of Jaden's group, or had Jaden and the others not entered the dungeons yet?

'That is not the mission of the Agnus Dei,' cried a young Sister from across the room. Charlie realised she had missed the other Agnus members, looking quite rattled, lined up against the west wall, cowering away from the scene before them. 'Our cause is to *heal* these children of their curse. To prepare them to re-join society, or... or to keep them safe, away from society.'

'Stupid is as stupid does.' Deimos snorted. Before anyone could react, he'd closed the distance between them and pulled out the Sister's heart, shock still plastered on her face as the rest of her crumpled to the ground. The others screamed, but Deimos only stepped, light-footed, across student bodies until he stood in the middle of the room. He threw his blood-covered hands up towards Charlie and her crew on the balcony.

'If I were you, I'd run.'

Just then, Jaden and his group burst through the open door of the dungeon and threw themselves on the werewolves, weapons lifted over their heads. Charlie's insides erupted with glorious happiness that made tears spring from her eyes, but the feelings weren't hers. Vanilla had caught sight of Jaden coming towards the cage to break her free, and the love the two felt in that moment was so apparent and overwhelming that it banished the last vestiges of misery from everyone in the room, lifting their lethargy and infusing them with new energy. Bolting upright, the students looked at each other with confusion. Tyler had a goofy grin on his face, and the Order members behind him seemed inclined to put their weapons down and hug each other. But Charlie remained grounded, and Deimos had already told them what to do.

'Run!' she screamed at the top of her lungs, and the enchantment was broken. Immediately, a wild panic spread, and students and grown-ups alike stormed the main staircases. Charlie and her crew had to be quick to exit the castle as to not be trampled.

'Charlie!' Tyler shouted from the front garden, pointing down to the beach. Figures were rising from the sea, armoured and carrying heavy weapons. 'They're coming through the sea passage!'

Belting out of the main doors behind them, students stopped in their tracks, pointing in horror at the oncoming beasts. Some Agnus members, to her surprise, started pushing the youths behind them, as if ready to defend them, while others simply darted for the woods. Cowardly as it was, they had the right idea.

'Run! Hide!' cried Charlie to students around her and then picked up an abandoned cane from the ground. 'Ordo Vitae, I need you to fight and protect us!'

The Order members raised their weapons once again but with less confidence. *They're afraid they'll hurt their children*, Charlie thought. Or anyone's children. She frowned; there was no way the mutants would stop and show mercy.

As she expected, the beasts raised their weapons over their heads the moment their feet hit firm ground. Batallion roared as he led the way, making the ground shudder with the stomp of his heavy minotaur feet. The harsh sound of metal against metal rang over the screams, and soon axes and swords were flying as much as bodies and magically enchanted branches and rocks.

The grounds were a blur of steel and fur – red, brown, and black – scales, feathers, deerskin trousers, battling men and women, boys and girls, and creatures of all shapes and sizes. Tyler and Batallion went head-to-head while Ava fought Roxy by setting fire to her bushy tail, preventing her from sinking her teeth into the slithering snake that was Venus. The last fighters seemed to have left the castle now, realising that the real battle was outside. Order members struck and made countermoves expertly, but the mutants were strong and the Order members' magic rusty. Whirls of wind and razor leaves spun towards the attackers, not enough to seriously harm but enough to hold back or blind them.

Bes crouched and leapt into the air, shifting into his golden suit, and attacked the mutant army's right flank. His giant paws knocked sprawling mutants to the ground, and a mighty snarl sent two fauns sprinting for the treeline. Charlie wanted to call for him to be careful, but there was no time. She dodged a sword swung by a centaur and threw herself to the ground, narrowly dodging an arrow flying over her head. It hit a mutant square in the chest, red gushing from the wound. She felt no triumph and stifled a sob instead, knowing the boy within would not have been in the battle had it not been for her. But this was not the time for guilt either.

They were being destroyed.

Running between the wounded, attempting to heal them enough so they could keep fighting or defend themselves, Charlie could barely patch one up before there was another. Meanwhile, Desdemona, having joined up with her army, kept on advancing. While the mutants were ruthless, all with teeth and claws and inhuman speed, their mistress was far worse. It took a large number of allies just to contain her from running wild, draining her opposition of blood or snapping their necks like toothpicks. All the Firelings tried to wall her in with towering orange flames, but Desdemona merely cackled within them, waiting for her mutants to attack the Maglings from behind. Once free, she began her slaughter all over again, leaving bodies in her wake.

Brave Withdrawers, Charlie realised, threw themselves before their magical comrades, armed with the Agnus' weapons of copper whips and tasers. Her eyes met with Albin's, who fervently pointed to somewhere behind her. Grabbing a tighter hold of her cane, Charlie spun around, blocking a blow from a satyr last minute.

It stepped back and tried again, swinging its bat over her head as she dodged and ran around it. But it followed suit, the two of them sparring feverishly until some buoyant crowing made the hairs stand up on her arms, and she turned around to see Caden running down the path of Mythos, purple orbs launching from his palms and firing into the ranks like cannonballs. Panic momentarily paralysed her, filling her with dread that something would happen to him, or that something had happened to Sophie.

Distracted, she failed to notice one of the satyrs spinning his bat around, hitting her hard. She went flying, the silver chain around her neck disappearing over her head as she landed in a heap on the ground, her fingers grasping around her wrist and spindle pin in agony.

Caden shouted her name – a warning – as he snapped his fingers into fists, dark violet sparks appearing between his knuckles. The satyr collapsed by her side while Bes, still in lion form, leapt on another heading her way. Tipped off by his growl, the satyr threw him off and raised a spiked club – only to be thrown to the ground by a lioness coming to Bes' aid. *Rowena.*

Charlie's heart filled with relief, and she took the short moment of reprieve to look around.

The battle was still going strong, although Caden was knocking mutants out left and right. An unforgiving Jaden held Deimos bound to the gazebo with his vines, while Tyler came running towards them with a sword raised.

But Desdemona did not seem to notice. Instead, she was eyeing Maddison's necklace, striding towards the place it lay twinkling in the grass, her long black dress whipping back and forth in the wind. *The necklace... Maddison's family heirloom...* Charlie saw the silver thread shimmering around the violet vial, bound like thread around a... spindle.

Realisation dawning upon her, Charlie threw herself to the ground and crawled towards it, racing the strides of Desdemona with her elbows and legs, her abdomen burning.

Everything else seemed to fade to the background as her fingers closed around the vial – everything but Desdemona's bloodthirsty expression of triumph as she neared, picking up a spear along the way.

Charlie ripped her spindle pin off her sleeve and felt it grow in her palm, but Desdemona's tall figure was already looming above her.

'Any last words?' she hissed, raising the spear.

'You're prettier than your illustrations, but that's about it,' Charlie snarled back.

With a scoff, Desdemona drove the spear down just as something black appeared between them.

Charlie's brain could not comprehend it at first.

There was no pain. No coldness as death should have claimed her body. Only Maddison's stunned expression and the tip of the spear protruding between her ribs. Despite the pain evident on her face, her lips mouthed words only Charlie could read.

Where there's a will, there's a way...

As if Charlie's energy reacted before her mind, the necklace's silver thread released the glass vial and started encircling the rounded wooden rod instead. Their strong power coursed through her, back and forth, like an unbroken connection. Her hair flickered wildly around her, slashing the air like Medusa's snakes.

Eyes wide and teeth bared, Desdemona pulled out the spear, letting Maddison collapse to the ground with blood soaking her clothes.

Charlie glared at the Fate of Fortune, her insides burning with hatred but also with love – love for Maddison, love for her friends and fellow Maglings. She put everything she had into blocking the reality of what Lachesis had done, focusing her energy on the spindle and the thread instead, both items beginning to glow in her hands.

An odd shudder came over Desdemona's face before she gave a bone-shattering shriek that was echoed by every mutant on the ground. The vampire fell to her knees, tugging at her head, looking immensely vulnerable.

Charlie threw the spindle and vial on the ground as she twisted and turned for a weapon when her eyes landed on one particular boy. 'Caden, *kill* her! Kill her now!'

But Caden only stopped, apparently dumbfounded, casting uncertain glances between his hands, Desdemona and Maddison. It infuriated her. Why wasn't he taking the opportunity? 'Kill her!'

But there was something different in Desdemona's eyes. Where before there had been only menace, there was now a certain awareness – and it was crippled by dread and horror, mirrored in the beasts coming to a halt around them.

Where there's a will...

They were all getting their free will back, but with that, empathy, awareness, and consciousness seemed to follow.

Desdemona's face was a mask of unyielding anguish, and Charlie could only imagine the images that were playing in her newly awakened mind. The many things she had done to create an army for the benefit of the very forces Desdemona had fought against before. The sacrifices it had required. The revulsion in Desdemona's expression told Charlie she was right as Desdemona turned to face her husband slunk against the castle wall, Tyler's sword now protruding from his chest, and then refastened her eyes on Maddison lying pale and drained, barely breathing by her feet.

Please, Charlie mouthed to Caden once more. *Kill her.*

Gritting her teeth, Desdemona snatched up the Fates' totems and Maddison in her arms. Charlie grappled for her friend's lifeless legs, but in an inhuman instant, the vampire and raven girl were gone.

The child of Life was left on the ground, crestfallen and surrounded by still mutants looking terrified, bloodied Ordo Vitae, and Agnus members, students, and friends – all looking relieved the battle was over. Rowena and Bes transformed back to themselves while Caden stood motionless by Charlie's side. Staring around in shock and exhaustion, Charlie's eyes landed on the patch of blood in the grass, and the first sobs escaped her.

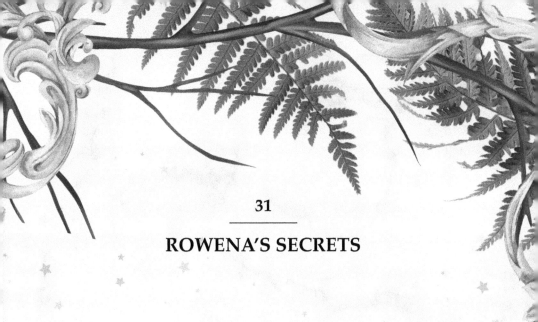

31

ROWENA'S SECRETS

'THERE YOU ARE.' Charlie sighed in relief, her voice hushed. She had searched for Caden all over the school before it occurred to her that he might not be *within* the grounds.

Caden turned around, acknowledging her as she stepped out of the folly.

There'd only been a couple days since the battle, but he looked clean and healthy with a fresh glow to his skin and dimples having returned to his smile. His eyes, however, were solemn upon Gilly sitting next to him. They could have been two perfectly normal friends resting in the grass – if it weren't for Gilly's ghostly complexion.

'Hey, Gilly, how are you?' Charlie carefully arranged her skirt as she sat down next to the pair.

'Still dead, but other than that, great,' Gilly chirped, tilting her head, a genuine smile playing on her lips. 'How are you holding up? Caden told me about your sister ... and Maddison.'

Caden hid his face. He'd apologised many times for not killing Desdemona, and she had apologised for even asking it of him in the first place. It didn't change the fact that Desdemona had escaped and taken Maddison with her, but there was little they could do about it without any trace of where in the world they could have gone. Bes had called in an anonymous tip to the authorities who had raided the experimental station. The horrific findings had been spread far and wide in various newspapers, pinning it all on the lingering laboratorians found on site. According to Bes, they had all been compelled not to say a word, and the investigation had been closed and put down to the result of a group serial-killer sect of some sort, with the remaining carcasses declared as victims.

'I'm okay. I just wish I knew what happened to them.'

Gilly gave Caden a meaningful look, and he sighed, pulling something out of his trouser pocket. A piece of thick paper that he folded out like a map. It was the painting from Mythos' hut, its grass-clothed valley and mountains as vivid as she remembered them from her first practice alone with Tyler.

Apparently, Sophie had spotted the picture as Caden and Rowena carried her into the hut. They had barely turned their backs on her before she leapt off the bed meant for her to rest in and – to the best they were able to describe it – dived into the picture, letting it swallow her, much like when someone went through the passage.

'I've been studying the picture,' Caden said. 'And I'm pretty certain I know where it is – although I have no idea how Sophie knows or why she would go there.'

'Where?' Having rested her chin on her knees, Charlie's head perked up with curiosity.

'Home. *My* home.'

'Your, err, kingdom?' Charlie pondered, remembering what Caden had spilled that night at the beach.

Caden nodded. 'Mhm. Caladria. It's'—his face contorted into a grimace—'in another realm. My father, the king, presides over its western territories. We have another painting at our home in Bath that takes us back.'

At once, Charlie felt sure he was talking about the same portrait that Maddison had wanted her to steal. If it was, had she known? Had she suspected that it would lead her to Sophie? After some thought, she turned back to Caden, realising that he was watching her with an eyebrow raised, perhaps waiting for a reaction, or a question, even.

'I don't know what to do with that information,' she stuttered, and Caden repocketed the picture.

'That's okay. I'm going back for Jaden's wedding at Solstice. I'll look for her there. You concentrate on looking for Maddison here.' He patted her hand, and Charlie smiled gratefully.

'I think I have to deal with the funeral first.' Under Rowena's administration, they were to hold one large funeral for all who had fallen during the Battle of Soli Gloria, and the very thought of it put them all in a rather sombre mood.

Gilly wrinkled her nose after a while. 'I wish I'd had a funeral.'

Caden turned to her. 'What did they do to your body?'

She nodded towards the folly. 'The Agnus put it in an unmarked grave behind the stables. I guess it's their tradition where Defectives are concerned, but I wish they would've tossed my body into the sea.' She sighed, observing the River Plym now high with the tide. 'It's where I belong.'

Nature herself seemed to join them in mourning on the day of the funeral. The sea lay calm, the wind low amongst the grass, and snowdrops by the thousands popped up to pay their respects. Even the sun appeared muted, and the various nymphs awakened once more to sing hymns at the burials.

Some of the dead received burials from Earthlings who made the ground tear open, creating holes like the ones in their hearts so that they could fill them with their fallen comrades. For those with Dryad blood running through their veins, they grew trees out of their cremated ashes. The ashes of fallen Airlings were spread with the wind before the last remaining bodies were placed on small boats and pushed towards the open sea.

Firelings raised one hand, palm up, in salute, with a torch in the other, while balls of fire shot from their fingers and set half of the boats alight as they sailed towards the horizon. The rest were sunk into a watery grave by Tyler and the other Waterlings.

As those gathered bowed their heads in respect, with tears glittering on wet cheeks, Charlie spotted a slim figure staggering through their ranks and into the water. Caden was covered in dirt, sweat glinting on his forehead. In his arms, something long was wrapped in a swathe of silk and, as he rolled it into the deepest end of the sea, Charlie realised he had dug up Gilly's body. She lifted her chin at the splash and projected her farewell on the breeze. *Now*, Gilly would be at peace. Charlie wondered whether the same could be said for Maddison.

She glanced at Bes and Rowena standing side by side, hand in hand, and Brimley standing with the mutants that remained to pay their respects, making up her mind that she would confront them all after the funeral. It was time. Time for them to tell her everything.

———

She didn't need to spend much time with Brimley to realise there wasn't much to be said. Without Maddison as the glue, it became clearer than before as they strolled through the hallways of Soli Gloria that whatever friendship had existed between them had only been a feeble extension of their affection for their mutual friend. He told her what little he remembered of what happened after the night they were all caught, and she told him what little she knew about the raven girl's current whereabouts – which was nothing. At least, in Maddison, they could find a common subject of interest, and when Brimley voiced his intention to go into the world and hunt her down, Charlie did not discourage him or attempt to sway him to stay.

'I'll take some of the mutants with me,' he said as they came to a halt before the infirmary door. 'Those who desire to leave rather than stay. If she's alive, I'll find her.'

Charlie nodded, her arms awkwardly folded around herself while she waited for the right moment to bid him goodbye. 'That sounds like a good plan.'

Brimley cleared his throat and dipped his chin. He almost looked like himself again, although there were some signs of the trauma he'd been through that could not be erased from his features. Unlike the other mutants, the werewolves had been able to shift back to their human forms once their free will had returned, but their wolf-shapes remained mutated.

Awkward silence ensued where neither looked as if they knew what to say, and it was a relief when the infirmary door swung open, and Rowena peeked outside.

'Ah! We thought we heard voices. We've been waiting for you.'

Charlie forced a smile, suddenly caught between the ambivalence of facing her grandparents and staying outside the infirmary. 'Well, then,' she said, turning to Brimley. 'Safe journey. Let me know if you find her.'

'Of course.' Brimley bowed and left, leaving her with Rowena who beckoned her inside and to an empty chair by her desk. Bes stood ready by a tray of tea and biscuits. Neither of the three addressed the empty chair that Sophie should have occupied. Instead, Bes handed her a cup of tea as Charlie settled in her own.

'Whenever Clotho spun a new thread for a new life,' Bes began, not beating about the bush. For that she was grateful. 'We, Beset and I, were sent to make sure mother and child had a safe birth. Our job became increasingly more difficult the larger the population grew of course, and sometimes we came too late. But nothing made our job more complicated than the evil Atropos set into the world.'

Rowena looked at her hands. 'So many innocent souls were lost to war and famine, sickness and despair.'

Bes continued, 'When the One True Divinity decided to step in, we would be reborn with Clotho to help her. The last time, we were born into these human bodies. We found each other at Nettleheys and grew up to administer the place, protecting orphaned Maglings along with the Magless.'

'We thought that was our purpose,' Rowena chimed in, and Bes took her hand. 'To be the opposite of what the Agnus was. It seemed big enough for us.'

'Sometimes, when you are reborn, it takes a while to understand your purpose and remember the lives that have been.'

'Some never do...'

'One day, a couple appeared on our doorstep with a young girl. They seemed delirious, as if they didn't really know why they were there, but the girl was clear-eyed and firm. She touched our foreheads and showed us a vision. Two young people falling in love and fighting on the side of the witches in Salem. We recognised them instantly. Our son, and another girl in our care – Hazel – in their past lives.'

'And the girl who showed you the vision,' Charlie breathed. 'Was it...'

'Yes, Charlie. A young Desdemona, as you call her. *Lachesis.* Powerful, even then.'

'Was she like that back then as well? Vampire-ish, I mean.'

Bes and Rowena exchanged a look of deep concern.

'Creatures of Night ... they were soulless creatures, created by Atropos, like the Creatures of Destruction. They were under her control and a vital part of her army during the Salem witch-hunts. She would let them loose at night, scaring witless country people away from the occult and into the waiting arms of witch hunters.'

'But Lachesis was never one. Which makes me think something must have happened when...' Bes went quiet. 'For years, the Ordo Vitae have been trying to keep tabs on Atropos, but eleven years ago, in Norway, it was as if she suddenly disappeared underground.'

'That's when Maddison's family was split apart.'

'Yes. I'd imagine Atropos must have found Lachesis and captured her. I believe she had caught Deimos before that and, if so, she must have turned him into a creature of the night already then... but it doesn't make sense why she would turn Lachesis.'

'Doesn't it?'

'No. If Atropos caught Lachesis, I imagine she would want to keep her for her fortunes. But a gift of the Fates can't reside within a soulless creature, and so Lachesis would have lost her celestial powers the moment she transformed.'

'Then there is the price,' Rowena added more solemnly. 'There's an ancient power that binds the Moirai, strengthening their powers when they're united. Using their powers against one another would come at a great cost.'

'Like Atropos' deathlike sleep?' Charlie bent forward in her chair, staring into her cup of tea as if she could see the Fate of Death amongst the swirls of liquid.

'Quite possibly.'

They were quiet, thinking it through, when Rowena clasped a hand to her mouth. 'Perhaps that's it. Perhaps Lachesis tricked her into turning her.'

Realisation dawned upon Bes. 'Of course. She'd be putting Death out of play while her gifts would pass on to her daughter.'

'A sacrifice,' whispered Charlie, thinking of Maddison during the battle of Soli Gloria. At the experimental station. Like mother like daughter. 'Fate must run its course.'

'That was her prerogative. Even from the very beginning, when she appeared on our doorstep as a little girl, Lachesis was always adamant that our purpose was to stop Atropos.'

'Everything we did from then and onwards was following her visions, her instructions,' said Rowena. 'Knowing Hazel and Thomas would end up here, I changed my name and left Nettle-heys to take the nurse position at Soli Gloria. That way, I would be there to receive them without anyone suspecting that I had any connection to them. I was able to keep them safe, until they ran away.'

Charlie recalled the night she had shown her their photos – her mother's pregnant belly, her father's protective hand on her mother's shoulder.

'I had the news that she delivered twins only a couple weeks after that, and news again from your grandfather barely a few months after with an encrypted message of what had transpired in the end.'

'So, when I came here...'

'I had been waiting eighteen years, hoping to see you.'

'But you never told me.' Again, the same old sense of betrayal flared within her.

Rowena's features grew solemn. 'I wanted to protect you. I loved Hazel and Thomas with all my heart, and what happened to them broke it. They were so much more than their destinies, but they never saw it.'

Once again, Charlie thought of the Quinseys, their entire lives steered by fate. 'Perhaps Sophie and I can? Turn our backs on all of this.'

Bes and Rowena glanced at each other once more, and in that look, a whole conversation seemed to take place. Charlie wondered if it was something that came after being together for as long as they had, or if, thinking about Vanilla and Jaden, it was the mark of true love.

'I don't think you have a choice anymore. Now that Atropos has been awakened, I'm afraid dark times lie ahead. Not only may there be consequences for what you did at the experimental station...' Bes let the words hang heavy in the air. 'But she'll come for you again now, knowing where you are.'

Shivers ran down Charlie's spine.

'Perhaps, there's still hope,' Rowena said, clutching her husband's hands. 'Atropos wasn't in the battle. There must be a reason for that. Perhaps she's still recovering.'

'Why?' Charlie said, her voice clipped. 'Why is she so adamant about coming after us?'

'Because you're the key, Charlie,' Bes said, his old eyes solemn. 'You're the key to end the war of the Fates and put a stop to her regime.'

And the best way to remove a key was to destroy it.

32

SECOND CHANCES

A NEW ERA dawned at Soli Gloria after the funeral. Under Bes and Rowena's leadership, the school was claimed in the name of the Ordo Vitae. The Agnus Brothers and Sisters who had not fled or left swore their allegiance to the Order to take up new positions at the school and work towards their redemption. Many of the Maglings remained sceptical of this, but it was not up for discussion. Rowena remained certain that there would never be peace between the two groups until they learned to live side by side with one another.

'I can tell what you're thinking, Charlie,' Rowena had said and raised an eyebrow the day she told her. 'But let me remind you of their history. These men and women have been exposed to the same mind manipulation and misinformation as you have. They *thought* they were saving students' souls and they *did* try to protect students during the battle. These individuals care, and we must show them a better way to act on it. There's been enough prejudice and misery. We'll need all the unity we can get for what lies ahead.'

New programs were planned and tested as winter turned to spring. The new year would have biology classes to teach the new and old students about the different kinds of Magling heritage, and history lessons based on all religions and mythologies. Psychology and meditation classes would be taught so that everyone would have the tools to empower their own psyche, as well as creative studies to fuel everyone's inner energy. Former divides based on gender would also be changed.

Last but not least, there would be new programs suited for the individual elements: gardening, forestry, environmental and conservation lessons, marine studies and oceanography, coalmining and firefighter training, and meteorology. The latter would be taught by Lady Harietta, who'd happily ditched her shopping cart when the Ordo Vitae came to visit her in Bath.

'What will happen to the rest of the Withdrawers?' Charlie asked during an Order meeting.

'There are programs in society more suited for their symptoms,' Rowena said.

'No,' Charlie simply stated, observing Albin helping a former Agnus swap out their old black leather tomes with books of various literature. His wings would never grow back to what they had been, Rowena had asserted, but he still kept hope that he would have magic again. 'I just have to believe it's there, even without my wings, and connect with it again,' he'd said one day. 'And when I do, I'll be a Magling again. A stronger one, despite my disability.' He had nudged her with his shoulder, and she'd chuckled. She'd told him everything that had happened at the experiment station, and he'd understood something important in a way regular Maglings couldn't.

Now, everyone around the table looked up at her, but Charlie only stuck her chin out. 'They need one *here*. One that will give them extra attention from individual advisors, adapted to their needs. More time.'

Tyler and Jaden exchanged glances, and so did many of the adult Order members. Some even turned to Bes as if wondering how much longer he would allow a young girl to dictate the meeting. But Bes looked at her as if he was seeing an old acquaintance from his past sitting before him. An entertained smile hid in the corner of Caden's mouth as well, and she knew he, like her, thought this was something Gilly would have approved of.

'Time to do what?' Sister Lucy piped up. She was dressed in a white blouse and teal green skirt; her cheeks had grown more apple-round, and blonde ringlets framed her face. In such little time, she was entirely altered – almost.

'To reconnect them to their magic,' Charlie replied.

She's lost her mind, the Order members' eyes seemed to say.

'Withdrawers don't reconnect with their magic,' said an Order member.

'I did. I was shown patience, support, guidance, and care.' Charlie and Tyler's eyes met.

'But you had not yet withdrawn?' countered Sister Lucy.

'Hadn't I? I had withdrawal symptoms, and I still have, and there were moments I didn't have magic, yet now I do. Which begs the question: do we ever really withdraw? When magic can skip genera-tions and reappear, does it ever really leave us? I don't believe there's such a thing as a *Withdrawer* or *Magless*. I think all of us have magic inside, somewhere. And if I'm right,' she shot in before the others could object, 'if we can help all who have had their magic suppressed by the Agnus'—she raised an eyebrow at Sister Lucy who looked down into her lap— 'then we could bring magic back to Earth. For real.'

'I say it's worth a shot,' Caden chimed in matter-of-factly, pursing his lips, eyes twinkling mischievously back at her under his fringe.

'So do I. Excellent suggestion, Charlie,' said Bes, and that decided it.

––––––––––––

'You did a good thing with the program,' Caden said out of the blue, taking her by surprise as they looked across the rocky point jutting out below the girls' cliff, where ten people moved about playing a sport from Caden's home.

A warm, fluffy sensation bubbled within her at the gentleness in his voice, and she stuffed her hands into her pockets, pulling her shoulders up to her chin.

'You think so? Don't you disapprove of magic anymore?'

Caden ruffled his hair, letting the sun turn it into white gold.

'I've come to realise that while it can be used to harm, it can be used to save someone too. Besides, some seem to think a life without magic is worse than death – who am I to deny them?' He dipped his head wistfully.

Death. She gave him a smile, yet her stomach dropped like a stone thinking about some deductions she had started to make. More than anything, she wanted to ask him if her suspicions were right. But, watching him in the thin morning light, looking like an extension of the sun rays themselves, it seemed mindboggling that she could be anything but wrong. And, on the off chance she was right, would it not be better to spare him the knowledge if he did not know? Yes, it would be better not to ask.

'So, this game, care to explain it?' she asked instead. His face lit up with his grin.

'It's called Elementorum, and it's a bit like *Battleship*, if you've ever played it?'

Like the game, two groups would be stationed at an arena but unable to see the opposition. Being dependent on their skills and ability to channel energy, they would try and attack or defend themselves with moves and countermoves.

Charlie watched him wave his hands enthusiastically, all the while pushing down the thoughts trying to intrude on her bliss. He had come up with the idea of making Elementorum a sport taught at Soli Gloria as a way of commemorating the secret duelling and quiet resistance that took place at Mythos while the Agnus held the school, and she reminded herself of the soft pink that had flooded his cheeks as Tyler complimented him for it. His joy at being recognised by his brother was so pure, that she wondered how she could ever have thought him cold and dispassionate in the first place.

In the same way, Caden's eyes sparkled with life and innocence as he now launched into new stories of the many matches they had played at home and the many incredible strategies he and his brothers had pulled off.

Charlie listened with bated breath, talking herself into conviction. No, there was no way that he could be...

Could he?

By April, Bes received good news from spies and scouts working on transforming the Agnus Dei from the inside. There were more allies within the Order than they had ever dared to hope, and some even spoke of new pockets of resistance building in other Magling communities around the world. Neither had they reported any sightings of Atropos, making her but a mare in Charlie's nightmares.

Although she often thought of Maddison, and wondered whether or not Brimley had found her, Charlie felt there was something tranquil about being without them, and it was hard feeling morose as she and her fellow students relaxed under shaded trees, drinking lemonade and watching the Waterlings turn the sea into a waterpark. The world seemed a little lighter without them, and it was only guilt keeping her from lowering her shoulders completely. Guilt and the thought of Sophie.

'Where's your head at?' Vanilla asked one day and took her eyes off her engagement ring. They were sitting on a picnic blanket with Caden and Jaden, either watching Elementorum or admiring Vanilla's ring. To no one's surprise, Jaden had taken the first opportunity after the battle to pop the question, and it would not be long until they left for Caladria to prepare for their wedding.

'Sophie. She should've been here, enjoying the peace and strengthening her magic.' *With the new programme,* Charlie's thoughts finished. Caden draped his arm around her and squeezed her shoulders.

'I'll find her, then she'll do all of that stuff.'

Charlie watched his lips curve in amusement at his players rumbling about in the arena and felt his heat radiating from his body. Her heart skipped another beat. The memories of all the kindness he'd ever shown her resurfaced. How he'd tended to her by the folly, protected her during the arrival feast, and stood up for her against Tyler – and of the ferocity with which he'd done it all. Suddenly, she was certain he had never looked more handsome or dearer to her than in that moment.

Her mouth opened and closed again, uncertain about the feelings swirling in her heart. Uncertain whether there was space there where Tyler still resided. And even if she found some, there was the tenderness that appeared in his eyes whenever she mentioned Sophie. Perhaps he would be the love she was looking for. Perhaps he would be more hurt.

'Caden—'

'Oh, no!' He jumped up and rushed down the uneven side of the cliff to help a player having stumbled and dived headfirst into the sea. But a giant wave lifted him up and replaced him, soaking wet, onto the stony surface before Caden reached him. Both Caden and Charlie turned, seeing Tyler coming towards them. He stopped, bit his lip, and then gave a jerk with his head as if asking her to come over to him.

Curious and perplexed, Charlie got up and walked over, leaving Jaden and Vanilla in their embrace of one another.

'How's the game going?' he asked, his hands stressing left and right as if he did not really know where to put them.

'Alright now I think, looks like you came at the right time.' She turned towards the others, seeing Caden back by the picnic blanket picking a flower and using exaggerated hand gestures to explain something about it. Jaden and Vanilla laughed. Clearly, he'd told a joke, and she longed to hear it herself.

'I miss you.'

It was so random and so soft that she thought she must have misheard him. Her head snapped around, but his face was blank.

'I miss you,' he said again, probably seeing the puzzled expression on her face. This time she saw his lips move. He'd really said it. 'I can't stop thinking about that time in the sea. More than anything, I want to put my arms around you like I did that night, and all those times after.' He took her hands, squeezing them tightly. 'There's something I didn't tell you before. Charming you *was* a task, at first. Something I did for the sake of the rebellion. And I did notice that you were becoming attached, but... I was too. I didn't understand my own feelings then, and quite frankly, I didn't want to. I'm a warrior, not boyfriend material. And then that incident in my cave happened.' She looked down, but he put a finger under her chin and lifted it so that her eyes met his. 'I was embarrassed, but not for the reasons you think. I was ashamed over my own behaviour and deceit. It was easier to push you away than to admit that. To tell you the truth.' *That I'd fallen for you,* his eyes seemed to say. But she couldn't be sure. She had been wrong before.

'I know I have a lot to make up for, both in words and actions, but I'll spend every day doing that if you say you'll be mine.' His blue eyes were wide and full of hope as if she were his light at the end of a tunnel. Her heart ached at how much she had missed being looked at that way. 'You don't understand. Just standing here with you now, seeing you, talking with you, I feel... excited. Alive. I haven't felt this way since before the uprising and it makes me smile. You, Charlie, make me smile – and I'm not the smiling kind of guy.'

'No, you're kind of broody,' Charlie joked, her throat dry.

Tyler snorted, his smile widening. 'Be mine, Charlie, will you?'

Her insides were in turmoil, a maelstrom of longing and rational thinking. They were the words she had longed to hear for so long, yet he'd hurt her so much. She *knew* he wasn't entirely good for her. Could she look past that? Could she believe him?

She shook her head, struggling to filter her thoughts and

emotions, fear and want. 'I-I can't,' she stuttered, hardly believing the words coming out of her mouth. 'I can't know that you mean it. I'm sorry.'

Turning away from him, Charlie rushed dizzily back to the others, feeling her surroundings sway underneath her feet. Caden saw her coming and straightened his back, a suspicious frown narrowed at his brother. He would guard her if she went to him. And yet, she felt a pull, her pace dragging, as if Tyler had thrown out a fishing bait and hooked her on a line. She felt it tightening the farther she walked from him, reeling her back. Her mind kept racing. Had she made the wrong decision? Would she regret her answer? After all, Tyler had practically sworn he would prove himself; what if he really could make up for all the things he had done?

Every daydream she'd had regarding the two of them resurfaced. They could all come true if he held his promise. If she had said yes, it could've been him and her sitting beneath a tree, her head resting in the nook of his neck, his lips kissing the top of her head.

If she said yes, she could finally be loved.

'Charlie, are you alright?' Caden called. Vanilla looked at her wistfully. She knew. Did she also know the right thing to do? The Liosalfar shook her head, probably sensing Charlie's confusion and desperation for an answer all the way from where she was sitting. Or simply reading it on her face.

'Yeah, no.' Charlie panted. 'I, ummm—'

'Charlie!'

She whirled around, realising Tyler had followed her.

He raised his arms in surrender. 'I'll repeat it before them all. I'll tell the whole school that I'm yours if you want me to. Anything you want as long as you say yes. Please, Charlie, just one more chance?'

She groaned, trying her best to ignore the intensity in his eyes, the reminder of a burning desire she once would have done anything to bask in. *Still* would do anything to bask in. Her mind told her to repeat her refusal, but her heart was so much louder. Here was a boy asking her to be his girl, something she had dreamed about her entire life – who knew how long it would be until it happened again?

She thought of Maddison, a slave to her rational mind, and contemplated the butterflies she felt in her own stomach. In this moment, Tyler was causing her... joy. Happiness. Her feet could have jumped and carried her into the skies on this elation alone. Was it so wrong to chase that? Was it so wrong to let her heart lead the way? Perhaps she would rather regret something she had done than something she didn't do, wasn't that how the saying went? Well, there was only one answer she truly wanted to give.

She bent her head shyly, still scared to say the word.

'Okay.'

Glancing at him from her tilted gaze, she saw his lips explode into a smile, his whole face brightening with relief and happiness. He covered the remaining distance between them in one stride and picked her up in his arms. Soft and warm, his lips found hers, and her heart stood still, the whole world disappearing as they kissed. Slowly, through the pink fog in her mind, it dawned on her what it meant. This. Them. It was happening.

'About time!' Jaden shouted, and the bubble burst. The rhythm of their kiss was broken, their laughs muffled by each other's mouths. Then her eyes caught Caden's, and he gave her a soft smile as if to say, *As long as you're happy.*

Feeling grateful, she turned back to Tyler.

'You're radiant,' he murmured, paying no attention to the others – only her. Charlie.

The child of Life.

RETURNING TO HALLOWS GROVE

SURROUNDED BY BLOSSOMING FIELDS, Charlie found herself looking up the long driveway to Hallows Grove, its brown-brick stone houses and white-framed windows visible from afar in the dim morning light. She didn't know what she had expected after so long, but the grounds' eerie atmosphere caught her off guard. Everything was quiet, asleep perhaps, or listening with bated breath. There was no sound of children crying or canes whipping through the air, but still the hair stood up on the back of her neck. The front door had been wrenched open and was barely hanging on its hinges. The windows were shattered, shards scattered around the flowerbeds underneath.

Somehow, she did not think anyone was sleeping. She did not think she would find anyone at all. Perhaps it made it easier to enter the old building, its many painful memories threatening to sweep her off her feet. Tears welled in her eyes as the smell of faeces and blood forced itself up her nose, but she kept on walking, stepping over large concrete pieces from where the walls had been torn and collapsed, her footprints abandoned in the dust.

Mother Agnes' office was empty, save for the same old plaquette and Charlie's troubled ghosts of the past. Her own childish, pleading voice filled her ears as she continued upstairs.

Things were in even worse disarray than downstairs. White feathers decorated the floors like the feathers of a hen house where a fox had snuck in. Ripped sheets hung off the beds, some with blood and others with abandoned dolls or stuffed animals. She picked up a familiar one – an old teddy that had once been hers and someone else's before that – and felt dread thinking of what might have happened to its latest owner.

Charlie searched the room for a quarter of an hour or so, looking for anything of Sophie that she might have left behind when she was taken. Anything that could tell her a little more about her sister – or help Caden find her. Yet there was nothing, and she headed downstairs again, catching a glimpse of the dining room through the open doorway. She neared the chaos of thrown chairs and broken tables, her foot crunching on broken glass as she stepped over the threshold. Something shifted, and she jumped, realising a figure sat by the windows.

Her hair, usually braided like a halo around her head, was now thrown in disarray, her few grey hairs having turned into many, although whether that was from the years gone by or dust, Charlie did not know. Likewise, her skin hung tiredly down her cheeks, big bags of shadow lining her eyes.

She gasped, her inhalation rushing down her throat like the howling wind outside. 'Charlie! You've come to haunt me, you wretched child!'

'Mother Agnes,' Charlie replied, stepping into the room, eyes wary upon the woman. She looked like herself, yet she didn't, as if she had one day sat down in the chair and aged every day since amongst rubble and dirt.

'See what you brought upon this house with your return.'

'I never returned, Mother Agnes. It was my sister.'

The old headmistress of Hallows Grove cackled, a hint of hysteria coming over her. 'Lies and falsehood. You did nothing but.'

'Now who's lying?' Charlie gritted her teeth. 'But then that's what you did, wasn't it?'

Mother Agnes turned to look out of the window once again, clenching a piece of crumpled paper in her hands. 'I should have let *him* take you, but I thought I could drive the devil out of you. Sickly creature you had become.'

'The devil was never in me,' Charlie said, her breath shaky and her words unsteady as they took their first steps into the world. 'Which is more than I can say for you. The things you did... don't you have any remorse?'

But Mother Agnes did not seem to listen. 'There was a time when your kind were dealt with swiftly. A quick hanging or burning at the stake. It would be impossible today without facing the wrath of the unenlightened. And so, we fell short in our task to put the sinful to death.'

'To him who knows to do good, and doesn't do it,' Charlie heard Sister Lucy in her head, *'to him it is sin.'*

'Now we must pay,' Mother Agnes said and gestured to the broken interior of the room, as if to indicate it reflected the world or her own broken self. 'The anger of God has come upon us, and it's coming for you.'

With trembling hands, Mother Agnes tossed something at Charlie's feet, and the sight of it sent a bolt of shock and discomfort through Charlie's system. A wooden flute and the piece of crumpled paper. The flute exactly like the one Mother Ratchford had used. Charlie picked up the items with the sleeve of her sweater and unwrapped the paper, recognising the letter she had given Deimos to find Sophie. The memories from the experimental station flashed before her. The operation theatre. The mutants. The girl pretending to be her mother.

Charlie pushed it all further back in her mind and sighed, wondering like many times before if anything would have been different if she never had trusted him. If she had never gone to Mother Ratchford's office. Would Maddison still be with them?

Would she be with Tyler if she was? And Sophie... If she had managed to escape Hallows Grove on her own, or learned about their grandparents, would she have found Charlie before she was taken?

Mother Agnes' face contorted into a satirical grimace, mistaking Charlie's silent inner torture for surprise. 'To get in bed with monsters is to cause one's own undoing.'

'It is,' Charlie said, raising her head. 'I'm glad you've learned that.'

For a moment, Charlie thought of the rebels after the uprising and of the mutants, brought to life by her. That they had the capacity to do bad things was undeniable. But then she thought of Caden. And Gilly. And even Tyler, and she felt certain that most people weren't hurting others because they were trying to be evil, but because they were trying to be good. *Treat a person like your enemy, and they will become one.* Charlie fixed a firm gaze on Mother Agnes.

'Monsters are created, not born, so being of my *kind* has nothing to do with it. The good news is all can be monsters. And if all can be monsters, then all can be human too.'

Mother Agnes' smirk fell into an eyeroll, and she turned back to the window, staring absently at her own reflection. Charlie gave her a nod upon her departure, knowing that any redeeming reunion was futile. Mother Agnes' validation and acceptance of her would never be given.

Perhaps for the best, Charlie wondered, knowing that in her own mind, the headmistress had done what she thought was not only right but good. That the end had justified the means, and Charlie was perfectly aware it was not a thought inherent only to the Agnus, nor that she could do anything to persuade her differently. So, she left her there, liberated in the knowledge that she was more than Mother Agnes' idea of her. In fact, she was quite free of it.

A fresh breeze blew past her as she went outside, and she exhaled to the first sound of birds waking underneath the dark sky. It was a brief moment of tranquillity, where she considered the best way to get back to Bath and her new home at Tyler's place, when a splitting headache tore through her head and her vision swam. Her ears filled with a sound, as if someone had just switched on the radio inside her head, a woman's voice humming eerily.

'We are nought of a fairy-tale.
Behave, be safe,
Lil' darling, Atropos hunts at night.'

High heeled stilettos marched down a concrete aisle, strays of dirty gold hay scattered next to small stains of blood.

'Rest assured,
Lachesis' measure does not fail.
As certain as day follows night,
Clotho brings life at light...
So, sleep, little magic pea
And a new day shall come to thee.'

'Please, don't hurt me!' said a male voice, and her vision changed entirely.

An Agnus man quivered on the floor, staring at the tall, slender figure looming over him. 'I was only following orders – your ord—' He didn't manage to say more before a boot kicked him in the chest and rolled him onto his back. Desdemona Quinsey hovered her foot over his throat, her sharp heel pressing against his Adam's apple.

'Where is she?'

'In one of the cells.' He gestured so wildly that he could have pointed her north or south, east or west.

'Was it successful?'

'Y-yes, please, by the love of God—'

'The man you pray for does not exist and, in any case, his love you've long since abandoned – so neither can save you now.' Desdemona set her foot down. The man's scream drowned in gurgles. She marched

down the corridor, leaving him to bleed out, stopping only at a large wooden door.

Its small window, blocked by bars, was the only means of looking in. Lit by the torchlight, a silhouette shifted on the bed within the cell. Desdemona ripped the lock open with brute force, and the door sprung away from its frame, creaking on its rusted hinges. Inside sat a huddled creature. The emerald-green sheen in her feather blanket shimmered with every movement, even in the feeble light. Rocking back and forth, the mutant-girl cupped her hands before her lips, tiny black feathers framing her thin face. Small, sharp cries escaped her, like those from an injured animal. In between, she whispered frantic words that disappeared between the chattering of her teeth. Then her eyes, previously emerald-green now turned pitch black, shifted to her onlookers – and Charlie's sight returned to normal, seeing the rolling green hills of the parish before her. Sweat rolled down her temple, and a new voice haunted her mind. One of a raven girl, reciting a prediction over and over again.

> *'A mother lives again*
> *A sister dies for love,*
> *Death follows where the son goes*
> *A twist of fortune you shall have*
> *when all unite as one.'*

Follow Charlie and the other fated heirs in

SCISSORS OF DEATH

Find out more on
www.chaselouiseqvam.com

AUTHOR NOTES

Thank you, dear reader, for reading *Spindle of Life*. I hope you loved it enough to join us onwards for the rest of the trilogy.

While its magic and main characters have been with me since the earliest years of the millennia change, I didn't begin to actually write and structure this series before 2015. With my emotional anchor suddenly gone, I was dealing with twenty-something years' worth of trauma catching up to me, new chronic health issues, and the steady deterioration of my mental health.

I will save you the nitty-gritty emotional details for the lines between some of my pages, but this was the first time in my life where my Death Anxiety no longer concerned itself with keeping me alive. I rather would have welcomed death at this point, actually. To distract me from this – or because of this – I immersed myself in my world. I had a story that needed to be told; I needed it out of my head and down on paper in case, one day, I would no longer be here to tell it.

In the end, I spent the entirety of the following years in therapy writing this series.

It was always going to be a series with my favourite tropes, such as the Chosen One, elements from mythology, folklore, elemental magic, romance, and captivating settings, but it became something much more personal than that.

Through Charlie, I have undoubtedly explored many of my own emotional responses, mental health, and personal wounds that I've carried with me since childhood. For now, I can't say much more without spoiling things to come, but ultimately, I hope Charlie's story will help those of you who find it relatable to feel less alone, more empowered.

Finally, please note that, while I've sometimes drawn from my own experiences when writing Charlie, all other characters remain fictional inventions.

Creative Licenses

With the majority of Charlie's story set in our world (except for her time at Soli Gloria, which all happens in a different realm), I've done my best to try to keep everything as true to the places mentioned as I could. There are, however, a few instances where I've taken some creative liberties, the first being the statue of Prince Bladud in Bath's Parade Garden. Unfortunately, it was not placed in the park until 2009 (while Charlie visited the park in 2000). Upon discovering my mistake, however, I decided to leave it in so that eager readers would be able to trace Charlie and Maddison's walk into town towards one of my favourite spots in Bath.

Secondly, with Charlie's story being set on the precipice between the real world and alternative realms, there are some places that might be more real or reminiscent of somewhere real than others. Like any other author, I've found inspiration in many of the places I've been to, but I also need to reiterate my disclaimer at the beginning of the book: This *is* a piece of fiction, and any likeness to real world places is purely coincidental or real but fictionalised for the sake of the story.

I *suspect* the third item to be a creative liberty. You see, it was in 2009 as I passed through Plymouth on the train that I spotted the amphitheatre of Saltram Park flashing by and thought: *There. That's the entrance to my magical world.* Before 2022, however, I'd never actually seen the folly up-close, and when I finally went to see it, there was a fence before it, and I, a stickler for adhering to rules (much like Charlie), did not dare cross it to step through. Whether it be placed there by Maglings, the Agnus, or the right authorities, I'd like to take the opportunity to discourage anyone else from crossing the fence to see if they will be able to cross through "the passage". I'm sure it's there for a reason.

As you can see, my work is heavily influenced and inspired by mythology. That said, it is important to understand that my version of the Fates and other twists on lore is my own and may not be historically accurate according to those cultures whom the myths originally came from. The different take on lore in this book is based on my own musings and hypothesises made as a child (including the philosophical speculations creating the theory of trinities and the One True Divinity), making it the fourth creative liberty I've taken.

My fifth creative liberty might be the most important one to mention. While the Agnus Dei do intentionally mirror the perils of extreme ideologies and belief-systems, they and their properties are not intended to represent any one specific religion, organisation, or institution. Nor do they, to my knowledge, exist in real-life.

As stated in the book, the Agnus Dei are a [fictional] faction broken off from the witch hunters of old; their name suggested to me by a sensitivity reader due to its translated meaning: Lamb of God. Should there exist a religious group or Order with the same name, it has evaded both my awareness and research on the matter.

The same goes for Soli Gloria, which was a play on "Soria Moria", the name of a fairy-tale castle from one of our Norwegian folktales. It was only when *Spindle of Life* was complete that I learned that Soli [Deo] Gloria is a Latin term, meaning "Glory to God alone". If there is a higher power, I take it as one of the many signs I've been given along the long and winding path of writing this book that it ought to be written. The way the many different super-moon lunar eclipses in the last century have lined up for the precise dates needed, is another.

While I've also volunteered at orphanages and street children programmes, I'd like to emphasise that I've been lucky to never set foot in an institution such as that of the Agnus Dei's. That is not to say that they do not exist. Throughout history, children's homes and orphanages have been notorious for what we today would consider emotional neglect and even physical abuse. While most organisations and homes have changed with the times and increasing knowledge of the importance of psychological wellbeing, there are still places and communities around the world where physical and psychological abuse or neglect of young, vulnerable people still occurs, particularly including that of conversion therapy. I think (and hope) it goes without saying that *Spindle of Life* champions for the emotional and physical well-being of young people, as well as their right to grow up safe, loved, and free to explore their own paths in life. Lest their magic be quenched.

To learn more behind-the-scenes secrets, find art, or discuss *Spindle of Life* and the rest of the series, make sure to join my exclusive readers' community by visiting www.chaselouiseqvam.com

ACKNOWLEDGMENTS

"Thank you to me, myself, and I for being stubborn enough not to quit" is pretty much how I feared I'd have to sum up these acknowledgements years back. I will be the first to admit that writing can be an excruciatingly lonely journey that leaves you feeling stranded on an isolated island. I never made myself a volleyball friend, but I came pretty close.

All of this began to change, however, once I braved the waters and started sharing my work with other people. Today, I have quite an extensive list of names to mention, and my only fear is that I might forget one or two. There is no disclaimer that can excuse that, so in case this happens, I hereby admit, I am a truly awful human being and I'm deeply sorry. Please forgive me and know that I appreciate every single one that has helped me in one way or another on this journey!

Okay, let's start at the beginning.

Thank you to the teachers who fought for me, believed in my voice, encouraged me, and who said I could write when others said I couldn't.

To any aspiring author who has found themselves crying in hallways or other places because you've been told you'll never be good enough for your dreams, I'll pass on the words said to me by one who helped me rise again:

If you want to be a writer, you'll be a writer. Just go on and do it.

Thank you to my late stepdad who taught me to chase my dreams, even if it means establishing one's own business so that one can make it happen [insert semi-disgruntled grumbles here].

Thank you to my professional support team. Seven years in therapy means that you see a lot of therapists and helpers come and go, all who've helped in one way or another, but I'd particularly like to thank Anniken and Kristian, who helped make it possible for me to see my writing through these last couple years, knowing how important it was for me and my well-being. You saw me as an individual human with individual needs, not just a case number in a system, and for professionals such as you I'm eternally grateful.

Thank you to Natasha Bell for guiding me with best practices when writing from own experiences, and for feeling so strongly when I read you a scene from *Scissors of Death*. However nervous I am to share it, I know in my heart now that I have to, for all the readers that might need it.

Thank you to my former teacher Kim and historian Hannah Pringle for contributing with useful information, research, and verses that helped make the Agnus Dei solid and realistic.

Thank you to my editors over the years: Lara Ferrari, Philip Womack, Laura Bennett, Andrew Hodges, Nastasia Bishop-McHugh, and Rachel L. Schade. I once wanted to publish traditionally so that I would have a team of editors to help me make this book the best it could be. I guess I ended up having one either way!

Thank you to all my alpha, beta, and sensitivity readers to whom I could entrust this book: Tana, Andy, Synne, Kim, Nick, Magda,

Erica, Jessica, Hannah, Rai, Martin, Isa, Ann Mari, and Lily. Your feedback and enthusiasm have been invaluable, and you're every bit part of the team that has helped me see this project to completion. Extra shoutout to those who've dropped everything to help me brainstorm my way out of a corner or read the hundredth version of a chapter. I'm humbled by your love for this book.

Thank you to the friends who allowed me to use their family names, to business mentors and coaches, and to my two loves, Ole and Tigris Athena, for putting up with my long office hours, feeding me with food and love, and generally believing in me even when my own faith wavered.

Thank you to the Bookstagrammers that have stood by me and continue to stand by me, eagerly awaiting the publication of this book, and particularly my fellow authors such as Rachel L. Schade and C. M. Karys. You're beacons of light and inspiration for the community, and your kindness knows no limit.

Finally, thank you to you, dear reader, for picking up this book, and every person I've had in my life or met along the way that has given me encouraging words and excitedly asked how the book is going. It's a teeth-grinding question, but your excitement has been the whip I needed. In particular, I'd like to single-out an old acquaintance that threw her arms around my neck one night at a party and declared she'd fought and won against her cancer to one day read my book. We'd both had a little to drink so maybe you just said it to be nice and maybe I even misheard you, but there were times, when the writing became a little too hard, a little too uncomfortable, and I truly wanted to quit and give up, that I remembered what you said, and it kept me going so you'd have something to read. That "one day" is here.

I dedicated this book to everyone who's ever had their magic suppressed and who's kept on fighting, but it is also dedicated to every single one mentioned in these acknowledgements (and anyone I might have forgotten).

From the bottom of my heart, by the Fates, I **thank** you.

We made it!

ABOUT THE AUTHOR

C. L. Qvam has been lost and found on several occasions, and this time she's been found by you!

Drawn to everything British and lore infused stories that explore the morally grey, Chase moved across the pond at a young age to write the story in her heart. Since then, the mixed-race Norwegian author has identified as an English rose and defies the barriers of her first language and dyslexia to write in her preferred language on the daily.

While pieces of it have also been built and drafted all over the world, Chase is now putting the finishing touches on her first trilogy back home in Norway, living with a very patient boyfriend and furbaby.

When she's not writing, she spends her time illustrating the stories in her head, recovering from a rough start at life, and checking her email for letters from excited readers.

If you loved this book, please consider letting others know with a review on Goodreads or your favourite retailer!

Socials:

instagram.com/chaselouiseqvam
tiktok.com/@chaselouiseqvam